LYON'S ROAR

ZODIAC ASSASSINS BOOK 1

ARTEMIS CROW

LYON'S ROAR
Copyright © 2015 by Leslie Bird Nuccio

All rights reserved. This book or any portion thereof
may not be reproduced or used in any manner
whatsoever without the express written permission
of the publisher except for the use of
brief quotations in a book review.

Printed in the United States of America

First Printing, 2015

ISBN 978-0-9966003-0-9

DEDICATION

To my mother for passing down her love of books and nurturing mine. To my husband, my Treasure, for never doubting.

A percentage of the author's process will be donated to a national animal rescue group and an animal shelter.

1

LYON HOBBLED DOWN THE round stone passageway, his loose robe bunched up in his shackled hands, his bare feet sinking into a cold carpet of foul mystery muck that squished between his toes. The clank of the chains dragging behind him nearly masked the drip-drip-drip of fat water droplets as they lost their war with gravity.

Bands of iron chafed the scar tissue girdling his ankles and wrists. Lyon tested the metal of the chains, and the mettle of his escort. The two grey and white fenrir-wolves growled and held Lyon fast, the length of enchanted, braided red string encircling their necks restraining them as surely as the shackles bound him.

A spontaneous rumble bubbled up from his chest, the alpha riposte as long and low and lean as the canids flanking him, but he cut the provocation short. He, too, was an animal in a cage, poked and prodded by the dungeon guards, and trotted out for pit death matches for the amusement of the masses. As satisfying as it would be, he refused to subject the beasts to the same. "No voice, no choice."

Man and beasts rounded the corner. In the distance, a thin ring of light surrounded a black bullseye. A jolt of adrenaline woke the piece of demon soul attached to his. Lyon fought to wrestle it back into dormancy, but the darkness gripped him tighter, like a python suffocating its prey.

The drips of water thundered when they hit the ground, the iron links in the chain slammed into each other, the booming out-of-sync *lub-dub* of the fenrir-wolf's heartbeats vibrated through his body. The deep dark of the tunnel softened until he could see details, each unique surface enshrouded in vibrating glimmers of different colors. Add to that the scents of woodsy mold, miasmic excreta, and wet dog smell and he was swamped with a helluva miserable sensory cocktail.

Rivulets of sweat ran down his spine and flanks and belly. Lyon stopped moving and concentrated on shoving the demon soul to its origin in the middle of his back. The sensory overload eased, but the demon soul bombarded his brain with images of past kills, each scene shifting and changing like a kaleidoscope with varying shades of one color: blood red.

The demon soul was growing stronger each day. Isolation sucked, but it slowed the spread to a crawl. Yet, even at a crawl, Lyon knew he was running out of time. He needed a miracle, and soon, or his soul would be consumed and he would cease to be.

The fenrir-wolves jerked on his chains, pulling him back to the present. He shuffled to the threshold between light and dark, and cocked his head to listen.

The scrape of the bolt sliding across stone jacked his heart again. The screech of the ancient, tortured hinges heralded the start of the pit death match. The door yawned wide. He cocked his head to one side to see past the edge of his hood, and scanned the paranorms gathered to witness his impending success or demise.

Fucking vultures.

A red and yellow molten glow bathed the voyeurs who hugged the rim of the pit, highlighting the crags and valleys of their tight, bloodlust-filled faces. Their hunger for gore a sign of the festering malignancy that had metastasized throughout the many paranorm species, corrupting the InBetween while Lyon moldered in his cell.

Four hooded figures adorned in black velvet cloaks with unfamiliar sigils sewn onto the cloth in red thread pushed their way through the fog-enshrouded crowd. Even when the four reached the large hole in the cavern floor that separated the spectators from the combatants, Lyon couldn't make out their faces.

Inside the hole, heat burned away the mist to expose a flat, round slab of rock thirty feet lower than the crowd, levitating on shimmering waves of searing heat that rose from a river of lava a mile below.

Gremlins raced around the floating rock, picking up pieces of the loser from the previous match and popping the flesh into their mouths, while others swept the pool of blood over the edge. Nice try, but nothing could remove the permanent black bloodstain.

Lyon stepped out of the darkness into the light, his hands raised to shield his hypersensitive eyes. The full fetor of sulfuric brimstone slammed into him, stinging his eyes. Tears welled; his nose drained. A lifetime wouldn't be long enough to get used to the rotten-egg stench.

Lyon scanned the shadows to his left. "Hood," he said, his seldom-used voice breaking like a stripling mounting his first female.

A troll emerged from the dark and lumbered over, his filthy loincloth barely covering his male bits, while nothing hid the acres of fat rolls and pimpled skin. He pulled Lyon's hood back, exposing his face.

Lyon held out his shackled wrists.

The troll looked across the pit.

Lyon followed the creature's sight line and saw one of the hooded figures nod. Permission granted.

Who is that? A dignitary of some back-cavern 'burb, one of the ruling Twelve...or maybe a wealthy human who'd bribed his way into the InBetween to see the paranormal monsters get their kill on? Humans, so easily electrified by the *snap, crackle, pop* of blood, brutality, and butchery.

The troll leaned close.

The sharp, raw reek of troll mixed with a brimstone chaser singed Lyon's eyes and nostrils, ratcheting up the waterworks and snot. He inhaled through his mouth, then held his breath while the troll freed his wrists and ankles, but he could still taste the foul odors on his tongue.

The iron dropped to the stone with a soft rattle and clunk, and the fenrir-wolves backed away. Lyon stalked to the edge of the pit like his namesake predator, his head low, his eyes moving around the cavern, gauging the crowd and the two exits on the spectator side.

Tall, slim elves dressed in earth-tone garments decorated with precious stones stood together but apart from the rest of the paranorms. Haughty species, the lot of them. Two Memoria soul-keepers with crowns of butterflies in the colors of the family they served hovered on the edges of the pit, while red-headed Bathory Berserkers, the InBetween Os Mage with her bag of bones, and delicate fairies with shimmering wings and sparkling skin made up the rest of the throng.

The cool of the cavern at his back and the shimmering heat of the lava flow warming his front, defined the dichotomy of Lyon's life. Dark and light, good and bad, lauded killer and reviled prisoner—he was all those things and more. But here, now, he was simply back in the pit, ready to play grim reaper for the masses.

Fists pumped in the air. The crowd chanted, "Lyon. Lyon. Lyon."

The bet-makers worked their way through the spectators, the hum of their singsong voices punctuated by the tinny clink of coin being exchanged. Humans may have created gambling, but the subterranean world of the InBetween, haven to all creatures paranormal, had embraced it.

Two of the four robed visitors pushed back their hoods. Lyon's blond-haired, amber-eyed father, Llewellyn, stood next to the biggest Corvus Ward warrior Lyon had ever seen.

The warrior dropped his robe, spread his legs, and crossed his arms over his now-naked chest. Only a few long wisps of black hair were left on his scalp, but he wasn't bald. Black feathers, one for each kill, had replaced the missing strands, and this warrior had a full head of feathers. That was the Corvus Ward warrior way. Almost as tall as Lyon, with ropes of muscle everywhere, the warrior was impressive, but it was his yellow eyes that captured Lyon's attention.

A chill radiated from his chest. Had Llewellyn continued melding paranorms and demons? Creating the Zodiac Assassins hadn't been enough of a clusterfuck to convince his father to stop his cruel experiments?

Lyon had believed the rumors of an unholy union between Corvus warriors and demons were just whispers in the night, a tale told to frighten little snotlings. For goddess sake, he'd never seen one…until now.

Llewellyn raised both hands to quiet the crowd, his mouth turned down in a deep frown of disgust for the paranorms surrounding him. The man could never quite contain his revulsion for the creatures that flowed into the InBetween, seeking freedom from human persecution. It didn't matter that the goddess blood inside Llewellyn made him a paranormal too. Perhaps it was being a Leo that made him feel so much better than everyone around him, Lyon reflected, or that gave him that corrupting I-want-what-I-want-when-I-want-it attitude. Really didn't matter—either way, the man was an arrogant son of a bitch.

Lyon stared at his sire, willing the man to acknowledge his own flesh and blood but, as usual, Lyon was doomed to disappointment.

"Tonight," Llewellyn said in a deep baritone, "we have a very special match to celebrate the beginning of a new era. But, as with any beginning, sacrifices must be made. Champions must be tested. So tonight, our reigning king of the pit," he gestured to the Corvus warrior, "will face an opponent you haven't seen in many months. The winner will go to the Overworld and bring back that which we need to reclaim our heritage."

He paused and looked around the cavern. "Many would see us remain hidden, buried in the dark while the humans plaguing the Overworld infect every corner, believing they are free to steal what is most precious to us all. But they have forgotten that we ruled the earth's surface first!"

The paranorms roared.

Lyon's gut clenched. Sweat broke out. The Overworld? He tried to inhale but he couldn't relax enough to let his lungs fill. He'd only been among the humans once, but that sole contact had resulted in disaster. Everything that had gone to shit in his life traced back to the Overworld and what happened there.

So it's the Overworld or death. He was screwed.

"Out of the darkness! Into the light!" Llewellyn yelled.

A gremlin banged the brass gong tucked in one corner of the cavern. The deep bass vibration hummed through his body, triggering a prickle that started at his scalp and raced south over his sweaty skin like an electric current, until it crashed into his feet.

The troll yanked on his robe.

"Yeah, yeah." Lyon dropped the robe to get the beast off him, happy to be rid of the itchy wool that was banned in the pit to keep the fights fair—nowhere to hide a weapon when you're nude. That and, no warrior wanted to win if it meant leaving the pit without their mightiest weapon hanging heavy front and center.

The Corvus male cocked his head at the levitating rock, an invitation for Lyon to go first.

Lyon rolled his neck, dread weighing him down. He backed several steps and ran at the hole then leapt through a curtain of blistering air and dropped thirty feet. He landed on the edge of the levitating rock, tipping it slightly. He pinwheeled his arms to stay on his feet, then walked to the opposite edge and looked at the still-hooded guests.

Lyon focused on the smaller guest. He tried to suss out a face, but inky-black shadows made it impossible. The guest turned toward Lyon, and a blast of deep cold and suffocating despair filled him.

The pit disappeared from view.

Lyon stood in white nothingness, a woman a few feet away, her features out of focus. He took a step in her direction and a high-pitched screech exploded in his brain. The tinny taste of blood filled his mouth. He fought the pull of her power until his body arched away from her. He dropped to his knees and held his head with his hands, his scream involuntary, uncontrollable.

The screech stopped. When he looked up, the pit had snapped back and he was still on his feet, his hands at his side. The blood in his mouth was gone. The hooded guest looked away as if nothing had happened, and the crowd showed no alarm—no response at all.

He took a deep breath. Witch. Most believed a witch could affect time but what they really did was affect the perception of time, or anything else they desired. This witch had power he'd never seen before, though. To take him to another place without anyone noticing…

Whatever his father had planned, Lyon had no doubt it wasn't for the benefit of the InBetween. Llewellyn's pretty speech about new beginnings and leaving the dark was borne on the back of the powerful witch standing next to him.

It shouldn't have come as a surprise.

A snarl exploded from Lyon. His body twitched with the desire to leap the thirty feet separating them and wrap his hands around the bastard's throat. But before he could give in to his baser instinct, Llewellyn raised a hand and dropped it. The gong pealed a second time. The match was on.

Stop thinking, and start doing.

Lyon backed to one edge of the rock. It dipped slightly when the Corvus warrior landed, but righted when he walked to the opposite end of the arena.

Lyon waited, his feet braced against the slight shifts in levitation. He clenched his fists and choked back the hot, demanding hunger to leap on the man and pound his flesh and bone into the stone until all that remained was a bloody smear. Despite his effort to retain control, the black demon soul inside him slithered through his gut and seized his bowels in a vice grip, its classic go-to bid for possession. Cold sweat coated Lyon's skin. He struggled to breathe, his control over the demon soul thinned.

The Corvus warrior ran straight at him.

Hell of a rookie move for a champion.

Lyon waited for the man to get closer, then pivoted and grabbed for the warrior's neck. He caught nothing but air.

The warrior dropped to the ground and kicked both feet into Lyon's groin.

Lyon fell on his side, unable to breathe. He curled into a ball, his hands cupping his stick and stones, paralyzed by the pain radiating through his body.

The warrior jumped up, clenched his fists, and raised them above his head. "I thought you'd make this interesting, Zodiac." He slammed his fists down.

Lyon rolled his body into the warrior's legs, and used his momentum to back-swing one leg hard and high into the male's chest.

The warrior hit the rock flat on his back. The air in his lungs exploded out with an audible 'whoosh.'

Lyon got up and staggered away. He braced his feet and crouched, ready for attack, when he saw the warrior's eyes. The yellow now glowed from lid to lid. Even the whites had surrendered. Only his pupils remained untouched, huge and black and empty.

Not screwed—double screwed with a demon on top.

The Corvus stalked Lyon, head down, limbs long and relaxed, the evil possessing him in complete control. "Come, come, Lyon," the warrior said in a thick, bass voice. "I can feel that sweet little piece of my demon king's soul inside you scratching to come out and play." He stopped walking and tilted his head. "You prideful little vessel. You're too afraid to stop fighting and embrace your potential. Don't you long to be free of the dungeons, of this limited life?"

Lyon bared his teeth. "I'm not afraid of anything."

The warrior's demon smirked. "So pathetic to waste your energy on lies."

Lyon's skin burned. Potent shame and rage honed his focus. He charged, hit the man's waist, and pushed off with his legs. Locked together, they slid across the rock until the edge loomed.

Lyon wasn't ready to go out in a blistering fall that ended in instant combustion, a burp of steam the last evidence of his existence. He freed his left hand and leonine claws erupted from his nail bed. He scraped the curved keratin daggers on the rock to stop them but the claws snapped off. Both men tumbled over the edge.

The crowd screamed.

Lyon gripped a tiny ledge of rock with the tips of his fingers, his digits blanching from the men's combined poundage. The burn of his muscles competed with the searing waves of air that rose from molten rock flowing beneath him. The twin fires rolled up his body, while his sweat rolled down. Salt burned his eyes. Wet slicked his hands.

The warrior below him writhed, his skin steaming.

The levitating rock tipped a millimeter, then another, creeping toward vertical. If they didn't get to the surface soon, the rock would roll until the Lyon and the warrior both went *poof*.

Lyon's fingers slipped. He looked down. "Move your ass before you kill us."

The warrior raised his head. "Let me go."

Lyon's fingers slipped again. "No. Climb!"

The warrior hesitated, then gripped Lyon's arm with both hands and pulled. He climbed up Lyon's body until he could hook an arm over Lyon's shoulder.

Lyon grabbed the ledge with his newly freed hand. He took a deep breath and let it out slowly. *Too fucking close.*

The warrior heaved, and his upper body landed on the rock. He planted his feet on Lyon's shoulders and pushed. The Corvus got to his knees and looked down before grabbing Lyon's wrists and pulling him up. They fell back, their bodies shaking from the effort, their heels dug into the sloped rock until it leveled out.

Like a drowning man flailing to rise to the surface for a precious gasp, Lyon fought for every breath until the fire in his lungs cooled. He got to his feet first, and helped the Corvus warrior rise.

Lyon didn't speak. He didn't have to—this changed nothing. They walked to opposite sides of the rock and faced each other. Lyon watched the Corvus, using the passing seconds to rest and gather his wits.

The warrior charged.

Lyon waited for the man to pull some fantastic move out of his ass, but he just kept coming. Too fatigued to control it, Lyon's instincts engaged before his brain. Claws emerged from the nailbed of his right hand, sending his fingernails flying. His canines doubled in length, and he barely registered the pain and gush of blood in his mouth.

Lyon grabbed the man's neck, raised him high in the air, then slammed him down on the stone. The demon soul battered against his defenses but Lyon pushed back to stop it from ripping apart this man like it had so many others. He sat on the warrior's chest and held his claws to the man's throat

"Kill, kill, kill," the crowd chanted.

The warrior gripped Lyon's wrist, holding it in place instead of pushing it away. "Do it. Make it look good. Quick, before my demon takes control again."

"What the hell are you talking about?"

"That's the deal. My life to save my son, Collas."

"Llewellyn wouldn't make that deal. He'd rather see me dead." Lyon released the man's neck. Before he could gain his feet, the warrior grabbed Lyon's wrist and jerked his hand down. Lyon's claws disappeared into the meat and bone of the warrior's throat before hitting the rock on the other side. Jets of bright red blood sprayed Lyon's face signaling a lethal bleed.

The warrior grimaced and released Lyon. "Llewellyn didn't make the deal."

Lyon ripped his claws out of the man's neck and sat back on his heels. In all the years he'd fought, no one had ever asked to be killed. They cried for their life, or pleaded to be spared while pissing themselves. It was pathetic and embarrassing. But this man's plea to be killed went against what little honor code Lyon had left.

This was no great match to name a champion. It was suicide by assassin to save a child, and it stunk.

A bubble formed on the ragged edge of the warrior's slashed windpipe before a final gurgle escaped him. The dying Corvus raised an arm as if reaching for something, or someone, then dropped it and died.

Lyon threw back his head, and roared until his lungs were empty.

The gremlins danced from foot to foot at the edge of the pit, waiting for the signal to jump in and clean up the mess. Their beady eyes glittered. The slash that constituted their mouths exposed nasty needle teeth that dripped with saliva and disease.

The warrior deserved honor. Instead of indulging the crowd and ripping the warrior apart or letting the gremlin crew eat him, Lyon picked him up, carried his body to the edge of the floating rock, and released him. The last evidence of the man's existence was a puff of steam that shot out of the lava for a microsecond before being consumed.

Lyon watched an iridescent blue-black butterfly float away from the lava on the hot air currents until it reached the level of the crowd. A Memoria soul-keeper with a towering crown of identically colored butterflies separated from the rest and held out a delicate hand. The butterfly fluttered to her and landed on the tip of her forefinger. The soul-keeper raised her hand to her crown and the Corvus Ward warrior's soul joined those of his ancestors.

Lyon turned to the crowd, searching for the maestro of this travesty, but Llewellyn and his two hooded guests had disappeared into the roaring spectators.

The energy of the pit had always been feral, but a certain honor was demanded of the fighters, especially in the death matches. At least, that had been the case when Lyon last competed. Now, it seemed, something had changed, and not for the better. The air was thick with sulfur and malice, the rage was predatory and consuming and wrapped around a dense layer of desperation and fear.

Lyon swayed before the rabid crowd, and shook his head. He was done. He jumped out of the pit, walked through the combatant entrance, and left the fevered horde behind, the fenrir-wolves trotting after him.

He was a killer. Check. He was proud to be the best. Check. Winning a rigged match? Even he had to draw the line somewhere.

2

PERSEPHONE PICKED HER WAY along the deer track that wound through the dense stand of pines and oaks, a pack of moon-picked herbs on her back. She stopped and listened for the call of owls, or the phwap-phwap of bat wings. Nothing.

Silence ruled this night as it had the previous fourteen.

The crisp tang of pinesap and the cool, quiet nights of the East Texas autumn usually gave her the succor she needed to white-knuckle it through the nightmares and paralyzing visions that came with the darkness. But the forest failed to soothe her. Tonight would be a bitch.

For two weeks, she'd seen things she couldn't explain, heard screams and whispers in a language foreign to her. Torturous dreams of a shadowy monster dragging her down a long dark hole was the crap icing being piled on top of her rapidly deteriorating sanity.

Normalcy eluded her. It had danced just outside her grasp since her earliest memories, despite the love and acceptance of her best friends, Taryn and Abella.

But now? Normalcy didn't just elude her—it had escaped to another hemisphere. Her world was going to hell, and she had no idea why.

She'd just taken a step toward home when excruciating pain gripped her thighs. She stumbled and fell to her knees. She ran her hands over her jeans, but found no reason for the waves of agony. Her stomach roiled, and her mouth filled with saliva. She swallowed several times to keep from vomiting.

She got to her feet, but hot fatigue swept through her body. The rapidly narrowing tunnel vision of an approaching faint forced her to lean on the rough bark of a pine tree. It didn't help. She held out her hands, took a step toward the next tree, and fell into darkness.

Her hands brushed something warm and solid. She grabbed it to stop her fall then opened her eyes and screamed. The forest was gone, replaced by craggy rock walls bathed in a red-orange glow. She looked down then back up. She was sandwiched between two horrors. Below her was the scorching heat from lava; above her, the obscured face of the monster from her nightmares. Only this time, her night terror was her lifeline.

He frowned and yelled something, but she couldn't hear him, could only see long blonde hair hanging in sweaty hanks. Tears welled, and she couldn't catch her breath. Full-blown, 3-D hallucinations, now? How much more was she expected to take?

He turned his head away, and in a blink she returned to her world. Her arms were wrapped around a large root, her body dangling over a deep ravine. She climbed hand over hand up the steep, slick slope and belly flopped onto pine needles, cones, and dead leaves, her body trembling, her heart hammering in her chest. She curled into a ball and rocked, sobbing.

Tonight. She had to tell Taryn and Abella about the visions and nightmares tonight, preferably after several batches of margaritas.

The three women had been together since they'd ended up in the same orphanage as newborns. They were her sisters, by choice, not by blood and she couldn't bear the thought of losing them. Her stomach lurched from a fresh surge of adrenaline; the resulting sweat chilled her. She had procrastinated long enough, and this latest batch of weird showed no signs of stopping.

Persephone rolled into a sit and dropped her head into her hands. She'd always been the eccentric of the trio, mad as a hatter most said, resulting in a revolving door of foster homes until, at fifteen, the three women decided to bid the system a not-so-fond farewell.

She'd known why she'd been booted from every home—watched the fear in her foster families eyes morph into anger. Dreaded that moment when they vented that anger in an imaginative variety of physical and mental punishments. How long before she saw the same fear in Taryn and Abella? How long before they rejected her?

Persephone stood and spread her feet for balance. She wiped off the dirt and twigs and leaves from her clothes, trying to ignore the perfect example of her madness hanging heavy and menacing in the night sky. Was the huge, blood-red full moon actually there, or just another figment?

"I should have bought more tequila."

Heavy wings flapped behind her. She whirled, then staggered back. The oaks and pines she'd passed moments before now glowed white. She stared at the bizarre sight, too frightened to turn away. The trees cracked and screamed as they bent far to the left, then the right, as if they'd turned to rubber, sending pieces of bark flying like shrapnel.

She backed up several steps. One by one, the trunks of the trees she passed changed from dark brown to a glowing white. The faster she moved, the faster they changed, until she was surrounded. She stumbled over a branch and felt it wrap around one ankle, binding her. She kicked at it until she freed herself, then bolted for home.

She ran into the kitchen and dropped her backpack on the island. She locked the windows and doors and turned on all the lights, then worked her way through the sprawling ranch house, chasing away the terrifying darkness until she came full circle. She dug through the pack for her phone, her hands shaking, her fingers numb.

"Come on, come on, COME ON."

She dumped the contents of the bag onto the kitchen island and pawed through the mess. Before she found her cell, the electricity blinked out, leaving her stranded in the darkness relieved only by the blood-red moonlight that stained every surface.

3

LYON FIDGETED WHILE HIS OLD healer barked orders at the guard coating his wounds with an unguent that reeked of the anal-gland discharge of a striped polecat. She swore the foul goop worked miracles on bruising and open wounds, but who cared about miracles if it meant no female would spread her legs for him? Not that he'd plowed anyone in years.

"You still won't let me tend to your wounds?" She flung out a hand at the guard. "I would have been done by now."

Lyon scowled. "I have enough blood on my hands, I'll not add yours to the list."

"By the goddess, my touch isn't going to make you lose control."

Lyon raised his hand to stop her. "Enough. Let it rest, hag." He rolled his shoulders and cracked his neck.

She lowered her voice. "I heard about the pit match."

Lyon remained silent and tuned out her chatter. Why he put up with the hag was a mystery. Maybe because she wasn't afraid of him, despite his nasty temper and sullen silences. That was gutsy, impressive even, but more impressive was her penchant for InBetween gossip. The first few years after losing his mother and his freedom, Lyon had said nothing to the woman, so lost in his grief and shame and anger he could barely breathe, much less get words out. But the woman's incessant magpie chatter about the goings-on outside his cell finally broke through his pain. They'd had one conversation; now he couldn't get her to shut up.

"There was a woman. I think it was a woman. Hooded, so I couldn't see a face but her power was beyond anything I've felt before."

"I've heard your father brought a woman to the InBetween recently. Her identity is a mystery, even to your father's servants. But you shouldn't worry yourself. Today you're the champion."

"No. Not today." He looked away. "Today, I was just a weapon."

She handed him a warm, wet cloth. "Your face."

He stood and pushed the guard aside with his forearm. "Leave," he said with a growl. The guard handed the unguent pot to the hag and left the cell in a rush.

Lyon turned to the small mirror on the wall. A single vertical crack in the glass split his face in two. He cleaned the dried blood from his cheeks and forehead, each swipe of the cloth revealing more of the network of scars that covered his face and traveled south down his neck. He removed as much blood from his tawny, mid-back-length hair as he could, then stared at the pale skin, squared jaw, and full lips that were identical to his father's. They could be twins, save for the scars and the height difference. Llewellyn towered over most and liked it that way, but Lyon was a head taller, forcing his father to look up. Height was definitely Lyon's favorite feature.

The hag droned on about winning matches, but Lyon froze when he saw the folded vellum peeking out from under his pillow. He clenched his fists. The fear that he would lose the woman he was trying to draw if someone else saw her was fucking nuts, but there it was in all its obsessive glory.

"Have you been dreaming about her again?"

"Her?"

"The woman you're drawing on that vellum you think is so well hidden."

Lyon dropped the dirty cloth and walked to his bed. He opened the folded paper, and studied the curve of her high cheekbones, the straight hair that spilled over her shoulders, the jut of her chin. But the real details, the eyes, the mouth, the nose that would define her, had so far escaped him. "She won't leave me alone, but she won't reveal herself to me, either."

The healer leaned over his shoulder, her breath tickling his ear. "I can imagine that she's lovely."

Lyon jerked away from the hag and closed the vellum. He glanced around the cell for a better hiding place. In his experience, that which meant the most to him was always lost—at least until he stopped allowing himself to care. "Don't care, don't get hurt" headlined his hard-and-fast list of rules. But this woman... Hell, just the outline of this woman's face opened a door to feelings he couldn't allow.

The hag tapped on a stone in the corner opposite the cell door. "Here."

He joined her and traced the slight curve of the cool stone with his fingers until he felt the cracked seam. He slipped the vellum inside, leaving only a tiny corner poking out so he could retrieve it quickly.

She stepped away.

"Are you done?" he asked, his back to her. He squared his shoulders and waited for her answer, his face hot, his teeth clinched.

"Yes."

"Hag?"

"Yes?"

He ground his teeth, the two words so foreign and bitter he could barely get his tongue around them. "Thank you."

She said nothing. The *thunk* of the dungeon door closing ended the uncomfortable silence.

Lyon touched the vellum once more, the woman's indistinct image a talisman against the dark of his cell, the dark of his soul. But that's all she would ever be: just a drawing of a dream of what his life could have been.

After the ritual that made him a Zodiac, his life had become one could-have-been moment after another, until the weight of his regrets threatened to suffocate him. But for the past two weeks, he had dreamed of a long-haired woman, her hands outstretched to him. Every day, he woke up with hope and dread competing for his heart. Dread for another day of endless deprivation, and hope that the woman would appear to him for the hours he slept. He was a fool.

He made a fist and plowed it into the wall. The skin over his knuckles split on contact. Warm, red blood splattered across the cold, grey stone. He dropped his head, his arms dangling by his side until the pain subsided. *There is no hope, no hope, no hope.*

He turned to his bed for some much-needed sleep and slid under the covers. The aches in his body throbbed in sync with his heart. The pain pulled at him until he sagged. He closed his eyes and fell into the fatigue.

Before oblivion took him, the dungeon door opened, and three very tall, very thin creatures of a species foreign to Lyon entered his cell. The black color of their skin rippled in response to the differing illumination between the dark hall and the slightly brighter candlelit cell, shifting like a humanoid chameleon.

Lyon's sister followed the men inside, her hand hovering over the long dagger sheathed at her waist. Her animosity flooded the small space with an oppressive weight that demanded Lyon acknowledge it. He crossed his arms over his chest and studied the dark red flush that highlighted the four thick, diagonal scars marring her otherwise perfect face.

Lyon raised his chin and girded himself against her hatred. "What do you want, Leona?"

"As champion," she scowled, her lips thinned as if she had bit into a bitter orange, "you've been summoned to attend Llewellyn. My punishment is to get you there in one piece. The Creepers are here to ensure that happens."

After the Creepers hustled Lyon out of his cell, Leona took the lead, her head down to avoid the rough ceiling. The bizarre-looking males followed Lyon, so tall they had to hold their arms up to keep their knuckles from dragging. Freaking goblins slaved these passages, carving them out for bodies the size of human children. Of course, it could have been worse. He could be a troll, and have to crawl through the muck.

After winding up and up from the deepest bowels of the dungeon, they reached a set of steps. Lyon stopped. Carved out of stone centuries earlier, the risers dipped in the middle from the wear of boots and bare feet, cloven hoof and paw. The day he'd first descended the steps, his world had changed from purpose and luxury and love to a dark, barren cell punctuated only by an occasional death match that kept him from perishing of boredom.

A sharp sting between his shoulder blades jolted him back to the present; Leona had poked him with the tip of her dagger.

She removed the blade and passed him. "Move it," she said over her shoulder. The group climbed the stairs and entered a hall. Leona picked up the pace until she was several feet ahead of Lyon.

"You've turned into a royal bitch, little sister."

Leona stopped, and bowed her head. She whirled to face him, one arm raised, her palm facing him. Her fingers curled inward and blanched as if wrapping around something more substantial than air.

Despite the distance separating them, he could feel her squeezing his throat tighter and tighter, until no air passed. He clawed at her fingers, gouging deep tracks in his flesh to gain purchase but there was nothing to grab, only five depressions in his skin. His heart raced, his ears buzzed. The hall faded to black in his narrowing vision until all he saw was her savage expression. He fell to his knees.

Leona's hand followed him down. Her amber eyes shifted to a glittering gold, her face turned blue. She finally dropped her hand, breaking the attack, and collapsed to the ground.

Lyon keeled back, both hands around his neck. He sucked in air, then coughed until he dry heaved. The Creepers grabbed his arms and forced him to his feet.

One reached for Leona, but she slapped him away. Bright red lines appeared on her neck, as if her assault had ricocheted.

"What the hell, Leona?" A chill gripped Lyon. The power she'd used on him wasn't natural to her, and she now reeked of the all-too-familiar sulfur and rotting flesh. The realization stole Lyon's breath nearly as effectively as Leona's magic: the demon king Asmodeus had corrupted her. He'd gobbled her up, and spat out the creature lying on the ground before him. He'd hoped his little sister would escape the legacy of the House of Leo, but she'd chosen her path just as he had, and the evil they'd embraced would kill them both before their time.

"Just keep your damn mouth shut."

Lyon understood her rage. He'd wallowed in hot, consuming anger for so long the emotion had permeated him, leaving no room for kindness or compassion.

After becoming the first Zodiac Assassin, his teenaged little princeling self had been so beyond arrogant in the belief that he could handle anything, that he never stopped to think about what could go wrong. Now, he'd just seen the same arrogance in Leona.

She rose, and staggered a couple of steps before righting herself. She continued down the passage, one hand sliding along the wall as if needing the solidity of the stone to maintain her balance. "If he lags behind, kill him."

Lyon forced his shaky legs to move to the light ahead; the great cavern was close. His heart lurched in his chest as they passed under the arched entrance, his attention drawn to the foot of the dais at the opposite end of the huge space. He had spent hours there playing with Leona, pulling her long blonde braids, slowing so she could keep up as he raced around the many InBetween guests, her infectious laughter and boundless joy never failing to make him smile. It had been so long since he'd heard her laugh—heard anyone laugh—that he wasn't sure he would recognize the sound. His hands itched to reach out and tug on the long, thick braid hanging down Leona's back, but he shook his head. Her joy was gone, replaced by a creature unknown to him.

He looked to the dais again. The heavy gold table and kingly chairs triggered other good memories from his childhood—his mother's golden hair, her blue eyes, her soft smile, the scent of lavender that tickled his nose when she tucked him into bed at night. Those memories quickly morphed into the horror of everything that came after: his mother's dead eyes, her lips drawn tight, exposing her teeth like she was caught in a silent, eternal scream. The cloud of death and decay that had enveloped him when he was allowed to say his last goodbye.

Even now, the memory of her blue eyes filled with love and forgiveness as she slid into death cut him to the core just as surely as his claws had cut open her flesh.

He drew a ragged breath to banish the image. Love had killed her, and it would kill him if he indulged in the emotion. Love made you weak, weak made you vulnerable, and vulnerable made you dead.

He clenched his fists, his newly grown fingernails biting into his palms. He looked away from the dais to take in the massive cavern.

A showcase for the most precious of the InBetween's treasures, the space elicited the awe the Twelve intended, an ego fuck wrapped in a shiny, gold-and jewel-encrusted bow, as if they gave a damn about the aberrations under their rule.

The candelabras and chandeliers scattered about the huge cavern had once held dozens of beeswax candles, the soft light of their flames bouncing off the hundreds of amethyst and citrine crystals embedded in the walls. In those days, shimmering rays of purple and amber painted the paranormals, making even the fiercest of them beautiful and enchanting. Coupled with the sweet scent of honey, his young, unrefined senses had been intoxicated, drunk on the magical sights and scents.

The past faded when he blinked, leaving behind the current grim reality before him. The amethyst and citrine crystals had been plundered, leaving the walls pockmarked and cold. The candelabras and chandeliers held only cobwebs and dust now. The smell of mold and fear and sour, unwashed bodies hung in the air, blanketing the space so thoroughly that no number of candles could cut through it.

Worse still, the few hushed, furtive creatures huddling in small groups in the shadows flinched when he passed, as if he'd managed to do something more horrendous than usual while confined to the dungeons.

A scream pierced the oppressive quiet, the wail so shrill that Lyon had to cover his ears. A Corvus Ward female ran at him and collapsed at his feet, followed by a male. He glanced up and recoiled before grabbing the woman's upper arms and tugging on them to pull her away.

"Stop." Lyon sneered. "If I was going to kill you, you'd already be choking on your own blood. Why is your woman screaming?"

The male blinked and steadied himself. He placed a hand on the woman's shoulder and squeezed. The simple touch stopped her screams, but she still sobbed. "She is my sister. The male you killed in the pit was her mate."

"Then she should be happy her son was saved." Lyon leaned closer. "That was the deal, was it not?"

"What deal? Their son is gone, like the others—like mine," the male Corvus said.

"Like the others? Clarify."

"Children have been disappearing for months."

"Corvus nestlings?"

"Not just Corvus nestlings—all the paranorm children. Slowly at first, but now all of our children are gone." The man looked away. "The gods and goddesses are angry, and we don't know why."

Lyon looked into the female's swollen, tear-drenched face, her desperation a mirror of her mate's.

"Help us," she whispered.

Regret slammed into him, the feeling foreign and weighted. He leaned over until the female's face was only inches from his, but he had no words of comfort to offer.

She leaned closer, her totally black eyes eerily similar in appearance to that of a mid-level demon. "Please. You took my mate." She held out a tiny black feather. "Find my child. Save Collas."

Two Creepers grabbed Lyon's arms. He palmed the feather before they could drag him away, while two others backhanded the Corvus male and female, sending them sliding across the ground.

"That's enough, leave them alone." Lyon gained his feet and jerked free of the skeletal creatures. "Call off your dogs, Leona."

She snapped her fingers and the Creepers returned to her, leaving the Corvus pair to help each other to a dark corner.

The Creepers flanked Lyon and pulled him along behind Leona to an ornate arch at the beginning of a passage.

"Disappearing children?" Lyon asked. *And suicidal warriors*, he could have added, but he wanted to keep that information to himself for now. 'Never show all your hand' was another hard-and-fast, a painful lesson learned in the pit, as evidenced by some of his worst scars.

Leona ignored him, her stride increasing.

"Leona?" A deep male voice called out from their right.

She stopped and turned, her face flushed crimson. "What do you want, Sag?"

Sagittarius stepped out of the shadows. His face was tanned and unlined save for the tiniest of crinkles radiating from the corners of his dark green eyes. Straight black hair brushed broad shoulders grown thick with muscle from drawing a bow, while his thighs and calves were long and lean like those of a distance runner. Sag, the archer, a lethal genius with anything sharp and pointy, whether it was a weapon, a retort, or his cock if the rumors were to be believed.

Goddess, how Lyon hated him.

Sag scowled at him. "You dare be in her presence?"

"She came to me. Can't control that."

"That's always been your excuse."

Leona shoved the two Zodiacs apart. "Why are you here?"

"Why is *he* here?" Sag demanded.

"Llewellyn summoned him."

Sag took her upper arm and pulled her into his chest. He traced the scars that crossed her face with his fingers, then dropped them to her throat and skimmed the bruises blooming on her delicate skin. "Did Lyon do this?"

She struggled against his hold. "Get off me."

Sag tightened his grip.

She cried out.

A hot, swift rage slammed into Lyon's gut. He may not have any say in Leona's life after what he'd done to her so many years ago, but he'd be damned if he'd stand by and watch her be manhandled. "Take your hands off her." Lyon stepped closer.

Sag pivoted, and cold-cocked him. Blood exploded from Lyon's mouth and nose. He rocked back, but stayed on his feet. A low growl vibrated deep in his throat, then increased to a rumble. The demon soul was a sneaky bastard. The tickle of its perpetual search for a foothold erupted into a full-on assault of his body. Lyon came prepared for anything in the pit, but he hadn't seen Sag's chicken-shit punch coming.

Pressure built inside him. His limbs twitched with the need to move, but each brush of his robe against his sensitive skin spurred a fresh wave of agony.

This is gonna be a bad one.

Leona glanced at Lyon, then did a double take. "Shit, his eyes are glowing gold." She broke free and glared at Sag. He reached for her, but she shoved him out of the way. "Back off." She turned to the Creepers. "Get him to Llewellyn's quarters. Go!"

The Creepers hissed and pulled on Lyon's arms.

He writhed under their grip. His stomach lurched. Sweat coursed down his face and body, and he bit his lower lip to stem his rising gorge. They rushed him out of the great cavern through an arch. Lyon's vision narrowed until the rich colors of the tapestries and thick wool rugs blended and shifted as they ran through the hall.

The Creepers stopped in front of a jewel-encrusted door.

"Leona, please," Sag said.

She unlocked the door, and shoved it open. "Get Lyon inside."

The Creepers pulled Lyon through the door, then turned to Leona for orders. "Drop him."

Lyon sagged to the floor, and rested his face against the cool stone. He watched Leona advance on Sag, her back and shoulders stiff, her hands clenched into fists. "You touch me again, and I'll kill you." Sag backed through the door. Leona slammed it in his face.

As if trapped in the Stevenson tale his mother used to read to him, the demon soul playing Hyde was racing to claim Lyon's Jekyll. Hot pain seared his mouth. His canines elongated, stretching the margins of the gum tissue until the flesh ripped open and blood flowed. The claws on his right hand extended; the claws on his left hadn't finished regenerating yet.

Son of a bitch, he hated these explosive possessions.

The Creepers backed away.

"Come back, you fools," Leona ordered.

Lyon curled into a ball, wrapped his arms around his knees, and pulled them tight into his chest. He hadn't been this close to losing complete control in years, not since he was a stripling. The colors in the room went beyond the normal spectrum, shifting to an unnaturally brilliant hue. A glimmer haloed the furniture, the low ambient light brightening until it blinded him.

A low whisper slithered through his mind like a snake. *"Lyy-oon. I'm coming."* In seconds, the demon soul would take control.

4

A WALL OF COLD AND MENACE PRECEDED the hooded figure that walked into Lyon's sight line. His skin tightened, his muscles twitched. The cold he felt in the pit was a crisp autumn chill compared to the arctic cold that enveloped him now. The frigid air washed over him, flash freezing his sweat. His body shook, and he gasped for air.

The witch from the pit stood over him. Even this close, Lyon couldn't see her face through the inky shadows, just a black, malevolent aura vibrating around her. He wasn't an auramancer, but a black aura couldn't be good.

She squatted. A slender hand and forearm emerged from a sleeve and pushed her hood back. Deep red hair flowed over her shoulders, her dark green eyes glittering as they roved over his face. Pale skin stretched tight over her high cheekbones, a high forehead, and strong jaw. A beauty for sure, but laced with cruelty, and molded with malice.

She reached for Lyon, but he pulled back. "Don't touch me."

She grabbed the front of his robe and jerked him closer, like he weighed no more than a suckling. She ran a hand through his hair. "You are delicious, Lyon."

Her fingers hovered millimeters above his scars. Multiple zings of blue current arced between them, like static electricity. "Llewellyn, dear. Make your pet demon release him."

"Asmodeus isn't here."

"Do not lie to me, I can feel his presence." She released Lyon and pulled out a folded piece of vellum. She leaned closer to Lyon. "You know what this is, don't you?"

Lyon grunted and swiped at the vellum, but the witch jerked it away. She opened it and ran her fingers down the image. She turned it around and showed it to Llewellyn. "Your son is connected to her. I'll not tolerate that connection being muddied by the black stain of demon soul inside him."

Lyon panted, the witch's statement rattling about his brain, but before he could make sense of it, the demon king Asmodeus squatted next to him. "Got yourself in a pickle, boy."

"Make it stop. Now," the witch ordered.

Asmodeus laid a hand on Lyon's upper back, between his shoulder blades. In seconds, Lyon's body relaxed and the knots in his muscles released. The demon soul scratched and clawed at his bowels in a panicked bid to regain traction, but finally receded. A bone-deep weariness rolled through him, and he sagged.

Lyon unfurled his liquid limbs, his eyes half-closed. "Shoving the genie back in the bottle. You must teach me that trick," he said.

The vellum fluttered down and landed next to Lyon's face. The witch stepped over him like he was no more visible than a dust mote. "Handle this," she said to Llewellyn. She left the room, followed by the demon.

"Don't go away all vexed." Lyon wanted to stay on the floor, but he forced himself to stand. He picked up the vellum and folded it before clenching it in his fist. Leaning wasn't too grave an admission of weakness, so he braced his body against the fireplace mantle, the warmth of the fire raising goosebumps on his skin.

Demon possession exhausted him; the deeper the possession, the weaker the Zodiac. It was a serious flaw in the grand demon design for Lyon and Scorpio, the only two Zodiacs who had not assimilated their souls.

As soon as the room stopped glowing, Lyon looked around Llewellyn's quarters, taking in the countless treasures his father had stolen from paranorms and humans. Silks and velvets in deep blue and green, and crimson and gold, were draped over dark, heavy furniture, and hung on the walls. Huge hand-loomed wool rugs covered great expanses of cold stone floor. Gold and silver tea services, crystal decanters filled with his sire's favorite whisky, ancient amphora jugs… Everywhere Lyon looked he saw a fortune. Obscene didn't quite cover it.

He crossed his arms over his chest, and raised an eyebrow at his scowling father.

Llewellyn walked to his wet bar and poured three fingers of single malt. "Leona, leave us."

"No, not this time." She placed a hand on Llewellyn's arm.

He finished the whisky in one swallow, set his glass aside, and backhanded her face, knocking her into the closest wall. Leona slid to the ground, a smear of blood on the stone marking her descent.

Llewellyn grabbed her throat, forced her to her feet, and backed her to the door.

Lyon growled.

His father raised Leona by the neck until her feet left the floor. She slapped at his hand. "Take a step, boy, and I'll snap her neck. You want her death on your hands, too?"

Lyon shut his mouth. He'd already caused Leona enough pain.

Llewellyn opened the door, and threw Leona into the hall. "You can train and fight all you want, but you'll never be good enough. Hell, I'd sell you to one of the Twelve, but they want virgins and we both know that's ancient history. Guess I'll have to sell you to some wealthy human instead."

"I'd rather die."

"That can be arranged." Llewellyn slammed the door, and returned to the bar. "A man just wants children who can help him advance in life. What do I get? A son with so little self-control that he can't be trusted to do anything but kill, and a daughter with the mental capacity of a snotling and legs that won't stay closed."

"She loves you. But that's not enough, is it?"

Llewellyn poured another whisky and downed it before throwing the crystal glass across the room. It hit a tapestry depicting the resurrection of the twelve human princes by the goddess Hecate, and exploded with a crack. "Love makes you weak. It's an artificial construct that makes you vulnerable to the whims of another. It was love for you that killed your mother and ruined Leona."

Lyon clenched his fists, and took a deep breath to cool down. Losing his temper wouldn't gain him anything but more contempt from Llewellyn. "Who's the witch?"

"Not your business." Llewellyn took a deep breath and waved a hand at a chair. "Sit."

Lyon lifted his chin. "I'll stand."

Llewellyn scowled. "You weren't supposed to win."

And there it was, all the hate Llewellyn had for him clearly illustrated in only five words. Lyon stood taller, and schooled his face against his father's venom. The old man still had the power to hurt him. *Gotta work on that.*

Llewellyn pulled a small piece of paper from his pocket and threw it at Lyon.

Lyon caught it and saw an Overworld address. "What's this?"

"That's your assignment. Get the three women living at that address and bring them back to me. Alive."

Lyon's gut clenched. A buzzing started in his ears. Going into the human Overworld, the place that kick-started the string of horrible mistakes that had defined his life, was impossible. Unthinkable. "If I can't be trusted to do anything but kill, why the hell would you give me a babysitting job? In the Overworld."

"You weren't my choice."

"Naturally." Lyon wadded the paper and threw it back. "The answer is no." He walked to the door and opened it.

"You'll do it if you want the demon soul removed," Llewellyn said.

Lyon froze and choked back the snark poised on his tongue. His heart raced neck and neck with his thoughts. No more parasitic demon soul leeched on his. No more dungeon cell. No more death matches. Freedom. A surge of hope raced through him until he squashed it. Hope was a subset of caring, landing it square at the top of his hard-and-fast "don't" list.

"If you refuse, if you fail, I'll bury you in the lower dungeons so deep it'll make your current cell look like it's fit for a king, with only the demon soul inside you for company."

Lyon fought the urge to squirm. No way was he going back to the small, dark, dank holes of hell where he'd spent the first several years of his imprisonment, his flesh fodder for his rat and cockroach cellmates. Pitted against the prospect of going into the Overworld, the lower dungeon won out as *the* last place he wanted to experience for a second time.

He swallowed hard. *Never let them see you sweat, or they'll make sure you bleed.* A bastardization of some slogan that had been written with his world in mind.

"That's what I thought," Llewellyn said. "This is a quick, clean retrieval job. Get the women. Bring them back here, preferably with a minimal body count, if that's possible. You do this right, you're free." Llewellyn grabbed the whisky bottle and a fresh glass, and took a seat on the brown Chesterfield sofa in front of the fireplace. "Get out."

Lyon picked up the address and walked to the door.

"One more thing," Llewellyn said. "They have to be here before the waning moon."

Lyon white-knuckled the knob. "That's less than a week from now."

"Then you better hurry."

Llewellyn didn't look when his door opened. He downed another shot of whisky instead. He hated having to deal with his children. Lyon should have been killed in the pit, and Leona… Well, her challenges over the past few weeks had grown tedious, but she'd never pushed so hard. He slumped into the sofa and rested his head, his eyes closed.

His favorite memory flooded his mind, pushing aside his anger. Beams of light streamed into the royal House of Leo throne room, filling the space with a golden glow. Warm and bright, the sun enveloped him, the eldest prince of the House of Leo, as if anointing him. He was young, cocksure, and in love with a mysterious, sensuous visitor named Circe. If only he'd known that she would be his downfall, that she would rip him away from his true destiny, perhaps he could have ignored her seduction. *Aw, hell, who was he kidding?*

The click of a door closing jerked him out of the memory.

Asmodeus sagged into a club chair across from Llewellyn. "Why are you sending him?"

Llewellyn sipped his drink to hide his irritation. "It wasn't my choice."

"What a shame. I've made a lot of money off his wins in the pit. Watching him shred his opponents was the icing on that stack of cash."

Llewellyn remained silent.

"But when he loses control to my itty bitty bit of soul inside him?" Asmodeus wrapped his arms around his chest. "Mm, I can almost taste his adrenaline and fear. Potent, heady, far more delicious than the rest of the Zodiacs combined." He waggled a forefinger. "Except, perhaps, Scorpio."

"Enough!" Llewellyn stood. "Take your freak show somewhere else."

"Me? A freak? What about you?" Asmodeus rose and stepped toward Llewellyn, poking the man in the chest. "You were human, a prince, when that witch goddess Circe killed you. Aw, poor bitty baby."

He pressed Llewellyn harder, forcing him to back up. "Then her mummy, Hecate, resurrected you with her blood, and created the InBetween for you and the eleven other princes her daughter killed. But you weren't content to stay put, so you summoned me here—which I do thank you for, by the way."

Asmodeus sighed. "I made you twelve of the best warriors in any of the four worlds, and you turn them into assassins to line your pocket with human coin."

He crowded into Llewellyn's personal space until their chests bumped. "But the riches weren't enough, so what did you do? You freed the witch who killed you." The demon king laid his hand on Llewellyn's heart. "I believe you are far more deserving of the moniker 'freak.'"

Llewellyn bared his teeth and shoved Asmodeus back, once, twice. "Get off me, you filth. You were nothing before I summoned you. I opened the door for you to rise to heights you'd have never known without me, and you've gorged yourself on souls *I* made available. You've lacked for nothing and now that I want to take away just one of your play toys, you pout like a whiny little bitch."

Asmodeus smirked. "I see Lyon comes by that rage naturally."

Llewellyn took a deep breath. "Lyon may be your favorite, but know this. When he does his part? You'll have two worlds flooded with adrenaline and fear on which to sate yourself."

"Now, isn't that just a delightful thought?" Asmodeus plopped back down in Llewellyn's club chair. He scooted it as close to the fireplace as possible, and held his hands only inches from the flames.

Llewellyn sat on the sofa and sighed, wanting to be alone to plan for the return to his rightful place as king, but the demon was a chatty bastard who never took a hint.

Asmodeus sat back and stared. "Just one question. Why Circe? There are many powerful witches here and in the Overworld."

"None as powerful as her. Besides, there's a kind of poetry to having the witch who stole my destiny be the one to give it back."

Asmodeus sat quietly for a moment. "Has she told you why she wants Lyon?"

"She says he's connected to one of the women, but I don't know why that matters." Llewellyn stared at the fire. "Don't get too comfortable, we have a lot to do—starting with my eleven brethren. It's time for a meeting." He waved his hand in the direction of the door. "Go fetch them."

Asmodeus lowered his head, his lips peeled back in a scowl. The skin on his face bubbled and shifted between the pale white of his human facade and the black-lined, deep red skin of his true demon form. "Be careful, Llewellyn. Goddess blood in you or not, if you continue to disrespect me you may not make it out of the InBetween alive."

Llewellyn waited for the demon to leave before swigging the rest of his single malt. *What else will I have to deal with before I get my fucking due?*

Before he could gather his thoughts, Circe slithered into the room. "Has Lyon agreed?"

Llewellyn sat back and crossed his legs. "He refused until I dangled the freedom carrot. He jumped on it just as you predicted."

She moved around the room, a hand drifting over sculptures and vases. She stopped at a large painting. "I've been thinking about Lyon." She picked up a citrine crystal and bounced it in her palm. "I selected him because he has a connection with one of the women, and because he's desperate to be free." She faced Llewellyn. "But I want insurance that I'll have the women in time."

Llewellyn held perfectly still, and willed his mounting frustration back down until he thought he'd choke on it. "What do you suggest?"

"Dangle the same carrot to the other Zodiacs."

"I doubt they'll all respond to the same carrot."

She slammed the citrine down so hard it shattered in her hand. "Then find out what carrots are needed, and dangle them."

5

SAGITTARIUS BANGED HIS FIST ON Leona's door, steeled for a fight, but the heavy wood opened with a creak. He pushed it further until he saw the whole of her living space. The furniture was dark but feminine, throws and rugs brightening the space, but it was the table in one corner of the room that drew his attention. Covered by a deep purple cloth with an intricate sigil he'd never seen before, the table held candles and tools of a practitioner of dark magic.

He walked to the corner and held his hands just above her altar, too afraid to actually touch the material or tools that would be infused with Leona's intention—one he wasn't sure he wanted to learn. Even from inches away, he could feel the darkness, the weight. This wasn't a place of good. He looked up at the few books dotting the bookshelves to his right and backed away. Dark magic practiced with blood and bone and hate…

"Leona?"

She appeared, a wet cloth pressed against her left cheek. "Go away."

He swept his hand toward the altar. "What is this? Leona, please. Talk to me."

"Did I not make it perfectly clear that I have nothing to say to you?" She shoved him out of her room and tried to slam the door.

It bounced off his chest and opened wide again. "Let me see your face."

She pulled away from him and pushed the door harder, but his foot blocked it.

He forced his way back into the room and took the cloth from her. A large red blotch surrounded a jagged cut on her cheek. Swollen blue lines ran across her throat. He touched the evidence of Lyon's abuse. "Why? Hasn't he hurt you enough?"

Red blotches appeared on her face and chest. She moved back, her face angled away from him. "Keep your hands to yourself. You forfeited the right to touch me when you chose killing over me all those years ago."

"Hell, Leona, you know I didn't have a choice. Why won't you tell me what happened, what I did wrong? Goddess knows you've held it over my head long enough."

She shook her head and backed away.

Sag held up his hands. "Okay, stop. I've resigned myself to the fact you'll never tell me what I did wrong all those years ago. I'm here to find out what's happening to you now. You look terrible, and I've never known you to be so angry." He glanced at the altar. "And now you're dabbling in dark magic?"

"Go to hell and don't come back." She retreated to her bathroom and slammed the door behind her.

She's killing herself, but how? Anger, fear, love, and sadness were clumped together in his gut like a giant emotional Gordian knot that, when it came to Leona, would never be unwound. But at the moment, the winner by a TKO was hate. That son of a bitch Lyon was the root of all her pain, and now he was hitting her? Choking her?

Sag laid a hand on the closed bathroom door, and bowed his head. "He will pay for the wrongs he's done you. I'll see to that."

The Creeper escorts backed out of Lyon's cell and closed the door.

The old healer stood on the other side of his bed.

Lyon rubbed his temples. "Why are you here?" He heard the scuff of her slippers on the stone and looked up.

"You can't do this."

"Do what?" It was a game they had played for years—her fussing about whatever, him feigning ignorance. You'd think she was his mother the way she acted, but this time he wasn't in the mood.

"You're not deaf, boy."

"And you have no say in my business."

"Nothing good can be gained by going among the humans."

He glanced at the mound on his bed. "This isn't up for discussion."

"You won't be able to control yourself."

"Don't you get it? I have a chance to be free!" He advanced on her until she was cornered, then grabbed her upper arms. "The demon soul is growing stronger every day, I'm running out of time. If I don't do this, my soul will be consumed. I will cease to be."

She whimpered. "Lyon, please."

He blinked and looked down at his hands. The fragile skin covering her thin upper arms had blanched under his tight grip. He released her with a growl and backed away until his legs hit the bed. He swiped at the sweat rolling down his face and turned away, unable to look her in the eye. The image of his mother dying at his feet, her chest slashed to ribbons, stabbed at his brain and made his stomach flip. *Not again, not again.* He pressed his palms to his temples. "Get out."

"Lyon?"

He pushed harder, until he thought his head would pop off. "Out!"

"I'm sorry I meddled. Please, let me help you get ready."

He dropped his hands and looked at the hag. "If you stay I'll hurt you, and I don't want that."

She dragged a leather duffle bag out from under his bed and placed it on the blanket. "So," she said. Her voice was high and tight as if she was trying to pretend nothing had happened, but her vocal cords couldn't pull off the lie. "We need to get you prepared."

The woman knew how to push his buttons but she also knew how to calm him, to reach him when he was lost. All the times he'd returned to his cell bloody, wounded, out of his mind wired on adrenaline and demon go-go juice, she'd been there to put back the pieces of his body, his mind, his humanity that had been jumbled in the fray.

She dropped her head. "Please, Lyon. Just assimilate your two souls and find peace."

A growl bubbled up, but Lyon contained it. He grabbed the duffle handles and waited for the anger to dissipate before speaking. "I have a chance to be free of the demon soul—probably my only chance. There is nothing in the four worlds that will stop me from doing this, no matter the cost."

"And what if it can't be removed? Possession by a demon is one thing, but I've never heard of a spell that can remove a demon soul from a body."

The woman was a pain in his ass. The demon soul had been added to his soul, so surely it could be removed. Of course, that could be his hope talking. Lyon waved her off. It was easier to do that than face the possibility she might be right. "It has to be possible. I can't live like this anymore."

She pursed her lips for a moment before speaking. "Well, if you're going to be a fool, at least be a prepared one." She lifted a long box and laid it next to the duffle.

"You take too many liberties, hag," he said to ease the tension. He flipped the lid and found all-black urban survival clothes. Lyon removed them and spread them out. Wool cargo pants, a tee shirt, a long-sleeved wool shirt, a down vest rolled into a tube, a sweater, military boots, and a long leather coat lined with pockets and holsters for all manner of weapons. *How does she always know?*

He whirled a forefinger in the air. "Turn around."

She clucked, then closed her eyes. "As if I haven't seen every inch of you already."

He dropped his robe and eased into the new clothes. "What else you got?" He found a bug-out-bag, a staple of urban survival, in the bottom. He opened it and dumped the contents on the bed to see what else she'd brought him. A variety of daggers and sheaths, meals ready to eat, a compass and maps... Everything an assassin needed in the field. "Where'd you find all this?"

"I figured the other Zodiacs wouldn't miss them."

"You stole from them?"

"Yes."

He reloaded the bag and stuffed it in the duffle. A flash of light caught his eye. A multi-tool with the gold words Dolce & Gabbana inlaid into the grip had been caught in a fold of his blanket. He held up the tool so she could see it. "Libra?"

She nodded.

Lyon snorted. "He's gonna shit himself." He grinned and pocketed the tool. "I like."

She reached into her voluminous robes. "One more thing." She pulled out a pair of dark sunglasses. "You have clung to the dark for too long. The light will burn your eyes, and you will not be able to see the truth of things. Wear these, and you will."

He took the glasses and slipped them on. "What the hell do you mean by 'the truth of things'?" He turned, but she was gone.

6

LYON TRAVELED SOUTH THROUGH the InBetween cave system via an underground river. Punctured by the beam of a small Maglite, the darkness folded back to reveal shattered limestone columns, decay, and thick mats of mold.

He had hopes for this mission but no illusions. This was it for him. If he failed, then he might as well gank himself on the spot. Fending off the demon soul wasn't getting any easier—he was baked beyond crunchy from the effort.

A tiny bright spotlight announced an armory so rarely used it had been forgotten. A wizened old man caught the line Lyon threw him and tied the inflatable dinghy to what could only be called a board, not a dock. A shack, set several feet back from the water, leaned hard to the right, and looked too small to house an armory and two people.

Lyon climbed out, his duffle on one shoulder, and nodded to the couple. "You still in business?"

"Depends," the old man croaked, his eyes squinting to see. "What do you need?"

The old woman smacked him on the back of his nearly bald head. "Where are your spectacles? You never have them on when you need them."

The old man winced away from her broad, flour-coated hands, and patted his pockets front, back, north, south.

Lyon pointed to his neck. "They're on that string."

The man squinted harder, then cupped his ears. "Huh?"

"Oh, for goddess' sake, Hiram." The woman lifted the bent and cracked glasses to his face. "You're going to be the death of us."

Hiram slid his specs in place and looked at Lyon. "Ahhh! Run, Fessa!" The pair turned and wobbled back and forth in a run a sloth could best, their bodies in sync left-right-left-right, their feet scuffing across the hard-pack.

Lyon's lips twitched. "Stop."

The couple halted just shy of the door. They hunched their shoulders around their ears as if anticipating a blow. Hiram turned back to face him. "Please, don't kill us. Spare our lives, and I'll let you have...I'll let you have the sex with my wife."

Fessa turned and crossed her arms. "You would, wouldn't you? You would let this cretin rape me to save your scrawny butt."

Hiram clapped both hands over his bottom. "What? You think he wants the sex with me?"

Heat flooded Lyon's body—not from rage or lust, but embarrassment. He cocked his head and frowned, as if contemplating Hiram's offer. "Though it pains me to deny myself the pleasure, I haven't the time to lay with your woman nor the desire to have the sex with you. I'll have to make do with supplies for the Overworld instead."

"Well, then." Hiram opened the armory door for Fessa and Lyon. "Whatever you need. We have guns, we have knives."

Lyon shook his head. "Don't do guns. I have daggers. What else?"

Hiram snapped his fingers under Fessa's nose.

She cocked one eyebrow. "I know that's not for me."

Hiram grunted. He frowned for a moment, then smiled and waved Lyon over. "Here, we have human coin." He pulled out a dusty shoebox and flipped the lid.

Lyon lifted a wad of bills, but they crumbled in his hand.

Fessa punched Hiram's arm. "I told you to put them in a can."

Lyon dug through the coins in the box until he unearthed a small red velvet bag. He emptied the contents into his hand. Twenty gold coins, shiny and pristine, clinked together. He picked up one coin and studied the Grecian woman on one side. He flipped it and saw an eagle in flight. "What are these?"

Hiram gasped and turned his back on Lyon. "I moved those to another box," he hissed in Fessa's ear.

"And I moved them back. The boy needs them more than we do."

Hiram huffed off.

"Ignore him." Fessa watched her husband for a second before giving her full attention to Lyon. "They're called double eagles."

"They look expensive. Where'd you get them?"

Fessa reached out to pat Lyon's hand, but stopped when he jerked it back. She wiped her apron, as if the lapse never happened. "Teddy Roosevelt was a friend."

"A friend, my tuchus, he was your lover," Hiram groused.

"Yes, and a mighty fine one for a human," she snapped back.

"Keep them." Lyon said to stop the argument before it delved deeper into information he did not want to know. "I can steal whatever I need."

Fessa shook her head and clucked. "Oh, no, no. Not these days, Zodiac. The humans have machines everywhere that will record your image and get you caught. And you? In a human prison?" She leaned close and lowered her voice. "Handsome boy like you would be mounted within hours." She put a finger to her lips. She reached around him, and handed him a small box of condoms with the name "Trojans" on the lid. "Just in case," she whispered, and winked.

Lyon cleared his throat before pocketing the condoms, noting an expiration date circa the 1970s. "I think that's enough to get me started."

Hiram wobbled back. "You shouldn't do this, Zodiac. No, no, no. The human world has changed since you were last there. The noise alone will overstimulate your senses and you will fail. Go back. Let someone else do this mission."

Lyon said nothing. If he listened to them and turned down the mission, he would be thrown in the armpit of the dungeons, alone save for the demon soul and its assault on his waning defenses until it possessed him. If he ignored their advice, however, he risked losing control in the Overworld and killing the three women.

Hiram's insistence that the mission would lead to disaster, coupled with the hag's warning, scared the crap out of him—but the threat of being dominated by the demon soul scared him more. He had no choice; he had to try.

Any cost, right?

Lyon pulled the sunglasses out of his pocket. "I've been told these are my secret weapon."

The couple looked at the glasses, then each other.

Lyon held them out to Fessa. "Here, take them. They're not as valuable as gold coins or condoms, but maybe you can barter them."

Her eyes widened and she backed away, pulling Hiram with her. "No, you keep them. They'll help you see more clearly."

Lyon pocketed the glasses, puzzled by the fear in their eyes. "Okay. Let's get this done."

Hiram unlocked a cabinet and Fessa removed an old iron band covered in symbols. Lyon offered his arm, and she clapped the band around his thick wrist. She held it with both hands. "Do not lose this. It's your only ticket home."

She led Lyon to a small curved niche carved in the wall. He stepped inside and a glass door closed with a quiet *whoosh*, separating him from the couple.

"This new?" Lyon asked as he looked around the claustrophobic tube of glass and metal, empty save for a pair of curved brass tubes on either side of his hips.

"Not so much," the couple said together.

"How's it work?"

"Place your hands on the two brass handles and hold on, dearie," the old woman said.

"No, no, don't listen to her," Hiram corrected.

A deep hum started at Lyon's feet and rose up the wall until it reached the full height of the tube. It shook harder and harder, until the hum became a din. Lyon leaned forward and yelled, "What?"

The old man cupped his mouth. "One hand on a handle, the other on your—"

In a gut-bottoming lurch, the tube shot up and the couple disappeared.

"—balls," Hiram hollered.

Fessa waved away the dust and smoke. "How many times have I asked you to fix it?"

Hiram threw up his hands. "How did I get stuck with such a shrew?"

"She's inserted herself in Lyon's life." Fessa frowned. "Giving the boy *those* glasses, what was she thinking?"

"What was *she* thinking? Hah! That's a trifle compared to what Llewellyn is doing." He snorted, his dour expression that of a man long beleaguered. "Our world is about to change, mother, and in a biggity-bad way. It may be time to pack up and leave."

The tube slammed to a halt. Lyon's head jammed into the top, and pain exploded behind his eyes and neck, but it was his nuts that hurt the most. "Shit me," he said as he adjusted the offended stones.

A deep *thunk* at his feet vibrated the tube and his insides. The tube rotated slowly, revealing the exit tunnel inch by inch. Narrow and crudely carved out of bedrock, the cave was coated with dust and cobwebs. Bones from small animals were strewn around the floor. The space had been staged to turn away even the most inquisitive humans.

Lyon's heart raced. He clenched his fists, and pressed his forehead against the cool glass. Anything to get out of the dungeon cell he called home, right? *So, why is taking this first step so hard? And why does this whole job feel so wrong, like it's the beginning of my end?*

"Fuck it." He gripped both brass handholds again. Air escaped with a hiss, and the glass opened. Lyon took a deep breath and stepped out. As soon as he cleared the rim of the chute, the glass door closed. The tube rotated until all he saw was metal, and then, in the blink of an eye, the tube dropped, disappearing on its journey back to the InBetween. A slab of rock slid over the tube opening and closed with a *clunk*, disguising the chute so effectively that even Lyon had difficulty seeing it.

He turned from the rock and squinted to protect his eyes from the blinding light, but tears still rolled down his face. He slipped on the sunglasses, dimming the light to a tolerable level.

Time to get on with it.

He took a step, then another one. His steps became treads and his treads became strides until he reached the opening to the Overworld.

Lyon paused at the exit. He rolled his shoulders, and ignored the warning buzzing in his head until it became nothing but background noise, no more important than the squirrel chewing on a nut in the tree in front of him, or the soft hiss of the wind that ruffled his hair.

One more step, and he'd be back in the world that had cost him so dearly—but not this time. This time, he would reclaim everything.

He opened his arms, and roared.

7

LYON SHIFTED HIS BODY TO EASE the cramp in his left leg. He'd been on his belly on the small rise above the house for hours watching one of the women with his binoculars. A hat covered her hair and blocked the top half of her face as she clomped through the woods, a bag over her shoulder. She stopped and leaned against a tree, rubbing her left thigh.

A frigid wind blew the fresh smell of rain over him. His body shook. His skin prickled. The dungeons were cold, but they didn't have wind and rain. Clouds rolled in and blocked the moonlight. Lightning flashed. He flinched when the thunder boomed—the storm was almost on top of him. "Get a grip, man."

The trip from Kentucky to Texas had been short but miserable. Hiram had understated the noise, and he hadn't even bothered to warn Lyon about the smells or the blistering sun. At least it was dark now, and Lyon could see.

Suddenly, the woman jumped and turned around.

Lyon trained his binoculars in the direction she was looking, but he saw nothing unusual. By the time his gaze had returned to her, she was running for the house.

She disappeared inside. He tracked her movement through the house by the lights flicking on.

This was too easy. He scanned the house perimeter, then the surrounding land. The snap of a twig drew his attention back to the house in time to see a large figure easing around the right corner. Abruptly, the lights inside winked out. The figure paused at the large bay window. A flash of lightning revealed the prowler's face.

Lyon's heart flopped in his chest. "Scorpio. Shit."

Scor climbed the porch steps, then rushed the front door and broke it open with one shoulder, the deadbolt no match for his mass.

Lyon dropped his binoculars and raced down the ridge. Lightning flashed and several more figures emerged from the tree line. A few feet from the front porch, Lyon heard the woman scream.

Llewellyn had betrayed him. He'd sent the other Zodiacs, and they were advancing on the house—poised to steal Lyon's prize.

Persephone felt her way through the kitchen and down the long hall to the breaker box in the garage. Dratted house was so sensitive to weather, wind, whatever, that the power went out regularly. But she shouldn't complain: Abella had won the one thousand-acre ranch in a game of strip Texas Hold'em, because the man was so distracted by her La Perla-covered tits that he'd lost his focus, the hand, and probably his marriage.

Persephone turned to enter the windowless utility room but stubbed her toe, and then her nose on the door trim. She hopped on one foot, her hand extended out to feel for the wall while the other cupped her throbbing nose. "Ouch."

She limped to the breaker box, but none of the switches were tripped. She popped the master off and on again. The fuses weren't the problem. A chill swept through her. This was the second time in as many days that the electricity had gone out, but it wasn't the breakers. She hugged the wall and used her hands to feel her way as she made her way back to the kitchen. She reached for the landline phone, but before she could call Taryn and Abella, there was a soft creak outside the kitchen door. Someone was on the back porch.

Liquid heat exploded inside her. Her fight-or-flight instinct pegged on flight. She covered her mouth with trembling hands and backed down the hall to the front door. She whirled around to make her escape when a movement beyond the frosted glass panes in the front door caught her eye. The outline of someone very large appeared. She screamed and turned to run, but her feet lost traction. Her palms and knees slammed down on the wood floor but the pain barely registered. She pushed off and ran for the kitchen, her heart in her throat, choking off her air.

The door exploded inward. A huge man chased her down the hall.

She looked back.

He lunged for her.

She screamed again, and tried to escape but he grabbed her from behind and pulled her into his chest. Her legs lost feeling and she sagged, but he gripped her tighter.

"Scream all you want, little girl, no one can hear you," he whispered in her ear. "Now, tell me. Where are your roommates?"

Lyon rushed through the front door in a crouch, a dagger in hand. He scanned the room to the left. Living room. Empty.

He started down the hall when the woman screamed. Scor had her in the kitchen, the view blocked by swinging doors.

Lyon backtracked to the living room. He skirted around the furniture until he reached a corner that divided the living and dining rooms. He heard the clatter of metal, the bang of a drawer hitting the floor—Scor was searching for something. Lyon dropped into a crouch and balanced his weight on the balls of his feet. He peeked around the corner.

The door to the kitchen was open. Scor had an arm across the woman's upper body, squeezing her back against his chest, his attention on the contents of the sink.

The woman's struggling slowed. She inhaled sharply. She had seen him.

Lyon held a forefinger to his lips.

She stopped moving for the span of a breath, then kicked and clawed harder.

Lyon shook his head, then jerked back when a knife flew past his nose.

"I've got her, Lyon, and I'm cashing her in."

"Can't be about money, you were never interested in that."

"You know nothing about me. Not anymore."

Lyon chanced another look, then froze. Scorpio's eyes glowed. His skin rippled in places, as if something was crawling just under the surface. But it was the large patches of ink-free skin that chilled him. Scor's tattoos were coming to life—several had already dropped off his body.

Seriously bad shit.

The scorpions were quiet, and as deadly as they come. One sting could kill a human in seconds. The woman was out of time.

Lyon heard a faint skitter. At the transition from kitchen tile to dining room carpet, a palm-sized black scorpion faced him, frozen as if awaiting orders.

The woman whimpered. Several more scorpions crawled over her face and upper body, their tails curved over their backs, their needle-like stingers poised to strike.

Lyon held his hands out and dropped his dagger. "Stop. I'll back off."

"No! Please!" Tears garbled her panicked plea.

Scor backed out and disappeared down a hall.

Lyon ran into the kitchen. He searched the cabinets next to the stove, under the sink, rushing until he found the canister he needed in the back of the pantry.

Glass crashed in another room. The other Zodiacs had breached the house. He was out of time.

Lyon worked his way down the hall. His instincts screamed for him to rush this—and he would have if it were any other Zodiac, but Scor never gave a second warning and had no compunction about killing. Lyon wasn't afraid of anyone, but Scor did give him pause.

"Come on, woman, make a noise. Tell me where you are," he muttered.

He heard a scrape behind the second door on the right. He lifted the canister and pulled the pin. Another scrape. Scorpio cursed. Lyon raised his right leg and kicked the door at the strike plate.

The woman was covered with scorpions, but damn if she wasn't biting the shit out of Scor's forearm.

Lyon sprayed Scor and his bugs with the fire extinguisher. The scorpions fell to the floor, stunned by the cold blast, while Scor released the woman and backed away. New scorpions erupted from his skin and he flung them at Lyon.

Lyon ducked and spun under Scorpion's arm, then bashed him in the head with the extinguisher. The Zodiac dropped.

The woman scrambled to get away, but Lyon grabbed her by the waist and carried her kicking and screaming to another bedroom. He closed the door and locked it. It wouldn't hold back the Zodiacs for long. He checked the front yard, then opened the window.

She clawed his face as he carried her through. He dropped down behind the shrubs and clamped his hand over her mouth, only to have her bite his palm.

"I'm trying to save you, damn it," he hissed in her ear.

She released his hand and stopped struggling, but her body shook.

"Do you have a car?"

She nodded.

"Where?"

She pointed to the right.

He released her mouth. "Are the keys in it?"

"Yes. Visor."

"Can you run?"

She opened her mouth to speak.

Lyon heard the soft *swoosh* of footsteps in grass. He held his forefinger to her lips and shook his head.

She nodded.

Clever girl.

He peeked through the dense leaves.

Taurus rolled his wide, thick shoulders. He scanned the yard from the front porch, then closed his eyes and sniffed the air. The Zodiac's senses were off the charts. Thank the goddess Lyon and the woman were downwind. If Lyon could have stopped his heartbeat for a few seconds, he would have, but a clap of thunder distracted Taurus. He descended the stairs and walked past them.

"Now," Lyon whispered in her ear.

He pulled the woman through the shrubs and held her hand tight as they sprinted to a land-yacht-sized sedan sitting under a huge oak tree. Lyon opened the back door and threw the woman onto the seat, then climbed in the driver's side and dropped the visor. The keys bounced off his lap and fell to the floor. Lyon picked them up and grimaced when he saw the woman in the rearview mirror, scrambling for the tree line, the door still ajar.

Not so clever after all.

"Arg." Lyon chased her into the woods, and grabbed her waist. She clawed at his face and kicked his shins, each blow punctuated by her growl. He covered her mouth and carried her to the car.

He glanced behind him. The other Zodiacs had heard them. They were closing fast.

The *tink-tink* of metal hitting metal sounded around him. He pushed the woman against the car and wrapped his body around her. Something small and hot slammed into his lower back, just left of his spine. His body jerked, and the sharp pain made him sag. He was hit. He gripped the door handle to stay on his feet and opened it for her.

"Get in."

She climbed in and slid to the passenger side.

He got behind the wheel and started the car.

The Zodiacs were only yards away when Lyon saw movement in the side mirror. Scor staggered out of the house, a rifle in his hands.

He pushed on the woman's neck. "Get down!"

The rear windshield exploded. She screamed. Lyon gunned the beast and they roared out of the yard, careening their way down the long gravel drive until they reached the highway.

"Go left."

Lyon took a right.

"Why'd you do that?"

"Because I'm not stupid. The sheriff's office is to the left."

"How did you know?"

"I scoped out the area. Where are the others?"

"Others?"

Lyon grimaced and shifted in the seat. Warm, sticky blood had bonded his T-shirt to his skin. "Don't screw with me, I'm in no mood. Your roommates, where are they?"

The woman crossed her arms and said nothing.

"You may think you're being loyal, but those men aren't going to leave your house. Do you want your friends to meet them?"

She checked her pockets, then pulled out a phone.

Lyon snatched it from her. "Not so fast." He looked at the screen, then handed the phone back.

"It's shattered."

"Exactly." Lyon slowed the car. They edged past old brick-and-mortar buildings so tightly packed together it looked like they were huddling for warmth, the owners and shoppers gone for the night. In seconds, they passed the last building and the rural countryside resumed its reign.

A few miles later, Lyon saw the dilapidated house on a small hill a hundred yards from the road. He turned onto the overgrown, dirt drive and they bounced on the bench seat as the car dipped and swayed through every rut and pothole until they reached an old shed behind the house.

He climbed out of the car and waved at the trembling woman to scoot across the seat. "Out." She slid over, then grabbed the steering wheel, pivoted on the seat, and kicked him in the gut.

He grunted, took one step back, and growled.

She paused, her mouth open, her eyes wide.

He grabbed her ankles and jerked her out of the car. She landed on her butt with a grunt, and her cap fell off releasing a cascade of long silver hair. He gripped her arms and pulled her to her feet. "Will you cooperate, or do I have to drag you to the cabin?"

"By my hair no doubt, you cretin," she blurted.

"By the hair, over my shoulder, whatever works." He tightened his grip and pulled her to the cabin. "Which one are you? Abella, Persephone, or Taryn?"

"Who are you? What's going on?"

"Where are your friends?"

She remained silent.

"Fine." He pushed her inside the one-room cabin, locked the door with three brand-new double-cylinder deadbolts, and pocketed the keys. He went to the open kitchen and lit a candle. A stack of wood sat by the fireplace. White pillar candles dotted the space, and several full plastic grocery bags sat on the floor, their contents spilling out. No one had lived there in a while, but it looked like they'd left in a hurry: furniture and pots and pans had been left behind.

The woman took a step deeper into the cabin. "You planned this."

He looked at the supplies. "This? Yes. The attack? No." Lyon lit the kindling and waited for the fire to spread to the logs. "What's your name?"

A rush of movement caught his attention. He pivoted on the balls of his feet, and an iron skillet hit the side of his head with a deep *gong*. A bright flash of light preceded the dark. He fell to the floor, hitting his head on the warped wood right on the rapidly rising knot.

"My name is Persephone, and no one forces me into a box, not again," she said, her voice a hiss of fear-laced defiance. She patted his pockets until she found the ring of keys. She tugged on the ring, but couldn't break it free from the fabric.

Lyon's foggy head pounded, but his limbs still worked. He gripped her bare wrist and wrenched it away. A zing of electricity arced between them. They stopped tussling for a moment, both surprised.

The woman resumed fighting his grip, but she was the size of one of his thighs. He pulled her down to the floor and rolled his bulk on top of her. She grunted and pushed at his shoulders, cursing his lineage, but he let his weight do the talking.

She relaxed a little. He raised his upper body so she could breathe and was rewarded with a hard bite on the tender flesh of his neck, so he flattened her again and waited. She would either stop fighting or stop breathing. Right now, he wasn't sure which he preferred.

Her hands slapped and scratched and pulled at his skin and clothes and hair. After several seconds, she stopped. Her arms dropped to the floor and she lay still, her heart pounding against his chest, each pull of air a battle that she would soon lose.

"If I let you up, are you going to behave?"

She nodded her head.

"Just so you know, I'm not here to harm you. I'm not interested in locking you in a box, either. Understand?"

She nodded harder, her hands fluttering around his shoulders.

Lyon pondered how much easier it would be to let her pass out before he rolled off of her. Her cooperation would be assured, and her mouth would be shut, but…

He rolled off the woman and latched his hands on the vertical stones that formed the fireplace chimney. Hand over hand he rose to his feet, the warm sticky blood in his hair pulling at his scalp and its undoubted laceration.

The woman coughed and gagged. She'd been a lot closer to passing out than he'd realized. A cold chill swept through him.

Women. Bane. Yeah.

Since becoming a Zodiac, he'd had plenty of offers for 'companionship' from women who wanted a taste of mortality with the 'Beast of the InBetween.' He could accept the random, anonymous sex—a guy needed to pop his top occasionally—but the women's demands for choking or beating during the act triggered both his greatest rage, and his greatest fear.

After a time, he'd given up women, tired of their fetishes, fixations, and fierce drive for self-destruction, until ultimately, he couldn't stand to be in a woman's company for any longer than a few minutes, much less touch their naked flesh. The old hurts and anger that boiled just under his skin demanded release. Women were a trigger that could open that door. It became easier to avoid them altogether and use the savagery of the pit fights to burn back his encroaching darkness.

He shook his head. Clear out the maudlin cobwebs, man. No time for this foolishness.

He pulled her to her feet. She swayed a bit, but didn't buckle. He brushed the dust off her clothes, ignoring her recoils when he touched her and the stunned, unblinking stare. He backed her to a chair and pushed her down. "My name is Lyon." He picked up the box of tinfoil and went to the closest window.

"You installed metal bars," she said, her voice a raspy whisper.

"At every window."

"What's going on? Why am I here?"

What would he gain by telling her the truth? Maybe some cooperation? Could the truth be any scarier than what she'd already been through? He pulled down the shredded drapes, then covered the pane with the foil. "I've been ordered to bring you and your friends to my father."

"Why?"

"I don't know."

"Well, what does he want with us?"

"I don't know."

"What *do* you know?"

"I was given an order. End of story."

She burst out of the chair, ran to the door, and pounded it with her fists, screaming for help.

Lyon covered his ears to block the shrill noise. He tried to push her away from the door with his body, but she just ducked under him and went to the nearest window.

She clawed at the tinfoil, then struck the windowpane. The glass shattered.

Lyon grabbed her arm.

She turned on him and punched.

His flank wound exploded with fresh torment. He wrapped an arm around her waist, dragged her to the bed, and threw her down. "I didn't want to do this."

She bucked and flailed her arms.

He opened the sole nightstand drawer and removed handcuffs.

"No, no, I'll stop. I promise. Please, don't."

He cuffed her left hand to the metal headboard. He disappeared inside the bathroom and returned with bandages, a tube of ointment, and wet cloth. "Behave and I'll leave the rest of your limbs free."

She scrambled away from him when he sat on the bed.

He waited in silence to give her a chance to calm down. The wan light from the fire painted her face in dark shadows and flickering orange, obscuring her features, but something about her seemed familiar. He studied her closely for a moment before shaking his head. What she looked like didn't matter as long as she was one of the women Llewellyn wanted.

When she stopped panting, he showed her the supplies in his hands. "I just want to clean and bandage your wound."

"What? Wound?" She stared at her bloody wrist for several seconds, then held it out to Lyon.

He cleaned her wrist and hand, dabbing at the fresh blood welling up with gauze until it finally clotted, before wrapping it. "That should do."

"Please, let me go. I won't report you."

"I have a job to do. As for reporting me, there's not a human out there who can stop me."

She pulled her head back, her eyes widened. "Human?"

Lyon pushed off the mattress and stood. He dragged the ancient recliner across the room, placed it next to the bed, then eased into it, surprised that the ugly, puke-green dinosaur was so comfortable. When he was free, he may have to come back and take the thing.

The woman turned her head away. That was for the best—he had no answers for her. Hell, even if he did have answers, he had no interest in quenching her curiosity.

A tickle started in his side and traveled south. He lifted his shirt and twisted at the waist. A fresh round of bleeding had started. He touched the small hole and blood poured out. Sweat ran down his face as a new wave of hot pain surged through him. The deep dark of unconsciousness made a strong bid, but he staved it off by thinking of his impending freedom. *It will be mine, no matter the cost.*

8

T HE ZODIACS SURROUNDED SCORPIO.

"What's going on, Scor?" Taurus asked.

"Was that really Lyon?" Pisces added.

Libra pushed through the other Zodiacs. "I was ordered to get three women to Llewellyn in the InBetween."

"Ditto," Capricorn said.

The remaining Zodiacs nodded their heads.

Scor snarled at the men. "So we were given the same order. Quit your bitching and help me figure out where Lyon went." He sniffed the air and caught a hint of metallic.

He walked around the front yard in a grid pattern, looking for the origin. The metallic smell disappeared. He doubled back to the west side of the house, where the car had been parked. A flash of light on the ground caught his eye. He squatted and touched it. A thick, sticky fluid coated his fingertips. He raised them to his nose and sniffed. "Blood and sulfur. Lyon was wounded." He ran his fingers through the grass to clean off the blood. "He won't get very far without help."

The low purr of a car engine brought Scor to full alert. "Cover!"

The Zodiacs scattered and disappeared around the house. Scor sprinted across the front yard and squatted behind a shrub, his view of the drive and the front door unimpeded.

A gorgeous, black 1971 Hemi 'Cuda rolled past him and stopped at an angle in front of the house. Some humans had a bucket list of things they wanted to do before they died. As a paranorm, Scor would live much longer than the inferior little meatsuits walking around in the Overworld, so he made his own version. Parked directly in front of him was the number-one item on that list. If the male driving it tried to keep him from taking it, Scor would end him.

A short, ebony-haired woman got out of the passenger side, chattering away about something. Pretty, loud, and dressed like a frump, Scor dismissed her immediately. His attention turned to the driver's door. Adrenaline spiked his heart rate, his muscles tensed. His scorpions writhed under his skin in anticipation of an attack.

The car door opened and a long slim leg, ending in a spike-heeled shoe, appeared. A second leg joined the first. A woman emerged.

Scorpio sucked in his breath. She was the tallest female he'd ever seen. He started at her feet and worked his way up her luscious body until he reached her face. Pale skin covered a bone structure that a goddess would envy, framed by red hair cut close to her skull. Scor wasn't a fan of short hair on a woman, but for this woman it worked. He blinked and shifted his hips to relieve his instant boner. Her rare beauty made him forget about her height, or her hair... Forget about everything except pounding her.

The short woman was still blathering on, but his focus was so tuned into the redhead all he heard was *blah-blah-blah*. The women walked to the porch steps. The short one went on to the front door, but the redhead stopped on the stairs, her attention on something at her feet. She bent over, exposing the longest, loveliest real estate Scor had ever seen, shooting his imagination into the porn stratosphere. Those long legs wrapped around his huge body while he impaled her sex over and over until she exploded beneath him. Oh yeah, he definitely needed to make that fantasy a reality.

Then she picked up one of his scorpions, and his fantasy screeched to a halt.

"Do you see this, Taryn? I could swear…but it's not possible." She held her hand up, her voice dropped to a mutter. "It looks like a species that's been extinct for centuries, which is surprising because they were one of the top predators of their age. When you get inside turn on the porch light, will ya? Persephone must have forgotten it again."

The woman called Taryn pushed the door open, then stepped back when it wobbled on its damaged hinges. "Uh, Abella, I hate to interrupt your creepy fascination with all things predator but we have something more pressing."

The redhead cupped the dead scorpion and laid it on the porch railing with a reverence that startled Scor. Most women shunned him. They couldn't stand to look at his tattoos, much less touch them. The few exceptions were bat-shit crazy, good for fucking but little else. But this woman not only touched his dead scorpion, she was gentle with it.

She's just another split-tail, Scor, and you've got a job to do.

Abella ran her fingers over the broken strike plate and shattered wood. She reached around to the small of her back. "Shit, my gun is inside." She grabbed the short woman's arm. "Get behind me."

"Are you kidding? We're still going in?"

"Persephone might be inside."

The shorter woman closed her mouth and nodded.

Scor stood and cleared his throat.

The two women whirled around.

"No need to go inside. She's not in there."

Persephone threw her pillow at the cretin to stop his snoring before it brought the rickety shack down around them. The pillow bounced off his face and landed on the floor. He snuffled, swiped at his face, and snored louder.

"For god's sake." She yanked on the handcuff, but it didn't do any good. "I should have hit him where it counts."

She rolled to the edge of the bed and saw his blood pooled on the floor. Who were these men, and what did they want with her and her friends? Tears welled. Anger, fear, and frustration melded together until she thought she'd explode. She writhed on the bed, fighting her need to twitch. *Restless Leg Syndrome, ha*. Restless Body Syndrome was a better description of how she felt.

After escaping the foster system, Persephone, Abella, and Taryn had promised each other they would never again allow anyone or anything to make them feel afraid and powerless. Persephone had worked hard to live up to that promise, but being shackled triggered long-buried childhood memories and shattered the illusion that she'd ever had any real control. She cowered in the dark, a frightened little girl again, praying for the boogie man to forget she was alive.

If only the darkness would cede to the light.

She closed her eyes and forced her body to relax. Indulging in panic wouldn't help her find a way to get loose, and it sure wouldn't help Taryn and Abella.

She opened her eyes and found the light. Hours must have passed. She rolled her head. The sun had not risen but a recently stoked fire flared high, giving her enough illumination to see the rough outlines of the furniture in the one-room cabin. Another recliner sat alone by the fireplace, a twin to the one Lyon was slouched in. Two bistro chairs were tucked against a small round table. A 1960s-era avocado-green stove and refrigerator ate up most of the designated kitchen space.

She turned her attention back to the man responsible for this current cock-up. Déjà vu swamped her, and she struggled to understand why. Long tawny hair covered much of his face, but she could see full lips and a web of scars that split his exposed eyebrow and marred his nose and chin, then ran down his neck and under his shirt. Tall as a basketball player with thick muscle covering his well-proportioned body, he was only slightly less massive than the monster in her nightmares. The seams of his black T-shirt strained to contain his pecs and biceps but were on the verge of failure. Scanning parts south proved the same was true for his pants. She'd no idea material could be stretched that far by man bits and thigh muscles without splitting.

She forced her eyes back to his face. Her cheeks flamed when she saw a stunning amber eye watching her. A surge of heat zinged her sex; the sensitive flesh contracted. *Don't need Kegel exercises when you have a man like that around.*

"Like what you see?" Lyon said in a husky voice.

She tried to think of something snarky to say but, as usual, no go on the comeback. "No, I don't. You're bleeding."

He raised his shirt and twisted.

Persephone couldn't help staring at the scars that covered his belly, or the dark-blond trail of hair that divided his eight-pack then disappeared under the waist of his pants. She shook her head to get rid of the lust fog.

The wound in his back was still bleeding, and she smelled a slight hint of infection. "Are you a hemophiliac?"

Lyon frowned. "No, I like women."

Had she not been attacked, rescued, kidnapped by her rescuer, and shackled to a bed by the same, she would have found his answer funny. "I mean, do you bleed a lot when you get hurt?"

"No, I'm not a bleeder."

She rattled the handcuff against the brass headboard. "Release me so I can take care of your wound."

Lyon dropped his shirt. "No."

"So what happens when you bleed out with me still cuffed?"

Lyon pushed off the chair and hobbled the four steps it took to get to the kitchen. "We both die."

Scorpio paced in front of the two women while Libra tried to get a fix on Lyon's phone. They were bound and finally quiet after his threats of bodily harm.

"Can't we just slit their throats?" Scorpio asked the other Zodiacs. All but Libra nodded their assent.

"Llewellyn wants these two alive." He turned in the chair and looked up at the men. "Do you want to tell him that we caught the women, then let Scor kill them?"

The men grumbled.

Libra sneered. "I didn't think so."

Scor grunted. "They're not talking. Time to do it my way."

"What are you suggesting? Torture? How any of you ever found your marks is beyond me," Libra said. He typed on his iPad for a few minutes, then slammed his fist on the kitchen table. "His phone must be off. We'll have to wait."

Taurus snorted. "Does he even have a cell? Last time he was topside, phones numbers were a mix of letters and numbers."

The redhead cleared her throat. "Topside? What the hell does that mean?"

Scor glared at the woman. He grabbed her chin and angled her face up. He studied the hot flare in her huge green eyes, her defiance as intriguing as her beauty was formidable. Too bad the woman would be collateral damage—he would have enjoyed breaking her. Of course, there was a lot of time between now and then.

"Whatever happens, this woman is mine," Scor said.

She jerked her head away and bared her teeth. "My name is Abella, not 'woman,' and I belong to no man."

"You think I give a shit about your name?" Scor rolled up one of his long sleeves, exposing his scorpion tats. He held his forearm close to her eyes and waited for the screams to start, for the sweet tang of her terror to waft up his nose. To his surprise, she leaned closer and studied the tats writhing under his skin. Where were the tears and terror that fed him?

"Stop playing with your food, Scor, and let me think. In fact, if all of you would kindly shut up…" Libra said.

Scor rolled his sleeve down. "Go get some sleep. Lyon and his woman won't get far if the blood in the yard is any indication. I'll take first watch."

The other Zodiacs left the kitchen. They weren't gone for more than a few seconds before an argument started over who got the bed, who was relegated to the couch, and which men had to sleep on the floor. A crash heralded the beginning of a fistfight.

Scor snorted. That didn't take long. Not surprising, considering the Zodiacs always worked alone. He settled on the floor in a corner of the kitchen, a scimitar across his lap, and waited for the house to quiet down before he pulled out a burner phone and sent a text. With that done, he pocketed the cell and closed his eyes, but an itch started at the back of his neck. He looked up. The redhead stared at him, her head cocked to one side as if studying him like a bug under a microscope.

"You harm Taryn or Persephone, I'll track you down and kill you."

He sneered and shook his head. "Words."

The woman leaned as far forward as the duct tape would allow. "Not words, that's a promise."

"You're welcome to try. Now shut your smart mouth and get some sleep."

Sunlight roused Lyon, but the hot jolt of pain spearing his flank woke him fully when he sat up.

I'm screwed.

Injured and babysitting only one woman out of three, the mighty—and mightily feared—Lyon had fallen far. To add salt to this snafu, he had no clue who these women were or why Llewellyn would send Lyon to retrieve them, then send the other Zodiacs. What was the point?

Dried blood coated the back of his shirt and his butt. He was stuck to the recliner fabric. He peeled it free and stood, each breath puffed out of him like steam venting. The air in the cabin was chilly and stale. He cracked the front door, then threw more wood on the live embers in the fireplace. He dropped the pieces of tinfoil from the windows to prevent the reflected sunlight from signaling their presence to everyone in the county. Bright light streamed in. His eyes watered.

"Shit." He re-covered the windows, dimming the sunlight so he could see.

He returned to Persephone, and unwrapped the bandage covering her cut hand. She flinched and moaned. The laceration should have been stitched, but the first aid kit in his bug-out bag was in his stolen car near her house. He still had the duffle, but losing the BOB was a setback.

After he finished rewrapping her hand, he reached for the pillow covering her face, but before he could remove it and get a better look at her, she rolled out from under it, opened her eyes and screamed.

She scrambled away as far as the cuff would let her. Typical response. He'd dealt with screams, tears, begging all his life. Can't expect warm fuzzies when you're a killer, but it did get tiresome when everyone had the same reaction. He crossed his arms and waited for her to simmer down or faint—whichever came first, as long as she stopped.

She grabbed the small lamp and threw it at his head. He ducked and turned. The lamp missed him, but it ripped the tinfoil and shattered another window. The sun blinded him again. He covered his eyes with one arm and backed toward the bed. "Damn it woman, I'm trying to help you."

The sheets rustled. "You scared me."

She touched his bare wrist and a jolt of electricity stabbed him. The sharp mix of pleasure and pain sent a shiver through his body. He jerked away from her. "Don't."

"You need help. Release me so I can get the bullet out before you bleed to death."

Lyon turned and froze. The morning sun danced across her cheeks and lit up her unusual purple eyes, her pale blonde eyebrows, and the bow of her full lips. Her long pale hair shimmered and flowed over her shoulders and chest like molten silver. Unease gripped him; he knew this face. The long straight hair, the curve of her high cheekbones, the jut of her chin. Exactly like his drawing, exactly like his dreams.

He backed into the sunlight, and the beam lit his features.

Persephone pushed into the headboard and pulled her feet into her chest. "I know you…don't I?"

Lyon grunted when his back hit the wall but he remained silent. She'd already verbalized his thoughts as if she could read his mind. What more was there to say?

9

Llewellyn stood next to the fireplace, his left hand braced against the pink and grey marble, his fingers drumming the cold stone. Circe and Asmodeus sat behind him, hatching goddess—only—knew what kind of personal plans. Betrayal had always been his meat and potatoes; you didn't stay alive this long in the InBetween without being the best. But betrayal, greed, and horror swirled around the demon king and the resurrected witch goddess.

A tap on the door brought him out of his reverie. "Enter."

A servant scurried across the room, his head bowed. He held out an ornately carved gold tray with a note on it.

Llewellyn snatched it. "Dismissed." He read it, then tossed it in the fire. "Lyon has one of the women. Scorpio doesn't know where they've gone, but he has the other two and will use them to complete the set."

Circe paced the room. "Unacceptable. You assured me that your Zodiacs are the best." She frowned. "I'm not happy. And you know how hungry I get when I'm not happy."

Llewellyn was well aware of her appetites and what stimulated them. Since raising her, he'd made sure she was sated in every way so he didn't end up on her menu.

Asmodeus steepled his fingers. "What about the Twelve? Time to light a fire under the Zodiacs?"

"Yes," Llewellyn said. He opened a drawer in his huge desk and pulled out a leather glove with Lyon's broken claws attached to the fingertips. He presented it to Circe. "For you."

She slipped the glove over her elegant hand and wiggled her long fingers, making the claws go *clack-clack-clack* when they struck each other. She touched one tip to her bare forefinger and giggled when a drop of blood formed. She licked her finger clean.

"I have a meal that should slake your hunger in this troubling time," Llewellyn said.

Circe caressed his cheek with the back of the claws. "I thought Lyon would be…well, more. So, imagine my disappointment." She sniffed a claw. "I need the women, and I need them soon."

"And what exactly do you need them for?"

Circe leaned close. "Be careful, my pet. I'm so very hungry, I really don't care who sates me," she whispered.

Llewellyn swallowed hard. He snapped his fingers and his servant pulled aside a huge tapestry that hung on the back wall of Llewellyn's quarters, exposing a small door.

The servant unlocked it and held the tapestry to one side while they entered. Circe looked inside the large chamber and gasped. Eleven men sat around a huge table, two Creepers per man to hold them in place.

"Will this offering satisfy you?"

"Mightily," she replied with a lusty sigh.

Llewellyn left her side and went to his wet bar. He poured four fingers of a rare fairy liquor. He had summoned Asmodeus, thinking a demon king would have the juice to break open the InBetween. But, even with a host of souls to burn through, Asmodeus wasn't enough.

So, Llewellyn had spent years looking for Circe, the witch goddess who had killed him—the same woman who had started the chain of events that resulted in his banishment to the InBetween. When he found her, he resurrected her. The witch goddess was proving to be effective—but he had to be a thrall to her every whim to avoid her ravenous, indiscriminate hunger.

He looked into the mirror above the bar. Circe still stood at the door to the meeting room, her back to Llewellyn and Asmodeus. She threw off her robes, revealing the luscious body that had entranced him as a young man. Her deep auburn hair tumbled in waves down the length of her long, cream-colored back; she could have been posing for a pre-Raphaelite painting. But the years had tempered his lust for her, hell, washed it away. No longer could he be blinded by her beautiful shell and not see the monster inside.

"You may leave, demon," she said. "Llewellyn. You will be here to service me when I'm done?"

"Of course," Llewellyn said.

She disappeared into the room, and the servant closed and locked the door.

Llewellyn and the demon looked at each other, but said nothing. Asmodeus shook his head and left the room.

Llewellyn took a seat. A few seconds later, the screams started. Fists pounded the door, voices begged for help, but he couldn't bring himself to care. Whatever it cost, whoever had to pay, it didn't matter as long as he reclaimed his rightful place as king.

Several minutes later, silence jerked him out of his reverie. He rose, pushed the tapestry aside, and entered the room.

Circe lifted a severed head in the air. The white of her fang-filled smile contrasted sharply to the bright red sheen of her blood-coated skin and hair. She giggled as she tossed the head and picked up an arm. She threw her own head back, unhinged her jaw like a python, and swallowed the limb whole. She belched, then threw out her slender arms and twirled among the carnage. "More, more, I need more."

Llewellyn looked at the dead and dying members of the Twelve. He had no problem killing his prey, but toying with it—especially with such psychotic glee—was just crass.

Circe held up her gloved hand, admiring the tight-fitting, claw-tipped weapon. "These claws were Lyon's?" she asked.

"Yes."

"I must have a matching pair."

"After the ritual. Where is the spell book?"

Circe finished her snack. "It's in the Pondera secret reliquary. With that book, the end shall begin."

"The Pondera will never let me take the book."

"True, but I know just who to have fetch it for us. But first, I must finish here."

Llewellyn worked his way through the detritus and returned to his quarters; he had no interest in watching her finish her meal. He stared into the fire until the tapestry moved, and Circe stepped into view.

The tip of her pink tongue lapped at the fresh blood on her bare forearm. Blood matted her hair to her head and coated her body. Her stomach was ridiculously flat considering she'd just consumed eleven men.

"Come, Llewellyn, you know what I need."

Llewellyn stood and disrobed, his limbs heavy. He knelt in front of her, reached around her hips to grip her sticky buttocks, and pulled her close until her sex was next to his mouth. He hesitated.

Circe grabbed his hair and jerked his head back. "Say it."

Llewellyn ground his teeth before speaking. "My queen. Ruler of the above and the below, of the light and the dark."

Circe threw her head back and laughed. She pulled his head back to the juncture of her open legs.

Hatred, fear, and relentless ambition entwined in Llewellyn's gut. One day very soon, she would be the one on her knees—and it wouldn't be to suck his cock. It would be to lose her head, and be gone for the whole of time.

He attacked her sex while sweet visions of her decapitation danced in his head.

Leona turned away from the peephole into Llewellyn's room. Her rage flared hot, causing beads of sweat to break out on her forehead and back. The man she thought to be stronger than any living being was on his knees to another. *Not only is he no better than any of us, he's worse—far worse.*

Weak and cruel, a tyrant who would do anything to achieve his goals, including promising Circe that which had been promised to her, his own daughter. Everything she'd done had been to prove her worthiness to him. Every sacrifice he demanded devoured her chance at happiness one bite at a time, but still she stood by his side, hand feeding him pieces of her soul for the rare kind word.

She had learned a hard truth today.

Her devotion hadn't worked, blood hadn't mattered to him. Power was all. But Llewellyn was weak, weaker than he had proclaimed her to be, and she had just seen the proof. It was time to get the power she needed to destroy her father and any other man who betrayed her.

She stalked through the maze of secret passages inside the walls until she reached Asmodeus' quarters. She opened the bookcase and found the demon king lounging on a sofa watching a writhing orgy of three succubi and three human men on his bed, as the succubi devoured each man's life force. Deep bass moans reverberated around the room. The men were so overwhelmed with pleasure they had no idea that death was imminent.

Leona walked between Asmodeus and his erotic tableau. "I'm ready."

He patted the sofa.

She sat next to him and crossed her legs. Her focus now was on getting Asmodeus to finally fulfill his promise to her. "I need to be made before Llewellyn figures out what we're doing."

Asmodeus raised a finger to his lips, then snapped his fingers. "Leave us, ladies."

The succubi scowled but obeyed, leaving the writhing men behind.

As soon as the door closed, Leona spoke. "Circe has castrated Llewellyn in this life, as well. She's going to be the ruin of us all if I'm not strong enough to stop her."

Asmodeus stood, and walked to the closest man. He laid a hand on the male's head and light exploded out of the human's eyes, nose, and mouth. The man jerked and twisted, foam pouring from the corners of his mouth until he collapsed, dead but grinning. The other two men whimpered, but were too weak to escape. Asmodeus finished them off, then turned to Leona.

She cocked one eyebrow. "Will I be able to do that when we're finished?"

Asmodeus sat next to her and pushed a lock of her long tawny hair behind her ear. He ran his fingers along her jaw.

She shuddered. It was growing harder to hide her revulsion for the demon king and his disgusting tastes.

"Is that what you'd like? To kill with one touch?"

"It would be a good skill to have."

He parted her lips with his thumb, slid his fingers in her mouth, and opened it wide. He leaned in and covered her open mouth with his.

A piercing cold flooded her. It ran down her throat and filled her lungs until she felt she might drown. Just when she thought she was going to faint or worse, the cold warmed and filled all of her senses. Her skin expanded, as if the souls of the men Asmodeus had just devoured were fighting to meld with hers. Memories not her own raced through her mind: images of children and school, of women young and old; mansions and cars and demonic pacts for wealth and fame made with the blood and bone and body and soul of these men and their families.

The sticky wet of her own blood tickled her skin as it flowed out of her nose, ears, and mouth. Her body jerked with heat and sex, until the explosive integration of her soul and the souls Asmodeus had fed her ignited an orgasm.

"That's just a taste of the pleasure you'll experience when we're done."

Too sated to speak, she nodded and sagged into the soft leather.

Asmodeus cut along the vein in his left wrist and held it to her mouth. She grabbed him and suckled hard, pulling and swallowing his blood until he shoved her away. She growled and launched herself at the demon, but he pushed her off the sofa. She landed on the floor with a grunt, then wiped her mouth with her fingers and licked them clean.

She smiled wide. "When?"

"Soon, little kitten. Very soon."

10

PERSEPHONE'S HEART POUNDED until all she could hear was the *whoosh-whoosh* of the blood in her ears. She pointed a trembling finger at Lyon and panted through her fright. "Who are you? Have we met somewhere?" She squinted, "I could swear we've met."

Lyon worked his way around the room, his eyes wide, his mouth opening and closing like a suffocating fish. "Who the hell are *you*?" He rushed the bed, teeth bared. "Is this some kind of spell?"

"Spell?"

He grabbed her T-shirt and pulled her close. "My gut is flopping, my heart is pounding. What kind of curse is this?"

"Are you mental?" She slapped at his hand. "Get off me." He released her but stood over her, his head cocked like a vulture assessing its meal. "Great. I'm trapped in a cabin that could be a set for the next *Texas Chainsaw Massacre* with a kidnapper I don't know, who's now yelling about spells." She closed her eyes and rubbed her forehead with her free hand. "I'm not nuts," she muttered under her breath. *Yeah, you keep telling yourself that, girlie.*

Lyon lifted a section of her hair and stared at it. "If you didn't cast a spell, how have I been dreaming about you? Your long hair. The outline of your face." He dropped the strands and stared at her mouth, her eyes. "I couldn't have drawn the rest, even had my dreams shown me all of you. Your full mouth," he whispered as he held his fingertips just above her lips. He looked up. "Your purple eyes, so sad…" He blinked and shook his head. "It doesn't matter, I have a job to do." He staggered away.

"Lyon?"

He closed his eyes and rubbed his forehead, unconsciously mirroring Persephone. "What?"

"You can't get across this cabin, much less finish this job you keep talking about. I need to look at your wound."

"If I release you, you'll just run."

"No. I won't. My friends are at the house and if those men are there too, I need to help them. You got me out, you can help me get them out, too."

Lyon studied her, his expression sour, then pulled out the key and released her.

She rubbed her wrist and rolled her shoulders to work out the kinks. "Where are the bandages?"

"They were in the bathroom, but I used them all on you."

Persephone looked around the room. Not much to choose from, so she jerked the top sheet off the bed and bit one edge to tear it into large strips. "Take a seat. Use one of the dining chairs so I can get all the way around you."

He grunted but did as she asked.

After she finished ripping the bright floral sheet, she gathered together tweezers, a near-empty bottle of alcohol—everything she thought might help. She dropped the tweezers in the alcohol and washed her hands.

"Sit," she ordered. "Shirt."

Lyon pulled off the black T-shirt revealing comic-book-sized broad shoulders and thick muscle friggin' everywhere. The sight of him rocked her body and sent a hot blast straight to her woman bits. She'd been attracted to men before, but nothing like this. Lust overwhelmed her senses, filling her body to bursting. His scent, the waves of heat radiating off him like a kiln, even the unending scars that marred his pale skin didn't stem her longing.

"Holy hell." She traced a web of thick scars on his back, her hands trembling over his twitching muscle. "No one should have to endure this."

He rolled his shoulders, shaking her hand off. "It's nothing. Just make it quick."

She found a ragged hole just a few inches left of his spine. "Something pierced your skin." She looked around and checked his belly. "No hole here. Whatever it is, it's still inside you."

She probed the wound with the tweezers expecting to find a bullet, but she couldn't feel anything. She pushed deeper and swept the tines back and forth.

He groaned.

She pulled the tweezers out. "I'm sorry. It must be in there, but I can't find it."

"Leave it, then." He growled as he shoved her away.

Why am I helping this man? She knew nothing about him or why she'd been forced to run from her own home. Danger oozed from his every pore, almost as fast as the flow of his blood. She picked up the sheet strips and did her best to make a pressure bandage to stop the bleeding. "Who are you?" she asked. "Why did that man try to take me?"

"Are you done?" Lyon stood, his arms crossed over his chest.

"You're insufferable. Get in bed." She shoved him.

He moaned and collapsed back.

Persephone covered him with a blanket. "You need to rest."

"You can't leave here. You're not safe with anyone but me."

Persephone leaned over until their faces were only inches apart. "I won't leave without you, you're my ticket to saving my friends." She stood tall and planted her fists on her hips. "We're not going to be rid of each other until that's done."

Lyon opened his eyes. Night had fallen; he'd slept all day. His heart flopped when he didn't see Persephone, then he heard humming. She appeared in the bathroom mirror. The reflection of her washing her bared belly and breasts caused his sex to twitch.

Her back muscles rippled under her creamy skin. Slender arms, tiny waist, she was nothing like the Amazon women he had preferred in the past. With their larger size and warrior attitudes, he was free to be as vigorous as he liked. Persephone would be crushed by his bulk, but that logic didn't trickle down to his cock. It tented the blanket as if trying to poke through the material and reach the woman standing a few feet away.

Ambitious bastard.

He'd just shifted to relieve his discomfort when his body got tangled in the blanket and gravity got the better of him. He rolled off the bed and landed facedown, erection first. The world disappeared, forced out of view by the breath-stealing pain. "Uhhh!"

Persephone ran to his side. She yanked the blanket binding his feet, and his body pivoted in a circle, his now-uncovered cock a fulcrum being twirled over the warped and splintered wood floor.

"Stop! You're killing me." He rolled onto his back, knees in his chest, both hands covering his tortured flesh. He opened his eyes and saw firm breasts topped with pale pink nipples only inches from his mouth. What a fucking waste. The pain was so bad he couldn't give a shit about the view.

She pulled on the blanket again and he jerked it out of her hands. "Leave it."

"It's not like I've never seen a penis before."

Lyon untangled himself enough to crawl to the bed, but couldn't muster the strength to stand. He curled back into a ball and waved at her. "Go away. And put on a shirt."

She looked down and squeaked. She covered her breasts and ran to the bathroom, then returned with her chest covered, her face flushed an impressive red. "I need to check your wound."

"If I let you, will you leave me alone?"

"Yes, I promise." She leaned over his bandage, and unraveled it. Her long hair swept over his bare chest. The rich sweet scent of her sex tantalized him. Blood rushed back to his insulted, yet far from incapacitated, manhood. *Seriously?*

"The bleeding has slowed but not stopped." She replaced the dirty, improvised bandages with clean ones.

"Who the hell are you?" he asked.

Persephone retied the bandage. "You crashed into my life, so you can go first."

Lyon growled.

She crossed her arms, but her trembling hands and wide eyes belied her jutted chin and thinned lips.

Lyon was flummoxed. Never, ever, had his best growl not sent others running. Even massive trolls would shit themselves as they fled. Of course, with a troll, how could you tell if they'd soiled themselves or that was their normal stench? But this slip of a thing was standing her ground in spite of her fear.

"Spill it," she demanded.

He ran through the short list of whys and why nots, but couldn't find a good reason not to tell her the truth. "I come from a world called the InBetween. It's a subterranean world that a goddess named Hecate created for the persecuted paranormal creatures of the earth."

Persephone's eyebrows arched. Her mouth twitched, but she managed to contain a laugh. "Okay, I'll bite. Why?"

"Hecate had a daughter, Circe—a witch goddess. She was jealous of Hecate's love for humans, so she killed the first-born princes of the twelve royal houses on earth. The kings called for Hecate to bring back their sons, but the best she could do was resurrect them, and take them to the InBetween to rule the paranorms."

Persephone sat on the end of the bed. "Well, sure," she said with a shrug of her shoulders. "That makes sense. If the princes showed up alive after they died, it could be a problem."

He nodded slowly, not sure if she was mocking him. "The princes are called the Twelve. They're still in power after centuries because of men like me. I am the son of one of the princes, and the first one to be made an assassin to serve the Twelve's needs. I am known in the InBetween as a Zodiac Assassin."

Persephone crossed her arms and leaned away from him. "So this Twelve—did they send you?"

"Only one of the Twelve gave me the order. I don't know why."

She looked away and said nothing for several seconds. She shook her head and started laughing. "That's preposterous, but what a great idea for a movie. What about the other men? Are they assassins, too?"

Before Lyon could answer her question, his phone rang. "Damn it." He threw off the blanket. "Don't answer that."

Persephone dug through his leather coat and pulled out a light grey rectangular piece of plastic the size of a brick. It rang again, and she flinched. "What's this?"

Lyon jumped off the bed.

Persephone backed away, pressed the 'send' button, and held the relic to her ear. "Hello?"

Lyon stalked to her. "Damn it, woman, give me the phone."

She gasped and averted her eyes from his naked body before handing it over.

"What?" he growled into the phone.

"Missing something, Zodiac?"

"Scorpio. You have two somethings that belong to me."

"Belong?"

"Cut the crap, Scor."

"Bring the woman, and her friends will be spared. Refuse to comply and I'll make a bloody mess of them."

"Damn you."

"You have one hour." The connection ended.

Lyon dropped the phone on the floor and stomped on it. "No more phones."

"Was that one of the Zodiacs?"

"Yes, Scorpio."

"He has my friends, doesn't he?"

"Yes, and he's not alone." Lyon dressed, grabbed his duffle, and filled it with the remaining food.

"How are we going to save Abella and Taryn?"

"We're not. I'm going to get you as far away from here as I can in the next hour."

"What will he do to them?" she asked, her voice high and tight.

"The same thing he'll do to you if I hand you over."

"He'll hurt them?"

"Probably."

"No."

Lyon brushed past her and bundled up the remaining sheet strips. He stuffed them in his coat for later. "What does that mean?"

Persephone crossed her arms. "I'm not going with you. I'm going to help my friends."

Lyon grabbed her arm. "You will go where I tell you."

Her faced paled, but she lifted her chin. "No."

Lyon leaned close, bared his teeth, and growled.

She cowered from him, her body trembling. "No."

He crushed her against his chest and pushed her chin up so she could see his face. "I'll just throw you in the trunk and drive away."

"No."

He released her arm and backed her into the closest wall, pressing the length of his body against hers. Her pupils dilated until the black pushed out the purple. Her nostrils flared, her mouth opened. Lyon breathed deep and nearly smiled when the bitter scent of her fear shifted to the musk of her sex weeping with lust.

I have her.

She shook her head. "You can't keep me in the trunk forever. You'll have to let me out to eat and go to the bathroom, unless you want a horrid mess. Plus, my car is so old I'll probably die from carbon monoxide poisoning."

Son of a bitch, I lost her.

"You're a fool. Your compassion is a weakness that will get us all killed."

"Then go—or stay here, I don't care. I'm going after my friends."

He shoved off the wall and roared his frustration. He ripped the locked door off its hinges and walked outside, where he paced back and forth in the yard. "Damned insufferable woman."

It was a long trip back to the InBetween, and her cooperation was crucial. There was no way he could fight her and eleven highly trained assassins at the same time. But how could he rescue the two women from the Zodiacs? For the first time, he was at a loss for a strategy. This fucking mission was full of firsts: first babysitting job, first rescue mission, first—and probably only—chance to earn his freedom. But to earn that freedom, he needed all three women.

His options were few, and decidedly grim. If he tried to get the other women from the Zodiacs by infiltrating the house, he'd be going against eleven highly trained assassins. He could take Persephone to the InBetween to secure her and try to steal the other two women from Scorpio in transit, that's if Scor didn't actually kill them like he threatened. But the waning moon wasn't far away and this going back and forth would chew up time that was in short supply to begin with, not to mention, Persephone would be so uncooperative about leaving her friends that he'd die from the dart before he could get to his healer.

The screech of the screen door's rusty hinges alerted him to Persephone's presence. He turned. She crossed the yard and stopped just outside his reach, her purple eyes glowing like they were lit from within. The moon bathed part of her face in cool silver that matched her hair, while shadows enveloped the rest of her in fierce black.

His heart slowed. The anger in him cooled. The wind stopped and Lyon struggled to breathe. The world fell away, leaving only her. He wanted to freeze this moment so he could figure out why it felt so important. The answers were right in front of him, but...

Persephone squared her shoulders like the bravest warrior, yet her hands trembled like the fallen facing death. "I know what to do."

Her words snapped Lyon back. "Zodiacs are not totally human. We're enhanced, making us the best assassins in all worlds. These men could kill you and your friends without a thought."

"But I thought you were supposed to get us to the InBetween alive."

"Those are *my* orders."

"But you don't know about the other Zodiacs?"

"Yes."

"What about the man who attacked me?"

"Scorpio."

"He could have snapped my neck and walked away. Why didn't he?"

"I don't know."

Persephone sagged, as if giving in to the weight of the unknown.

He didn't expect her to have anything of worth to offer, but his curiosity and no small amount of desperation made him indulgent. "So, what would you do?"

Persephone looked at the ground. "I don't think I can explain it, you'll think I'm crazy. But when Abella, Taryn, and I get together, especially lately…um, things happen."

"Things happen? You want to go up against eleven assassins with 'things happen'?"

Persephone scrunched up her face and shrugged her shoulders. "They're really good things?"

Lyon stared at her, thinking. The woman was nuts, but this whole situation didn't sit well with him. Llewellyn had no interest in humans; he considered them to be a stain on the planet. How could three humans have possibly caught his attention?

Lyon shook his head. The why didn't matter. Confronting the Zodiacs alone would be a disaster that would cost him Persephone and his freedom. "So your plan is to walk into the middle of a house filled with most highly trained killers in any world, get your friends, then waltz out? Do you have a death wish? Or are you just that foolish?" He sighed, his mind made up. If he could get Persephone to the InBetween in the next few hours, he could turn around and try to run down the other two women. "No, we're running."

Lyon turned away, but stopped when she placed her hand on his arm. Her casual touch made him shudder.

"My friends that you dismiss so easily? They're my family. They mean everything to me."

He whirled on her. "Family?" He leaned into her, his body trembling, his flash-fire rage all-consuming. "These people called family, they sidle up and say 'I love you' over and over until you believe it, until you relax and trust that they'll be there when you need them most."

Persephone backed up but Lyon followed her, pressing into her space. He wagged his finger. "But that's when they have you. That's when they rip your heart out and stomp on it. Family." He stopped advancing and dropped his hand. "You better run as fast as you can away from them, before you learn this truth the hard way."

Persephone shivered. She wrapped her arms over her chest, as if that would protect her. "Don't you have anyone you would lay down your life for?"

Lyon clenched his jaw. She didn't get it, and he had no interest in answering her question with a pathetic 'no.' At one time he would have sacrificed his life for Leona, but their relationship ended when, with one vicious swipe of his claws, her face was ripped open and her life's promise closed. In the span of time between one breath and the next, Leona's old life as the most beautiful young woman in all the worlds had been shredded and her new life as the "Untouchable" was carved into her soul.

His life of privilege as Llewellyn's only son and the esteem afforded him as the first Zodiac had evaporated, leaving in its place a beast worthy of nothing more than deprivation and hatred. But, while he may not believe in sacrificial love, this woman did. Add in no good alternative solution to the problem, and he made his decision. "So if I agreed to this, what would you need?"

"You get me in the same room with Taryn and Abella, and we'll take it from there."

11

ABELLA WORKED HER ARMS, pulling and tugging on the duct tape, but all she accomplished for her trouble was burning muscles, raw and bloody skin, and tape rolled up so tight it might as well have been handcuffs.

Taryn, however, snored to raise the dead.

Abella wanted to kick her awake, but she resisted the urge. How the woman could sleep when they were tied up in a house full of massive maniacs was beyond her. Hell, the cloud of testosterone alone was enough to gag a girl, but no, there Taryn sat slumped, her eyes shut while death sniffed around them like a randy dog.

Abella shifted in the chair. She'd earned the nickname 'Ice Queen' for her habit of walking away from any man without the typical womanly hissy fits. But the big bad secret she guarded so vigilantly was that she was afraid. More like terrified, if she was honest. Her fight-or-flight instinct was always on deck, but she managed to mask it by shoving and stomping the fear down so deep no one could see it. Between denial and using her looks to distract the opposite sex so she could make her literal and figurative escape, she'd skated through life pretending to be someone she most definitely was not.

The pale grey light of pre-dawn softened the shadows in the kitchen, giving Abella a better look at the man called Scorpio. Well over six feet tall, his long limbs were heavy with ropes of muscle. Pale olive skin was stretched tight over the harsh angles of his square jaw and high cheekbones. His long, thick, black hair made him look like a Goth wannabe, until the first time he looked through Abella with a deep-set hazel glare. There wasn't a single 'wannabe' bone in this man's body. He was the real thing—whatever that thing might be.

Raw, hard, brutal: the kind of man who could see through her bullshit and demand that the terrified little girl cowering inside her crack the façade and crawl into the light. That and the bone-deep surety that, given time, she would crawl anywhere for him, landed him squarely on top of her most-dangerous-man list and meant he should be avoided at all cost.

He lay curled in a corner with his back against the wall, a curved sword in his hand. The skin of his forearm stretched and undulated as if something lived under it. *Not just something*, she corrected herself. *The impossible.*

She'd held a huge, black scorpion no one had seen for centuries. A scorpion that started as a tattoo on his skin, then somehow came to life. If this weren't so real she'd have thought they were filming a Syfy movie—except *Sharknado* had nothing on this guy. If anyone told her they'd seen such a thing, she would have laughed as she sidled away from their lunatic selves. But last night, she became a full-fledged member of the government conspiracy, alien abduction, Loch Ness monster kooks club she so assiduously avoided at cocktail parties and poker games.

So, of course, her false bravado flared and she taunted the man with her eyes when he placed one of the scorpions on her face. She stared at him, waiting for the pain, but when it didn't come she 'hmmphed.' Her single sound trumpeted her victory over his attempt to intimidate. But when he placed the same scorpion on a terrified Taryn, Abella backed down. She wouldn't risk Taryn's life to win a war of wills.

"You shouldn't stare," Taryn whispered, her eyes still closed. "You might wake him."

"You okay?" Abella asked, not bothering to ask how Taryn knew. Strange was the one trait that had brought the three women together as children, and the same one that kept them together as adults. No one could possibly understand how strange they'd become—hell, she didn't understand it either, especially lately. Strange may have brought them together, but love was the Gorilla Glue that bonded them.

"Other than having an overly full bladder, I'm the picture of health."

Abella looked at Scorpio again. "Should I wake him?"

"It's gonna get really messy if you don't."

Abella nodded. A bathroom break sounded good and, beyond all reason considering their situation, she was starving. Before she could decide what to do, Scorpio's breathing changed.

"You're awake, aren't you?"

He opened his eyes.

"We need a bathroom break." Abella's stomach rumbled. "And food and drink. Preferably alcohol."

He unfurled his body and loomed over Abella, so close she could feel his heat. She tilted her head back and looked in his eyes. Like a push-button ignition, her body flared to life, hot and tingly and wanting. His scent went straight to her brain, making her woozy while her body screamed for its fair share of the heady mix. She took a deep breath.

Without breaking eye contact, he reached around his back and pulled a blade as long as her forearm.

She pressed back into the chair. Her bowels loosened. *This can't be it.* So many things she wanted to experience in her life: the downy silk of her infant's hair, a mate who was her equal in bed and in life. Despite her fear, she couldn't stop her snark defense weapon. "Seriously? You would kill me for requesting some common courtesy? Does the Geneva Convention ring a bell?"

Scor laid the flat of the blade against her face, the tip so close to her eye she was afraid to move or speak. Her nose began to itch. If her allergies kicked in and she sneezed, bam, instant cyclops.

"Leave her alone, Scor."

Abella rolled her eyes to see who spoke. The lofty, urbane, suit-wearing man named Libra strode to Scor and crossed his arms, his dandified airs of last night gone. Instead, he frowned at the taller Scorpio, the pair in a silent battle of wills.

Scor bared his teeth and pressed the blade deeper. "Screw you, Libra."

Abella opened her mouth and panted, partly out of fear, partly because she couldn't breathe through her nose.

"Don't push me," Libra said in a baritone that was octaves lower than his voice was last night.

Abella blinked and looked at Libra again. The light must be playing tricks on her, because she could swear there were waves of energy pulsating out of him. There was more to this man than just the constipated persona he presented to everyone.

Scor removed the knife from Abella's face and retreated to his corner.

I'll be damned.

"Please forgive him, he's never been around a lady." Libra pulled a large Swiss Army knife out of his inside pocket and opened a blade with a flick of his thumb. He cut the duct tape binding her ankles and her wrists, freeing her. "I keep requesting a muzzle for the man," he said with a shrug.

She rotated her raw wrists and stiff shoulders. "Thank you."

He touched her wrists. "You're hurt."

Abella jerked free of his gentle hold. "Free Taryn."

Libra glanced at Taryn. "Must I? She's so…unkempt. Are you certain she won't give me lice? Or scabies?"

Abella remained silent.

"Oh, all right."

He bent over Taryn and cut the tape, his charm absent.

When he stood, Taryn opened her eyes and hissed. He looked her up and down, then snorted. He held out his hand to Abella, but she ignored it as she stood. "You okay, T?"

"Bathroom. Now."

The women led the way to the closest bathroom with Libra and Scor trailing them. Scor pushed to the front of the group and opened the door. He walked inside, stopped at the miniscule window, and ran his fingers around the edges of the pane.

Abella couldn't stop herself. "I'd take your scrutiny of the window as a compliment to our svelte figures, but since you obviously aren't the type to offer a woman honeyed words, I have to assume you have no idea how small a woman would have to be to climb out that window. Let me make it easy for you. If you cut off my left arm and leg and I didn't eat for a week, I'd still have to be greased up like a pig to get out that way."

Scor dropped his hand. He crossed the bathroom and stopped inches from her. He braced one hand on the wall behind her and leaned in. His heat and scent enveloped her; his hazel eyes held her in thrall. For the first time, Abella wanted to open herself to a man. No fear, no games, no manipulation, but the thought of the vulnerability that would require nauseated her.

Scor lowered his head. His long hair fell forward, blocking out Taryn and Libra, narrowing the world to just the two of them.

She rose onto her toes until his lips were so close she could feel his breath tickling her skin.

His lips parted.

Abella closed her eyes.

"More like both arms and legs and those delectable breasts," Scor whispered in her ear. The knuckles of his free hand brushed one of her erect nipples before he pushed off the wall and walked away.

Abella struggled to figure out what had just happened, until her feet cramped and she realized she was still on her toes.

Taryn pushed Abella deeper inside the bathroom and slammed the door in Libra's face. The click of the lock snapped Abella back. She smiled for a second, then started laughing. Long, loud whoops that brought tears to her eyes.

"Zounds girl, there's a man on the planet who didn't turn to mewling mush around you. This one's for the record books."

Abella laughed even harder, tears flowing down her cheeks.

"We're captives of the biggest, baddest men I've ever seen and you're laughing." Taryn shook her head. "You have lost your mind." She lifted her colorful gypsy skirt and sat on the toilet. "Privacy, please."

Abella stuck her fingers in her ears and turned away. Yep, she'd lost her mind but, damn, she couldn't help but be drawn to the irascible Scorpio. What that said about her was something she didn't dare ponder.

12

LYON BELLY CRAWLED TO THE RISE overlooking Persephone's house, until the front and right site lines were visible. The place was a strategic nightmare. Forest surrounded it on three sides, while the gravel road and the front yard were open, save for shrubs against the house and more dotting the yard. The trees offered the best cover, but they provided the same cover for the Zodiacs.

In addition, there was too much open real estate between the trees and the house, and the sun was rising too fast, leaving Lyon with no shadows in which to work. Goddess, how he hated the blinding, burning sunlight. At least it was to his back, giving him the advantage for the next few minutes.

Persephone plopped down on his left. "So, what's the plan? Bust down the front door? Throw smoke bombs and choke them out?"

"What the hell? I told you to wait until I signaled you."

She shrugged. "I'm not good at taking orders."

"I'm getting that."

She poked her head above the vegetation.

"By the goddess, get down before you're spotted." He pulled on her arm until she got on her belly. Humans and their movies. Hell, the woman had no idea what to do with a gun, much less anything else that went boom.

"So that's a 'no' to an all-out assault?"

Lyon grit his teeth. "Yes, that's a no. Subtlety is key with these guys."

The squeak of the screen door drew Lyon's attention back to the house. Taurus stopped at the edge of the porch, grabbed his master-blaster-sized cock, and peed.

"Do you at least have an action plan? Oh, my…who's that? Doesn't he realize he's naked?" Persephone whispered, her eyes wide. Her mouth dropped open.

Built like a Sherman tank or a 'roided linebacker, Taurus had barely-fit-through-the-door shoulders and solid hips that were only slightly narrower than his shoulders. But Persephone wasn't focused on his shoulders or his hips.

"Give the man some privacy."

"If he wanted privacy, he should have put on some clothes. Or used a toilet."

"Nudity is common in the InBetween." Lyon grunted, more than a little peeved at her penis preoccupation. "Is this going to be a problem?"

Persephone ducked her head, and flushed. "Not looking, not looking." She cleared her throat and glanced at the house again. "Wait, look."

Lyon heaved a sigh. "So. Problem."

"No. No penis…I mean problem." She pointed to the right side of the house. "Look."

Streams of toilet paper flapped in the breeze.

Lyon snorted. "Must be your friends. No Zodiac would use a roll of ass-wipe for an SOS."

"They *are* resourceful."

"Is that window big enough for them to fit through?"

"Not even close."

"Then how is that helpful?"

"I just need to touch them."

"If I can get you to that window, will you be close enough to do your thing?" Lyon asked.

"Yes."

"And you don't plan on sharing what's going to happen?"

"It's not that I *won't* share what will happen so much as I *don't know* what's going to happen."

Lyon closed his eyes. *Goddess, give me patience.* This was going to be a clusterfuck, he could feel it in his bones. "Last chance."

Persephone shook her head.

He weighed his options. He couldn't leave her alone, she'd be ripe for the plucking. Taking her with him was even riskier, but in this case that old 'bird in the hand' saying was a crock of shit. One bird wouldn't buy him freedom. He needed both hands full of birds and a clear path to the birdcage.

The lengths of ass-wipe flapping in the breeze heralded his only choice. He took in Persephone's expression, a mix of earnestness and terror, and his heart flopped once in his chest. His decision was made.

Lyon rolled into a crouch, but kept his head down. He held out a hand and pulled her into a crouch with him, ignoring the chill of her shaking hand. *It's a miracle she hasn't soiled herself yet. The real test is coming, though: how will she handle herself when this all goes to hell? 'Cause, go to hell it will.* He expected nothing less from these men.

He waited for several seconds after Taurus had gone inside, to make sure none of the others planned a porch piss. "Your friends were smart enough to bring a roll for the shit storm about to hit us." He glanced at her. "What have you brought to the party?"

She frowned, and stared at him for several seconds. "You."

That single word hit Lyon like a punch to the gut. He swallowed hard. A sharp pang of longing rushed through him before it shattered against his thick layers of pain and regret. "Then you're fucked."

She gasped.

Before she could say anything else distracting, Lyon jerked her to her feet. He raced down the rise with Persephone in tow, then jumped the last few feet and landed on flat ground. They ran to the side of the house and pressed their backs against the limestone wall. He paused, listening for a shout of discovery, but the only sound he heard was the whisper of leaves.

"That was easy," Persephone whispered.

He decided not to share the reality. Was it quiet because the Zodiacs hadn't detected them? Or were they baiting a trap?

Lyon got on his hands and knees and crawled under a large window, Persephone close behind. He heard several voices. The Zodiacs were milling around, but at least they weren't swarming out of the house. Their senses were dulled and their reflexes sluggish this early in the morning, but that still made them faster and more deadly than the most dangerous human. If only he could nab one of them, so he could get some answers.

First things first, though, gotta rescue two more damsels in distress. Lyon helped Persephone to her feet. He sidestepped to the toilet paper and stopped, then waved her over and traded places. "Look," he whispered in her ear.

Persephone took a quick look inside the bathroom. She nodded. She shook her hands, then rubbed them together.

"What's wrong?"

"Nothing. They tingle when I'm this close to Abella and Taryn."

Lyon nodded. "Stay here." He worked his way back to the corner of the house. He checked the front. No Zodiacs yet.

He looked back at Persephone. The rising sun painted her face and form, dust motes dancing around her like she was a fairy. Her silver hair and purple eyes glowed in the soft golden light, and for the first time he saw the brave, beautiful woman underneath the pain in the ass. Her world has been turned upside down but she hadn't complained—at least not much. She'd tended her wounded captor and when she found out her friends were in danger, she hadn't hesitated to jump into what could be a trap, no matter how terrified she might be. Foolish? Definitely. But he admired her love for her friends. If he'd had the same, perhaps his soul wouldn't be so blighted that it would take a pack of sin-eaters to cleanse it.

He blinked to break his reverie and nodded.

She flashed a smile and reached through the open window with both hands. He could see her lips moving, but couldn't hear the words. Persephone shook her head vigorously and frowned.

He flinched when the hairs on his neck stood at attention. An electrical charge danced across his skin and tickled his scalp, the tingle not unpleasant. One of the Zodiacs shouted. Lyon heard banging and other raised voices.

Lyon checked the front yard. No one…yet.

He looked back at Persephone. The electric charge faded away as the wind picked up, but someone forgot to tell the trees: they weren't moving. The wind had contracted into a very discrete space around the women. The speed increased until a screaming vortex formed, half of it surrounding Persephone, the other half inside the house. The invisible force ripped through the limestone, drywall, roof tin, and wood like a hellhound shredding a man's chest before dragging him to the black abyss. Dirt and grass and leaves were sucked into the funnel. Within seconds, Persephone disappeared inside the maelstrom of debris.

Lyon took a step in her direction when the screen door squealed. Someone was leaving. He peeked around the corner.

"Shit."

Taurus, Libra, and Sagittarius stood in the yard in various states of undress, swiping at the delicate arcs of blue electricity dancing across their skin. The door slammed open and the rest of the Zodiacs poured off the porch.

Only Scorpio was missing.

Lyon grabbed the corner of the house and held tight against the pull of the widening vortex. "Persephone. Hurry!"

He had no idea if she heard him above the deafening noise, but the Zodiacs did. They turned and spread out, using the house and the shrubs for cover. Lyon unsheathed his longest dagger. He looked around the corner to assess the situation, when the ground vibrated under his feet. He braced his legs to maintain balance.

Before the Zodiacs could close in, the ground bucked and a loud *boom* knocked the men into the dirt. A fissure formed in the front yard and disappeared under the house, separating Lyon and the woman from the Zodiacs.

Lyon scrambled to his feet. A second buck bounced Lyon, but he was ready for it this time.

The shrill screams of twisting metal and explosive snaps of breaking wood sounded the knell for the dying domicile. The house sagged in the middle. The ground on either side of the fissure rose one foot, two feet, on and on. Wood studs snapped, windows exploded, shards flew. The two halves of the house leaned away from each other, hovering on the precipice of complete separation, held in place by wiring only.

Lyon dropped to all fours and scrambled for Persephone. He grabbed her waist. Excruciating electric shocks exploded through his body. His muscles seized. He couldn't release her, but he couldn't move her either. He was frozen in place until his body weight and the laws of nature did what he couldn't. He fell and pulled her down with him, severing the women's connection.

An immense release of power blew Lyon back with Persephone cradled against him. They flew down the growing incline. Lyon's back slammed against the hard ground, the blow knocking the air from his lungs. A blessed silence blanketed him. He fell into it, his eyes closed, his frozen lungs and spasming muscles on full strike. The wound in his flank screamed about the fresh insult. Let the world go all to hell, as long as he didn't have to move or fight or run for the next few minutes.

Persephone's back was pressed against his chest, her limp body draped over his. He opened his mouth to speak, but he needed air to push out the words. For the moment, he was mute.

A groan pierced the silence. The house shuddered as the ground pushed it higher and higher above them. The two halves leaned away from each other until they reached an apex and gravity took hold. Wires snapped, the pops sounding like a small-caliber gun.

Too close, too close, too close.

Lyon barrel-rolled to the left, one arm around Persephone's dead-weight torso, his opposite hand shielding her face. Over and over he tumbled, the remains of the house looming closer. He jolted to a halt against a stump. The house fell, fell, fell.

"Fuck me." He rolled Persephone under him and rose onto his forearms and lower legs, shielding her with his back. If he was going to die, at least he could save one life.

A final dull *boom* and the house smashed down inches from Lyon. Dust washed over them, choking him. Exhaustion and adrenaline devoured him until he was hollow. He collapsed to one side of Persephone and saw the Zodiacs littered across the front yard, some unconscious, others struggling to rise. Inside the peeled remains of Persephone's home, two women stood shivering, millimeters apart but not touching, drenched by the spray of the broken water pipes.

Lyon touched Persephone's shoulder and shook it, but before he could rouse her he smelled the strong odor of natural gas. He staggered to his feet and yelled at the women standing stunned in the rubble of their home. "Hey, get out of there."

They didn't acknowledge him.

"Snap out of it," he yelled. He skated over the shifting rubble and offered a hand to the closest woman, a short, sodden, black-haired little thing whose clothes were so colorful it hurt his eyes to look at them.

"Move!" he bellowed.

She remained frozen, her eyes glazed in shock.

"Go, go, go, go, go," he said under his breath. There was no time to indulge in niceties like introductions. He hoisted the woman over his shoulder and ran down the incline. The fumes choked him. His eyes watered, obscuring his vision. He set the little woman next to Persephone. He took a deep breath and hurried back for the redhead.

Libra and Sag caught his eye. The two Zodiacs picked up the pace. They hurdled the downed porch railing and skirted around the twisted metal roof, making a beeline for Lyon.

Just when he reached the redhead, the bathroom debris shifted. Lyon had just scooped the woman into his arms, when Scorpio emerged from the rubble, scorpions dropping off his body and skittering in all directions.

Lyon raced away from Scor's bugs, set the redhead down next to Persephone, and looked back at the house. Scorpio had pushed aside most of the wood and drywall, but otherwise hadn't moved. A huge wood beam had pinned his legs to the ground.

Libra and Sag were within feet of Scor when they stopped. Sag raised an arm and stopped Libra. They smelled the gas, too.

Lyon pulled the multi-tool out of his pocket and gripped it, his thumb on top. Time to bluff. "Could be a spark from this lighter will ignite the gas and we'll all be mulch…or not. Wanna find out?"

The two Zodiacs raised their hands. Libra jogged off, but Sag hesitated. "Your reckoning is coming, and I'll be first in line." He headed for the tree line.

Lyon turned to Persephone and her friends. The three women looked stunned, but at least they were on their feet. He opened his arms to herd them. "Let's go."

Persephone frowned, her focus on Scorpio. "What about him?"

"No time."

The women exchanged a glance. The redhead crossed her arms.

"We're not leaving without freeing him," Persephone said.

"I don't know, he's kind of a horse's ass," the black-haired woman said.

Lyon loomed over the women, trying to intimidate, but they just stood there, chins jutted, refusing to obey. He wanted to throw them over his shoulders and haul them away, but these women had proven to be uncommonly stubborn. Once again he was backed into an action against his will and common sense.

"Son of a bitch." Lyon strode to the beam.

The women trailed him.

"We can help," Persephone offered.

"No."

"But—"

Lyon turned on Persephone, his frustration finally bubbling to the surface. "You said 'things happen.'" He pointed to the remains of her home. "You decimated your house. No control, no focused strike, just complete destruction in seconds. You and your friends are a menace."

Persephone backed away, her eyes wide, tears on her eyelashes threatening to spill down her cheeks. She tripped on a wood stud and sat down hard. Her friends gasped and took a step toward her, but Persephone waved them off. "I'm fine. We wouldn't want to accidentally destroy something else."

Lyon ground his teeth. He hated dealing with women and their messy feelings. He rolled a shoulder to slough off his irritation and climbed the incline.

"Are you ready?" Lyon asked the Zodiac.

"I don't want your help," Scorpio said.

"Fuck you, too." With any luck, he could tap into the demon's strength without letting it have complete control of his body. The ever-present ache of the demon piggy-backing him exploded into a fiery burn. The demon writhed and scratched as if it knew Lyon was about to call for it to come out and play. He wrapped his hands around the wood, bent his knees, and heaved.

The beam only moved an inch. Lyon released it and stood.

"Persephone?"

"I'm here."

"Come to me."

She came up behind him.

He looked around the ground and found a long length of wood. He handed it to her. "Take this."

She took the wood from him.

"Point it at my head."

"What? No."

He leaned close to her. "Hear me, Persephone."

She swallowed and nodded.

"There's a darkness inside me. It's strong and savage," he said. "If I'm to help Scorpio, I have to tap into it."

She shook her head. "What am I supposed to do with this?"

Lyon rolled his shoulders. The demon scratched and tested him, impatient to crash the party. "I'll try to control it, but if it takes me and I can't get back, you need to knock me out. That's the only way to truly stop me…stop it…from hurting you when the darkness has control."

"No. I can't." Persephone tried to hand the wood back. "Please don't ask me to do this."

"This is what you have demanded. Now be prepared to defend yourself." Lyon waved her off. "My head. Now."

The other two women came up behind Persephone. They didn't touch, just stood quietly behind their friend.

Lyon looked at the redhead and the brunette. "If I turn on you, you have to drop me. Understand?" The women nodded but remained silent.

The redhead held out her hand. "Give it to me, Persephone, I can do it."

"No, he asked me to do it," Persephone said through her tears. She squared her shoulders and raised the wood. "Why give me a weapon? I could knock you out right now and we could run."

He studied her for a moment. "Because at least I'm a known." He nodded at Scor then glanced at the Zodiacs hovering at the tree line. "They are not."

Persephone pursed her lips and nodded once.

Lyon took hold of the heavy beam that pinned Scor. He closed his eyes, and concentrated on the foreign part of his body, willing the demon soul to stretch, to seep into every cell and cohabit his body. For years, he'd battled to keep the demon at bay, hating the forced connection, but hating himself more for the truth he suspected—that the demon was merely a manifestation of his true nature.

Pressure filled his body. *He's coming.*

His extremities tingled; canines and claws erupted. A low growl started in his belly, the rumble growing in strength and volume until it reached his vocal cords.

The demon roared in triumph.

"Lyon?" Persephone whispered.

He opened his eyes and winced when the world exploded into glaring, brilliant colors. A tinny *wha-wha-wha* seeped through the pounding in his ears. He turned to the sound and saw Persephone.

"Are you in there, Lyon?" She stepped closer.

"Persephone, get back," the redhead warned. "Look at his eyes."

Persephone gasped and staggered back.

He knew what she saw; he'd seen it many times before. Gold eyes ablaze with light, swirling shades of gold that blanketed the white and danced around his pupils. He sniffed the air, and the raw scent of her fear washed over him. The little piece of Lyon still present fought the demon's desire to attack the woman, clawing at the need until he turned the demon's attention to the beam.

He grabbed the wood. Man and demon lifted, one inch, two inches, six inches, until Scorpio's legs were free.

Scor pulled himself out, gained his feet, and looked at the redhead. "You should have let me die." He leaped over the fissure in the earth and limped away.

Lyon scratched and clawed for control, but a loud buzzing in his head stopped him. When he tried again, the buzzing grew to a shriek. He dropped to one knee and grabbed his head. "Persephone."

She dropped to her knees in front of him. "What do you need?"

"Hit me, knock me out."

"I can't."

"I can," the redhead offered. She grabbed the wood out of Persephone's hands and lifted it over her head.

"Abella, no." Persephone covered Lyon's hands and pulled his head into her chest.

The shrieking rose an octave. Lyon screamed. He batted at her hands, but Persephone squeezed him tighter. The black of unconsciousness flirted. The demon demanded dominion. Lyon was ready to give it to him when he heard a voice say, "Make it stop, make it stop."

The demon quieted. Lyon stilled. The voice repeated, "Make it stop, make it stop."

Lyon heard a loud pop, and the demon soul retreated. Quiet enveloped him and he held his breath, waiting for the demon to return. Nothing happened. He opened his eyes to find Persephone's wet face only inches from his. He pushed her silver hair back so he could see her eyes. "I'm okay."

She nodded and hiccupped but before he could sit up, she dropped his head, rolled away, and vomited.

The redhead closed in on him. "What the hell was that?" she demanded.

Lyon ignored her. He wanted to join Persephone's heave-fest, but they weren't clear of danger yet. He got to his feet and waited for Persephone to finish, then helped her stand. He had so many questions, but they would have to wait. "Can you walk?"

They nodded.

Lyon pushed through the rolling waves of exhaustion and limped to the rise. He waited for the women to pass him, watching for an ambush while they climbed. As soon as the women were clear, Lyon crawled to the top of the incline.

He passed Persephone, eager to get to the car and out of the area before law enforcement showed.

"Did you hear that?" Persephone asked.

"Hear what?"

"Down!" Persephone tackled him. Lyon fell into the other two women and they all hit the ground.

A massive explosion shook the ground. A shockwave of hot air, fire, and debris shot up the ridge and blew over them for a second, then sucked back down the rise.

Persephone jumped up and offered Lyon a hand. "Are you all right?"

He ignored her offer and rose. He staggered a few steps before Persephone wrapped her arms around his waist. "I'm fine," Lyon said. "How did you know?"

She looked back at the burning rubble that once was her home. "I have no idea. I saw the explosion and just knew what to do."

"That's nothing. I think I'm the one who made the ground split open," the brunette said, pointing in the direction of the decimated house.

"I'll see your ground splitting and raise you with, 'I didn't shit myself.'" the redhead said.

The group looked at her.

"What? I think that's fucking miraculous."

Persephone pointed to the redhead. "Abella." Then the brunette. "Taryn. This is Lyon."

"We need to get out of here before the Zodiacs regroup," Lyon said.

The women followed Lyon to Persephone's car. Abella and Taryn climbed in the back while Persephone took shotgun. She turned to her friends, and the three started talking over each other like a bunch of hens.

Lyon slid behind the wheel, inserted the key in the ignition, then sat back.

"Lyon?" Persephone asked.

"There's a creature I met once, years ago, who lives just a few hours from here. He might give us shelter."

"So. Let's go," Abella said.

"It's been a long time. Didn't part well."

"For god's sake, pick him some flowers," Taryn groused.

"And chocolate. Everything is better with chocolate," Abella added. The three women giggled.

Lyon slammed his hands against the steering wheel. "Enough!"

Persephone flinched. "We're tired and hungry and flying blind here. We need a place to hide and figure out what's happening." She turned in her seat to face her friends. "And Lyon? You need to tell them what you told me. They have a right to know, so they can decide if they want to be part of this journey or go their separate ways while there's still time."

Lyon didn't have the energy to tell them the whole truth, much less deal with their inevitable questions. How do you say, 'Sorry, girls, you don't have a choice. You're going to a world you didn't know existed, with creatures from your nightmares, facing goddess only knows what kind of fate'?

He gripped the wheel. "The Red Cap it is, then. He's the closest. But be warned, he may look harmless, but he's one of the deadliest creatures I've ever met."

"And you pissed him off," Abella said. "Imagine that."

13

THE ZODIACS GATHERED TOGETHER in a forest clearing several yards from the destroyed house. They circled each other, silent, predatory, each waiting for the others to attack.

Libra and Scorpio came together and stared for a moment before Libra started laughing.

"What the hell is so funny?" Scorpio demanded.

The rest of the men stopped their posturing.

Libra laughed harder. He bent at the waist and held up a hand. "Oh, he is good."

Scor growled and advanced on Libra.

"Stay back, bug boy, I'm not laughing at you." Libra stood tall and shook his head. "Lyon. The bastard isn't out of his cage for more than a couple days, and already he's got us going after each other."

Taurus pushed his way to the front of the group. "The question is, why are we all here? For a simple retrieval? I don't think so."

Sagittarius crossed his arms. "As long as I can have a go at Lyon, I don't care why we're here."

"Oh please, do bore us again with your pining," Libra said.

"Shut it, you over-groomed ninny," Scor said.

Libra turned to Scor, his amusement gone. "What did you say?"

Taurus looked to the sky. "All of you, quiet." He pointed.

A small black spot in the distance danced in the radiant blue, increasing in size as the seconds went by.

"What *is* that?" Libra asked.

The eleven men instinctively fell into an inverted 'V' attack formation and waited. The spot became a cloud. Then, the cloud separated into eleven individual birds.

"Shit me. Hermes hawks," Scor said.

The black hawks slowed as they approached the group of men. They formed a circle above the assassins and glided on the thermals.

"Messengers," Pisces said. He stepped away from the others. One hawk tracked him. When the Zodiac was several feet away from the others, it dropped a small, brown pouch from one of its talons, then did a slow turn and flew away.

Pisces caught the burlap and pulled on the purse string. He removed a small grey item, rock hard and covered with black spots, along with a tiny scroll sealed with red wax and stamped with Llewellyn's crest. Pisces read the message and frowned. He raised the grey rock to his nose and sniffed, then threw back his head and howled.

The remaining Zodiacs quickly separated. Pouches rained down, and the hawks flew away. One by one the men read their message, sniffed the blood on the grey object, then roared their anger and agony.

Scorpio waited until the others were done before he cracked the wax. The message consisted of a single line. *Your sire is dead.* He brought the grey object to his nose and sniffed. The image of his father cut and bleeding swamped him. This was his father's blood, no doubt. Rage filled every cell. He closed his eyes and forced his breathing to slow. He wouldn't mourn his father—he'd hated the bastard. But someone stole his chance to carve a pound of flesh out of the man, and that wasn't acceptable.

Scor studied the object. "Give me your pieces," he said without looking up.

"What the hell for?" Aries asked. Two pointed bumps rose out of his skull and pushed through his hair. They arced steadily, until his ram horns had thickened and curved around the sides of his head.

"This doesn't make sense," Libra said, his face ashen. "Lyon is here now." He looked around the ring of silent Zodiacs. "When was the last time any of you saw your fathers?"

A heavy silence fell. Not even the sound of the wind rustling dead leaves or the chatter of birds punctuated it.

"Screw that. This is my chance for payback." Scor held out his hand, the movement a demand, not a request. "Give me the pieces."

The men handed over their fragments and Scor took a knee. He lay all the pieces on the ground and put them together like a jigsaw puzzle.

The Zodiacs leaned in.

"What does this look like?" Scor asked. No one answered.

Libra cocked his head to the left, then the right. He dropped down next to Scor and elbowed him out of the way. He rearranged the pieces until he had four parallel lines, slightly curved, ending in sharp tips. "Claws."

"And we know someone with claws, don't we?" Libra asked as he stood.

"Lyon," Sag said.

"Llewellyn sent the messages," Pisces said.

Scorpio smiled. "Yes."

"Why are you smiling?" Sag asked.

Scor's smile widened. "Llewellyn has removed our gloves."

"What about the women?" Libra asked.

Scor opened the one-line message and held it out for everyone to see. "Fuck the women. Lyon is our mark, sanctioned by Llewellyn himself."

Sag stepped up to Scor and held his message high above his head. "Lyon."

The rest of the Zodiacs raised their messages.

"First, we pay our respects." Scorpio crumpled his piece of parchment and threw it away. "Then, we go hunting."

★ ★ ★

Lyon turned Persephone's land yacht onto an unkempt, hard-pack dirt road. The sparse city lights of Sonora, Texas, had given way to the deep dark of the desert, save for moonlight and a thick dusting of stars.

Beyond all logic, he had reclaimed his tickets to freedom from the Zodiacs. Now he needed to get the women to the InBetween. It would be faster to travel topside, but far safer to go subterranean. So, underground it was.

A microburst of cold and hot zinged through his gut, but this time it wasn't the demon. Hell, he was excited—hopeful, even. Where would he go when he was free of the demon soul and the dungeon? Not here in the Overworld, not in the bright light, among smelly humans hell-bent on destroying each other and themselves. He may be from the House of Leo, but he didn't belong here. The sun may rule him, but he blistered under its exposure. He was forged in darkness, and that's where he needed to stay.

He turned off the headlights and slowed to a crawl to avoid driving off into a ditch or worse while his eyes adjusted to the blessed dark. The twisted shapes of cacti rose and fell, eerie, stark, and dangerous.

He rounded a corner and stopped. The road ended at a ramshackle house built only a few yards from his destination. Barking erupted and two dogs rounded the front corner, one large and red, the other extra large and black. They dropped their heads and stalked toward the car, teeth bared.

He reached under the driver's seat and pulled out two machetes, then he climbed out of the car and waited for the dogs to reach him.

"No," Persephone yelled. She climbed out of the car and ran to Lyon.

"Get back."

"Don't hurt them." She placed herself between Lyon and the dogs.

Lyon grabbed her arm and pulled her behind him. The moment he loosened his grip, she jerked free and went around him again, wide enough to avoid his reach.

He growled at her.

"Shush." Persephone turned her body sideways to the dogs and dropped her head. She crooned, her voice deep and quiet, her body relaxed, her arms by her side.

"What the hell?" Lyon asked.

Abella climbed out of the car. "No. Give her a chance. She's got a mojo with animals like I've never seen."

"Dogs? 'Cause right now it looks like they're ready to eat her."

"Not just dogs, all animals."

The dogs slowed and raised their heads.

Persephone waited.

The black dog approached her.

"Are you kidding me? She's going to lose a limb."

"Just wait," Abella whispered.

Lyon watched the large dog closest to Persephone, waiting for it to lunge for her throat.

The dog sniffed the air, then took the last step separating them and nosed her hand. Persephone raised her other hand to the dog lagging behind. The old red female walked over and sniffed her thoroughly, then sat by Persephone's side politely demanding her due.

"Dobermans," Persephone said softly. "A male and a senior female, judging by the grey on her muzzle." She squatted down and stroked their heads.

"Insane."

The dogs snuggled up close to Persephone. She glanced at Lyon. "You can put your weapons away, they won't harm us."

Lyon snorted.

Persephone walked back to the car, trailed by the two dogs. She opened the glove box and retrieved a flashlight. When the light hit the dogs, she gasped. Their eyes were huge in their craggy skulls. "Oh, you poor babies." She ran a hand over their protruding spines, ribs, and hips. She lifted the heavy chain wrapped around their necks and dragging on the ground behind them, a carabiner attached to the last link. "There's a lock on the collar."

"Damn, I don't have my lock-picking kit," Abella said.

"Leave them. There's nothing you can do for them." Lyon hit the top of the car to wake the sleeping gypsy girl. "Let's go."

"So, where are you taking us?" Persephone asked.

"Somewhere we'll be safe from the Zodiacs."

Abella pointed to the house. "As long as I get a go at this Red Cap for his cruelty to these dogs."

Lyon glanced at the house. "He doesn't live there, and these aren't his dogs."

"How do you know?" Persephone asked.

"They'd be fat and ripe for eating if they were his."

Persephone pulled the dogs closer, her lips thinned.

Abella grunted. "Oh, man, you shouldn't have told Persephone that."

"We don't have time to debate this."

The three women walked by him, and gathered at the trunk while Lyon donned his weapon-laden leather coat. He joined them, then stopped. The women had removed three backpacks and were slinging them over their shoulders.

Lyon shook his head. "What the hell? Where'd those come from?"

Persephone shrugged. "We have backpacks with some essentials in all our cars."

"Always be prepared," Abella said.

"Do you have heavy coats for the cold? Do you have food? Water?"

Persephone and her friends stared at him.

"Put the bags back. This isn't some camping trip. You can't afford to weigh yourselves down."

The three women snorted in unison.

Abella tightened her hip strap. "Honey, this stopped being about recreation when you snagged Persephone and left us knee deep in a turd floater of bad guys."

Persephone's chin rose. "Yeah."

Taryn and Abella looked at Persephone, then burst out laughing.

"You go, baby girl," Abella said.

"I don't see why we left with this man in the first place, much less why we're still with him, heading off to god knows where," Taryn groused. "I was nursing such a jones for margaritas and guacamole."

"I don't think we have a choice until we understand what's happening," Persephone said.

Abella pointed to Persephone and nodded.

The crack of a shotgun shell being chambered stopped the conversation. A man walked out of the dark. Filthy clothes, balding head, and scary-ass teeth, the man was so rank Lyon wondered why he hadn't smelled him in advance. This was why he didn't babysit. Too many damned distractions. Shoot and scoot was a Zodiac's number-one rule.

The man aimed at Lyon. "Step away from the car." He pointed the shotgun at Persephone. "Drop the backpacks and kick them over here."

Lyon's hands itched. He could feel the dagger handles pressing against his body. He weighed the odds that he could grab the daggers and throw them faster than the man could pull the trigger, but dust exploded between his feet. His question was answered.

"I ain't asking again."

The women unbuckled the packs and dropped them at their feet. Lyon raised his hands and walked away from the car, putting his large body between the man and the women.

The man smiled. "That's right, boy. You may be big, but pipe," he said, nodding to the barrel of his rifle, "outweighs might." He scowled at the dogs standing behind Persephone. "You dumbass curs. Get to the barn, I'll deal with you later."

The dogs cowered.

Persephone placed her hands on their heads. "No. They're mine now."

"They ain't yours to claim." He raised the rifle and pointed it at her face. "Meat's been scarce this fall, could drive a man to try some long pig." He grinned and scanned her, lingering at her breasts and the juncture between her thighs. "Your friends can keep the dogs, if you take their place. I been wantin' me a good breedin' bitch."

Persephone's shoulders hunched. She crossed her arms and dropped her head.

Lyon couldn't believe this submissive, frightened woman was the same one who'd given him shit this whole time.

The man cackled and licked his cracked lips.

Lyon hissed and took a step.

The man turned his rifle on Lyon again and shook his head. "Don't."

Abella stepped in front of Persephone and the dogs. She ran a hand up her neck and through her short hair. "I wager it gets lonely out here with no woman to cook your meals." She opened the first two buttons of her shirt, exposing her cleavage and her lack of a bra. She moved sideways, away from Persephone. She slid a hand inside the silk, cupped her full breast, and gave it a gentle squeeze.

The man pivoted with her, his eyes wide. He grunted and gripped his groin, riveted.

Abella prowled to one side, moving and taunting the man. She glanced at Lyon.

He sidestepped to the trunk, and grabbed the ancient jack, watching her performance and waited for her signal. Man-eater, no doubt. *Goddess help the man she decides is her mate.* Lyon eased back to Persephone and the dogs, placing himself between the rifle and her.

Abella removed her hand from her breast, slid it over her belly until it disappeared under the waistband of her short skirt. "No woman to mount." She bit her bottom lip, then sucked it inside her mouth.

The bastard's breathing increased to a pant.

If the situation weren't so dire, Lyon would have laughed. It only took the woman seconds to drive the man to the verge.

The barrel of the rifle dipped until it pointed to the ground.

Abella removed her hand and crossed her arms. "Well, darlin', your dry streak isn't getting broken by me or my friends."

Before the man could raise the barrel again, Lyon threw the jack at his head. The metal connected with the man's temple and he dropped into an unconscious heap on the ground.

"Damn, Abella, a Bathory Berserker couldn't have done better." Lyon took the rifle and checked the man for more weapons.

"What's a Bathory Berserker?" Abella and Taryn asked at the same time.

"What are you going to do with him?" Persephone asked.

"Castration sounds good," Lyon said.

Taryn pushed the man's hips with a toe. "Do any of you really want to touch him…down there?"

Abella and Persephone shuddered.

"Next best thing, then." Lyon grabbed the man's collar and dragged him to the back of the house.

A tiny doghouse listed to one side between two scraggly trees, topped by a patchwork of junk lumber with broken roofing tiles that did little to protect the dogs from cold or rain. Inside, the dirt floor was so packed down that concrete was forgiving by comparison. Large rings of eroded bark marked the use of heavy chains. A single hubcap with a little water in the rusty bottom lay just inches outside the dog's reach.

Memories of Lyon's least-favorite torture swept through him. Heat flushed his skin; beads of sweat formed. He knew all too well how maddening the thirst had been for the dogs.

The man stirred. He pushed off the ground and rose to his knees, but before he could stand Lyon placed the barrel of the rifle against the back of his head. "Stay down."

"Please don't kill me, mister. You can have the dogs."

"Oh, I'll take the dogs and whatever else I want, starting with the keys to the locks on the chain."

The man's hands shook, but he managed to pull a ring of keys out of his pocket. He threw them to Lyon.

"Good boy. Now go get the chains."

The man scrambled to the metal on hands and knees.

"Bring them to me."

Lyon rested the rifle in the crook of his arm and ran his fingers along the doghouse roof until he found a nail. He gripped it between his thumb and forefinger and pulled it out of the wood. He pulled a second nail free.

The man crawled back, the chains in his hands clattering behind him. He quivered. Tears ran down his face, cleaning the filth in parallel tracks. A snot bubble formed and hung on his upper lip. The sharp tang of fresh piss assailed Lyon's nostrils when the man stopped at Lyon's boots.

Lyon laid the rifle on the ground. He looped one chain tight around the man's right wrist and secured it with a nail. He chained the man's other wrist, then stepped back. "Well and truly trussed."

"Ya can't leave me like this," the man protested. "It ain't right."

Lyon picked up the rifle. "You're right, no creature should be left to rot with no shelter, no food, no water. Suffering the cold and the heat, vulnerable to every predator. What makes it worse is, if given the chance, those dogs would lick your hand and be happy you deigned to let them. A piece of shite like you doesn't deserve love or devotion, only a long, painful death. Or not." Lyon swirled a forefinger in the air. "Turn around."

The man moaned but obeyed.

Lyon pressed the barrel to the back of his head.

The man sobbed, collapsing forward until his forehead touched the ground.

Lyon aimed and squeezed the trigger.

The buckshot grazed the side of the man's skull, obliterating his left ear before penetrating the dirt. He slumped in a dead faint. *Bullies make the worst victims.*

"Asshole." Lyon dragged the unconscious man to the doghouse and stuffed him inside. If he was lucky, someone would find him in time. If not, Lyon couldn't bring himself to care.

He sniffed the cold air. Mesquite and cedar, clay and rain mixed with dog waste, topped by the overwhelming stench of human detritus. Goddess, he hated humans.

Light, swift footsteps preceded Persephone. "You killed him?" she said, her voice high, breathless.

"You don't think it was warranted?"

Persephone covered her mouth with both hands. "Oh, God."

She assumed he'd ended the man. Lyon grit his teeth against the hurt. "You would feel sorry for a man who did this to his dogs? Who would have raped the three of you?"

"I don't feel sorry for him. His cruelty and neglect are evil, but I couldn't kill him, either."

"Only hours ago, you said you would lay down your life for your friends. Would you not take a life to save theirs?"

Persephone shook her head. Her tears glistened in the light of the moon. "I...I don't know."

He walked around her and headed for the front of the house before he said anything else. If he weren't so desperate to be free of the demon soul, he would leave her here. He made it to the corner before her soft voice stopped him. "What have you done to survive?"

He didn't turn around. He didn't want to see her cower away from the truth. "More than I could ever be forgiven for."

His skin crawled with disgust at his unwillingness to spare Persephone, but she needed to understand. Every day, sweet little morsels like her were snatched up and savored like rare ambrosia until they were consumed, body and soul. The thought of her being harmed by the monsters lurking in the shadows of the InBetween doubled his disgust.

But he was by far the most dangerous monster, because he was about to hand Persephone and her friends over to his father to buy his own sliver of happiness. *Freedom at any cost, right?*

The great black of her unknown fate loomed and kick-started a flutter of emotion he had thought stripped from him with every lash of the whip, every strike of the chains, every recalling of his failings. "Don't care, don't get hurt" may have been at the top of his hard-and-fast list, but that didn't stop a single word from bubbling up from somewhere around his heart.

Inamorata. Beloved.

The ramification stunned him. "What the hell am I supposed to do with that?"

14

LEONA PACED IN HER ROOM, ignoring the crunch of broken glass and the strips of shredded canvas strewn over the floor. She stopped at her most cherished treasure, a portrait of her dead mother. She ran her fingers over the beloved face, every crack and swirl of the paint memorized. "You left me when I needed you most."

She ripped the ornate gold frame off the wall and threw it to the floor. She unsheathed her dagger but hesitated, her body shaking, until rage eclipsed her love. She slashed and ripped the portrait into tiny pieces, then threw her mother's ruined face into the fireplace and watched the flames devour her.

All the years she'd tried to catch her father's eye, to gain his love by giving him a progeny he could be proud of to make up for Lyon's failing and her unfortunate gender, were just a waste.

Then she made the ultimate mistake, at least in Llewellyn's eyes. Leona opened a tiny white marble chest on the fireplace mantle. She removed a clipping of dark brown hair held together with a tiny pink bow and held it to her nose. "You left me too, but it wasn't of your making." Leona folded a handkerchief of linen and lace around the lock of hair and slipped it into a leather pouch around her neck. "You will be my good luck, my muse, my strength."

She hovered at the apex of her rage as she slipped the pouch inside her shirt, then let herself tumble over. She trembled, her belly clenched until she thought she would vomit, her eyes hot but dry. No more tears. It was time to take control of her destiny. To do that, she needed a powerful ally. Sagittarius loved her and would do anything she asked. She'd known about his feelings for years, but she was the "Untouchable" and he was only a Zodiac, not nearly powerful enough to sate her ambitions. Only the demon would fit the bill. He could give her the power she needed. "No more waiting. It's time."

She kicked aside the rubble and finished dressing before leaving her rooms.

Leona stood inside a huge sigil painted on the bare floor, her naked body trembling from the chill of the cave. She looked around the small space and scowled. The other Zodiacs were created in the great cavern surrounded by riches, lauded with elaborate ceremonies and witnessed by the Twelve. The pageantry was glorious and spoke to her need for recognition. But for her there was no pomp, just a demon and his personal servants in the dingy dark surrounded by a circle of mirrors so she could watch her metamorphosis.

The demon king stepped inside the circle. The last mirror was placed, enclosing them. He walked to Leona, a smile on his face, his eyes glazed with excitement. She'd seen that look before, just before he sucked the soul out of some human. A jolt of concern ripped through her body, but she squelched it before the concern could morph into fear. This was what she wanted, *nulla materia sumptus*—no matter the cost.

He pushed a lock of hair behind her ear. "Are you ready?"

She nodded, not trusting her voice.

Asmodeus took a few steps back and crouched. He balanced on the balls of his feet and bowed his head. A flash of fire and smoke exploded around him, obscuring his body. It dissipated in seconds, revealing his true demonic form, sans clothes.

The horror show slowly unfurled, revealing a massive body with a chest wider than that of the largest troll and tree-trunk-sized arms and legs. The eight-foot-tall nightmare towered over Leona, panting so hard her hair moved with each breath.

"Hands and knees," he ordered, his voice octaves lower than normal—so low that it vibrated inside her.

Leona dropped down, then pivoted away from him. Her heart pounded, her body trembled, until she saw her reflection in the mirror. Who was that woman looking back at her? The scars on her face blazed a white trail across her flushed skin. Her blonde hair was disheveled, her eyes bloodshot. Her bones pushed at her skin, blanching it at each protuberance.

She looked away from her reality and focused on Asmodeus.

The fingernails on the demon king's huge hands blackened and shriveled. The ruined keratin fell to the ground next to his molted toenails. He raised his hands to eye level and watched and waited. The ends of the demon's fingertips pulsed for several seconds before they burst open. Black blood sprayed across the demon's chest and face. Long claws punched their way through the gaping flesh.

Thick black lines formed sigils that covered the demon's rippling crimson skin. Ropes of double muscle flexed when he crouched again, an evil grin on his face, his solid red eyes glittering with pleasure. He threw back his head and laughed, exposing grisly, jagged teeth. "Are you sure? There's no going back, my pet."

"Get on with it, demon."

Asmodeus closed his eyes and began the ritual. He stroked Leona from the small of her back to her neck with the back of his claws. She arched her spine into his caress, his touch soft, loving even. Then, in a lightning-fast move, he rotated his wrist and gouged four deep lines in her skin and muscle.

Leona screamed and tried to crawl away, but he wrapped an arm around her waist and held her in place.

Asmodeus giggled. He removed his claws from her flesh and licked them clean. He held his left hand above her head, the other over her slashed back. The black sigils covering Asmodeus' body writhed. A tiny ball of blue electricity emerged from his left palm and hovered between them, sizzling and popping as it expanded until it enveloped them in a bubble. The mirrors rippled; her reflection was softened by the blue sphere. Leona's muscles twitched. Her bones ached with the desperate need to run, but her brain ordered her to stay. *This is what I want. This is the road I must take.*

The bubble exploded. Asmodeus roared with pleasure, then punched his right hand through the skin and flesh and bone of her back. Just as quickly, the demon pulled back, dragging Leona's writhing, pale-white soul out of the torn skin.

She screamed again, her back arched away from the demon. Her body involuntarily twisted and bucked as if fighting for its very essence, regardless of her wishes.

With the claw of his left forefinger, Asmodeus ripped her squirming soul and pulled slowly until, with a small pop, he tore a piece away. He threw back his head, opened his mouth wide, and slurped it down like an oyster.

He belched and swiped at the corners of his mouth with the back of his hand. "What a delicious pound of flesh. Your turn, my pet." Asmodeus turned his claws inward and pressed them hard against his belly until they penetrated his dark red skin. Black blood oozed down his arm, but still he pushed deeper, his head cocked to one side, a vague smile on his face.

He stopped just shy of his elbow. He grunted, twisted his arm, and backed it out, a huge handful of a thick, black, gelatinous blob in his fist. He held the quivering mass high, closed his eyes and chanted the words needed to bind his soul with that of the assassins. When he finished, he pressed the black mass against the hole in Leona's soul and waited for the tendrils of his corruption to penetrate her purity. He released his grip on the demon-tainted soul and it disappeared inside Leona with a hiss.

Asmodeus waved his bloody hand over her back and the wound knitted together. "You are Leo, the lioness, the first female Zodiac." He held out a hand.

Leona clasped it and rose into his arms.

"You are mine, and I am yours," he whispered in her ear.

She clung to him, her body numb, her heart frozen. Just like that, all the pints of demon blood he'd made her drink, all the times she'd given him her body, all the humiliations and degradations were over. The first major step toward her evolution was done: she was the first female Zodiac.

"I need to rest while I assimilate," she whispered.

Asmodeus clapped his hands. Servants ran to her and guided her out.

Asmodeus finished his hot shower and walked into his main room, a towel wrapped around his waist. A woman sat on his sofa, her arms draped across the back, her red hair flowing to the floor.

She turned her head so he could see her profile. "Is it done?"

He took a seat in his club chair and relaxed back. Making a Zodiac was exhilarating, but exhausting. "Yes."

Circe leaned forward and rested her elbows on her knees. "How much soul did you give her?"

"Three times what Lyon received."

Circe frowned. "Can she handle that much without going off the rails? I can't use another Lyon."

Asmodeus dropped his towel, and held out his hand. When she took it, he pulled her up and led her to his bed. He lifted her in his arms and set her down gently before climbing on top of her luscious, writhing body. His heavy sex swayed above her open thighs, his lips suspended over hers. "That's why I've fed her a steady diet of my blood."

He didn't trust this witch. Even being a demon king, he'd never met a more powerful creature, and that scared the crap out of him. Goddesses and demons don't mix well, but for him, in this situation, it was a case of the devil you know.

Add Llewellyn to the mix and Asmodeus didn't see it ending well for him once the gates of hell were opened and his army rose. There would be too many opportunities for "friendly fire" in the ensuing chaos.

So, when Circe had cornered him and revealed that she knew what he was doing to, and with, Leona, he'd welcomed her into the fold. One, to keep an eye on her and two, because she was a beautiful woman who loved sex. No self-respecting, black-blooded demon could refuse that.

"Enough talking, demon. Give me what I came for."

He positioned his sex, and buried it inside her with one thrust.

"Leona!" Sagittarius banged on Leona's door but no one answered, not even a servant.

He punched the wood and walked away. He'd returned to the InBetween to find out the truth of what had happened to his father and to speak with Leona, but she wouldn't see him. Hell, she wouldn't even yell at him through her door.

His sire was dead. He had hoped a mistake had been made, but the truth gut-punched him when he opened the small box and saw the remains of his father's head.

With his sire gone and Leona not speaking to him, there was only one thing left to do before he left the InBetween. Sag walked through the bleak dungeon passages until he reached Lyon's cell. Why would Lyon commit such a heinous act? The Zodiac was a killer for sure, and Sag hated him for what he had done to Leona, but how could Lyon be that far gone? What could he gain from murdering the Twelve? Libra's question about seeing their fathers hit home: it had been weeks since he'd last seen his sire. But it had to be Lyon—why else would Llewellyn still be alive? Right?

He scanned the passage before slipping into Lyon's cell. He shut the door and locked it, then searched the space until he looked under Lyon's bed and found a small wood chest with iron bands and a lock in the middle.

Sag pulled out a blade and started on the lock, but before he could pick it, someone opened the cell door.

Lyon's old healer woman entered the room. "What are you doing here, Zodiac?"

He bristled at her impertinence, but decided to overlook it for now. Each Zodiac had his own personal healer, so this woman would know more about Lyon than anyone. He stowed his anger and decided to tell her the truth.

"I'm trying to find out why Lyon killed my father."

The healer opened the door wider and stepped to one side. "You need to leave."

Sag patted the top of the chest and jiggled the heavy lock. "What's this?"

She swept her hand to the door. "Please, leave."

Sag tucked the chest under his arm, stalked to her, and crowded her space. "Okay. I'll leave."

She blocked the door. "I can't let you take that."

Sag growled in frustration. He ripped her hood from her head then staggered back when he saw her face. Wrinkled skin and cloudy eyes were framed by sparse grey hair—so familiar, but he couldn't place her.

The hag grabbed the chest from him and placed it on the bed.

Sag rubbed his forehead. "What's in the chest?"

She stared at him as if trying to decide if he could be trusted, then sighed. She pulled out a key on a piece of string from inside her clothes, unlocked it, and opened the lid. Then, she brushed past Sag, closed the cell door, and leaned against it.

Sag lifted a leather glove coated with black splashes and spots. A quick whiff confirmed his suspicion: dried blood. Cold sweat coated his skin when he smelled his father's blood mixed with many others. He threw the glove on the bed. "This proves Lyon's the killer. Why would you show this to me?"

"Smell it again."

"I don't need to smell it a second time. This glove was worn during the murders of the Twelve."

"Smell the inside of the glove."

Sag grit his teeth. He wanted to walk out and show the proof of Lyon's guilt to the world. Rid Leona of the burden of being his sister. Maybe then she would see how much he loved her. But he couldn't understand the why of it. It was that doubt that drove him to do as the healer asked. He took a quick sniff, then a deeper one. "Shit. A woman wore this glove."

The healer nodded.

"Lyon is innocent?"

"Yes. Exactly."

"Holy crap, the Zodiacs are out for his head. I have to go." Sag placed the glove in the chest. He closed the lock and shoved it under the bed. "Wait, do you know who the woman is?"

"I have an idea, but no way to get close enough to her to confirm it."

"You'll keep the glove safe?"

"I'll keep it safe. You just keep Lyon alive."

15

S**EVERAL YARDS FROM THE HOUSE**, Persephone, Abella, and Taryn raised their flashlights from the dusty single-track and studied the small opening in the tall, horizontal, raised shelf of rock that appeared out of nowhere.

Persephone squatted and ran her hand along the edge of the crack. "This is the main entrance? It looks more like a fracture."

Abella and Taryn looked inside the entrance, then disappeared inside.

Persephone turned her body sideways and inched her way along the crack until she reached the other side. She raised the beam to look around and pointed it into Lyon's face.

He threw up his hands. "You trying to blind me? Get that light out of my eyes."

"Sorry," Persephone mumbled.

"Turn off the lights and wait."

The dark had blanketed the group for several seconds when long threads of blue light appeared, suspended from the ceiling. Lyon raised an arm and touched the bottom of the longest strands. They undulated, and the blue glow brightened.

"What is that?" Abella asked.

"Gleam worms, but I've never seen them this close to the surface." He ran his fingers along the walls and growled. "There used to be dozens, hundreds of crystals here." He shook his head. "Let's keep moving."

They worked their way through the debris-strewn floor of the small cave until they reached an yawning hole in the wall that led to an endless black.

"We're going in there?" Persephone asked, her tight throat choking her voice into a high squeak. "I can't see the bottom." She turned to Lyon, her normally manageable claustrophobia now paralyzing her. "I can't see the bottom," she repeated.

"I know where the bottom is." Lyon offered his arm. "Who's first?"

Abella took it and followed him into the dark.

"Abella?" Persephone called out several seconds later.

"I'm at the bottom. It's a steep slope, but not too long."

Lyon reappeared and looked at Persephone. He offered his hand. Her heart fluttered in her chest, and she fought for every breath. She took a step back, and shook her head.

He turned to Taryn. She took his hand and they started down.

Persephone took another step back, her body shaking.

"Persephone?" Lyon called, returning once more.

"Take the dogs first. Please."

He picked up the old female and laid his hand on the male's head, then squatted low and slid down the rubble.

Moments later, like a beast rising up out of the dark, Lyon slowly reappeared. "It's time."

She nodded, then gasped and shook her head. She wrapped her arms around her body and whimpered. "This…this is my nightmare."

"What," he asked, "this cave?"

"Not the cave—well, maybe, but not. I'm not making any sense." She took a ragged breath, and blinked. "It's the dark…and you. You are the monster who dragged me down into the dark."

Lyon had no words. What could he say to that? *I'm not a monster?* Lying wasn't his style, and he wouldn't change that to make her feel better. He *was* dragging her down into the dark—she just didn't know how far.

He peeled Persephone's right arm free and led her to the beginning of the incline. "First thing we need to do," he said, "is wash those dogs."

The corners of her mouth curved for a second, but she didn't look away from the dark, staring as if in thrall.

"Persephone?" She looked at him and blinked, her eyes glazed. "Keep your eyes on me. I'll protect you."

He walked backward, watching her tight face, willing her to trust him. The urge to protect her, to ease her fears, brought him up fast. He was perilously close to a serious breach of his number-one hard-and-fast, and that was unacceptable. He needed to purge any shred of caring before it brought him down, like a preemptive puking of a tainted meal before every orifice blew. *Emotional bulimia, son of a bitch. Just keep a lid on it, man.*

"This isn't so bad," Persephone said, her voice tight.

Before Lyon could reply, she lost her footing and plowed into his chest. Lyon flew through the air and landed on his back on the incline. They slid faster and faster, Persephone clinging to his chest, their combined weight shredding his shirt and grinding rubble into his skin and the hole in his flank.

They reached the bottom, then stopped when gravity lost its fight against the level floor, but Lyon continued to grip Persephone's trembling body tight against his. "Are you okay?"

She nodded.

They stared at each other, mouths open, lips almost touching, bodies melded.

She wrapped her arms around his neck, pulled her body across him and kissed his cheek. "Thank you."

"Screw that. This is a proper thank you." Lyon slid his fingers through her hair. He raised his head and met her full lips with his own. Their breath mingled. Her warm essence tickled his lips, his skin, but he waited, giving Persephone a chance to pull away, to escape.

Instead, she ran her fingers through his hair and pulled him closer.

"Ahem," Abella said. "Can we turn on our flashlights?"

Persephone gasped and wiggled to get away.

Lyon closed his eyes and rolled his body to the side to deposit Persephone in the dirt before she put any more pressure on his savage boner. He sat up, straightened his shirt, and rolled his shoulders to reengage his brain.

The old Doberman hobbled over to him. She sniffed his face, licked it, then plopped down next to him and put her head across his legs as if claiming him.

"Come on, old gal, I need to get up."

She lifted her head—releasing him—and watched him rise.

Lyon leaned over to ruffle her red fur, but a shooting pain in his back forced him to stop. When he touched his shirt, his fingers came away wet and sticky. He wiped the blood on his pants. Nothing to do about it now.

Lyon slipped on the sunglasses to protect his vision from the flashlights, and scanned the space. He was stunned by the changes. The entire roof of the cave was covered with long stands of gleam worms, providing low light. Cool air, dripping water, and a confluence of rock and dirt and crystals formed over centuries filled the space. Tiny white lights with the occasional dot of blue and red danced along the walls. He ran his hands along the wall and found more holes than crystals.

He looked at the women and his heart went thud. Swirling lights danced around their bodies. Dark green and dark blue surrounded Abella, while Taryn had a lighter green, like moss, and dark brown. But it was the pale blue, purple, and gold surrounding Persephone that stole his breath. The old healer had told him he would see the truth of things with these glasses. Now if they could only tell him what he was seeing. Aura? Possession? Gas?

He shook his head. It didn't mean a damn thing, just some trick.

The women joined him and he pointed out the pockmarks. "There used to be huge crystals in these holes. Humans have been poaching these stones as well."

Persephone ran her fingers inside a hole. "What about the Red Cap? From what you told us, I thought he'd be too territorial to allow that."

"He is. Several humans disappeared when the Red Cap chose this cave, so the system was closed to the public." Lyon wiped his hands on his pant legs. "I'm surprised this entrance hasn't been sealed."

"What about that monster on the surface?" Abella asked.

"I have no idea why the human was allowed to live this close."

"Please, can we go somewhere that has more light?" Persephone asked.

Lyon touched the closest crystal, then sang a clear tone and held it for several seconds while it bounced around the space.

The stone flickered, then glowed. A few feet down the wall, another crystal came to life, then another and another until the small chamber was bathed in purple and gold and white. A tiny crack in the wall opposite them appeared, and the trail of crystal lights disappeared inside.

Lyon gestured to the newly revealed crack. "Let's press on to the next cavern. If memory serves, there's fresh water running through it. Oh, by the way, you better have a holy verse ready. If we run into the Red Cap and he attacks, a verse is the only thing that'll stop him."

Persephone stepped up to him.

He turned her body. "Go sideways."

She shimmied into the crack and disappeared, the dogs trailing after her.

Lyon waved Abella and Taryn over and they followed Persephone. Lyon looked around the cave once more and shook his head. So few crystals remained. Damn greedy bastards, plundering these gifts from the goddess.

He slipped inside the crack, but stopped short when it became impassable. He looked ahead, but the fissure just got smaller. He'd only been sixteen when he'd last traveled this cave—guess he'd grown a bit since then. He dropped to his hands and knees, then his belly, the lower half of the crack being the only part that remained wide enough for his huge body to pass. He grunted and cursed as more dirt and pebbles ground into his skin. Finally, he reached the next chamber. The women stood with their backs to Lyon.

"A hand would have been nice," he grumbled.

The women said nothing. The dogs whined.

The *pat-pat-pat* of bare feet reverberated from wall to wall. The women turned in reaction to each sound, but it was too fast, the light from the crystals too low to help. Whispering, giggling, hissing surrounded them.

Lyon stepped around the women and put them between his back and the wall. He crouched, waiting for an attack.

Heavy footsteps silenced the whispers. A flame erupted revealing a short, squat man with red eyes, filthy hands with long talons instead of fingernails, and a stovepipe hat perched on his head that dripped blood. The little man bared large jagged teeth at the women, but he growled when he saw Lyon. His eyes blazed a brighter red.

"You!" He ran at Lyon, his talons aimed straight for Lyon's heart.

"I am in pain and distress. May your salvation, O Goddess, protect me," Lyon yelled.

"Ahhh." The man slid to a halt, his hands cupped over his ears. He backed away from the group. "Why be here, whoreson?"

Lyon stalked the retreating creature, his head held low and his teeth bared. "You dare malign my mother?"

"Words, only words. What you did, far worse, far, far worse."

Lyon stopped. As much as he hated to admit it, the Red Cap spoke the truth of it. Lyon had done far worse than malign his mother. "We seek refuge."

"In my home? Oh, no, no, no."

"This cave system has far more room than one Red Cap needs. A couple hours and we'll be gone."

"No, no, no, too many. Too many here." The Red Cap removed his red hat and rotated it counterclockwise over and over. His eyes swept the cave. "Too many. Too, too many."

Lyon looked around. In the few seconds they had talked, the space had filled with dozens of bodies. Some tall, some short, with a variety of eye colors—red, black, pale blue, and green—that glowed in the dark shadows.

Lyon turned on the little beast. "What the hell are you doing with children?"

Scorpio sat by the dying fire in his dark, sparsely decorated room. *A bed, a chair, what more does a man need?* He took a pull on the cigar and blew smoke rings, his eyes half-closed, a small portrait of his father balanced on his knee. He tapped the cigar against the picture frame until the ash fell onto dear old dad's face. A couple more taps and the ash would obscure the bastard's smug mug.

Quiet reigned, soothing him, until someone pounded on his door so hard the hinges rattled and the wood bowed. His adrenaline spiked. A couple of scorpions jumped off his skin and landed on the floor.

"Enter!"

Leona stalked in.

Scor studied the beautiful woman. She had changed. Increased confidence, check, but it was more than that. Her body, her aura, or both had expanded, but not from gaining weight—her entire frame had widened, her normally lean muscles had thickened. But it was her dark intensity that caught his attention. He'd seen her around for years. She was a very unhappy woman, a walking black hole of need and insecurity. The creature standing before him was none of those things.

"What?"

"No niceties?"

He snorted.

She sat on the edge of his bed. "To the point then. You're the best tracker I know."

"Yes."

"I also know you're thorough."

"Your point?"

"I know you have a way to find Lyon."

Scor waited for the woman to finish. Goddess, how he hated conversation.

"I want you to take me to him."

"No." He gestured to the door. "Leave."

"Why?"

Scor laid the painting and his cigar aside, then slid to the edge of his chair. He leaned forward, his elbows on his knees. "Lyon is mine."

"He killed my mother."

"And he killed mine! What else you got?"

Leona sneered. "Your mother disappeared—ran away from you is what I heard."

Scor sniffed the air, then cocked his head: sulfur and blood and death. "What have you done?"

Leona ignored his question. "Take me to Lyon so I can bring him back here."

"I hear a lot of 'me' and 'I' in your request. Why should *I* help you?"

"Because I can convince Lyon to return. And when I'm done with him, he's all yours." She stood and walked to the door. "You have an hour to decide." She paused, her hand on the knob.

Scor picked up his cigar and ground it into his father's portrait, obliterating the man's face. "No need to waste an hour. Let's go."

16

"THEY'RE JUST CHILDREN." Persephone said.

"Chil…chil…children." The Red Cap shuddered. "Spawn, spawn of the devil. Yes, yes."

Persephone pushed past Lyon and approached the nearest child. Tiny, fragile, with black hair and glowing red eyes, the girl stood her ground.

"I'm Persephone. What's your name?"

The girl cocked her head.

Persephone stepped closer.

The girl hissed and black feathers snapped up out of her hair, like the hackles of a frightened dog. The girl scurried behind a larger child.

Persephone turned to another girl, older and taller than the rest, but she hissed and backed away until her left leg buckled. She fell to the ground and keened.

"She's hurt." Persephone dropped to her knees. She extended her hand again and held it a few inches away. "I won't hurt you. Will you let me see?"

Persephone leaned closer. She hesitated, then touched the child's skin.

The girl gouged tracks in Persephone's forearm. Persephone inhaled sharply, but didn't move—if she backed away now, the girl may never let her get close again.

The room exploded with chattering teeth and growls and caws like that of a crow. The other children stepped closer, bodies tense, fists clenched.

"Persephone?" Abella and Taryn said simultaneously.

"I'm good."

"Get away from her before she decides to really hurt you," Lyon demanded.

Persephone shook her head, but kept her eyes on the terrified child. "No. She won't hurt me again."

Persephone sat back on her heels and opened her backpack. She pulled out a large bag of M&Ms, poured a few into her hand, then placed them on the ground next to the girl.

"What are those?" Lyon asked.

"They're called M&Ms," Abella said. "They're candy."

The girl looked at the candy, then at Persephone.

Persephone nodded and smiled. "See? It's good." She flipped a piece into her mouth and chewed. "Mm, yummy."

The children drew closer to their injured friend to study Persephone and her offering.

"They're getting awfully close," Taryn warned.

Persephone ignored her. She pointed to the candy in front of the girl, then to her mouth, and smiled again.

The girl reached out and took a piece of candy. She rolled it between her thumb and forefinger, sniffed each side, then touched the candy with the tip of her tongue. Her eyes widened. She licked it, then slipped it inside her mouth. After a single crunch, she swallowed. Her eyes widened. She gathered up the rest of the candies and held her closed fists against her chest before looking at the other children. She unfurled her fingers, then doled out the M&Ms to the smallest children.

Persephone leaned closer. The girl grunted, but this time she didn't pull away when Persephone touched her injured leg. She straightened the girl's skeletal limb and found a large swelling that started at just under her knee, ran the length of her lower leg, and stopped north of her ankle.

"The water you mentioned? Fire to boil it with? Bandages? I need to lance this abscess before the infection enters her blood."

"I could go back to the house and check for a first aid kit," Abella offered.

"None of you are going back, I can't risk it. Water is through there, in one of the caves." Lyon patted a pants pocket. "And I have the sheets from the cabin. That'll have to do."

He joined Persephone and bent over to pick up the girl, but the other children keened and wailed. They advanced on him, poised to attack as a single unit.

"For goodness sake, back up," Persephone ordered under her breath.

He stepped back, but bared his teeth.

The children swelled around Persephone until he lost sight of her.

"Persephone?" Lyon called out.

Several children lifted the injured girl off the ground while the others pulled Persephone to her feet and gripped her hands, her clothes. The rest of the children surrounded the two dogs and cooed as they herded them. The mass walked to another opening in the stone that led deep into the belly of the underground, Abella and Taryn hot on their trail.

The Red Cap turned to follow them, but Lyon grabbed his shoulder and jerked him to a stop. "What the hell are you doing with these babies? Corvus Wards? Portends? Kellas Cats? I've never seen so many in one place, much less mingling."

The little man pulled his bloody hat down on his head. "Not mine, not mine. They won't leave." He shook his head and stamped a foot. "More, more, always more." He turned to Lyon and pointed, his smile and eyes wide. "You! You take. Take them all."

"Let us rest for a couple hours and I'll think about taking them."

"Reals? Really reals?"

"Yes, reals."

The Red Cap danced a jig as he sang. "Human is back, human is back, human is back on the menu."

Lyon pushed the nasty little man out of his way. "Yeah, yeah, human is back on the menu except for those three humans. You touch them, you die. Got it?"

The Red Cap stomped his foot. "Nasty man, mean and nasty. No humans here, no man-flesh meal for Red Cap here. But the doggies…"

Lyon walked to the crack. "Not gonna happen," he called over his shoulder.

Circe stretched and rolled in the tangled silk sheets on her bed. She had to give Asmodeus his due, the demon certainly knew his way around a female body. Males too, if she had to take a guess.

Centuries in a tomb tended to wreak havoc on a girl—her libido included—but her glorious body hadn't lost a step during the many years of her entombment. Hell, the nerves in her sex still pulsed from the last explosive orgasm the demon had elicited.

She pushed the sheets aside, got out of bed, and padded into the luxurious bathroom. Gleaming white marble surfaces, gold faucets, and floor-length mirrors dotted the space. She'd known Llewellyn was ambitious, so she wasn't surprised he had brought her back to help him reclaim what belonged to him. She stood in front of the closest mirror and admired her reflection. Long limbs, full breasts and a tiny waist; a thick curtain of auburn waves that ended at her lower back; dark green eyes and full lips. She was still a beauty.

Thick white bath sheets that were longer than she was tall and a shower enclosed in glass were new to her. They hadn't had any of this in her time. But her favorite toy was the deep tub with jets of water that tickled her in all the right places.

She cooed as she ran the tips of her fingers along the porcelain sides. "Get off and get clean at the same time. Genius." She closed the drain and started the hot water.

When the tub was full, she slipped into the heat and let it ease the tension in her body. She couldn't remember a time she'd been so sated. Killing the twelve human princes so many years ago had been delicious and filling in so many ways, but that was so long ago. This new world her mother had created after resurrecting the dead princes was yielding a feast of food and sex and blood. The greatest banquet, however, was coming soon.

She counted off the list of ingredients she needed for the ritual. There were only two items left: the three women, and the book. The women should be here soon, and she had the perfect person in mind to fetch the last item.

"Circe," a voice called out.

"Here."

Leona walked into the bathroom and stopped short. She turned around. "You asked to see me?"

"So bashful, child. Come, look your fill."

"I'd rather not."

Circe kept her anger in check. The impudent bitch would go down, but not before she had served Circe's needs. "So be it. I have a job for you."

"Pick one of your Creepers, or a Zodiac."

"They don't have your finesse, your passion."

"Doesn't matter. I already have a job."

"To find Lyon? Yes, I know about all that family drama. Luckily, the job I have in mind for you will have you crossing paths with your brother."

"So you know where he is?"

"I can't give you exact coordinates at the moment, but I can guess where he'll be in two or three days."

"Tell me."

"I'll tell you if you fetch a certain item for me."

"Done."

"The information you need is on the nightstand next to the bed."

Leona started to leave.

Circe laughed. "Oh, darling. I simply adore the new you."

17

PERSEPHONE SQUIRMED TO FREE herself from the children's grip, but they held her fast as they marched through the opening and descended into a large chamber. Finally, they stopped and released her.

She used her flashlight to look around the cavern. Where the others had few crystals embedded in the walls, this one was covered with purple, amber, red, and white stones. When the beam hit them, the stones flared to life and painted sections of floor, walls, and ceiling with shimmering points of light like a huge kaleidoscope that softened the hard edges of the broken stalagmites and stalactites.

More glowing eyes appeared on ledges in the wall and from around fallen rocks. The injured girl limped to Persephone and took her hand.

"No, don't walk." Persephone picked her up and cradled her thin, cold body against her chest. The girl's body tensed for a moment before she sagged into Persephone's chest and sighed.

Persephone turned to the Red Cap. "I need a fire and clean water."

Several children took Abella and Taryn by the hands and guided them to a charred stone pit with a small pile of wood stacked inside. The children pointed to the wood, then wrapped their arms across their chests with the universal sign for cold.

Abella patted her pockets. "I'm sorry, I have nothing to light a fire. Taryn?"

Taryn dug deep into the pockets of her floor-length gypsy skirt. She pulled out a small lighter. "Voila. Always be prepared." She tossed it to Abella, who gathered a handful of kindling and tucked it against the wood stack. She held the lighter out for the children to see, then flicked the striker wheel. A small flame erupted from the plastic body.

The children gasped.

Abella held out her free hand. "It's okay." She released the fuel lever and the flame disappeared. "See?"

The children drew closer.

Abella let the closest boy take the lighter. He examined it, then handed it back to Abella. He pointed to her hand and she flicked the lighter again. He pointed to the kindling. Abella held the lighter under the smallest twigs until they caught fire. The flames devoured the kindling, then grew greedy and engulfed the logs.

Persephone turned off the flashlight and watched her best friends with the children.

Taryn looked like a gypsy queen with her long, curly black hair, ankle-length skirts of the most outrageous color combinations, a no-holds-barred personality, and the uncanny ability to find anything lost. A five-four, curvy mother hen who never held back her opinion, never made decisions with her head. Nope, she was all heart and gut and would take down anyone who threatened her family.

Abella couldn't be more different. Six-foot tall, with a supermodel body and face, and a fiery red pixie haircut that was the antithesis of her calm, cool demeanor. Her fierce beauty alone would have been enough to make the world bow at her feet had she desired the adulation, but her physical assets were nothing compared to her intelligence. Her body and face brought rich men to the Texas Hold'em table. Her brains and the ubiquitous male ego kept them there until she fleeced them out of cash, cars, and real estate. The woman neutered the fools, one hand at a time, and they adored her for it.

The dogs plopped down as close to the growing flames as they could get without falling into the pit. The flickering yellow and orange light bathed the cave chamber, lapping at the crystals in the walls until a riotous explosion of yellow, purple, white and red painted everything and everyone.

Persephone had never seen anything so beautiful—until she looked at her patient. Pale white skin was painted with an ombre wash of pale pink on her forehead, the tips of her pointed and slightly furred ears, and her hands and feet. Huge, expressive eyes of pale green framed with thick, dark pink lashes and a stunning bone structure were the icing on this girl's unique look.

She laid the child on the ground near the fire and sat next to her.

"What's your name?" Persephone asked.

The injured girl cocked her head.

"She doesn't have a name," Lyon said from a dark corner of the cave. "None of them do."

"What? Why?"

"Because she doesn't have her familiar yet—none of these Kellas Cat children do. Only after her familiar is revealed will the goddess allow her parents to give her a name."

Persephone stared at him. Holy crap, that was another question to add to the long list she had for him.

"What?" he said.

"Well, I have to call her something. 'Hey, you' doesn't work for me." She looked at the Kellas Cat girl and almost laughed when she saw the girl digging in the backpack with one hand. As if feeling Persephone's eyes on her, she glanced up and slowly removed her hand.

Persephone reached over the girl and pulled out the bag of candy. The children around her stilled. She handed the bag to the Kellas Cat girl. "M&M, that's what I'll call her. Not a name, a nickname."

"Is there any difference?" Lyon asked from his corner of the dark.

She shrugged her shoulders. "You mentioned water?"

Lyon rose. "You have a kettle to boil water?" he asked the Red Cap.

The little man pointed to the largest boulder. "Behind that rock."

Lyon did a check of the space. Other than a couple of large boulders and several smaller ones off to one side, there wasn't much to see. A few horizontal cracks slashed the walls, but they didn't seem to go anywhere. That could be the reason the children were still alive with a Red Cap for a guardian—or a warden, depending on what was going on here.

He found a hodge-podge of items stashed behind one boulder. Pots and pans, a huge kettle, drinking glasses, newspapers, torn remnants of clothes, and other unrecognizable junk made up a pile that would make a hoarder twitch. He grabbed the kettle, a couple of pots, and several pieces of material that could be used for bandaging and returned to Persephone.

"I'm afraid it's definitely an abscess. Do you have soap and a scalpel blade?"

Lyon unsheathed his dagger and offered it to her. "No soap."

The children cried out, M&M whimpered. Persephone held her ankle tight. "Put that away, you're scaring the children. Don't you have something smaller?"

"Maybe." He dug through his pockets until he found Libra's fancy multi-tool. He handed it to Persephone.

Her eyebrows shot up, her mouth twitched with what he assumed was amusement. The glittery tool was ridiculous. "It's not mine."

She held up her hands. "Not my business."

"No, really, it's not mine," he ground out.

She looked away and opened the smallest blade. "This will work."

He grabbed the kettle. "I'll get some water." He walked a few steps before looking back at Persephone. "We're moving on as soon as you're done, two hours, tops. It's not safe here."

"I'm not going anywhere. These children can't travel. They're malnourished and filthy. Your injuries need care as well, and we all need rest."

Lyon gripped the kettle handle as a wave of heat burned a hole in his gut. He stalked away from the group and dropped to his knees next to a small stream. He splashed cold water on his face, closed his eyes. "Cool down, man."

When he'd gained enough control to breathe normally, he filled the kettle and placed it on the fire.

A hand landed on his shoulder.

He dropped and whirled, his claws extended, but stopped just short of eviscerating Persephone. The children screamed and ran, disappearing into hidey holes as fast as scat bugs. The dogs growled, their hackles up, their heads low. Too jacked to stand, he crawled to the closest dark corner and curled into a ball.

Persephone remained frozen in place.

"Honey, you're okay, please sit," he heard Taryn say.

Persephone collapsed to the ground.

Taryn marched over to Lyon. "What the hell is wrong with you?"

"I don't like being touched."

"You didn't mind her touching you earlier."

Lyon bared his teeth and growled.

Taryn rolled her eyes. "Huh. Frackin' 'roid head."

Lyon closed his eyes and willed the termagant to go away. She left, but the memory of his mother bleeding out despite his desperate efforts to save her played in his brain over and over. He couldn't stop it. He fisted his hands and dug his nails into his palms, hoping the pain would stop the fucking infinity loop, but the memory just shifted. Instead of his dying mother, Persephone lay before him, his claws buried in her belly, blood pouring out of her open mouth while her lips moved as if she was trying to say something.

Lyon pounded his fists into his temples over and over. "Stop, stop, stop," he hissed.

"What are you doing, Lyon? Trying to throw me off? I'll stop this misery, but only if you agree to owe me one," the demon whispered in Lyon's head.

"Yes, yes, anything."

The images vanished as quickly as they had started. Lyon sagged with momentary relief, but it was short-lived. The piece of Asmodeus' soul inside him had caused him untold misery over the years, but never had it talked to him.

Not until two weeks ago—at the beginning of his dreams of a mystery woman who turned out to be Persephone.

Persephone sat quietly, willing her shaking to stop, but it still took several minutes for her to gain control of her body and her emotions. *Not the time to fall apart.*

She piled this new hurt and pain and fear on top of the massive crap pile she'd been squirrelling away since the first time the trees had turned white and chased her to the house. Pretty soon she'd run out of room, and the emotional storm would be epic. Blow-the-margarita-blender-motor epic. No-guacamole-or-ice cream-in-all-of-Texas epic.

A soft touch on her shoulder brought her out of her reverie. M&M lifted her leg into Persephone's lap. As soon as the girl settled, the other children drifted back to the fire, but stayed as far away from the adults as possible.

"Hey, you okay?" Abella removed the kettle from the fire and poured the hot water into a pot until it covered the multi-tool and strips of cloth made from the discarded clothes. She sat and crossed her long legs.

Persephone nodded through the sudden prick of tears. She swiped at her cheeks and cleared her throat.

"If it's any help, I don't believe he wants to hurt you."

Persephone nodded, but couldn't trust her voice.

"Could he hurt you? Hell, yeah. His size could squash a bitty thing like you. And, oh boy, his scars alone scream he's majorly damaged."

"I think there's more to him than that."

"I agree."

"But, Abella." Persephone looked at her friend and chewed through the tears. "He killed that man outside, murdered him. How can you ignore the bad to reach the good?"

"I don't have an answer for that, love." Abella looked at Lyon, curled into a fetal ball and rocking, hugging the dark like a blanket. "But I think he deserves someone who'll try."

Persephone dropped her head. Abella was right. Lyon deserved someone who believed in him so strongly she would fight her way to his good. Everyone deserved that. But it wasn't her; she wasn't strong enough. He needed someone like Abella or Taryn.

Abella rose and ran a hand down Persephone's hair. Electricity arced between them and raced down Persephone's spine. Abella backed up. "Can't even touch your hair, now? Son of a bitch." She walked away, staring at her palm while shaking her head.

Persephone took a deep breath and turned her attention back to the girl, anything to smother her jumbled feelings. "You ready?"

M&M cocked her head.

Persephone pulled a strip of cloth out of the hot water, waved it in the air to cool it a little, and wiped the dirt off her forearm.

M&M nodded.

Persephone cleaned the dirt off her leg and palpated until she found the soft spot low on the girl's leg. "It's definitely an abscess." She fished the multi-tool out of the water.

The girl's eyes widened. She whimpered and struggled to get away.

Persephone held up one hand to ease the girl's fears. "We have to get the pus out."

"Here, let us help," Taryn said. Abella sat on one side of the child, Taryn the other, and they took her hands. Taryn pushed the girl's filthy pink hair out of her face and smiled.

M&M nodded again.

Persephone placed a thumb next to the soft spot and then, before the girl could get more agitated, she lanced it in one cut.

The girl cried out. The other children surrounded Persephone, their posture threatening.

Lyon growled from his corner, a deep bass that echoed through the cave. The children moved back and paced, keening and wringing their hands.

Persephone dropped the multi-tool and showed the children her empty hands. "I'm done. See, no more knife."

The M&M grunted at the pack of children. They stopped moving and fell silent.

Persephone started at the highest point on the girl's leg and gently massaged the abscess, working her way down to the ankle, then started at the top again. The girl leaned over her leg and watched the pus flow out with each pass of Persephone's hands. She poked her leg and grinned. She waved the other children over and they crowded around.

"Jeez, that's gross," Taryn said with a groan.

"Who knew children could be so entertained by gore?" Abella added.

When she had drained as much pus as possible, Persephone bound the girl's leg, then sat back and wiped the sweat off her face. She looked around and saw Lyon still curled in the corner, but he had rolled over and was watching her. "I've done what I can, but she needs a doctor and antibiotics as soon as possible."

He said nothing, just stared at her, silent and forbidding.

She shivered—not a scared or cold kind of shiver, more like an I-want-to-jump-his-bones kind of shiver. Her gut clenched. Her sex followed suit. Damn. He was the antithesis of everything she looked for in a man, not that she'd done much looking. So why, after witnessing his brutality and anger, after being enveloped in the darkness that swaddled him, would her body choose this man to lust over?

M&M climbed out of her lap and stood. She took a step, then another. Her face lit up and she danced in place.

"Go slow," Persephone said, but the girl was already surrounded by her friends. They clapped as she twirled and jumped.

Abella stood. "I need to clean the road funk off me. You ladies coming?"

Persephone waved her hand. "No, I need to rest for a while."

Abella and Taryn walked away, each with a strip of cloth in one hand and their backpacks in the other.

Persephone climbed to her feet.

Suddenly, the children stopped dancing. They ran to Persephone and formed a tight circle around her, touching her legs and hands. A soft growl rose around her but just from the children with pointed ears.

"Did I do something wrong?" Persephone asked Lyon.

He uncoiled his body and stood. "No. They're purring."

"That's a good thing?"

"If you're fond of Kellas Cats, then yes, it's their highest praise."

Persephone put her arms around the children.

"You should be flattered they've accepted you. Their kind refuse to mingle with humans, much less deign to accept them," Lyon added.

Persephone closed her eyes as the fatigue weighed her down.

"Hey, you okay?" Taryn called out from the stream.

Persephone nodded even as she swayed.

"Oh, no," Abella yelled. "Lyon, catch her."

18

PERSEPHONE CRUMPLED TO the ground before he could reach her. He lifted her off and cradled her against his chest. *How could such a fierce little creature be so scrawny?* He grunted at the children to move, carried her to a clear spot by the fire, and lowered her to the ground once more. She smiled at him and opened her mouth as if to speak, but no words came out. She closed her eyes and her body went limp.

Lyon jumped up. "What's wrong with her?" He paced around her, growling when anyone came close.

"When did she last eat?" Abella asked.

"She hasn't eaten since Scorpio attacked her."

"You mean since Scorpio attacked her and you kidnapped her?" Taryn asked.

"Saved her," Lyon snapped out.

"Enough," Abella said. "She needs food. She gets woozy if she doesn't eat often enough."

Taryn poked his shoulder. "She also needs to rest."

Lyon opened his mouth wide and hissed.

Taryn placed her closed fists on her hips and sneered. "You don't scare me, you overgrown oaf."

Lyon's hands clenched, his desire to ring her neck all but overwhelming. "You should be scared, little girl." The anger crackled between them until a hand gripped Lyon's calf and squeezed, distracting him.

"Tell us about your world, about these children. Who are they?" Persephone asked. Tears filled her eyes and ran down her cheeks.

An electric zing raced through his body, powering up waves of heebie-jeebies. "Oh, hell no. Not now, you rest. Food and rest. Yes." He backed away quickly, relieved he had a mission, something to do. Tears? Holy fuck, no. A mission? Fuck yeah, any mission, if it meant getting out of the vicinity of the tears. Lyon grabbed the Red Cap by the neck and pulled him along as he headed for the crack in the wall. "Come on, time to forage."

The two males emerged from the cave system and entered the dilapidated house.

The Red Cap licked his lips. "Human, human where?"

"The man living here?"

The Red Cap nodded.

"He's alive. Why the hell did you let him live so close to your territory?"

The creature winced and wrung his hands. "Secret, secret, a secret to keep."

"Have something to do with the children?"

The creature's right eye twitched. He opened his mouth, then closed it.

"Yeah, I got it, it's a secret." Lyon climbed the front steps and entered the open door. The stench of human washed over him. Body odor, dirty clothes and piss—no amount of cleaning would rid the house of the stench. The place needed to be burned to the ground.

He raided the kitchen and pantry and discovered some choice goodies, far more than one man could eat. The assbutt sure as shit wasn't feeding any of it to the dogs. After covering the kitchen table with a stack of food, he found huge black bags on the floor by an ancient washer and dryer. Long and rectangular, the bags were far heavier material than Lyon had seen before, with a zipper on one side in the shape of a long "U." He had pulled a second bag out of the box when he the saw the drawing of a human inside a bag, the zipper closed save for the head. The name "Coroner's Favorite" in large red letters. He threw the box down.

"Red Cap!" Lyon tossed the bags on top of the pile of food. "Get your ass in here, now!"

The heavy clomp of feet ran down the stairs. The Red Cap skidded into the kitchen, his hands filled with bedding. "What, what, what?"

Lyon shoved a body bag in the creature's chest. "Explain this."

He dropped the bedding on the floor and paced. "Garbage, yes, good for garbage."

Lyon grabbed his arm and jerked him into a kitchen chair. "That's a lie. It's a body bag." He shook the little man, hard, until his hat fell to the floor exposing greasy clumps of dark hair. "For dead bodies."

He sagged into Lyon's hold.

Lyon released him. "Why this scum of a human? What does he do for you?"

"He…brings me…humans…to eat. I give him pretty, pretty rocks."

"Where does he get the humans?"

The Red Cap shrugged as if he didn't know, but he dropped his head.

"So, since they're not invading your cave, this man is bringing you innocent humans?"

"Yes, yes, yes."

"Why?"

The Red Cap shrugged again. "I eat human. I no, no, no eat children."

"So, he brings you humans to eat so you won't eat the children."

The Red Cap grabbed his hat and jammed it back on his head, then nodded vigorously.

"What about these body bags? You don't need them for your meals."

"All, all, I eat them all up."

"Right, so the body bags are for the children."

The Red Cap remained mute for the second time.

"That's a yes."

"In the night, night, night, some children come and some go."

Lyon grabbed his throat and squeezed. "Why?"

The little man shook his head and clawed at Lyon's hand.

Lyon squeezed harder. "Why?"

The Red Cap's face turned crimson. He slapped at Lyon's wrist. "They don't share secret, secret. Red Cap must keep children, children, children in cave."

Lyon eased his grip on the creature's throat. "The body bags?"

"Some children are hurt, hurt or sick, very sick, sick, sick."

"Last question. Who are they? Who chose you to guard the children?"

He beat the side of his head with his filthy fists, then opened his mouth and wailed.

"Okay!" Lyon shoved the little beast away. They were going in circles—he wouldn't get more from the creature. Red Caps were at the head of the line when it came to asking no questions. As a species, they were immune to introspection, instead they relied on their most base instinct for survival. Eat, sleep and fuck, if they could find a female Red Cap who would deign to let them mount. They were slaves to their fight-or-flight impulses, self-preservation front and center.

Lyon slipped a hand inside his left pant pocket and rolled the tiny Corvus feather between his thumb and forefinger, then stopped. He turned back to the task before him. He couldn't afford to break his number-one hard-and-fast. The children weren't his problem. Caring about them wouldn't advance his mission success, but it could jeopardize it.

He knew what he had to do, but his great pronouncement of freedom at any cost suddenly felt a lot heavier.

He filled the body bag with the fridge and pantry bounty, then threw another body bag at the Red Cap. "Fill it up—bedding, blankets, whatever you can find."

"My human?"

"He's alive, chained out back."

The Red Cap dragged the chair to the window, looked outside, and waved. A muffled scream rose from the yard. The Red Cap smiled and chattered his long, sharp teeth. "Human back on the menu."

★ ★ ★

Persephone pushed herself up when Lyon returned, two huge black bags slung over his shoulders, a deep scowl on his face. The Red Cap trailed behind him, muttering and spitting and dragging a third bag.

The children parted for the males as they walked by. She didn't blame them—Lyon and the Red Cap were pissed about something. Rage rolled off them and formed a vortex of vexation that filled their wake. Lyon dropped his bags next to Persephone. He snapped his fingers and pointed to the ground. The nasty little creature growled but complied, dropping his bag where Lyon pointed, then stalked away.

"See what you can do with this," Lyon said before walking away to a far corner. He crouched, his back against the wall, and stared as they opened his offering.

Persephone, Abella, and Taryn opened the black bags and gasped. The children rushed over and surrounded them. The first bag was filled with blankets, pillows, towels, and soap. The second bag held an assortment of items: pots and pans, spices, fruits and vegetables, first aid supplies and piles of brand-new clothes—shirts and jeans and more, all with the tags still on them.

Abella and Taryn pulled out the pans and set them by the fire pit. Abella picked up her backpack. "I'm going to finish getting washed and change clothes. Taryn?"

"Right behind you." She followed Abella behind the largest boulder.

Persephone unzipped the last bag. The children gasped when the flap fell open and revealed food. Persephone emptied it and formed four piles. The first pile was meat—smoked ham, several cuts of steak, links of sausage, and chicken breasts. In the second pile, wax-covered wheels of cheddar, Monterey jack, and smoked Gouda. The third pile had bread in every shape and grain. The last pile contained boxes and bins of imported sweets: candy, cookies, pies, and creams. The man had been reprehensible but he had a helluva refined sugar palate.

"Come." Persephone waved over the children. They stared at the food, then looked at the Red Cap, shifting and whimpering as if afraid to eat in front of him.

"Ignore him. Eat, please."

A handful of children went to the piles and gingerly picked out some of the choicest foods. They placed ham and bread and cheese and a pile of cookies next to Persephone and backed away, their hands clutched to their chests with broad grins on their faces like the pile was an offering to a deity.

The Red Cap ran in and grabbed the loaf of bread next to Persephone. He reached for the ham, but the children stomped their feet and growled.

He dropped the food and backed away, his hands fidgeting with the brim of his bloody hat. "Ah, devil's spawn you are. Devil, devil, devil." He jumped on a rock and squatted, snarling and snapping.

The children settled down and pointed to the food pile, gesturing for Persephone to eat. Their earnest expressions and wide, bright eyes broke Persephone's heart. Who could have left these beautiful, generous children in the dark with a creature like the Red Cap? Sweet, frightened babies left alone, slowly starving, with no one to protect them.

"There's much too much food here. I don't need all this," Persephone said as she shook her head.

The children stopped smiling. They clutched their hands together and rocked.

"You're insulting them by not accepting their food offering," Lyon said.

"But I can't eat that much food."

"Accept it anyway, or you'll shame them."

Persephone took the large loaf of bread the Red Cap had dropped on the floor and brushed it clean. She broke off a small piece, ate it, and smiled.

The children smiled back and sighed.

Persephone waved them over and patted the ground next to her. The children closed in around her, jostling for the chance to be close. When they settled, Persephone held out a hunk of bread to the smallest girl.

The child's pale blue eyes widened. She pulled on strands of her long silver hair, then wound them nervously around her fingers as if she was afraid to accept it.

Taryn walked up and gasped. "Look at her. She could be your daughter, Persephone."

"What?"

"Look at her coloring. Other than a difference in eye color, you could be related." Taryn sat next to Persephone. "Mini-Me. That's her nickname."

"Seriously?"

"Hey, you gave the Kellas Cat a nickname. Why not this girl?"

Persephone shook her head. "Mini-Me it is, then." She held out the bread. "Go ahead and eat."

M&M touched the girl's knee and nodded. Permission given, Mini-Me took the bread from Persephone and attacked it like she hadn't eaten in days.

Persephone passed around piece after piece, working through the pile of bread until every child and the two dogs were chewing.

Then, she pulled the huge ham into her lap and looked around the cave. "A knife?" she asked Lyon.

He jumped off the rock and opened the left side of his leather coat. Sheaths sewn into the leather held blades of different shapes and lengths. He removed a machete and handed it to Persephone. "It carves up men just fine. Ought to be good for pig."

She looked at the weapon. "Is it clean?"

"Does licking it count?"

Persephone scowled. "That's disgusting."

Lyon stared for a few seconds, then ripped the machete and the ham out of Persephone's hands and stalked away. He sat down in a far corner and hacked at the meat until it was cut into ribbons. He held up a piece and offered it to the children, but they hovered around Persephone, too afraid to approach him. He frowned, dropped the slice, then wiped the machete on his leg before standing. He sheathed the blade, wrapped the leather coat around him, and left the cave.

Abella walked to Persephone, her skin clean, hair wet and slicked back, a fresh shirt, jeans, and tennis shoes on. "I think you hurt his feelings."

"Will you get the ham?" Persephone grabbed a wheel of cheddar and peeled back the wax cover. She broke off hunks of the fragrant yellow cheese and handed it out.

Abella squatted down and passed out the ham slices. "He did come back for us when he didn't have to."

"No, he *did* have to come back for us. I just don't know why yet."

Finally, after the children and the Dobermans had their fill, Persephone waved Abella, Taryn, and the Red Cap over.

The little man rushed the remaining piles of food and hissed at Persephone before filling his pockets and hands with as much as he could carry. "Devil's spawn you are. Devil, devil, devil." After chastising her, he hunched over his bounty and scurried away to a dark corner.

Taryn laughed. "Kind of a broken record, isn't he?"

Abella and Taryn sat closer to the fire while they ate.

Persephone sagged back, too tired to lift the food to her mouth. Abella scooted closer to her, but before she had a chance to help, Lyon appeared out of the shadows.

He growled at Abella.

"Okay, okay." Abella moved back to Taryn's side.

Lyon sat next to Persephone.

He picked out the choicest bread, cheese, and ham, shredding them into bite-sized pieces. If the woman was too tired to eat, she wouldn't be able to keep up the brutal pace he had planned.

"Open," he ordered.

She gently sucked the ham from his fingers. The touch of her moist lips and tongue on his fingers, the ticklish heat of her breath, woke the demon soul—and his cock. The first writhed inside him, longing to take control, while the one in his pants thickened and throbbed, seeking its own version of control. He struggled to quiet both, and kept feeding Persephone. Ham and bread and cheese and a creamy piece of pie that she licked off his fingers. His belly rumbled, but he refused to eat until she was full.

Persephone looked at him. "Are you purring?" She looked into his eyes and gasped. "Your eyes are glowing."

Holy shit. Lyon leaned back. The demon wasn't in control, yet it managed to make its presence and pleasure known. The demon was smitten with Persephone. *This is bad. Really, really bad.*

He stuffed a large chunk of bread into his mouth so he wouldn't have to answer, gathered an armful of food, and retreated to his corner.

"Did you see their eyes?" Abella said around a bite of bread.

"Which ones? They all have unusual eyes." Taryn wiped her hands on her jeans. "What about the feathers in the hair? It's like they're attached to their scalp."

"Better than any extensions I've ever seen," Abella added.

"You'd know with all the stuff you've done to your hair," Taryn threw in.

Persephone grinned. She avoided sparring, drama wasn't her thing, but her friends loved it. Usually they kept Persephone out of their sniping, but after what she'd seen and heard in the last couple of days, she welcomed a good old-fashioned spat. At least it would bring a semblance of normalcy to the insanity.

Abella ran a hand through her auburn pixie. "You got me there, after all the color and extensions this was the shortest I could go without pulling a Britney."

"So, is the red your natural color? It's been so long I can't remember," Taryn said with a grin.

Abella cocked her head. She pointed to Taryn's forehead and tsked. "Girl, when ya gonna do something about that unibrow?"

Taryn laughed and waved Abella away. "Get off me, woman."

Persephone laughed at her friends. It felt good to forget everything for a moment. She glanced up and caught the stares of the children. They looked appalled, like they'd never heard laughter before. M&M walked to her and cocked her head. She placed one hand on Persephone's throat and the other on Persephone's chest and grunted.

"What?" Persephone asked.

"She wants you to laugh again," Lyon said from behind her.

Persephone looked around. Lyon had left his rock and walked over without making a sound.

Predator.

There was no other word to describe him. She shivered as hot lust and cold fear combined and settled south of her navel.

M&M saw Lyon. Her eyes widened and she backed away, blending into the group until Persephone couldn't see her. Without a sound, the children retreated to horizontal cracks hidden from view while others vanished behind vertical fissures between rock faces. Only the dogs, Abella, and Taryn remained behind with Persephone and the men, the silence utter and empty.

Lyon stoked the fire and added several more logs. The flames flitted from log to log, flaring and popping when it encountered resin, lapping at bark and twigs until they were consumed.

He stood next to Persephone. "I know you have questions. What do you want to know?"

"Think you could sit instead of towering over us?" Abella asked.

The Red Cap sidled over and sat by the fire.

Lyon lowered his huge form to the floor and tried different positions before sitting cross-legged.

Abella and Taryn shifted so the group formed a circle.

Lyon rolled his shoulders. "Well?"

"Who are the children?" Persephone asked.

"The young children with red eyes and feathers in their hair are Corvus Ward nestlings before their maturation ritual. The older children with black eyes and feathers are Corvus Ward nestlings who have already gone through the maturation ritual but have not reached adult age."

"Corvus Wards? What is that?" Persephone asked.

"And what about the children with pale blue eyes?" Abella added. "Like Mini-Me?"

"Portends—" Lyon started to say.

"What about the kids with pointed ears, like M&M?" Taryn interrupted.

Lyon clenched his fists, his nearly depleted patience slipping further with every rapid-fire question. "Kellas Cats." He flushed, his anger mounting until a black, deadly rage oozed out of his skin with each drop of sweat on his brow. His right eye twitched.

The Red Cap grunted and slapped the floor. The women stopped talking.

"Start at the start," he said to Lyon.

Lyon frowned.

"Start. At. The. Start."

Lyon steeled himself and began. "Okay, he's right. I need to go back to the very beginning, back to when all of this started." He reached inside his coat and removed a large bottle of single malt he'd pinched from the house. He unscrewed the top, took a swig, and passed it to Persephone. "Drink. You're going to need it."

She sniffed, then drank. After coughing through the burn, she drank a bit more and passed it on.

Abella grabbed it and sniffed. She rolled her eyes and groaned her approval. "You've been holding back," she said, and took a swig.

Lyon waited for the women to gird themselves with the whisky before he began. "Have you heard the story of the goddess Persephone's abduction to the Underworld?

"I've read the story. Another goddess named Hecate witnessed the abduction and told Persephone's mother, Demeter," Persephone said.

Lyon nodded. "Yes. The two women found Persephone with Hades, and Demeter struck a bargain with him. 'Let me have my daughter half the year and she shall be yours for the other half.' He agreed, and Hecate chose to remain with Persephone in Hades as her companion."

"The gypsies say that the months of spring and summer are when Persephone and Hecate roam the earth. In the fall and winter, both are with Hades," Taryn added.

"Oh, come on, you're talking about mythology here, not fact," Abella said.

"After what I've seen the last two days, I'm willing to stretch my definition of possible," Taryn said.

"Honey, you believe in the boogie man—so that stretch ain't much of a stretch," Abella replied.

Taryn raised her arms and gestured around the cave. "Look around. I think this qualifies as me being right."

The women glared at each other.

Lyon grunted and shoved off the cold floor before his legs became permanently pretzeled. "Are you done?"

Both women nodded.

Lyon paced. "Hecate bore a child, a daughter she named Circe, and in celebration Zeus made Circe a witch goddess. When fall came, Hecate and Persephone had to return to Hades, so Hecate left Circe behind to be raised by witches."

Lyon took another swig of whisky.

Abella snapped her fingers and waved him over. He gave her the bottle and resumed his pacing.

"For years, Circe followed a good path, until she met a powerful sorcerer who had other plans for her. Nurturing the darkest recesses of her heart and soul, he turned Circe into a cruel, capricious sadist. By the time Hecate returned to earth that spring, Circe was no longer recognizable; she had been consumed. Circe begged her mother to stay on earth, but Hecate refused. If she didn't return to the Underworld, Hades would exact punishment, not on Hecate or Persephone, but on the humans they loved, for whom they spent half of each year deep in the belly of the earth."

"So Hecate chose humans over her child," Persephone said.

Abella snorted. "That sounds familiar."

Taryn sighed and nodded.

"That's exactly how Circe saw it, and the jealousy ate her alive. It only took her days to act on her mother's betrayal. The retaliations started small—the random human here and there. But eventually, Circe was killing whole villages."

Lyon looked at the women and almost laughed at their expressions. Persephone and Taryn were leaning forward, mouths open, but Abella had crossed her arms, a scowl darkening her face.

"This story got an end?" she asked.

"Coming to it. Eventually, Circe set her sights on a much higher class of human. At that time, there were twelve human royal houses. She infiltrated each of them and was a feted guest of the unsuspecting royals. As a huge 'fuck you' to her mother, Circe waited until just before Hecate was due to return to the earth's surface before starting her endgame, beginning with the House of Leo."

The Red Cap rocked and clapped his hands. "Good part, good part. Dead, dead, dead."

Lyon bared his canines and hissed.

The Red Cap stopped his singsong chant, but he continued to smile, exposing his disgusting, food-encrusted fangs.

"Long story short, when Hecate rose she learned Circe had killed all of the eldest sons of the twelve kings. Hecate was forbidden to intervene, but she couldn't turn her back on the anguished kings, so she used her own blood to resurrect the princes. She carved out a subterranean world for them to live in, and she welcomed any paranormal creature needing sanctuary."

"What about Circe?" Persephone asked.

"Circe was to be executed, but Hecate couldn't kill her only child, so she entombed Circe, hoping that—in time—the gods would lift the death decree."

"The subterranean world Hecate created—is that where you're from?" Persephone asked.

"It's called the InBetween. It's home to many species who used to roam the earth's surface—or as we call it—the Overworld."

"The prince from the House of Leo?" Abella prompted.

"My father."

"So, what about these children?" Persephone whispered.

"They are of the InBetween, but I've never seen so many gathered in one place, much less so close to the Overworld, and with a Red Cap to boot."

"Lyon?" Persephone said softly. "Why is all this happening?"

"I don't know."

Abella jumped up and dusted off her butt. "This has been a lovely diversion, but it's past time for us to leave. Let's go home, ladies. Oh, that's right—we don't have a home anymore, because you and your friends destroyed it."

Lyon stopped pacing. "No, you three destroyed it."

Taryn stood. "Only because you and your friends kidnapped and threatened us. I'd say that puts the blame back in your court."

"My order was to bring you three to the InBetween. Alive. The other men? I don't know why they showed. Are you willing to gamble that they have the same orders I do? If you're wrong, you're dead."

"According to Libra, their orders are the same as yours," Abella said.

"But Scorpio kept asking if he could slit our throats—"

"Orders change," Lyon interrupted. "You have two choices. Stay with me and stay alive, or take your chances that the other men aren't out to kill you."

Persephone rose. "I'm staying here."

"Persephone, no," Abella said.

"I'm so exhausted, I can't wrap my head around all this. I need to sleep."

Lyon pulled out an odd assortment of quilts, comforters, and pillows and laid them out, one for each woman. "You have two hours to sleep, then we go."

"She's going to need at least eight hours," Taryn said.

"Two hours. We've been here too long as it is."

Abella smirked at Lyon. "You might as well get used to it, big guy. Persephone isn't going to walk away when someone needs help. It's not in her blood."

He growled at the women, then walked to the entrance and sat with his back against the wall to keep watch while the women slept.

Abella and Taryn herded Persephone to the makeshift pallets. She settled in the middle and they took the outside. Abella used a finger to flick a lock of silver hair out of Persephone's face. She leaned close. "As soon as assbutt drifts off, we're out of here. Yes?"

Persephone nodded, too tired to speak, a sudden headache pounding her temples in time with her heartbeat. The firelight dancing on the cave walls was interrupted by three shadows moving across the stone. She looked around to see who was casting the shadows, but saw no one. She closed her eyes. *Nothing, it's nothing.*

The two dogs crept in and settled on either side of Persephone, their heads on her chest. They sighed and relaxed.

"Two new fans," Taryn whispered.

"Make that four," Abella corrected.

The Kellas Cat—M&M—and the tiny silver-haired girl, Mini-Me, squeezed between the women.

Abella and Taryn scooted over to make room for the girls as they bellied up to the dogs.

"And just like that, bedding for three becomes bedding for seven," Persephone said without opening her eyes.

Abella snorted again. "Sleep, baby girl. As soon as he closes his eyes, we go and make our way as we've always done."

19

LYON WATCHED THE WOMEN settle in. Then the dogs. Then two of the children. How did this simple assignment become such a free-for-all? He pulled in everything he knew and lined it up to make sense of the past couple of days, but his everything was too many facts short of clarity.

The children of three different species, maybe more, who never typically came into long-term contact with each other had somehow ended up with a Red Cap, a creature considered lower than the dung on a troll's backside. Portend children were independent at a young age, but they still didn't live apart from their clans. Corvus Ward nestlings and Kellas Cat singlets stayed with their parents for many years, much like human children.

So, why are these children alone?

From the moment he'd entered the Overworld, it had been one crisis after another. Hell, ever since he'd left his cell. Something had changed for the people of the InBetween, and Lyon was sure his father was involved. The only question he could allow himself to care about was, how would it affect his bid for freedom?

He closed his eyes for a moment, but when he opened them again the fire was almost out. Shit, at least a couple hours must have passed. He glanced at the pile of women, girls, and dogs. So much for their plan to escape while he slept. He shifted positions and a stabbing pain jarred him from his musing.

He lifted his shirt. He grit his teeth to remain silent as he ripped the encrusted makeshift bandage from his skin, but still, a hiss escaped his lips. The edges of the folded strip of bed sheet were black and crusted over, while the center was wet with fresh blood. Gore gushed down his back and soaked his pants and showed no signs of stopping. But it was the stench of infection assailing his nostrils that made him gag.

Damn Sag and his anti-coagulant, flesh-eating-bacteria-tipped darts.

Lyon was headed down one of two roads: exsanguination or infection, or both if he didn't burn his flesh to cauterize the wound and kill the bacteria. His gut clenched, and his sac tightened so hard it felt like his balls had disappeared back into his body. *This is gonna suck.*

The cavern was quiet, except for the Red Cap's snores. Lyon pushed off the floor and crept to the fire, careful to not waken anyone. After having his cock ground into a rough wood floor, and tweezers digging around in his insides, the last thing he wanted was more of Persephone's tender ministrations. He chose a long, narrow stick with a glowing tip and pulled it free from the burning pile.

The Red Cap snorted.

Lyon froze.

The monstrous little creature rolled away and settled.

Lyon waited a few more seconds before returning to his sentry position. He blew out the paltry flame, but the wood still flared bright red. He broke the stick in half and placed the cool portion between his teeth. He waved the burning end in the air to keep it red-hot as he rolled up his shirt. He twisted at the waist to see the hole. Then, before he could second-guess what needed to happen, he thrust the glowing ember inside his wound. The stench of burning flesh and infection was an afterthought to the searing pain.

Sweat poured down his face. He clenched his free hand into a fist and slammed it against the floor over and over until the burning in his back was replaced by the agony in his hand. He ripped the stick out and threw it across the cavern before falling over. He curled into a ball and fought the descending darkness of an impending faint.

When the cavern reappeared, he sat up and rubbed his salt-encrusted face with his hands. He opened his eyes and saw Mini-Me standing in front of him, silent and staring. Her cherubic face was solemn, her unblemished skin as white as alabaster, a web of blue veins beneath. But it was her huge eyes that claimed Lyon, drew him in. Irises so pale blue that they looked near-white, with a weary expression seen only in the oldest of souls. Framed by her long silver hair, the child was arresting, stark, and sad. There was no mistake. This child was one of the rarest creatures in any world: a Portend purebred.

Lyon pointed to the pile of women by the fire. "Go back."

Mini-Me took one step toward him, then two, but stopped just shy of his reach. She stared at him for several seconds, unmoving, barely breathing, before cocking her head to the side. She looked past him, to the crack in the wall that led to the human world. More seconds passed, then she raised a hand and pointed to the fissure—her body language screaming, *Something's coming*.

Lyon rolled and stood. He waved her back and she ran to the women. He removed a dagger from his coat, all the while watching and listening. Nothing. Lyon glanced at the little girl. She knelt between Persephone and one of the dogs, her hands pushing on Persephone's side to wake her.

Lyon picked up a pebble and threw it. It bounced off Persephone's head.

"Wha?" she sputtered.

The dogs jumped to their feet and growled.

Taryn, Abella, and M&M sat up and rubbed their faces.

"What's happening?" Abella said.

Mini-Me grabbed M&M's arm and pulled frantically.

The Kellas Cat rolled to her feet. She tried to put the baby Portend behind her, but the small girl grunted and pushed against the larger girl until she could see Lyon. She pointed to the crack and grunted again, her eyes wide in panic.

"Get up," Lyon hissed.

M&M gathered a handful of pebbles and threw them against the back wall of the cavern. Several heads appeared from the shadows. M&M pointed to the cave opening, then keened. Without a word, the children gathered together in a tight bunch, the youngest protected by the oldest, each child holding a sharpened stick or a rock.

The Red Cap sat up and looked around the space before he jumped to his feet and took two large flaming logs from the fire. He crouched in front of the fire pit. "What, what, what?"

Lyon held a finger to his lips to silence the creature. He called on the demon soul, but before he could benefit from its keener senses, a shockwave of air threw him several feet across the cavern. He landed with a thud next to another crack in the wall—one that led deeper into the cave system.

Piercing screeches preceded three figures. A whirl of clothing and mist obscured the faces of the attackers for a second, but the arctic cold that settled into the already-chilly cave told Lyon what he really didn't want to know. Wraiths. Three fucking wraiths had been sicced on them, and he could just imagine who'd done it: the cold-blooded bastard Scorpio. Yeah, that picture fit.

Lyon pointed to the Red Cap. "Get the children out of here. Now!"

The creature dropped his sticks and ran to the pack of children. He waved his hands and screamed until most of the children had disappeared around what must have been a false wall.

Outta sight, outta danger. Hopefully.

Lyon turned back to the wraiths. The specters had changed from apparition to solid form, and scanned the cavern. Tattered black robes were draped over their emaciated bodies. Abnormally long arms and legs extended beyond the material, their clawed fingers curved into weapons.

The wraiths were mere inches from the Red Cap, their hands raised to slice him to ribbons.

The Red Cap dropped to his knees, his hands over his ears.

Lyon waved his arms. "Hey! Over here."

The wraiths whipped around to track Lyon's shout. They opened their large, round, spike-filled mouths and screamed as they advanced on Lyon, their cries growing louder with each step.

The Red Cap staggered to his feet and launched himself on the back of one wraith, drawing the attention of the other two away from Lyon.

Lyon ran to the women, Mini-Me, M&M, and the dogs. He pointed to the small crack at the back of the cave. "Go!"

The group ran to the crack and Taryn disappeared inside, followed closely by Abella.

Persephone hesitated.

M&M pointed to the cleft.

Persephone shook her head and looked at Lyon. "Not without you."

M&M pointed again and stamped a foot.

Persephone tried to send Mini-Me after Abella, but the child wouldn't release her hand.

Lyon grabbed Persephone's arm. "The Portend's not going without you."

Persephone frowned, but nodded. She dropped to her hands and knees, Mini-Me in the same position between Persephone's arms and legs. The two crawled into the crack together.

The dogs barked and whined and paced in front of the crack, but they wouldn't follow the women.

Lyon had no time to deal with them. He turned to the closest wraith. The Red Cap had wrapped his legs around its neck, his fists beating the wraith's head. The wraith reached back, plucked the little man off, and slammed him against the floor. Blood exploded from his skull, mouth, and ears.

M&M howled. She reached for Lyon's blade.

"No," Lyon snapped. "You're hurt."

Her chin jutted, her head lifted. She shook her outstretched hand, her demand for a weapon clear.

As much as he wanted to, Lyon couldn't force her tiny ass through the crack. The girl wanted to fight, and he wouldn't deny her the right. He held the grip of the dagger out to her. "Buy me a few seconds, then get the hell out."

M&M grabbed the grip and nodded. She ran to the wraith that had killed the Red Cap and raised her dagger. Her expression was fierce, but her arms and legs shook like a stripling in its first fight.

A warrior disguised as a child.

Lyon pulled another blade from his coat. The other two wraiths keened as they flanked him, drawing his focus back to the rest of this clusterfuck. Lyon slashed the air to drive one toward its buddy. Better to have them where he could see them. "C'mon, you bastards," he yelled. He parried a swipe of the closest wraith's claws, then whirled and sliced open its belly.

It keened, then swung at Lyon, its claws ripping open four parallel wounds in Lyon's right thigh.

Lyon staggered but held his ground. He lunged under the wraith's arms and sank his blade to the hilt in the wraith's chest. It screamed and fell, took one last breath, and died before it could vanish in a puff of black mist.

Lyon turned to the other wraith, but it smoked out before Lyon could gank it.

Persephone screamed, drawing the attention of the last wraith away from M&M.

Lyon whirled around and saw Persephone's head sticking out of the crack. "Persephone, what the hell? Get out of here!"

"The dogs!"

Persephone scrambled out of the crack followed by Abella. Abella grabbed the male Doberman by the scruff and led him to the opening. He crouched and entered the crack followed by Abella. Persephone herded the senior Doberman to the crack, but she was too frightened of the dark and balked.

"Go to the other side and pull," Lyon said.

Persephone backed into the crack and pulled on the frightened dog, but she leaned back.

"Shit." Lyon ran to the old dog, dropped to his hands and knees, and pushed. Halfway through the passage, something hit the top of his head. He reached up and felt a thick, knotted rope hanging from above. He batted it away and continued pushing until he reached the other side.

"M&M?" Persephone asked.

"Going back for her now."

Lyon had just entered the passage to return for M&M when he saw her at the other end. He gestured her forward. "Come on."

She grinned and lifted her blade. The metal was coated with black blood. She'd killed her wraith.

"Good girl. Now take my hand!" He crawled a couple of feet into the tight, short tunnel through the rock and held out a hand to pull her through. She reached for him, but before Lyon could grab her, the wraith that had smoked out earlier reappeared just behind her.

It grabbed her legs and pulled her backward, shredding her skin and her bandage with its long claws. She screamed as it dragged her out of Lyon's reach. Her arms flailed to find purchase in the tiny passage. They brushed against the dangling knotted rope, and she grabbed it with both hands.

The wraith jerked her, but M&M's body stopped when the length of rope tightened. The monster shrieked and pulled again, but she held tight, two contestants in a grisly game of tug of war.

"Hold on!" Lyon lunged for her hands. Before he could reach her, the wraith jerked hard and M&M was pulled away.

A creak above his head was his only warning. He flung his body back just before a hail of large rocks and pebbles fell from above, blocking the passage.

A second shriek filtered through the rubble. Then silence.

Lyon threw back his head and roared.

"No!" Persephone ran to the crack and tore at the stone, pulling and clawing until her nails were shredded and bloody.

Lyon wrapped his arms around her waist and pulled her away. "It's no use, she's gone."

"No!" She kicked his legs and clawed his face.

He held her tight until she'd tired, then set her down. He grabbed her chin and lifted it. "Look at me."

She wrenched away from his grip. Only then did she look him in the eye.

He leaned over her, crowding her space. Fury and despair conjoined inside him, then, like an arrow, they shot out and hit the closest target. "There's nothing I could have done to save her—she was dead the moment we entered the cave. If you had listened to me and kept moving, she would still be alive. The wraiths would have ignored all of them in their pursuit of us."

Tears welled in Persephone's eyes. She backed away from him.

He stalked her. No way was she going to escape the truth of what her actions wrought. "You believe compassion costs you nothing, and family is everything." He pointed to the blocked passage. "Well, you're wrong. Your compassion just cost that girl her life. Maybe the lives of the other children, too, if the wraith finds them," he stabbed a forefinger at the now-blocked passage, "because wraiths don't leave witnesses!" he bellowed.

Persephone collapsed to the floor and sobbed.

"I'm done with stopping to help every wounded creature. We're doing it my way from here on out, unless you want to get your friends killed, too."

Persephone shook her head.

Lyon glared at Abella and Taryn, their red faces and open mouths signaling a coming argument. "Not one word," he ground out. "Get her up and keep her moving. The next one of you who lags behind or has a thought to stop and render aid or proffer up even a fucking kind word gets a new smile," he said as he drew his thumb across his throat.

He walked away, disgusted with the lot of them—but mostly with himself. He'd made Persephone the scapegoat when the reality was the girl died because he was more worried about earning his freedom than he was about saving her life.

'Freedom at all costs' sure the fuck wasn't pretty, but after coming this far he would sure as shit make it happen. To do anything less would make the girl's death meaningless.

20

GLEAM WORMS LIT THE SMALL CAVE, illuminating the stricken, tear-stained faces around Persephone. Mini-Me wiped away Persephone's tears, then climbed into her lap.

"You say the word and I'll throw a gypsy curse on him," Taryn whispered. "His man bits falling off should do the trick."

Persephone's grief sat so heavy and thick in her body that she fought to draw a breath. She shook her head. "No, he's right. If I had listened to him, we wouldn't have been there. A part of me didn't believe any of this was real. I was willful and dismissive and two people are dead because of it."

Abella raised her hands. "Whoa, whoa, whoa. We've been through some messed-up shit before, but we're running headlong down a dark, dark path here with a tour guide who's the definition of a dick. So why are we still here? Why don't we ditch this guy and take care of ourselves like always?"

Persephone held Mini-Me tight. "Because we're being hunted by scary men and monsters from a world we didn't know existed until now. I need to know why. I need to understand why we can't enjoy a simple touch without ripping a house in two." She took a shuddering breath. "I need to know why there are dozens of children hiding in the dark and cold instead of being with their families. If they're still alive." Her voice faded away.

Persephone dropped her face into the girl's thick silver hair. "No one should have the childhood we had. Wondering why they were abandoned, why they're not good enough to have their own family. If there's even a chance I can find *this* child's family, I'll go to hell itself."

The women said nothing. Only the *tap-tap-tap* of Lyon's dagger hilt on rock broke the silence.

Abella cleared her throat. "Well, I'm not sold on the hell idea, but if I can figure out how to animate tattoos like those scorpions, we'll be filthy rich."

Taryn snorted. "Animated? Dude, you got Criss-Angeled."

"And I never thought I'd see you wanna get plowed by a guy in a suit, but there it is," Abella snapped.

"That guy in the monkey suit fawning all over you?"

"Yeah, him."

"I'd sooner plow it with your bug boy than that girly man."

Abella cocked one eyebrow. Persephone's mouth dropped open.

"Yeah, maybe I'll throw that gypsy curse at all of them so none of them have dicks, like assbutt over there." Taryn looked at her friend's wide eyes and open mouths. "He's right behind me, isn't he?"

"This dickless assbutt found a way out of the cave, if you have a moment between curses."

Abella and Persephone followed Lyon. Taryn joined them, but stayed a step behind.

He picked up a large rock and slammed it against the wall. Two blows later, a puff of air blew back his hair. He squatted to get a look.

Mini-Me went to Lyon and leaned in with him, her hand on his shoulder. He twitched and glanced at the child. He frowned, but didn't push her away or growl.

Persephone sucked in her surprise. How could a girl barely bigger than one of his huge, muscular thighs, trust such a dangerous man?

Abella stepped up to Persephone. "You really need to give the girl a name. We can't call her Mini-Me forever."

"I vote for Candace." Taryn said. "It means 'pure white.'"

Abella nodded. "I like it."

Persephone walked to the girl and tapped her on the shoulder. When the child faced her, Persephone pointed to herself. "Persephone." The girl cocked her head.

"I am Persephone."

The child nodded her understanding.

Persephone pointed to her. "You are Candace."

The girl pointed to her chest, her head cocked to one side.

"Yes, you are Candace."

The child mouthed the name, then smiled. The newly named girl twirled and mouthed her name over and over. When she stopped, she looked at Persephone, but pointed to Abella.

"Her name is Abella."

Candace pointed to Taryn.

"She is Taryn."

Candace pointed to herself again.

"Candace," Persephone said.

The child danced around the women until her face was flushed, her smile wide.

Lyon shook his head. "You shouldn't have done that. Only her family has the honor of naming her."

"Well, I don't see any family here and I won't keep calling her Mini-Me."

He pulled on a huge stone blocking the narrow passage. "Her family is here, now. That's what you've done. If we manage to get through this, what will you tell her parents?"

Persephone swallowed hard when the gravity of what she'd done sank in, but she refused to be cowed by him—or her mistake. Instead, she jutted her chin and pulled Candace close. "I'll tell them that we're her family now."

"And just like that she will have been stolen a second time, as if being ripped from her parents wasn't bad enough."

Persephone remained silent.

Lyon rolled the stone away, then sat on it. He wiped the sweat from his face. "If you think the last couple of days have been bad, think again. My father wants the three of you alive, goddess only knows why. But a purebred Portend? If that wraith saw her, if it recognized her for what she was, the full force of hell will rain down on us all, Llewellyn's orders be damned."

A tense silence lasted several seconds.

"Let's go back to the surface. We can hide there," Persephone said.

"It's too late. Even if going topside was the best option, it'll take too long to get through the rock."

"Then we go deep—deep as it gets—and find out what's going on," Persephone said. "As for Candace, if anyone here can disguise our girl, it's Abella."

Abella grabbed a handful of red clay and spat in it a few times until it was moist. She rubbed both hands together to make a paste, then turned to Candace. "Well, it isn't Clairol, but it'll do."

Libra looked away from the computer screen long enough to drop some sour cream on the trout caviar on his potato cracker. He took a bite and chewed slowly, his focus on the single blip that flickered on the map. It jumped from place to place, then disappeared for several seconds before returning.

After paying his respects to the tiny box that held his father's remains, Libra had stayed in his rooms staring at the signal with no breaks, waiting for the LoJack he'd planted on Abella to pay off.

The blip finally stabilized long enough for his tracking program to zero in on a point several miles outside of Sonora, Texas. He tapped the screen and smiled. "Hello, beautiful."

He downed the last cracker and strode to the bathroom for an overdue shower. *Such are the trials of a computer geek.*

Towel-dried and smelling less like a musk ox, Libra fingered his favorite Gucci suit hanging on the back of his closet door. He touched the pristine blue cotton mohair, then shook his head. Lyon had taken the women underground, into the caves. *Gucci suits have no business in the dark.* This job was more suited to his Carhartt wardrobe. He selected the black heavy-duty work clothes, and dressed. He walked to his computer again and touched the blip. "Where there's Abella, the rest will be."

Someone knocked on the door. Libra opened it, then opened it wider. "Taurus, come in. I need your help."

Lyon sang for a purple crystal and waited for the interconnected stones to chase away the dark.

The Portend whimpered, then hiccupped.

"Candace needs to rest," Persephone said.

"We need to keep going."

"But—"

Lyon turned. "Not one word."

Candace was on the ground rubbing her eyes, a pout on her cherubic face. He picked her up and threw her over his shoulder, then trudged off.

The baby Portend giggled.

"No, no, you can't carry her like that," Persephone said as she chased him around and over the rocks.

"Why? You gonna say it's not healthy for her? None of this is healthy. No child should be shoved in a cage, thrown away for years, trotted out for the amusement of the masses…" He stopped and took a breath to stop his mouth from spitting out the litany of horrors in his past and present.

Persephone's eyes sparkled with unshed tears.

He growled and turned away when he felt Candace's belly heave. Before he could react, she urped down his back. Lyon turned slowly and glared at the women.

Persephone clapped a hand over her mouth. Abella and Taryn smirked.

Lyon pulled Candace off his shoulder and looked at her red face. She grinned, then yawned wide. He put her down, removed his coat, and wiped it clean on the ground. He picked her up and placed her on his hip. "Don't do that again."

She smiled, her chubby cheeks dimpled, then her head wobbled. She hiccupped.

Lyon's heart flopped for a moment. That simple expression of joy and trust sent a sharp pang of longing through him. He'd never thought about children before; they were so out of the realm of possibility for him that there had been no point. But with one smile, this little girl made him wish for more. He blinked and cleared his throat to rid himself of the unattainable before he choked on it. "When the time comes, little Portend, you're gonna be the death of your mate."

She snuggled into his chest, nuzzling his neck until she found a comfortable spot before her body went limp. She was fast asleep.

His skin crawled, and he fought the need to shudder. He'd never been one for affection, even as a child. He had been a proud and arrogant little shit of a prince, too lofty to be held—that was for babies who needed love and reassurance. He still couldn't abide touch, but for vastly different reasons. The shudder finally won and his body shook.

Candace's heart fluttered. Her breath tickled his skin, and he wondered if his revulsion was not because of his discomfort but rather the demon soul recoiling from the child's innocence. Either way, he'd rather be in the pit than have a child stuck to him like a tick. "Can we go now?"

The women fell in behind him.

"You were going to tell us about some of the paranormal species?" Persephone said. "What about Candace?"

"She's the rarest kind of Portend, a purebred. Most Portends are human children with one normal human parent and one parent who carries the Portend gene. These children can see paranormal creatures from the InBetween when no one else can. They're highly prized for their ability to communicate with the dead and predict events."

"Then why haven't we heard of them before?" Abella asked.

"Most Portends don't live beyond ten years old. The more they use their abilities, the higher the risk of a brain aneurysm and death. They're rare because when a Portend is found, they're sold to the highest bidder—who then uses the

Portend to gain power and wealth until the child dies. Kind of like the genie in the bottle: once you rub the lamp, you get three wishes and the genie goes back in the bottle. No more wishes. That makes Portends one of the most in-demand commodities in any world."

Persephone frowned. "You called Candace a purebred. What's the difference?"

"She is the daughter of two humans with the Portend gene." Lyon paused. How much should he tell them? *Tell the whole fucking truth, man.*

"My father has been breeding Portends like sheep and selling them to the wealthy, the influential, and the powerful. Trouble is, with such a small number of breeding stock, the Portends have become increasingly inbred, resulting in madness, shortened life span, unpredictable and sometimes uncontrollable actions, murderous rages, devastating birth defects, and stillbirths. But the worst problem in the inbred Portends is misinterpreting future events. When that happens, my father sends in a sweeper crew to make changes so it looks like the Portend didn't make a mistake. Then that Portend is put down."

"That's barbaric," Persephone said.

"That's the reality of the InBetween, and why Candace can't fall into his hands. He needs purebreds to revitalize his program, so to him she is worth far more than her weight in gold. But the demon king Asmodeus has hunted the purebreds for more vile reasons."

"What do you mean?" Persephone asked.

Lyon shook his head. "I don't want to scare the girl."

"Candace. Her name is Candace," Persephone said.

"And she's far more capable of understanding this conversation than you think." He settled a hand over her upturned ear. "She has two very powerful foes out there who want to hurt her. That's all you need to know."

Taryn cleared her throat. "M&M was a Kellas Cat."

"Yes, a Kellas Cat singlet. The Kellai look like humans when they're very young, but as they grow older they take on more and more catlike features—like their pupils change from round to a slit. Their skin is white with secondary colors that are dark at their feet and hands, but pale as they travel up the Kellai's legs and arms. Their hair does the same thing."

"It's called ombre," Abella said.

"Her ears were pointed with a small amount of tufted hair at the tip," Persephone added.

"Yes. And some develop tails. When the Kellas Cats reach maturity, a feline familiar—either a wilding or a milding—will choose them. After their bonding, the familiar takes on the color of their Kellas Cat."

"What are wildings and mildings?" Abella asked.

"Both are cats. The wildings are large cats, like tigers, lions, and panthers. Mildings are small cats like the ones humans live with."

"Domesticated cats," Persephone added.

"Do the Kellai and their familiar have an ability?" Taryn asked.

"The bonded pair is extremely powerful against demons—not only in their overall strength, but also for tracking low-level demons. The female Kellai are known for their beauty. They're as seductive as succubae—without the pesky aftereffects of soul-sucking death."

"Is there a purebred version of the Kellas Cats, too?"

"The purebred Kellai remain pure white as adults, and are nearly as valuable as the purebred Portends for their ability to track any demon, including demon kings."

Abella stopped walking. "Wait, did you say succubae?"

Lyon held up a fist. "Hold." The air was fresher, and he could hear water flowing. "Take a break, I want to see what's ahead." Lyon shifted the sleeping Candace from one hip to the other and walked away.

21

PERSEPHONE CRUMPLED TO THE FLOOR. Her body ached from the hours of walking, crawling, and scrambling over rocks and rubble. She watched Lyon move around the cavern with Candace sleeping against his chest, the child's trust in him complete.

Taryn plopped down and closed her eyes.

Abella sat next to Persephone. "He's a mystery."

"He's cruel."

"He was wrong to blame you for M&M."

"I don't know."

Taryn snorted. "Honey, how were we to know there was such a thing as a wraith? He's a horse's ass, simple as that."

"No," Persephone said. "Look at Candace. Whatever Lyon is, he's not simple."

He shifted Candace again, then rubbed her back when she stirred. His tenderness coupled with the sadness in his eyes broke Persephone's heart. Lyon glanced her way as if he felt her stare. The sadness gave way to a deep frown, and he walked out of sight.

"Did you notice that every time Lyon found something edible, he fed all of us—including the dogs—first? Now that I think of it, I haven't seen him eat since before the wraith attack," Persephone said.

Abella shuddered. "Ugh. I'll never be able to look at moss again without wanting to ralph." She laid back and closed her eyes. "I'm gonna get some sleep before he rousts us."

Taryn cleared her throat. "You know Candace has silver hair just like yours, Persephone. Wonder what that means?"

Persephone rested her back on a large rock. She closed her eyes and tried to relax, but sleep eluded her. Scenes from the past few hours flowed through her mind, but it was Taryn's question that made her heart flip-flop in her chest. *Could it be possible that she...? No.*

Before she could make sense of it all, Lyon appeared. "Come. The next cave—well, you just have to see it."

Persephone groaned, but got to her feet.

He led the way over a pile of rubble like a freakin' mountain goat.

Persephone stumbled after him, Taryn and Abella behind her.

He put Candace down and entered the narrow passage.

Persephone took the girl's hand and together they followed him into an opening in the wall that had a proverbial light at the end of the tunnel.

The next cave was small, but there was a light radiating up from a large crack in the floor. Above it, more long strings of blue gleam worms hung from the ceiling.

Persephone leaned over the crack. "Whoa." Water lit from within flowed past the floor opening. Like a kiddie pool, one side of the crack sloped gently, capturing some of the swirling water, slowing it. Then the rock dropped off sharply to the main body of water.

Abella smiled. "I'll be damned. The water's movement is causing it to glow."

Candace plopped on her belly and leaned over. She stuck a hand in the water and swooshed it around, creating an eddy of light. Her giggles echoed around the cave. The simple sound of joy soothed Persephone fears, calming her.

Lyon reached for the girl, but she rolled away and ran in a circle around the crack, the two Dobermans giving chase, evading all attempts to catch her. He grabbed for her but she jumped, and landed in the kiddie pool. The water exploded with blue-green light. Phosphorescence danced on the planes of the walls and ceiling. The red clay coating her hair swirled away, revealing her mane of silver.

Lyon flopped down and caught her. She squealed, then giggled again. "What the hell am I supposed to do with a wiggling, giggling girl?" He pulled her out of the water and held her wet body out to Taryn. When he pushed off the ground to stand, his right leg buckled.

Persephone grabbed one of his arms and steadied him. "You need to sit so I can check your wounds."

"Release me."

She pulled him to a corner of the cave and pushed on his chest until he settled on the floor. "Not until I've taken inventory."

"I'm fine."

She knelt next to him. "You've taken care of us, now it's my turn to take care of you."

Abella and Taryn walked the inquisitive Candace and the dogs to another corner of the cave to give Persephone and Lyon some privacy.

"Turn your back to the water so I can see better."

Lyon said nothing as he pivoted on his butt.

Persephone stripped off his coat and gasped when she saw rips in the back of the leather. She quickly removed the tee shirt and saw his shredded back. "Good god, when did you do this? It looks like road rash." She leaned closer. "And I see pebbles under your skin."

"Sliding down rocks on your back will do that." He shrugged her off. "I'm fine."

The memory of the slide down the gravelly slope came to her. A flash of the heebie-jeebies made her shudder. She'd caused this. She checked the wound in his lower back. "This wound is still bleeding. A lot. Wait." She leaned closer to the hole. "This looks burned." She sat up. "What did you do?"

"I cauterized it."

"Oh, good lord." She waved a hand at his pants. "You need to take these off as well, so I can see the damage the wraith caused."

"You don't want me to do that."

Persephone sat on her heels and planted her fists on her hips. "I need to see all of the wounds so I know whether you're going to be able to stay on your feet. We can't carry you."

"Okayyy…" He unbuttoned his pants and pushed them down. Persephone watched him fight to push the pants over his knees, then her gaze slid back up. "Whoa." She looked away, her face hot. "You could have told me you go commando."

Just one glimpse of his sex had sent her core into overdrive. Her body wept with need for his touch—any place would do, but one place in particular demanded first dibs. She cleared her throat and tried to make this clinical.

"Look if you want to, there's no call to be ashamed." He stroked her hair, then gripped her chin and turned her face to him.

Persephone glanced down at his rampant erection then gasped—mortified when his sex bobbed as if acknowledging her.

He released her chin and slipped his fingers through her hair. The pads of his fingertips settled on the back of her head while his thumb caressed the peaks and valleys of her ear before traveling to the lower lip she was biting. He pulled the swollen flesh from between her teeth and kissed her.

Persephone leaned closer, pulled by his heat, entranced by the softness of his lips, his slick tongue, his breath tickling her skin. She leaned forward and braced her hands on his thighs to keep from falling.

"Ah!" Lyon cried.

Persephone jerked away. "Oh, I'm so sorry." The heebie-jeebies raced through her body again. She shook her hands.

Lyon panted for a minute before speaking. "I'm fine. Really."

Persephone took a deep breath to get her body under control and forced her attention back to his injuries. "Your upper back isn't too bad, but the cauterized wound and these claw marks on your thigh are infected."

"Just clean them the best you can."

"You need a hospital. Antibiotics."

He stared at her, his chin set.

Persephone raised a hand. "I know, I know, you're fine." She cleaned his wounds with water, then helped him redress.

The Pondera Realm, Subterranean Yellowstone

Leona paced a sumptuous guest room, her fists opening and closing as she struggled to control her leonine temper. How dare the Pondera queen cut her off and hustle her away? The Pondera Novi were famous for offering sanctuary to any female. That was the beauty of her plan. Ask to become a 'sister' and she would have a free pass to all corners of the Pondera high command, including their reliquary.

But the moment Leona had started to plead her case with the queen of the Pondera Novus Ordo Seclorum, or Pondera Novi, she'd been escorted away by the queen's second, Ailith, and locked in this room.

The door opened. "You're dismissed," a voice ordered. Ailith walked in and closed the door behind her. Long, straight brown hair, vivid blue eyes: a hard beauty who didn't miss a thing. This woman could be a good second when Leona ruled.

Ailith stalked to her and grabbed her throat. She slammed Leona's back against the wall. "Who the hell are you and what are you doing here?"

Leona strained against the warrior's grip, but the Pondera warrior was strong, and Leona wasn't willing to flex her new Zodiac muscles just for the pleasure of kicking the woman's arrogant ass. She grinned.

Ailith pulled Leona forward and rammed her into the wall again. "Stop smiling and speak," she ordered as she squeezed Leona's neck.

"I'm Leona. I need sanctuary."

"Liar. Why are you here?"

"I told you."

Ailith squeezed harder, until Leona thought she'd pass out. "Speak the truth."

Leona wanted to take the bitch down, but she needed to wait. "I'm here on behalf of the witch goddess Circe."

Ailith stared into Leona's eyes, then dropped her. "That's better. I suspect there is more to it than that, though."

Leona coughed. Her throat burned. "As I suspect there's more to you than just being the queen's whipping boy."

The warrior circled Leona. "Your skin is covered with demon stink. Even your breath has that same rotten fetor."

Leona straightened her clothes. She rolled her shoulders and looked up at the taller woman. "I am Leona, of the House of Leo." She stepped into Ailith and opened her mouth. Her canines and claws elongated and she snarled.

Ailith didn't give an inch, but she did blink. "Your eyes. They're glowing gold."

"I'm the first female Zodiac—it comes with the territory." Leona caressed Ailith's long, lean arm. "And you are a Pondera Exemplar, a rogue warrior disguised as one of the Novi. Tell me, will you be the one to betray the queen? Are you here to kill her?"

She jerked away from Leona. "No. I am one of the good guys."

"As am I." Leona sat in a chair and crossed her legs. "Now that we know the truth of each other, we both have leverage. Will you help me?"

Ailith paced the room. "If I help you, what do I get in return?"

Leona smiled to herself. *Got her by the curlies.* "One, when we are finished, I will make you the leader of the Pondera Exemplars. Two, I'll give you the choice to fold all of the Pondera Novi into the Exemplars or kill them. I don't care." Leona examined her nails. "Last, cooperate or die."

Ailith stared at Leona for several seconds. "What if I want to become a Zodiac?"

"That's possible, depending on how well you perform. But know this: I am the First. No matter how many Pondera are following you, you will answer to me. Not negotiable."

Ailith bowed. "Welcome to the Pondera, Leona. We always have room for another sister."

Leona rose. "I need access to the reliquary."

"Done."

"And privacy while I'm in there."

The Pondera warrior's jaw muscles flexed. "Done."

"Last, when my brother arrives, you inform me."

The Pondera warrior grinned and bowed. "As you wish…my queen."

Abella, Taryn, and Persephone washed off the grime coating their skin and settled in to rest, their bellies empty and growling. Their backpacks and the food Lyon had found in the house had been were left behind in the panic to get away from the wraiths. The water was clean enough, but with no canteens and no idea when they might have access to water again, their choices were slim—and all were undesirable.

Lyon watched the women while he mulled. One, they could stay hidden in the caves and push forward to find food. Two, they could go back the way they came. Or three, they could leave the caves for the Overworld and try to hide in the light. Whatever they chose, they needed to do it quickly.

Persephone curled around Candace, and the old dog joined them. The big male sniffed Abella, then walked to Taryn. He plopped down next to her and draped his head across her neck. Lyon almost laughed when she gasped. He expected her to shove the dog away, but instead she wrapped an arm around him and closed her eyes, a grin on her face. *Wonders never cease.*

Lyon closed his eyes and fell into his exhaustion. He floated in a half-slumber but deep sleep eluded him. Several questions rushed at him, so jumbled they were nonsensical. He shifted positions to relieve his numb butt and heard a soft rhythmic clicking.

He opened his eyes.

The walls were moving.

22

"UP!" LYON YELLED. He ran to the women, then slid to a stop and turned back. "Shit."

"What's wrong?" Persephone asked, her heart pounding so hard that she could feel the blood pumping in her ears.

"Weapons."

"What?"

A shadowy figure landed on Lyon's coat. Lyon growled at the creature, his teeth bared. "Too late."

Candace slapped the surface of the flowing water and the phosphorescence lit up the cave. Skeletal creatures with skin the dark color of the stone dropped to the floor and hissed.

Persephone's belly bottomed out.

"What the hell are those?" Taryn yelled.

"Creepers," Lyon replied.

"Friend or foe?"

The Creepers formed a half circle and closed in. Even crouched in an attack position, they still towered over Lyon.

"Definitely foe." Lyon placed the others behind him and backed the group away.

Candace splashed the water repeatedly, illuminating the cave.

The Creepers advanced.

Candace grunted and keened as she frantically smacked the water.

"Shut her down," Lyon said.

"She's trying to tell us something," Persephone replied.

Lyon glanced at the girl.

The dogs were standing next to Candace, wagging their nubs, their focus on her face complete, as if she was communicating with them. Candace touched their heads and then jumped in the water, the dogs right behind her.

Abella and Taryn screamed and ran to the pool edge. "She's gone," Abella yelled. "Swept away."

Lyon and Persephone backed up to the pool. Persephone squatted, hoping to see the girl and the dogs, but they weren't there—the current had taken them.

"A current," Persephone said, "means an opening."

"Go," he ordered the women.

"Gladly." Taryn cannonballed in and swam away, trails of phosphorescent light following her sweeping arms and fluttering feet. Abella dove in after her, the surface barely disturbed by her slim body.

"Go, Persephone," Lyon ordered.

"Not this time. We go together."

"We have no weapons. Taking a stand is suicide."

"You mean weapons like these?" Persephone showed him a pair of long daggers. "I stole them from your coat."

He grinned as he took one of the blades from her, then grabbed the back of her neck and pulled her in for a quick kiss.

"You're enjoying this?"

He lunged for the closest Creeper. It scurried away. "I am now."

"Oh, lord, why did I ask?" Persephone said as she raised the dagger.

A Creeper lunged for her, but lost control and slid across the fine pebbles littering the floor. Persephone raised her hands higher and locked her elbows, her head turned to one side. The Creeper pinwheeled his arms, but kept sliding to Persephone.

The creature impaled itself on her dagger like a piece of meat on a skewer. Persephone screamed and jerked her hands away, severing the creature's throat. Black blood sprayed her face, arms, and chest. The Creeper crumpled to her feet.

She couldn't move. She gasped for air. Hot and cold vied for real estate on her skin. Her hands shook. Her fingers were numb. She lost her grip and the dagger clattered on the ground.

She looked for Lyon, but he was battling at least three of the skeletal creatures. Spinning, kicking, stabbing, the man was a whirling dervish, his movements fluid and efficient in a dance that was as beautiful as it was deadly.

Lyon hunched over and fell to one knee, an arm around his belly.

The Creepers keened.

Persephone saw more shadows skittering down the opposite wall. Too many for the two of them. "Lyon! We have to go."

She picked up her dagger and planted her feet next to Lyon. She pivoted, hacking and slashing at the air to keep them away. The creatures advanced, their focus on her.

Her muscles burned and quivered. The jelly phase would soon follow. She saw a movement to her left and turned to face the creature, but she was too slow. It slashed her forearm. She grunted from the impact of the blow. Her blade clattered to the ground again. Her butt followed. She was done.

"I'm so sorry, Lyon."

He looked at her and roared. His rage echoed around the small cave, wrapped around the group, and squeezed.

The Creepers stopped moving.

Lyon jumped to his feet and spread his legs, his stance wide and threatening. He released his blade and it landed on the ground with a clunk. His steady growl held the Creepers at bay for a moment, their hisses and clicks punctuating his threat.

"Lyon?"

He whirled.

Persephone gasped. His eyes were a glittering, glowing gold. Long claws had replaced his fingernails; his canines had lengthened, blood flowing down his chin. Lyon wasn't Lyon anymore. He had changed into a feral beast that stood only two feet from her.

One of the Creepers broke away and turned its attention on Persephone. It worked its way around until Lyon no longer stood between them. Persephone crawled to the blade and held it in front of her with her left hand, her injured arm wrapped around her waist.

The Creeper stalked her, its pointed teeth bared, a long white scar that split its face in two more defined in the phosphorescence.

Persephone backed into a wall. The creature's foul breath choked her. She turned her head away and pushed into the wall to shrink her body. Of all the ways to die, this was one she could never have imagined. The creature raised its clawed hand. She screamed.

Before it could strike, the creature stiffened, its mouth opened wide. Lyon's claws exploded from the back of its throat. Choking on its own blood, the Creeper wrapped its arms around Persephone, and they tumbled into the water.

Lyon eviscerated the Creeper in front of him, then turned to the next one in line. The demon's possession was pushing past the last reserves of Lyon's strength when Persephone screamed. The Creeper's long, filthy nails ripped Lyon's chest. He ignored the burning of his flayed flesh and stepped into the next blow, waiting for the sweet spot to present itself. The creature raised its hand to strike when Lyon sank his claws deep into its chest and ripped out the heart, killing the creature instantly.

Lyon staggered when he turned.

The last Creeper had raised a hand and was poised to impale Persephone. Lyon ran behind it, closed his claws to form a single solid weapon, and rammed them through the base of the creature's skull.

He jerked his hand back and waited for the Creeper to realize it was dead. The creature swayed for a second and fell forward, wrapping its arms around Persephone.

Before Lyon could get to her, the creature fell into the water, dragging her with it.

"No!" Lyon jumped in after them. Where the surface crack stopped, a deeper crack began. He dove down and entered a seam in the wall.

Just ahead, a flicker of light caught his attention. He surged forward, his legs cutting through the water. Within seconds his lungs ached, his need for air looming. A rhythmic throb started in his flank outdone only by the triple fires in his chest, back, and thigh. Lyon clenched his teeth and kept swimming.

The passage narrowed and then split, creating a fork. He looked both ways and saw a tiny light on the left. He followed the light for what seemed like eternity. His lungs burned; his head pounded. The pain in his side fell away. The muscles in his arms writhed in protest and he slowed. His vision narrowed.

His throat tightened, spasms pummeling his chest. The sulfurous stench of the hellfire of his rapidly approaching afterlife gagged him. A body slammed into him then rolled off, limp and lifeless.

Persephone. No.

Lyon grabbed an arm and relief flooded him. The sticklike limb belonged to the Creeper. Somehow, Persephone had escaped its grasp. He shoved the body away. Adrenaline surged and he shot forward. Within a few feet, the channel curved right, and Lyon saw a dot of light ahead. His vision narrowed as the black of unconsciousness slowed his brain. His limbs floundered, and his tight lips relaxed.

Breathe, breathe.

Just as he opened his mouth to relieve the agony in his lungs, something grabbed him and pulled until his head broke the surface. He sucked in stale air, his angry, seared lungs greedy and demanding. A firestorm coursed through him; agony and ecstasy merged. He scissored his legs and landed on the flat stone next to Persephone.

He cupped her delicate face with his rough hands. "Thank you," was all he could say.

Persephone sagged into him. "I...I thought I lost you." She hiccupped and her body shook as she sobbed.

He pulled her into his lap and held her loosely for fear he would hurt her. The demon stirred inside him. His canines and claws were already elongated but, for once, the demon didn't push harder. It hovered just below his skin, as if content to remain on the surface—a participant who just wanted to be close to Persephone, not an adversary fighting for possession.

She snuggled under his chin and curled into a ball. He held his breath and froze, not sure how to react, not sure he could handle the contact, but another part of him knew what to do and was starved for her touch. He fought through his discomfort and pulled her tight against him. Her heat warmed him and loosened the tight, protective coil of hate, rage, and self-loathing that had enslaved him for years.

She whimpered. "Oh, God." She pulled back and looked at him, the soft blue-green of the phosphorescence dancing across her bleak expression.

"What?"

"Where are the others?"

23

LYON HELD PERSEPHONE for several minutes, until she'd calmed. "We need to rest before we decide what to do."

"How are these monsters finding us?"

"Do you have anything electronic on you? Another phone, a pager, anything?"

Persephone stood and turned her pockets out, removed her pink hiking boots, and patted down her body. "Nothing. What about you?"

Lyon checked every pocket, and his boots. He shook his head, then looked away. "Abella and Taryn were with the Zodiacs for hours."

"You think they planted some sort of tracker on them?"

"That's what I would do."

Persephone smiled. "That's perfect. All we need to do is track them, then."

"It's not that simple."

"But—"

He pulled her back into his lap. "You need rest."

"What if they need our help now?"

"We need to help ourselves before we can help them. We need to sleep." Lyon held her tight, until he felt her body relax and her breathing slow.

"Why is your name Lyon instead of Leo?"

Lyon grunted. "Pure arrogance. I thought I was worthy of a more elegant name than Leo when I was made a Zodiac. Laughable now, in light of what happened."

"Will you tell me what happened?"

You tell her, you lose her.

Lyon's breath caught in his throat. Pain ripped through his gut at the thought and in a moment of cowardice, he flinched. "I can't. Not right now."

"How did you get so many scars?"

He hoped she'd stop talking, stop asking questions, and sleep so he could slide into blessed oblivion beside her. "You really don't want to know. It would only give you nightmares."

"I've seen the results. How much worse could it be?"

He remained silent.

"That bad?"

"Yes." Lyon pulled her closer, wanting just a little more contact to remember her by when her inevitable revulsion cast him back to the dark and the cold of his life.

Based on the events so far, the cold and dark were exactly where he was headed and undoubtedly belonged. This, his second mission, was turning out to be as spectacular a failure as his first. If he was going to be free of the demon soul, he needed to get the mission back on track, and fast—but how?

"Will you at least tell me why the Zodiacs were made?"

"Money, pure greed. Llewellyn convinced the Twelve to give up their eldest sons to make the assassins. He found a ritual to boost their strength and trained us to kill. Then, he hired them out to wealthy humans and governments who had problems that needed solving."

"Why Zodiac?"

Lyon hesitated. He'd managed to avoid telling her about the demon soul, and he had no intention of telling her now. "Centuries ago, the twelve human royal houses were named after the Zodiac signs. For instance, I'm from the House of Leo. So, a side effect of the ritual was that it exaggerated the dark characteristics of our signs. I have claws, elongated canines, and a leonine beast inside me. Scorpio has scorpion tattoos that come to life."

Persephone said nothing for a moment. "What about Gemini, the twins? How does that work?"

"Gemini has two people sharing the same body, a male and a female—like fraternal twins. When one is in control, the other is inside. So, if the male is needed in a situation that's who you see."

"And the woman shows up other times?"

"Yes."

"Do they ever appear at the same time?"

"They can, but there are time limitations. Aquarius has control over water, and you saw Taurus, he's built like a bull and is as strong as one. I once saw him—"

Persephone responded with a snore.

Lyon lifted her out of his lap and settled her on the ground. He prowled the cave for a possible egress, but found nothing until the faintest draft of air ruffled his hair. He looked up and saw a tiny corner of the moon above. This was their exit.

He lay down next to Persephone, draped an arm over her, and finally drifted away.

Abella shivered, close to Taryn but not touching. Her clothes had dried, so she couldn't blame the trembling on the water. More like her body was done, her brain soon to follow.

"Got any ideas?" Taryn snapped.

"We have no food and no way to communicate with the surface." Abella rubbed her upper arms to beat back the chill. "I've got nothing."

Taryn hiccupped. "Do you think Persephone is alive?"

"I have to believe it. I'd feel it if she wasn't."

"When did you come around to the supernatural dark side?"

"Yesterday."

Taryn snorted, then quieted. "Abella?"

"Yeah?"

"I'm scared."

"Me, too. Look, we have water and the air seems fresh enough. Let's get some sleep so our heads aren't so fuzzy." She scooted closer to Taryn. "Then we'll find a way out. Okay?"

Taryn hiccupped again. "Okay." She rolled onto her side. "But, what about Candace?"

Lyon woke Persephone after several hours. "Come, we can't carry water so fill your belly."

"What are you thinking?"

Lyon pointed to the natural vent. "If you look closely there's a light up there. So we climb."

"But there must be a way to find Abella and Taryn."

"They could be miles away." She opened her mouth to protest, but Lyon covered it with his hand. "You need to trust me. Someone is hunting us. I had hoped the Zodiacs wouldn't believe I'd go underground, but I was wrong. So, we need to adapt and hide in the Overworld."

Persephone nodded even as her tears fell.

Lyon squirmed. Weeping women always felled him. "They have a pure Portend with them. If there is anyone in all the worlds who can lead them to safety, it's that little girl. But we need to go now, before we're attacked again."

Persephone swiped at her tears. "Okay."

Lyon clapped a hand on her shoulder. "I promise to come back for them."

"Climb?"

"Climb."

* * *

Lyon held Persephone close to keep her on her feet. The climb had taken a hell of a lot longer than he had estimated, and he needed all his strength to keep both of them from falling. When they emerged, he was surprised that the sun was setting, but also relieved that he wouldn't be blinded by bright light after so many hours in the dark.

"Do you see anything?" Persephone whispered.

Lyon looked around the rocky, arid terrain and the surrounding mountains. "No, but I smell water. If we can find it, we may find humans."

Persephone sniffed the rapidly cooling air. "I don't smell anything."

"It's a Zodiac thing."

She stumbled over a rock and fell to her knees.

Lyon touched the top of her head and felt her body shake. "Are you crying?"

"No."

"C'mon, let me help you." He pulled her up and saw her face was wet with tears. He squatted. "Climb on my back."

"But you're wounded."

"The sooner we find civilization, the sooner you can clean the wounds for me."

Persephone climbed on his back, wrapped her legs around his waist and draped her arms over his shoulders. He gripped her wrists and rose. He hitched her body further up, then linked his hands under her thighs.

"Wow, I had no idea this was your view. How tall are you?"

"Taller than my father. Other than that, I don't know." The last time his height was measured he'd been a child. Every week, he'd begged his mother to measure him, his desire to be just like his father consuming his earnest, little-boy heart. The letdown had been monumental and scarring.

Persephone laid her head on his shoulder. In seconds she was snoring. He bit back a laugh and trudged on, his senses seeking the water source. He hoped the dark would reveal the artificial lights of a city, or a suburb—hell, he'd be happy with a lean-to at this point. They were in a desert, they were lost, and had no food or water. He was in dire need of more sleep, but they were exposed out here, vulnerable. Until he found shelter, he couldn't stop. To stop was to die.

Just when his legs were all but jelly, he heard a rhythmic squeak, too steady and too shrill to be an animal. He worked his way around the hill separating him from the sound and saw a farmhouse. Behind it was a tiny barn and a carping windmill, an alluring Siren call for the lost.

Lyon walked around the house and peered in every window, but no one was home. He laid Persephone on the porch and stretched his back before checking out the barn. Unimpeded winds had battered the structure until the decaying wood leaned slightly to one side. Inside, an old red truck was partially covered by a tarp that had shifted until it was inches from falling on the floor. The truck had no rust or dents. Someone had taken pretty good care of it.

He returned to Persephone and carried her inside the unlocked house. He used an elbow to flip the closest light switch, and a bare bulb illuminated the living area. The interior was slightly larger than the cabin he used in Red Bud, but the layout was the same. A living, eating, cooking area took up most of the space. The sole bedroom, a small bathroom, and a closet took up the rest.

He found the only bed and laid Persephone on it. "Persephone?" He shook her, but she just muttered and rolled away. The odor of dirt and her sweat and the sharp tang of fear had saturated her filthy clothes; they needed to come off. "Sorry about this."

He pulled Persephone onto her back and unzipped her vest, then unbuttoned her shirt and her jeans. He peeled off her clothes, leaving her pale pink bra and underwear—for her modesty and to rein in his libido, but the curve of her neck, and the jut of her ribs and hipbones taunted him.

Swaths of dirt covered her face. Lyon checked the bathroom and found towels. He ran water in the sink for several seconds, waiting for the rust color to clear before wetting a washcloth.

The wet rag erased the grime from her alabaster skin, exposing high cheekbones and delicate features. He traced each curve and hollow with his fingertips, the tactile sense powerful and defining; he would never forget her face. He worked his way down her body, checking her for wounds and cleaning away her time in the caves as if the water could purify her, but—beside the claws marks on one arm—all he saw were bumps and bruises. No serious injuries, no indication she had a tracking device on her. He covered her with a quilt, then left her to sleep.

He stripped and showered in the cold water to gain control of his throbbing cock, but it would take much colder water than the shower could provide to rein in the beast.

He dressed in the men's clothes he found in the closet and explored the cabin. It was fully furnished, right down to a full pantry, and the closet was filled with bedding and clothing as if the owners could return anytime. But what bothered Lyon the most were the two plates of half-eaten food on the kitchen table. He touched a piece of steak. Cold, but not rotten. Two people had been here only a few hours ago, and something made them leave in the middle of eating a meal without taking anything with them.

The place gave Lyon the willies. Why it had been abandoned worried him, but it was a gift he couldn't refuse.

He disposed of the plates and cleaned up a little—he didn't want Persephone to worry when she woke. Then he climbed into the bed, pulled her into his chest, and welcomed the dark.

24

ABELLA WORKED HER WAY around the small cave hand over hand along the wall until she made her way back to Taryn. She plopped down on her butt, fell back, and groaned. "Nothing. Not a fucking crack, or hole or sliver of a fracture to be found."

"I'm hungry," Taryn said, the complaint punctuated by a growling in her gut that sounded like two fighting grizzlies.

"Yep, heard ya the other three hundred and thirty-three times you said it."

"And yet, we're no closer to finding food. It's time to do something more proactive than play touchy-feely with the rock." Taryn sat up. "You think Persephone is okay?"

"Right now, I'm counting on her being okay. To think otherwise is not helpful." Abella sighed. "What do you have in mind? I don't think kicking the rock is gonna help."

Taryn stood. "Did you hear that?"

"Hear what? Your gut is making my ears ring."

"Shhh."

Abella sat up. She closed her eyes and listened. A soft noise broke through the ambient sound of the flowing water and the blood pounding in her ears. She scrambled to her feet. Silence. "Come on, come on. Don't stop now."

Suddenly, she heard dogs barking. "Holy crap."

Taryn squealed and jumped around Abella.

"Where's it coming from?" Abella asked as she pulled away. She walked to the closest wall and touched it with both hands. "Go left and I'll go right. Maybe we can isolate the location."

They worked in silence, stopping and starting with each round of barking until they met at a spot in the wall. They ran their hands over the rock.

"Shit. Nothing." Taryn scrubbed her face with her hands.

"Could be a thin spot."

"Do you think it's the Dobermans?"

"What else it could be?"

"I would have said the same thing a few days ago…"

Abella nodded. There was truth to her words, but this wasn't the time to dwell.

"You think Candace is with them?"

"Don't know. I *do* think your idea about touchy-feely with the rock is brilliant."

"What?"

"We have no way out of this cave and I'm not taking a chance with the water again."

Taryn whistled. "You want to touch? Our hands?"

"I'm thinking if we concentrate, maybe we can direct the energy at the wall and blow a hole in it."

"And ourselves."

"Possibly, but do you have a better idea?"

Taryn shook her head.

The dogs barked again, followed by the tinkle of a child's laughter.

Abella gasped and bent down. "Candace! Candace!"

Taryn squatted a couple of feet away from Abella and laid her palm on the wall. "Do it."

Abella said a brief prayer, then slapped her hand on top of Taryn's. Immediately, a surge of energy rocketed through her and the ground began to shake. Dirt and small rocks rained down on them.

Taryn cried out and tried to pull away.

"Hold on!" Abella yelled.

Pulses of light started in their chests and collided in their hands until they glowed a bright yellow. The entire cave shook. Large rocks and crystals tore free of the roof and walls and cascaded to the floor, kicking up dust.

Abella's hand grew hot and it felt huge, like all her blood had filled the flesh to near bursting. Just when she thought she'd pass out, she yelled, "Push!"

She pressed all her weight into Taryn's hand.

The light surged out, and the stone exploded into the next cavern. Both women screamed and fell to the ground.

Libra held the scanner close to the dirt and rocks that owned this stretch of Texas. The scanner beeped slowly as he turned in a circle.

Taurus tilted his head back and raised his canteen over his open mouth. A single drop fell onto his tongue. "Son of a bitch."

Libra glanced at the Zodiac. "Quit your bellyaching and help me find an entrance."

Taurus shook the now-empty canteen. "I'm close to drying out here." He ran his huge hand over his bald head to rid it of sweat and dust, but the heat and wind deposited more in seconds. "Your shortcut isn't working, Libra."

Libra scowled and hit the scanner against his open palm. "Damn thing can't get a lock with this much rock between us and them. A dying battery doesn't help, either."

Taurus shuffled his feet. "I need water, Libra."

Libra looked at him. "You really want to go the hard way?"

"The Sonora entrance that Lyon probably used is only a few miles from here. I say we go there and retrace his steps."

Libra pocketed the scanner. "That'll take longer. I don't know if they can last that long."

"But at least we'll be out of the damn sun, and, I'll be closer to the magnetic fields. If we're lucky, they'll still be vibrating from the passage of Lyon and the women. That *is* why you brought me, yes?"

Libra looked in the distance. The flat arid plain ended at the base of dark purple mountains, with not a single tree to offer relief. The sun would set in minutes, and his expensive and powerful equipment wasn't penetrating deep enough to be effective. He needed to get closer to Abella to find her. "Underground it is."

Libra and Taurus descended into the caves until they reached a huge space that smelled of fire smoke and blood. They separated and explored the cave, their LED headlamps lighting the way.

"Hey, there are large bags here, with food," Taurus called out. He grunted. "And body bags." He nudged the ashes in the pit with his toe. "The fire died hours ago,"

Libra stared at a small, bloody bundle on the floor. He nudged a red hat with the toe of his boot. "So did this Red Cap."

"There's a lot of dried blood on the ground in front of this crack in the wall," Taurus said. He squatted and touched the black streak, then followed the line that started at the crack until he had crossed the entire cavern. The blood ended abruptly behind some large rocks in one corner. He placed a hand on the wall and ran it forward until his fingers found the edge of a false wall. He looked around the corner. The crack was so small he wouldn't be able to squeeze through it. Children maybe, but not adults. He checked the ground. The blood trail continued on the other side of the crack before it disappeared in the deep black.

Libra appeared. "What is it?"

"The only place they could have gone is that hole," Libra said as he pointed to the crack blocked by rocks. "Looks like we have some work to do."

"What? And mess up your manicure?" Taurus said.

Libra looked back to insult the hulking Zodiac, but Taurus had disappeared around a large boulder.

Libra heard a 'whoop' and a splash. "Great. Leave me alone to do the hard work." He walked to the rocks spilling from the crack and began moving them to one side. "You know for an earth sign you have a strange preoccupation with water!" He placed a hand on one larger rock and felt it vibrate under his hand. The cavern quaked. The pile blocking the tiny passage shifted, loosened.

Libra jerked away from the moving rocks before he was crushed. "Holy mother. What was that?"

Persephone opened her eyes and looked around the small bedroom. Ramshackle didn't quite cover it, but she was happy to be out of the caves. She rolled onto her side, then realized she was in her underwear. "Holy crap!"

"You okay?" Lyon called out from another room.

"My clothes."

He poked his head in the room. "Your clothes were filthy so I removed them." He disappeared again.

Her face grew hot at the image of his big hands on her near-naked flesh. Creepy? Or hot? She stretched. Her sex pulsed. Hot, definitely hot. She wanted to lay back and indulge in some erotic daydreams, but she saw the pile of clothes in a corner by the bathroom. He wasn't kidding—she could barely recognize which clothes were hers or his. She lifted the sheet, got a whiff, and made a beeline for the bathroom. "You showered?"

"Last night."

She unhooked her bra and stepped out of her panties. "And you didn't wake me?"

"I couldn't wake you," Lyon said as he walked into the bathroom.

"Holy crap, what are you doing?" Persephone covered her lady bits and backed to the shower. She jumped in and pulled the shower curtain closed. She gasped when Lyon was almost as clear through the curtain as without. "Blasted transparent curtain. Turn around."

Lyon cocked one eyebrow. "I think we're beyond modesty."

"You may be, but I'm not. Turn around!"

"I just thought you should know—"

"Out."

"But—"

She gripped the shower curtain with one hand, scowled, and stabbed her free forefinger at the door.

"Okay." Lyon shrugged his massive shoulders and walked out.

She sat down hard on the side of the porcelain tub. She hated that she was so shy about her body. There wasn't anything to be ashamed of, but compared to Abella's statuesque perfection and Taryn's luscious curves, Persephone was just…average.

A handsome man like Lyon must have seen dozens of beautiful naked women. She imagined her body stacked up against that bevy and grimaced. No way could she ever measure up. She shook her head to clear her thoughts. Lust and sex weren't even on her list of worries. Right now, all she wanted was to get clean. Maybe a good scrubbing would wash away her confusion, as well.

A bottle of shampoo and body wash rested by the drain. She opened them and sniffed. Strawberry. *That'll do.*

She stood, turned the hot and cold taps wide open, lifted the lever for the shower…and screamed.

Lyon smiled, his back to the sputtering woman. "I tried to tell you."

"Three words. Just three. 'No hot water.' Is that so hard?"

He glanced over his shoulder. He'd never seen such a scowl. Persephone had a towel wrapped around her body. Part of her silver hair was piled in a gremlin's nest on her head, while the rest hung down in stringy sections. She looked like an indignant, wet Kellas Cat. She certainly knew how to yowl like one.

He bit the inside of his mouth to keep from laughing. "No."

She stamped a foot and marched back into the bedroom, muttering something about inconsiderate men.

A few minutes later, she reappeared dressed in a pair of hot-pink polyester pants with an elastic waist she had to pin to keep them from falling to the floor, and a circus-tent-sized shirt covered in bright, neon-colored flowers.

She raised her forefinger and wagged it at him. "Not one word."

He raised his hands in surrender. "Are you hungry?"

Her nose wiggled. She gave him one more frown, then followed her nose to the stove and peered inside the soup pot. She closed her eyes and groaned. "I'm starving."

Lyon heaved a sigh of relief. *All is forgiven, praise be to the power of food.*

He dished up a bowl of the stew of smoked ham, canned vegetables, onions, and garlic. "There's salt and pepper on the table."

They sat across from each other, eating in silence. Persephone finished before him. She stood, grabbed her bowl, and refilled it.

He grinned.

"What? Never seen a woman with an appetite?"

"I have, but I've never cooked for a woman before. It pleases me that you like it enough to go back for more."

"Well, then you're gonna be ecstatic because I'll probably be going back for thirds."

"So be it."

She looked around the cabin. "How did you find this place?"

"I heard the windmill squeaking and followed the sound. We're lucky no one is here, but I don't understand why they would leave so much behind."

Persephone slurped down the rest of her soup, then took both of their bowls and refilled them. "The whole country has fallen on hard times, especially in rural areas. Perhaps they didn't have a choice."

He remained silent. The only reason he could figure someone would leave so abruptly was if they were chased away. Or killed. *No need to tell Persephone about that.* "We can't stay here long. It's the only house for miles, the Zodiacs will find it."

"What about Abella and Taryn, or Candace and the dogs? We can't leave them in the caves."

"We can't go back for them, not without help, and not without finding out how we were tracked or we'll be in the same mess."

"Where can we go?" Persephone asked.

"I have an idea, but we need a couple days to rest before we go. There's a truck in the barn, I'll see if it starts."

Persephone collected the dishes and washed them. "I better come with you."

"Why?"

"You know anything about engines?"

"I can drive cars. How hard can it be?"

"Ah," Persephone nodded. "That's what I thought. We'll get the truck ready, then we leave tomorrow morning. Not in two days." She looked past Lyon. The haunted look in her eyes shredded him. "They may not have that long."

Taryn climbed through the newly blown hole, careful not to linger on the red-hot edges. Air passed over the sweat over the sweat on her face, cooling the skin. "Is your whole body hot? I'm sweating like a pig."

"You know I never—"

"Sweat, yeah, I know. You suck."

Abella chuckled as she crawled through the hole. She groaned as she pushed off the ground and stood.

Taryn joined her, and they took in the magnificent sight. The cave was massive. The floor sloped steeply to the center of the space, while the water burbled merrily to their left. The walls were studded by thousands of crystals. Gold and red and green light bounced around the cave in an all-natural kaleidoscope that could rival the best light show in Las Vegas. They looked up and saw a tiny dot of sunlight that acted as the catalyst for the spectacle.

"Guess we could have taken the wet route, after all," Taryn said.

"Either way was a risk, but I'm kinda glad we blew a hole in the bitch."

"Whhyyy?"

Abella held up her hands. "Because now we know we can direct this power—make it work for us."

The dogs barked again, and Taryn looked in the distance. "They sound like they're just beyond that wall."

Abella grinned and took off at a jog, Taryn close on her heels. They closed in on the source of the barking, then squatted by the wall.

"Ready to do this again?" Abella asked.

Taryn frowned, but nodded. She laid her hand on the rock just like before, then dropped her head. No sense getting your noggin crushed by a rock if you could prevent it.

Abella shook her hands, then placed one on top of Taryn's.

Nothing happened.

Abella lifted her hand and slapped it down again.

"Ouch," Taryn said.

They waited for several seconds but still, nothing happened. No shaking, no glowing, no blowing.

Taryn removed her hand and sat back on her heels. "What the hell?"

Abella laughed while shaking her head. "I think we blew our wad."

"What?"

"This power or energy or whatever it is, needs to recharge."

Taryn sagged to the ground and groaned. "So we wait."

"Yes, we wait."

The grizzlies in Taryn's stomach started a rematch.

"I know, I know, you're hungry," Abella said with a sigh.

Libra collapsed on the ground in the new cave and panted, his clothes filthy, his manicure most decidedly ruined. It had taken them hours to move the rubble enough for them to slither through to this cave. His stomach growled, but there wasn't time to eat or rest. He rolled up and turned on his flashlight. Nothing here, but another pile of rubble next to a different crack. "Thank you, Lyon. Your breadcrumbs are very much appreciated."

Taurus followed Libra to the next cave, then the next, until they reached one littered with dead Creepers. The stench of blood and death clung to the walls and hovered in the air. Libra moved through the dead bodies until he found black blood. He touched it with one finger. It was dry and that meant human, not Creeper.

"They were here. The Creepers attacked them here."

Taurus squatted next to Libra. "But they escaped."

The two Zodiacs looked around the space.

Libra stood. "Spread out. We need to find out how they got out of this cave."

The men searched along the walls until they met at the crack in the floor. They switched off their flashlights and waited for their eyes to adjust.

Libra sat on the edge of the crack and scooped out some water. Light flared in the water, illuminating the cave further. He sipped it out of his joined hands, then reached for more. "This is where they escaped."

Taurus walked around the crack, staring at the ground. He squatted and ran his hands over the stone. "There is quite a lot of blood here." He rubbed his fingertips with his thumb, sniffed the blood, then wiped his fingers clean. "Human and Creeper." He looked at the water bubbling along in the crack.

Taurus stared at Libra. "Why didn't you bring Aquarius, or Pisces? Water is their shit, not mine."

"You wasted plenty of time splashing like a little girl in the main cave."

"Answer the question."

Libra ran a hand through his hair. "You can move rock like I've never seen, and I don't trust Aquarius." No one messed with Aquarius, not when the Zodiac could drown a man from the inside out with a flick of a finger. *Seriously fucked up superpower, that.*

"And Pisces?"

"He'd demand coin for this mission."

Taurus nodded. "He *is* all about the money."

Libra dropped to the floor and laid on his belly looking for the passage. "I can't see anything up here."

Taurus jumped in, his knees pulled into his chest.

The splash drenched Libra. "Bastard," he muttered as he wiped his face.

In seconds, Taurus reached the surface. He grabbed the ledge and sucked in a great breath. "Son of a banshee, that current is strong. There's a fork in the stone just a few feet downstream."

Libra nodded. "You go left, I'll go right."

"Nope, I'm with you all the way."

"It'll take twice as long to search if we don't split up."

"You don't trust Aquarius, and I don't trust you. We go together."

Libra grit his teeth. Taurus was physically intimidating, obdurate as hell, and had an elephant's memory. No sense arguing once he'd made up his mind. "Fine, pick a tunnel."

"Right has always been my lucky fork in the road."

Libra dove over Taurus gave the water an extra kick to splash Taurus in the face, then headed down the right passage, hoping Abella had enough time for this one-off effort.

25

As THE SUN BEGAN TO DROP behind the hills, the temperature plummeted. Lyon held the front door open for Persephone. She walked past him. Even covered in grease and dirt, his body reacted with interest. They'd spent hours working on the truck, and Persephone had shown him what she knew about an engine. Together, they'd gotten the truck running and revved their libidos as well, if the scent of her aroused sex was any indication.

"Are you taking a shower?" Persephone asked, her eyes half-closed. Her hand covered her mouth when she yawned.

"You're tired."

"Long day." She rubbed her eyes and sagged.

He carried a chair to the fireplace, started a fire, and waved her over. "Sit." Once she'd settled, he filled the two largest pots with water, then placed them on the stove to heat.

He returned and knelt at her feet, making short work of her shoes and socks, clearing the way to run his hands over her calves, then stopped at her knees. "May I?"

She placed her hands on his, leaned in, and kissed him lightly on the lips. A shock arced between them. Persephone gasped and drew back.

A jolt of electricity raced from the top of his head to all points south, and threatened to incinerate his restraint. *Keep it under control, man.*

"The man who lived here must have been big." She released the top button of the worn canvas shirt. She fanned out her fingers and pressed her palms to the hot skin of his neck.

His pulse pounded beneath her touch. He could barely breathe. "Arggg." Lyon's muscles quivered. The demon scratched at him, demanding to get in on the good stuff. His body flooded with want, weakening his control over the demon's call. His brain flooded with images of him ripping her clothes off and mounting her tiny body. Pumping her like she was a whore. *No. No. No.*

"Stop." Lyon stood, bringing Persephone with him.

"What?" She looked into his eyes. Her dilated pupils and heady scent screamed 'take me.' "What's wrong?"

"I can't." He wanted to tell her how much he desired her, that every part of him needed her touch, that he was too afraid that he'd shred her if he lost control, but the words wouldn't come. The only thing he could do was take care of her needs. He backed away from her and busied himself until the water was hot enough for a bath.

"Come."

Persephone sat on the edge of the tub and ran her fingers through the water. She sniffled.

Tears? "Stop that."

"I can't help it." She swiped her nose with the back of her hand. "It's Abella and Taryn. I'm about to take a hot bath, there's food to eat, and I don't even know if they're alive." She stopped. Her shoulders heaved and several nearly incomprehensible words came out. "…Candace and the dogs. *Blah-blah-blah*…the other children…"

He backed out of the bathroom to escape before the crying turned to blubbering, desperate to find anything that would turn off the waterworks. A search of the kitchen cabinets yielded gold. He returned with two large round candles in tins and lit them. The small space glowed soft yellow.

Persephone stood and walked into his arms. He pulled her tight against him and just held her. If he were less of an animal, he'd know what to say, but pretty words weren't needed in a pit death match. Pretty words wouldn't keep you alive in the dungeons when the guards left barely enough food for six, in a cell that held twice that many beasts.

He released her and waved a hand at the tub. "You better…before it gets cold."

She looked at him and nodded, her purple eyes huge in her pale face.

Lyon had just opened the bathroom door when Persephone groaned. He looked back in time to see her frown and cover her nose.

"Jeez, what is that stench?"

A wave of sulfurous, thick stench hit his nose and eyes, and sent snot and tears into overdrive. "What the hell?"

Persephone grabbed the lids, looked at the writing, then swept the candles into the bath water before running out of the room.

Lyon followed her to escape, but the fetor billowed after them into the bedroom.

They ran to the fireplace but the entire cabin had been befouled. Only after running outside did they find relief.

"What kind of candles were those?" Lyon asked.

"Didn't you see the lid? It said 'Skunk.'"

"What the hell reason would there be for that horrible smell?"

"To scare away animals, maybe?"

Lyon turned his back to her, his embarrassment foreign and unpleasant. *Scare away animals, indeed.*

Persephone touched his shoulder. "Thank you."

"What? For driving us out of the cabin?"

"Your intention was sweet." She tried to disguise her laughter with a cough, but he could feel her derision. He turned around, ready to flay her, when he saw the humor in her eyes.

She grinned.

His lips twitched.

She covered her mouth, but she couldn't stop the laughter any longer. She wrapped her arms around her waist and howled.

He smiled, then chuckled. "It's not *that* funny."

Persephone wiped the tears from her eyes and laughed harder.

Lyon crossed his arms over his chest and frowned, waiting for her to regain her senses.

She raised a hand and caressed his cheek. "Oh, I needed that."

"What?"

"Something to laugh about." She looked at the barn. "I'll never be able to sleep now, especially not in there," she said as she pointed to the cabin.

"What do you suggest?"

Persephone looked out over the Texas desert in the direction of the caves for a moment, then back at Lyon. "Please?"

He sighed. She hadn't left her friends behind, despite eleven assassins being in the way—she sure as hell wouldn't let a desert and uncharted caves deter her from searching for them. Add in a bunch of lost children and a couple of dogs…

He was a fool to think he could stop her. "All right, let's load up. This may be a mistake, but you've proven to be uncommonly stubborn—"

Persephone launched herself at him.

He caught her when she hit his chest, and squirmed when she plastered him with kisses. He wanted to tell her to stop, but damned if he wasn't enjoying the slobbering.

She slid down his body and flushed a bright red that was visible even by the dim porch light. She cleared her throat as if to take her mind off the intimate moment, planted her hands on her hips, and looked at the cabin. "So, who's going inside for food and supplies?"

"Uh, huh." Lyon closed his eyes and sighed before taking a deep breath and running for the steps.

Libra used the current to carry him faster than he could swim, his limbs only needed to keep from pummeling into the stone walls while he looked for another crack that might lead to a cave…and air. His heart pounded, but he pushed harder.

He lifted his arms, feeling along the ceiling for an opening—no matter how small—that might have enough air for one quick breath. His head slammed into a chunk of stone that jutted out from the wall. He sagged. The lack of oxygen and a likely concussion took their toll. *This is it.* He drifted, ready for the inevitable, when hands grabbed him and pulled him to the surface.

He sucked in the air, relieved to be alive, then opened his eyes. Abella and Taryn were kneeling over him, frowning.

"Well, come on. Climb out," Taryn ordered.

The two women pulled on his arms until he was able to belly flop onto the ground.

"No reinforcements. Not even a scrap of food," Taryn said. "Great. Some savior you are."

A splash drew their attention, and they dropped his arms. Exhaustion washed over Libra and he sagged. A stabbing ache started in his back and radiated out until he was a throbbing pile of pain. He heard the women laughing. A sopping wet Taurus appeared in his dwindling field of vision. "You made it."

Taurus held out a hand to Libra. "Get off your lazy ass. We have an exit to find."

"Yeah, yeah, give me a minute." Libra croaked. He rolled onto his back, squinted for a second then pointed to the tiny bit of fading light in the ceiling of the cavern. "Huh. There's our exit," he said before he passed out.

The desert was still cloaked in darkness; the sun hadn't broken the horizon. Persephone and Lyon bounced around for hours, searching for the tiny hole they had crawled from to use as a starting point, stopping time and again with no luck. Persephone strained against the lap belt, her hands clinging to the dash, her eyes wide, her mouth shut.

"Stop!" Persephone grabbed his arm. "There. I think it's there."

Lyon stopped the truck behind one of the only hills around, the headlights pointed at the hole, and turned off the engine. The sudden silence was utter and chilling. Lyon sighed. He'd lost count several stops ago. The damn desert floor was riddled with holes that he didn't remember seeing when they'd climbed out of the cave a little over a day ago. They walked to the front of the truck and used the headlights to search for their tracks as they worked their way to the opening.

Persephone crouched and touched the ground. She looked up at Lyon, her face beaming. "Look, our tracks. You are brilliant." She stood and bounced on her toes. "So, what do we do now?"

Lyon scratched his head. "What we need is more of that ass wipe…"

"Ha, ha, funny guy." Persephone crouched down and looked inside the hole.

Lyon approached her, but before he could drop to a knee next to her, he heard the soft flap of wings a few feet above his head. He pivoted to see the bird but it had disappeared into the dark, a puff of dust the only physical evidence of its low fly-by. A frizzle of concern prickled his scalp and worked its way down his spine, but the night air was once again still, the desert silent.

Lyon shook his head and turned back to Persephone when he heard more flapping, this time from multiple birds. He whirled around. A wing brushed his cheek. He swatted at it, but got nothing but air.

"Son of a—"

Low growls sounded behind him. Coyote or wolf? Hell, he didn't know, but it wasn't good. "Persephone, we need to get back to the truck."

Her arm swept back and grabbed his lower leg. "Lyon."

He grabbed her arm and pulled, but she fought him. "Persephone. Now."

"No, look." She pointed to a spot a football-field length north of them.

A dark form rose to its feet, then leaned over and held out a hand.

Lyon jumped and landed on his belly. He pulled Persephone down until she was flat before pulling her into his side. In the span of a breath, the inky-black sky gave way to a dark grey.

"What are we doing?"

"Stay down and wait."

A long, slim arm rose out of the desert floor. The dark form grabbed it and pulled.

The sky broke with bands of blue and grey and purple. The cool colors held reign for a few more seconds before yielding to the soft pinks, then reds of the sunrise. The body of a long, tall woman emerged, her back to Lyon and Persephone. The sun's rays rushed across the flat desert floor and spotlighted her. She threw out her arms in a stretch and turned.

Persephone jerked against him. "It's Abella!" She fought his grip. "Let me go."

"And Libra." He pulled her tighter and clamped a hand over her mouth. "Wait, just wait."

They watched Taurus climb out of the hole followed by Taryn.

"Let me go."

"What? You think Libra and Taurus are just going to let the three of you go about your merry? They're here to take them to the InBetween."

Persephone leaned in and bit his shoulder, hard.

He released her and grabbed the offended muscle. "Shit!"

She jumped to her feet and started running for her friends.

Lyon rolled onto his back and saw a thick cloud of undulating black forms flying waist-high directly at him. He had to move—now. Wounded muscle forgotten, he jumped up and heard a chorus of snarls. A small pack of wolves appeared from behind the hill hiding the truck, their hackles raised and their heads low.

Lyon took off after Persephone at a dead run.

The wolves growled. Their claws digging into the hard-pack made a scratching sound that chilled Lyon to the marrow. "Persephone. Stop!"

Taurus grabbed Abella and Taryn around the waist, preventing them from running. Libra trotted toward Persephone, a smug grin on his face. "Ah, sweet reunion," he shouted.

Lyon increased his stride, but before he could make a dent in the distance separating him from Persephone, the cloud of birds swarmed past him.

A whole mess of Hermes hawks, more than he'd ever seen in one place—maybe all of the messenger birds from the InBetween—had been sicced on them. *Bad, bad, bad.*

Libra faltered and then started running, but before he could reach Persephone the hawks encircled her, going round and round in a tight formation that blocked her from view and from touch. Libra skidded to a stop, sending dust motes swirling in the sunlight.

A single bird separated from the group and dove at Libra. He stepped back. Another, then another attacked him with their wings and their claws, forcing him away from Persephone.

The wolves skulked around Lyon and the mass of hawks until they crouched between Libra and the birds.

Libra raised his hands. "Okay, okay, I've heard the will of the goddess." He laughed and ran back to Taurus and the women. "But fuck you if you think I'm handing these two over." The men pulled Abella and Taryn away, trotting further north until they were close to a rise of hills.

The group stopped. Libra raised his hands and a thick swirl of dust followed a blast of swirling energy. The son of a bitch never, ever used his power; he complained mightily about the balance of his dark and light. Using it pulled him deep into the dark side, and he was afraid that one day he would never find his way back to the light.

So to have him shoot off his blaster like it was a daily occurrence... Lyon squinted. "Shit me." The blast of energy must have had some serious hocus pocus, because a black Humvee appeared out of thin air.

One hawk flew free of the mass and toward Lyon, pulling his attention back to his most pressing situation: Persephone and the mass of birds. The hawk circled above Lyon before dropping a small bundle at his feet.

The messenger cried out to the others and the preternatural vortex immediately flew apart, the hawks speeding out in all directions. By the time Lyon looked at Persephone, the wolves had also vanished like a fucking mirage.

He snatched up the bundle and raced to Persephone.

She turned to face him, her face wet with tears, and pointed north. "They're gone."

He touched her shoulder and she sagged into him, grasping at his arms to stop the slide to her knees. The sobbing started when she reached the ground.

Lyon sat and crossed his legs, then pulled her into his lap and let her cry. Several minutes passed before she finally took a deep breath and hiccupped.

"We were so close," Persephone whispered in his chest.

"Yes."

"What happened?"

"I think the animals were protecting you."

"But who—"

"Some would say the goddess was protecting you, but I am not a man of belief."

Persephone sucked in a breath and let it out slowly. "What do we do now? How do we find them?"

Lyon showed her the bundle dropped by the hawk, then opened it and pulled out two messages. He unrolled the first. *The Twelve are dead by your hand, save for Llewellyn.*

Lyon ground his teeth. The message fell from his numb fingers. His mind raced trying to make sense of the murders, but the harder he fought to untangle them, the more snarled they became.

The second vellum was wrapped around a hard object. He uncovered a piece of grey keratin with black spots on it, sniffed it, then jerked his head back. He flipped the vellum over and saw just one word:

Run!

26

"WHY DID YOU LET THEM TAKE Abella and Taryn?" Persephone asked.

"I had no choice. The hawks and the wolves had you surrounded. They weren't letting anyone get close to you or around you. Between the animals and Libra and Taurus, it wasn't gonna happen."

"They'll be taken to the InBetween."

"Yes."

He shifted, but after so many hours of driving, there weren't any comfortable positions. Lyon desperately wanted to curl into a ball and sleep his way to clarity. He shouldn't have been surprised that Llewellyn would claim Lyon—his own son—had killed the fathers of the other Zodiacs. Now he understood why they had been attacked. As for who was sending the wraiths and Creepers, there were at least eleven choices—every one of them bad.

A hot panic choked him. Each attack was like a slamming door squeezing him, pushing him, until claustrophobia filled his body. It was only a matter of time before they caught him, and when they did, he'd be dead—literally. Hiding from one Zodiac was difficult. Eluding eleven enraged Zodiacs hell-bent on his destruction was impossible.

He couldn't stay in the Overworld forever. He had no idea how to function among the humans, much less keep the demon at bay permanently with all the stimulation. Pain and death—that was his life. It made him dangerous to everyone around him, unpredictable even to himself, and the last man who could be counted on for help.

But for the first time in years, he wished he were a better man. Not a hero—he wasn't made of that exalted stuff. Just...better. Witnessing the love Persephone and her friends shared, their willingness to risk their lives to save others, made him question his fundamental belief that he didn't need anyone. It made him long for more than the life he'd been living.

"Who the hell do you think you're kidding?" he muttered.

"What?" Persephone asked.

Lyon rubbed his temples to clear out the drivel.

Persephone shifted on the bench seat. "Have we made it to Wyoming yet?"

Lyon glanced at her. "We're better than that. Yellowstone is only an hour away."

"Does this neutral party you spoke of live near Yellowstone?"

"Not near, under. We're going back down into the darkness."

Lyon held Persephone's hand as they approached a broad, grin-like slash in a wall of rock, partially hidden by fallen trees and grasses.

Persephone sighed, and her stomach flopped. *Another blasted cave.* "Who lives here?"

"They're called the Pondera Novus Ordo Seclorum."

"That's a mouthful."

"It means, 'Balance of the New Order of the Ages.' The Pondera were put here by the gods to guard the balance of light to dark, human to nonhuman, ensuring that humans don't discover the paranormals and paranormals don't take advantage of humans. They're quartered all around the world, but their leaders live here in the caves surrounding the Yellowstone caldera."

Lyon pulled aside a stand of tall grass and held it open while Persephone entered the shadows inside the cave opening.

A layer of cool air washed over her, drying her sweat. The space was huge compared to the other caves they'd escaped, but still her heart flipped in her tight chest. Claustrophobia was looming. Before her imagination went into overdrive and panic swamped her, ten warrior women stepped out from behind the boulders dotting the cave floor, their long spears aimed at them, their scowls almost as piercing as the tips of their weapons.

"Halt."

The tallest warrior woman stepped closer. Her dark hair was pulled back and secured with a brown leather thong. Her pants and vest were made of the same brown leather and decorated with a layer of lacy dark green leather, in an ancient-looking pattern dotted with a variety of small gemstones in blue, red, and gold. She was broad-shouldered with thick muscles in her arms and legs, black eyes framed by crow's feet, and several conspicuous scars. The woman was older than the others, but Persephone had no doubt she could dish out some harsh punishment, even to Lyon.

Lyon tried to pull Persephone forward, but she put on the brakes. "They said halt. I think we should do what they say."

The older warrior closed in on Lyon and put the blade against his throat. "Listen to the woman if you value your life, Zodiac."

Persephone started. "How do you know he's a Zodiac?"

The woman turned her attention to Persephone without removing the blade. "I can smell the stench of demon on him." She backed up a couple of steps. "Let's go."

Persephone stumbled when Lyon started walking.

Demon? How could she have missed it? She thought his cryptic "darkness" and "beast" were just euphemisms for a bad temper. She'd known the human version of evil: monstrous creatures disguised as benevolent foster families who would give even Lucifer the willies. But *real* demons? From *hell* demons?

She pulled her hand free of his and fell back. Sweat drenched her. Fear scraped and ripped at her like a ship stranded on coral.

Lyon frowned.

She mustered a smile until he looked away. A snort drew her attention. The warrior smirked as if she knew what Persephone was thinking, and the falling dominos of doubt and fear were exactly what she'd planned.

What the hell are you doing, Persephone?

She put one foot in front of the other and followed the women deeper into the cave, her mind racing but her body numb.

Images of the wretched man with the starving Dobermans, the glee in Lyon's glowing eyes as he shredded the Creepers with a blade and then his claws, the thick and numerous scars that were a testament to his violent existence, it was all there, all the bits and bobs she needed to see the truth.

She'd had opportunities to walk away, but she had stuck with Lyon because of the arrogant idea that she could make a difference. That she could learn a long-sought truth about who she was—that she wasn't just another abandoned foundling with more questions than answers. She needed to help a man as lost as she was—even though she hadn't been able to help herself.

A hidden world, lost children, Zodiac Assassins, witches and goddesses... It was fodder for the worst nightmares and the best dreams. She couldn't deny her nightmares were true now, not in light of what she'd seen. *But, please, let the dreams also be true.*

"Persephone!"

She stubbed her toe on a rock and fell to her knees. Lyon held out a hand to help her up. She looked at his callused palm and long, scarred fingers. This hand had wrought pain and death more times than she could bare to contemplate, but it had also held her gently when she was frightened for herself, and for her friends. Lyon was not a simple man, and he was capable of great violence, but there was far more to him than just the darkness.

Make your choice. She lifted her hand and settled it into his. She may not know what would happen in the future, but what she wanted right now was to travel through the dark with Lyon until they found the light...together.

Lyon pulled her to her feet and kept her hand until she finished brushing the dirt off her now torn and bloody pants. "What?"

Lyon glanced to his left.

Persephone looked up and gasped. She was standing at the top of a switchback staircase that led to a massive cavern far below her. The steep descent ended in a smooth, light-grey granite floor with an intricate circular design of gold, red, and green etched into the entire surface.

Huge tapestries awash in bright colors hung from the walls. Chandeliers held thick beeswax pillar candles while candelabras were filled with tall tapers, the air honeyed and heavy. Persephone breathed deep the sweet scent as she looked around.

Dozens of women dressed in leathers like those worn by the warrior greeting party stood in front of a large wood dais at the opposite end, their various spears, daggers, swords, maces, and axes at the ready to protect the slim, elegant, grey-haired woman who sat on a simple gnarled-wood throne before them.

In the space between the guards and the older woman on the throne were several women dressed in rich gowns, their faces obscured by veils, bustling around the space as they directed the food-laden male servants to the dais table.

The warriors surrounding Lyon and Persephone stepped closer, crowding the pair without touching them.

Lyon pulled Persephone behind him and growled.

A tall warrior broke from the ring of guards and climbed the stairs. She pointed her spear at Lyon. "With me, Zodiac."

He growled. "Lower your stick, bitch."

"At ease, Ailith, lower your weapon. We have nothing to fear from our guests." The woman on the throne waved at Lyon and Persephone. "Come here, let me see you both."

The warrior arched an eyebrow in warning, then started down the stairs.

Lyon and Persephone followed. A dozen warriors, each more broad shouldered than the next, all with a deep scowl, stood at the base of the stairs.

After passing through the horde, Lyon and Persephone came to the dais steps.

The old woman was beautiful and graceful, but there was a hard look in her eye when she looked at Lyon. "You look just like your father."

She turned her attention to Persephone, and studied her the same way Abella studied predators—human, animal, and insect. "You've been on a long road, child. You and your friends."

"Yes, it's been a long few days."

The woman smiled. "I'm not talking about recent history. You all have been on a path since before you were born." She looked around the cavern. "Where are the other two?"

Persephone started. "How do you know about my friends?"

She held out a hand to Persephone. "Come with me, we have a lot to talk about."

Lyon grunted and wrapped an arm around Persephone's waist. "No. We stay together."

The old woman smiled, one eyebrow arched high as she looked at Persephone.

"Yes." Persephone said. "Together."

"I can't say that I approve of your champion, but perhaps…" The woman studied Lyon for a moment, her head cocked to one side, before blinking and gesturing for Persephone and Lyon to follow. "My name is Elona. I am the queen of the Pondera Novus Ordo Seclorum. A rather unwieldy title, I admit, but it is who we are. Come, let us go to my quarters so we may speak in private."

The group traveled down several passages before the queen's guard opened the double doors that led to tastefully decorated quarters. Persephone and Lyon were stopped just inside the room by the guards.

Persephone glanced at the feminine, muted colors of the many tapestries hanging on the wall, and the thick wool rugs worn from decades of footfalls. In contrast, the thick, dark wood furniture was solid and heavily carved and turned, very masculine—very yin and yang. It spoke volumes to Persephone about the dichotomy that was this woman, and made her harder to read.

After the queen took a seat, she waved Lyon and Persephone forward. "This is better. Even the Pondera have to worry about eavesdropping."

"Why are so many Pondera Novi amassed here?" Lyon asked. "You can't let the Exemplars go unchecked to spill blood as they will."

"You have been in the dungeons too long, Zodiac."

"True."

"The children of the paranormals have been taken from their families."

Persephone opened her mouth.

Lyon cleared his throat.

She glanced at him.

He frowned.

Persephone closed her mouth and smiled at the queen. She wasn't sure why Lyon didn't want to tell the queen about the children in the cave, but, demon or not, she trusted him more than these women.

"Then why are your warriors here and not out looking for them?" he asked.

"The Quietus is coming." The queen sat back in her chair and drummed her fingers on the arm. "Sacrifices must be made."

27

AILITH CHECKED THE CROSS hall, but it was empty. She unlocked the map room, then waved Leona inside and pointed out the secret door. "Your brother and his whore just arrived."

Leona snorted. "That's definitely not my brother's style. He's more the celibate type."

"There's a lot of animosity there."

"I have my reasons." Leona ran her fingers across the words and sigils carved into the wood. "How do I open it?"

Ailith reached over Leona's shoulder and used her forefinger and middle finger to pull on two books.

The scrape of a heavy bolt dragging across metal caused Leona's belly to clench. So close to success. "Leave me."

"But—"

"Find out where he will be quartered."

Ailith bowed and left Leona alone in the map room.

Leona pulled open the heavy door, waving away the years worth of dust that billowed around her. She stepped into the Pondera's greatest treasure, a secret reliquary holding dark and dangerous artifacts and tomes used at a time when the paranorms had lived among the humans. She dropped her head back and breathed deep the smell of old paper, mold, and power before pulling the door closed behind her.

She had lived and breathed the stories of why and how the paranorms ended up underground, the power of the gods and goddesses. But her childish curiosity morphed into obsession after Lyon killed their mother; after Llewellyn sent Sag into the Overworld to keep him away from Leona until time and distance and circumstance had killed their blossoming love.

She'd searched for years for the dark magic spell books that had been whispered about in the shadows. When she found out about the Pondera reliquary, she wanted to make a beeline there but as the daughter of one of the Twelve, there was no way she could gain entrance. It had taken a shitload of crazy turning the worlds upside down for her to finally get here.

Leona walked in a circle, taking in the books and scrolls that filled every shelf and cranny. The most powerful magical tools known in ancient time and since were only an arm's length from her. The Pondera had not only protected the balance between light and dark—they'd guarded the words and artifacts that could tip the balance and send all the worlds into darkness.

She ran her fingers across the book spines, reading the titles until she came to a book so old that the words and the gold leaf had faded away. She pulled it out and laid it on the small reading table before opening the cover. After the first two pages, she came to a title page that said, *Absolutum Dominium*. "Absolute dominion," she whispered as she ran her fingers over the printed words. "So shall it be."

She wrapped the book in an oilskin to protect it and slipped it into a pouch under her long, loose skirt. Her errand for Circe was complete.

"Now for me." She giggled, then clapped a hand over her mouth. "No, no, no. I'm perfectly sane, perfectly sane." She shook her head to clear out the itch emanating from deep inside her brain before beginning her next search. Of all the dark magic or mages in the worlds, there was no one more powerful than

Circe's teacher and lover, the sorcerer called the Dominus de Tenebris, or the Master of the Dark.

Leona hated Circe, but more insidious than that hot, jagged emotion was her envy of Circe's time with the Master, and the skills she'd learned from him. When the Master and Circe disappeared—both rumored to be dead—the Pondera had confiscated the Master's books and dark magic tools, leaving Leona cut off from the magic that she wanted above all else.

Any one of the Master's possessions would fetch her a fortune, but only two held any real interest for Leona…though, it wasn't for money. She rolled her neck and started searching the room. It could be a long few hours, but she wasn't leaving until she had what she needed.

"Sacrifices? What the hell does that mean?" Lyon demanded.

The queen shifted in her seat and frowned. "Why do you think you've been sent on this mission?"

"Don't know, don't care." He said the words because they came easily to him. He'd said them for years. But for the first time, he wasn't sure he believed it. He may not understand what was happening, but he damn sure cared. "Will you protect Persephone or not?"

Persephone jumped in. "Wait a minute, don't I have a say?"

"No, you don't," Lyon said.

"Yes, you do," the queen said at the same time.

Lyon took Persephone's arms. "You need to stay here, just for a while until I figure out what's going on."

The queen cleared her throat. "To answer your earlier question, Zodiac, my warriors are gathered because events around the globe have convinced me it's necessary."

"Events?" Lyon repeated.

"Can't you feel it? The weather anomalies, the panicked animals, the wars breaking out all over the globe?" The queen walked to Persephone and touched her face. "You've seen things. Inexplicable things."

Persephone nodded.

"So have I."

Lyon rubbed his forehead. "What are you talking about?"

Elona smiled at Persephone. "Trees turning white and glowing."

"And bending over so far that the tops touch the ground," Persephone added.

The queen held out both hands and Persephone took them. The queen closed her eyes. "A blood-red moon that's too large to be real. Animals fleeing."

Persephone nodded. "How do you know that?"

Elona squeezed Persephone's hands until the skin blanched white with an outer ring of red.

Persephone hissed and tried to pull away.

Lyon jumped up. "Stop. You're hurting her."

A deep thrum vibrated the floor.

The queen's head dropped back. Her spine cracked and curved until her skull touched her back. *"Eternus obscurum, Eternus obscurum, Eternus obscurum."*

Persephone struggled against Elona's hold. "Lyon?"

Before Lyon could reach her, the Pondera guard surrounded the two women.

"No." Lyon charged the guards, then rebounded off their linked arms. "Let me through," Lyon yelled.

"Lyon?" Persephone's voice was so soft he could barely hear it.

He stopped fighting. Blood drained from her ears and mouth. Her eyes were completely bloodshot; her tears ran red. The veins in her neck bulged as if a force was squeezing her throat. Her face turned blue.

"Persephone!"

He stumbled back. He opened his mind and demanded the demon answer his call. Nothing.

Persephone gasped. Then, she stopped breathing.

Panic flooded Lyon, swamping his desire for freedom, his need for a single soul. The demon roared front and center and Lyon welcomed it. His claws and canines extended. His body broadened, expanded. His senses blew out until he could smell the sex of every woman in the room. He could hear every heartbeat and every breath taken.

Except Persephone's.

"Last chance, ladies," he said, his voice octaves lower than normal.

The warriors shifted but held.

He stalked around them until he smelled the woman with the heaviest, sour scent of fear. Without warning, he lunged at her, picked her up, and threw her across the room. Fists and spears flashed at him, but he didn't feel any blow or stab. He whirled and kicked and clawed his way through the women until he reached the queen. He grabbed one of her arms and yanked, but she wouldn't release Persephone. He wound the queen's long grey hair around his left wrist, placed his right foot in Persephone's belly, and pushed.

The two women separated, followed by a powerful wave of energy that threw the warriors to the ground. Lyon jumped for Persephone. He wrapped his arms around her and twisted his body before landing on his back with Persephone on top of him, cushioning her fall.

Half the warriors went to their queen. The rest surrounded Lyon. He laid Persephone on the ground and looked for signs of life, but she remained limp, her skin blue, her lips almost black. "Damn you, don't you dare leave me." He gathered her to his chest and rocked her, keening for his loss.

A hand landed on his shoulder.

He snarled. "Get the fuck off me."

The queen squatted down next to him. "She is an extraordinary woman."

"I *will* kill you for this."

"Look at her, Zodiac."

He stopped rocking and looked down. Her face was pale, but no longer blue. He placed a hand on her chest. Her heart was beating, her lungs filled with air. He pulled her tight against his chest and panted as nausea, relief, and joy overwhelmed him.

"Lyon? I can't breathe," Persephone said, her words muffled by his shirt.

He loosened his grip so he could see her face. Other than blue circles under her eyes, her color had returned to normal. He scowled and tried to speak, but the tears choked him. "You. Don't you ever leave me again. That's an order."

* * *

The Pondera warriors escorting Lyon stayed outside of his range as they led him, with Persephone still in his arms, to a small but elegant room. The walls and floors were carved out of the stone, but warm to the touch from thermal vents routed around the living spaces. Living in a caldera had its advantages, and its downfalls—if you could count melting to death in a mass of magma merely a downfall, and not a scrotal-tightening, bowel-loosening, horrific way to die.

Several Pondera maids followed Lyon inside, their arms laden with clean clothes, hot water for a bath, soaps, shampoo, and salves and bandages for Lyon.

He looked around the room. "This will do. Get out."

The maids scurried around the tub, mixing the jugs of hot and cold water until it was perfect, then quickly made their exit. The warriors backed out last, their scowls deeper for the offense Lyon had perpetrated on their queen.

He waited for the door to close before dropping his scowl…and his clothes. He quickly removed Persephone's as well, and stepped into the water. He settled her between his legs, her back against his chest. His body hummed. "Bad timing, guy," he said to his crowing cock. He washed her hair and bathed every inch of her body, then sat quietly while she dozed, rehashing what had happened with Persephone and the queen as the bathwater cooled.

He'd never given the demon utter control before. He'd always been too afraid it would take advantage and he'd be assimilated with no ability to stop it. So, the rare times he did let the demon out, he fought like hell to maintain baseline control.

He dried Persephone carefully and carried her to the bed. He slid under the covers and held her body against his. For the first time in his memory, the demon was right there with him, holding Persephone, loving her as Lyon loved her.

Love? Holy fuck. He had nothing to offer her but a life underground, in the cold and dark of a dungeon cell, or a life spent on the run in the Overworld. How could he shackle her with either option? *Not bloody happening.*

It was good enough for him; it was the life he knew and functioned in. But it wasn't for her. The chill alone would enshroud her, stealing her warmth and spirit.

Llewellyn had it right. In Lyon's brutal world, loving her would make him vulnerable and being vulnerable was tantamount to death. For both of them.

Lyon eased out of the huge bed and tucked Persephone in. He stoked the fire to warm the room and sat in a chair watching Persephone sleep for several minutes. Then, he left. It was time to make the queen talk, damn the consequences if he offended her.

Persephone opened her eyes when the door closed behind Lyon. She pressed her fingers against her temples. The headache pounded and the *lub-dub, whoosh-whoosh* of the blood being shoved through her ears drowned out the ambient noise of the fire and the soft footsteps outside her door. She pulled the covers up to her chin and stared at the small iron chandelier hanging from the ceiling while the memories of the connection with the queen filtered through her mind. As if her brain was an old reel-to-reel tape deck, she was able to rewind and fast forward through the images until she found the start of the vision.

Shadows warred with the pale light of several candles. The inky darkness wound around and through the weak illumination, vying for dominance. Persephone looked around, unnerved by the silence. She stood in the middle of a massive cave, one much larger than that of the Pondera. The walls were far in the distance, the ceiling too high to see.

She pivoted. The vision blurred and shimmered, then settled. A raised dais covered in gold stood at one end. At its foot, several priests were carving a center, middle, and outside ring into the stone floor. To her right, a group of people huddled together, their faces tear-stained, their expressions desperate, their wrists and ankles shackled. Tall, skeletal Creepers herded them to the dais and fanned them out until they formed a living, breathing wall that enclosed the outer circle.

Just as Persephone decided to fast forward the scene, heads turned her way and stared at a point over her shoulder. Her gut clenched; her nape itched. She didn't want to look, but she had to see what was behind her. She closed her eyes and moved her numb feet. She clenched her hands into fists and opened her eyes.

Several yards away, three robed and hooded figures emerged from the dark, led by tall, skeletal Creepers. The small group walked to the circle and pushed through the prisoners until they gained entrance.

Persephone followed. She stopped at the prisoner line and watched the Creepers drop the hoods of the three figures, then gasped when she saw Abella, Taryn, and herself. They were part of this ritual. She tried to push through the line, but this was just a vision—she had no physical mass and no option but to watch.

A woman entered the circle. The Creepers strapped the three women down. The woman cut their wrists and stepped back as the red blood flowed.

The wall of prisoners stirred. Persephone looked to her left and saw Scorpio dragging a bloody Lyon to the circle.

Scor pushed him to his knees. Lyon's swollen face nearly obliterated his features. The Zodiac raised a dagger, and impaled Lyon's throat.

"No!" she yelled. The vision shifted, wavering like a sheet of water, then, with a *pop,* she was jerked back to the present.

Persephone rolled into a ball and cried.

28

"YOU WANT THE TRUTH, ZODIAC? Here it is. Your father and the demon king have freed Circe from her tomb."

"Circe, the witch goddess?"

"Yes. The one who killed your father and the others when they were human."

Lyon sat very still. The witch in the pit and in his father's quarters must have been Circe. *What the hell are you doing, Llewellyn?* "What about Persephone? Who is she? She's not one hundred-percent human."

"That is not for me to say. You'll know when Persephone is ready for you to know."

"She doesn't have a clue, or haven't you noticed?"

The queen remained silent for several seconds. "What about Persephone's companions?"

"Abella and Taryn are foundlings like Persephone."

"Have they any powers?"

"Like what?"

"Anything not human."

"Well, they touched and their house split in half."

She sat up and scooted forward in her throne, her eyes wide, face flushed. "You actually witnessed this?"

Lyon nodded.

"And it happened when they touched?"

"Yes."

The queen stood and started pacing. "Are there any others?"

Lyon shook his head, confused. "No others, just these three women."

The queen stopped in front of him. "Why are you doing this, Zodiac? The women, I mean. Who gave you the order?"

Lyon hesitated. Should he share this with Elona? Goddess only knew the whole picture and Lyon's part to play, but his ignorance grated on him. He needed answers. "Llewellyn told me to bring the three women to the InBetween."

"You didn't do this for nothing."

"The demon soul. Llewellyn will remove it."

The queen stepped back, a corner of her upper lip curled. "You stink of demon and desperation, Zodiac, but I didn't take you for a fool."

Lyon clenched his fists. "What the hell do you mean by that?"

The queen ignored Lyon's question as she gestured to someone behind him. The tall broad-shouldered warrior named Ailith strode across the throne room and took a knee. Long brown hair flowed over her broad shoulders. Her vivid blue eyes flared with fire when she looked at Lyon, her hatred hitting him like a slap.

"Take him to the healer, and have the tracker removed. Then show him to his new room."

"I already have a room."

The queen laughed. "Not anymore you don't. Persephone is mine now. She is a maid of Pondera."

"After what you did to her? I don't trust that she'll be safe here. I can take care of her just fine, I've kept her alive so far."

"Only by the greatest of fortunes have you kept her alive. Goddess knows how, with all your injuries and that tracker in your hand."

Lyon looked down. Outside of the copious scrapes, cuts, and bruises, the only mark was a scorpion sting on the back of his right hand. He rubbed the spot with his thumb. Shit. He'd been out of the game for too long.

"Go," the queen ordered.

The warrior snapped her fingers as she passed Lyon.

Lyon's temper flared as he caught up with the warrior. "You snap those digits again and you lose them."

The warrior snorted. "You followed me, didn't you?"

She pointed to another woman as they walked out of the throne room. The two women flanked him as they strode down a maze of passages until they reached an ancient, warped wood door.

Unlike the throne room's tapestry-covered walls, these walls were lined with bookshelves overflowing with tomes of every size. Rickety stacks of books covered most of the floor space and were piled so high that it looked like a puff of wind or a misstep would send them careening into their neighbors.

An ornately carved desk dominated the room, its surface worn and ink-stained from centuries of use. The warrior pointed to a chair and snapped her fingers again.

Lyon growled.

She grinned, as if she knew what he was thinking and didn't give a damn.

He sat and crossed his arms, unconcerned that he was acting like a petulant child. Circe had been resurrected and he'd been sent on a babysitting job, set up for the murder, chased, shot, had a tracker implanted with a scorpion sting... He'd been insulted, ignored, and more. Petulance was the least-negative emotion coursing through him at the moment.

A door in the back wall led to another, much larger space with more shelves, but these were filled with stoppered bottles of every color and size. A tiny, stooped woman scuttled through the door and snapped two black, sigil-covered curtains closed, blocking off the view of the other room.

She scrunched her face, accenting her numerous, cavernous wrinkles, and squinted at him, then patted her unruly nest of grey hair until she found a pair of glasses made of two monocles cobbled together with something that looked like string.

"He has a tracker in his hand," Ailith said. "The queen wants it removed."

The old woman patted the table surface.

He laid his hand flat on the table, palm down.

She set an old lantern next to his hand to illuminate the welt, then leaned close and studied it for a moment, one hand feeling the books on the table. She grabbed a large book, raised it high, and slammed it down on the welt.

Lyon yelled and jerked his hand, but the woman was tenacious and beyond strong. His nails and canines elongated. He longed to loose the beast on this bitch and rip her head off, but that would only alienate the Novi and give them an excuse to separate him from Persephone. The Novi didn't have much use for males except for breeding—they would send him packing if he caused trouble.

"Hold still or I'll give you another whack."

Lyon breathed through the pain and scanned the title of the book she'd used on him. *Chiromancy for the Modern Chiromancer,* and below that, in smaller letters, *Updated Methodology for the Hand Job of the Future.*

"Of course," he muttered.

The old woman relaxed her grip and turned his hand. There, in the center of his palm, was a tiny, black rice-shaped thorn. She pulled tweezers out of her hair.

"Good goddess, what else you got in there?"

"Whatever I need to be prepared." She plucked the device from his palm and held it to the light before setting it on the table and raising the heavy tome again.

Lyon grabbed the woman's arm. "Wait, I can use this."

"What could you possibly want with it?" Ailith asked.

Lyon picked up the tiny tracker. *Scor wants something to track? I'll make sure he has quite the chase.* "That's my concern, not yours." He tore a corner off the writing vellum to wrap the tracker and pocketed it.

Ailith snapped her fingers at the other warrior. "Take him to his room."

"First, the aviary," Lyon said.

She nodded. "Fine, but the aviary only, no other detours."

The woman escorted Lyon to the birdhouse. He selected a pigeon, tied the vellum-wrapped tracker to its leg, and sent the bird as far west from Yellowstone as it could range.

Leona hid beneath an ancient desk and watched Ailith search the reliquary for her. Finally, the warrior left the room. Leona released her breath, but waited several minutes before crawling out from under the desk.

Where the hell was the book? She'd been searching for hours. She leaned to the side and groaned as her limbs unfurled. Exhaustion weighed her down and she finally succumbed. The stone floor was uncomfortable, but she was too tired to care. She laid on her back for a few minutes, mentally ticking off the places she'd already looked. The Pondera were cautious with their priceless artifacts, but by the goddess, where the hell could they have hidden the two things she needed?

Leona sighed and rolled onto her side. *Time to go. Try again tomorrow.*

She rubbed her face, then planted her palm on the stone to push off the floor when she saw the corner of a box peeking out of the deep shadow under a rickety armoire. She crawled on hands and knees to the armoire and pulled out a dusty chest. A tingle danced down her spine. Her fatigue was swept away by the shot of adrenaline.

She palmed the lock, feeling its weight, and the thick, coarse layer of rust that covered it. She squeezed the metal and giggled when the lock disintegrated in her hand before she lifted the lid. Inside, dust covered a book. Leona stroked the cover clean and frowned at the faded script.

Thick, heavy... The only true account of the Countess Bathory and her practice of blood magic was priceless in any world. Highly sought after for the great power it bestowed on whoever claimed ownership, the descendants of the Countess—a women centric, warrior race called the Bathorys—would sacrifice any number of their own to acquire the grimoire of their high priestess, their mother. The book was a bonus, but not what she wanted.

She added it to her pouch, then reached for the lid when she saw another book—thinner, smaller than the Bathory grimoire. Her heart leapt in her chest, her breath caught in her throat. She closed her eyes for a moment. *Please.*

Leona removed the book and blew on the cover, sending dust up her nose and into her eyes. The adrenaline made her stomach roll. She touched the surface and smiled. *Human skin.* She opened it and gingerly flipped through the pages until she reached the middle, where a square section had been carved into several pages, leaving enough space for a large, heavy silver locket and chain. She lifted the locket, studied the ornate etchings filled with gold, then pulled the chain over her head and slipped the locket inside her shirt to lie against her warm skin. The metal hummed against her flesh as if alive and responding to her life force, ecstatic to be touching living skin instead of old, hand-wrought uterine vellum.

One step closer to my own goal.

She snorted. Llewellyn hadn't even noticed she'd changed. Asmodeus was smart enough to stay out of her way since making her a Zodiac, but she could see him gloating over what he had wrought out of her bone and sinew and odium. Circe had hinted that she knew, but she was wise enough to not challenge Leona now that she was a Zodiac. But her father? He was too busy scheming to see that the source of his impending destruction was one of his own.

After locating books similar in size, she placed them in the chest, and slid it back under the armoire. How did these stupid women protect anything, much less the balance between worlds?

Leona reached for the door and scraped her hand on the trim. "Ouch." A drop of blood appeared on the back of her right hand, but the pain was far deeper than a slight scrape would cause. She crossed the room to the sole light, swiped the blood away, and looked at the small patch of wrinkled, grey skin. She scratched an edge with her thumbnail and the skin peeled back, exposing red, raw tissue. She pulled until the dead skin had separated from the live. "Huh."

Her body was changing, no doubt. She could feel her bones expanding even as her skin contracted, and her swirling, jumbled intellect flew so far over the heads of anyone around her that they acted like she was spewing gibberish at them when she spoke.

She raised her hand and contemplated her molting skin. Evolution was a bitch, but it was her bitch now and she'd damned sure enjoy the journey.

She removed two orbs from her pockets, one small, one large, both half silver and half gold. She twisted the gold half of the small orb to activate it and placed it on the floor. She stepped out of the secret room, but paused before closing the door—she had to make sure the orb detonated. In seconds, the gold top opened like a lotus flower and a fine mist exploded out of the center, coating every surface in the room, obscuring the evidence of Leona's presence from any form of magical sleuthing. Seconds later, the orb shimmered then disappeared in a wink.

Leona quickly closed the door of the secret reliquary, then activated the large orb in the map room before slipping out and traversing the vast warren of passages. "Ridiculously piss-poor security."

She slipped inside her room and locked the door behind her before removing the books from the pouch and hiding them behind an assortment of books that were already in her room. Now that her desire to take her rightful place as Llewellyn's chosen one was gone, now that she had found the Master's most powerful spells and the locket to work them, she was free to soar to unimaginable heights. And if anyone tried to stop her—she covered her mouth and giggled. *They will meet a hot, sticky end.*

Dawn was hours away, and she needed sleep. She stretched out on the bed and smiled. Her job was done, and her brother was here. She patted the blade sheathed at her waist. Soon, she would start the search for Lyon. It was time for the family reunion she'd dreamed of for years.

29

THE WOMEN LED LYON DOWN several passages he hadn't seen before. By the time they stopped at a door, he was so turned around he didn't think he'd ever find his way out. *Probably part of the plan.*

The women unlocked his door and waited for him to enter. He sighed and stepped inside. The door slammed behind him and a pair of heavy bolts slid home. Locked up, again. He prowled around the room. At least the bed looked comfortable, and there was a fireplace with wood stacked inside. He lit a fire and watched the flames devour the starter twigs then lap at the logs, the warm light softening the craggy walls. Lyon had climbed in the bed and closed his eyes when the bolts squeaked and the door opened.

He lay still while the patter of feet crossed to him.

"Lyon?" Persephone asked. "Why are you here?"

"Apparently, I've been demoted. How the hell did you find me?"

"I don't know, I just felt you and the feeling guided me here."

Lyon pulled back the blankets.

Persephone took a step back. "Will you tell me about the demon...uh, inside you?"

Lyon sat up in the bed and stared at the fire. He had avoided this conversation as long as he could; he couldn't bear the thought that she'd turn away from him in fear or disgust. But, she had a right to know the truth, and he needed to know if she would walk away from him because of it. He took a deep breath and sighed.

"Yes, there is demon inside me—or more accurately, a piece of a demon's soul is attached to mine."

She sat down hard on the bed, her shoulders hunched. "Why?"

"The added soul gives us great strength, heightened senses, and, depending on your royal house—"

"The traits of your zodiac signs are enhanced."

"More like perverted, skewed to the dark side of our sign," Lyon clarified.

"But still...why? Why add demon soul to your own?"

"Money, power, influence from the humans. That's why I was created. Why the others were created."

"But you said you've been in a dungeon for years. Are all the Zodiacs kept in the dungeon?"

Lyon rubbed his face with both hands. "I made a terrible mistake after my first assignment, because I couldn't control the demon part of me. The dungeon was the only place to keep me. I wasn't safe then—and truth be told, I'm growing less safe every day. That's why I accepted the mission to take you and the others to the InBetween."

"What do you mean?"

"My mission was to get the three of you to my father. In exchange, he would remove my demon soul."

Persephone nodded. Her teeth ground together as if mustering the courage to say something. "So with us here and Taryn and Abella...not here—"

"My mission is blown. All I can do now is keep you safe."

"And find Taryn and Abella? And the children? We have to go back for the children and get them to safety."

Lyon nodded. He owed her that. "Yes, all of them."

Persephone studied him for several seconds without speaking.

He held his breath, waiting for her to make whatever decision about the emotions swimming behind her eyes. He expected her to weep, or run out of the room. He didn't expect her to slide under the covers and pull them up to her nose, much less snuggle up tight against his naked body.

The blankets settled around them. She placed a hand on his chest before her fingertips began tracing the old scars that marred his thick muscles. Her hand drifted down his abdomen.

He watched her mouth open, and her breathing increase. He had remained still while she explored; she'd had a bitch of a few days, including this latest confession. No way would he demand anything of her—she had to come to him. But the obvious signs of her arousal gave his cock hope of the carnal Holy Grail, not just a touch here, a caress there.

She ran the tips of her fingers along the length of him, then pulled back.

Lyon rolled on his side and stopped her retreat. He placed her hand back on his turgid flesh, then released it. "Don't be shy. Take what you want."

She gripped him, then gasped when the girth of his manhood surged. She looked into his eyes. Her longing and trust combined to create a potent mix that kick-started his passion, protective instinct, and animal nature and braided them into a knot in his heart and gut.

He palmed her cheek, his thumb under her chin. He lifted her head until her mouth was close to his, then stopped just shy of her lips. They parted for him, and he inhaled her soft, warm breath. An electric shock jerked his body, and he stiffened, afraid the demon would try to take over. It surged to the forefront, and Lyon readied himself for a rapid exit from the room. But the demon soul didn't demand control. Instead, it stayed just under his skin, humming with energy and hungry for more.

Persephone released him and ran her hand up to his chest, then thumbed his erect nipple.

A wave of heat started at the point of contact, and swamped the rest of him. His hips jerked forward, his thighs and ass clenched tight. The quiescent demon part of him howled to bury itself inside her. With one casual, fleeting touch she had brought him to the precipice of losing control. He ached for another stroke, another caress, but the intensity threatened to send Lyon over the edge with Persephone clutched in his arms—a fall into darkness from which they might never return.

"Stop. Stop." Lyon gently removed her hand and pulled away.

"What? Why?"

Lyon sat up. "We can't do it this way." He looked at her. "Have you ever?"

"I'm not a virgin, if that's where you're going with this." Her chin jutted. "And I'm not afraid of you."

Lyon stilled. He couldn't remember anyone saying that to him since being imprisoned, but her words didn't count. She had no clue how bad he could get, how out of control, how much blood he had shed. "You should be afraid."

"Of the demon soul in you?"

"Yes, and more."

She pushed up and sat cross-legged next to him, her eyes wide. "Then tell me."

"The demon wants you, too."

"Okayyyy."

"And, I haven't been with a woman…in that way, for a long time."

"And that's a problem because…?"

Lyon clenched his hands. *Why is this so hard?* "When I wanted sex, I would find a willing woman and fuck her."

"You say that like it's a bad thing. I've had sex just for the release."

He scowled, threw back the covers, and started pacing. "It's bad because that's all I've had, it's all I know. Just a release."

She rubbed her chin and cocked her head. "Well, after the past few days I've had…"

He stopped at the side of the bed and slammed his fists against the mattress. "No. No! I don't want to fuck you."

She leaned back and blinked. Her face reddened.

Lyon grabbed his hair with both hands and pulled. "Damn it. I'm screwing this up." He sat on the bed. "Look. I don't want to fuck you. Okay? What I want, what I need, is to make love to you. And, I've never made love to a woman before. I have no idea what to do…well, I know what to do—slot A and tab B and all that rot—" He dropped his head, mortified and unable to look her in the eye.

Persephone laid a hand on his shoulder and squeezed.

He glanced at her, then did a double take. "Well, hell, now I've made you cry."

"Stop your whinging and really look at me."

He raised his head.

"My tears aren't a bad thing. My tears are for all that you've lost, for what was taken from you. I'd like to show you what making love is about."

"But—"

She shifted and held up her hands to make him stop talking. "I get that you're afraid you'll hurt me. But if you're game, I have an idea."

He sucked in a breath. His balls tightened. "Anything."

Persephone looked around the room. "Do you trust me?"

"Yes." The word came out of his mouth before he had a chance to think about it. His ability to trust had ceased to be so many years ago that he barely remembered what it felt like. But this woman, something about her…he trusted her, plain and simple and undeniable.

She climbed across the bed and walked to a small desk. She rifled through the drawers and cubbyholes until she found a small set of shears and brought them to the bed. She laid them on the nightstand, then pushed Lyon's thighs apart. She stepped between them and raised her arms. "Remove my gown."

Lyon's desire nearly overwhelmed him. The thin fabric hid very little from his view: her breasts and hips, her erect nipples, the pale flesh he so longed to hold and touch for the rest of his life. He leaned over and placed his palms on her thighs and slid the gown up, memorizing every curve of her delicious body.

She squirmed when he stroked and squeezed, then sighed when he handed her the gown.

She cut the material into four long strips and held them up to him. "Are you sure?"

Lyon nodded, eager to do whatever she wished.

"Then lay down in the center of the bed."

Goosebumps covered Lyon's body. His desire had filled his cock to bursting.

"Spread your legs and arms."

He obeyed her command. He wanted to smile—hell, he wanted to crow, but instead kept his mouth shut and his expression serious.

Persephone wrapped the material around one of his ankles, then tied it to the bedpost. She bound his other ankle. "Now your wrists."

She tied one wrist, then held up the last strip as she walked around the bed. "Your last chance."

He smiled.

She snorted. "Not too tight?"

He shook his head. "No."

Persephone touched a forefinger to her mouth. "Okay, where to start?"

"Me buried inside you would be good."

"And rush this? Not gonna happen." She climbed into bed and sat on her lower legs as she studied Lyon's body. She lightly touched a scar on his chest, then another on his belly before placing her palm over his heart.

The muscle pounded. His adrenaline and lust triggered a sweat. Damn, if a simple touch could send his sweat glands gushing, this was going to be one bitch of a sweet, wet night.

She straddled his belly, ignoring his heat-seeking missile. It bobbed and danced for her, eager for her attention, but she was an elusive minx, bent on studying his everything else.

Persephone leaned over until her lips hovered over his.

He lifted his head and strained against his bindings, desperate for a taste, but she pulled back.

"Close your eyes."

Lyon dropped his head back and obeyed.

She shifted her body and leaned forward. Her warm breath tickled him for only a moment before she pressed her full lips to his. Tentative, soft, sexy as hell. She opened her mouth; he followed her lead. She nipped his bottom lip, then sucked it into her mouth.

His claws extended. His canines dropped. A low rumble started in his chest. The sound of hunger and need and desire vibrated them both.

Persephone growled back. She lowered her upper body until her nipples touched his, then slowly dragged them back and forth. She moaned as she exhaled, her want sweet in his mouth. She stopped the kiss and opened her legs wide to match Lyon's bound limbs, then slid down until her prone upper body covered his.

Lyon's cock bobbed. The tip glided through her wet sex until it found her entrance. He groaned long and low. All of his desire to be gentle had been scorched in one move.

She reached between them and positioned him so only the very tip of his cock rested inside her.

Lyon shifted his hips, desperate to bury his full length, but she rode out his every effort. "Shit," he groaned.

"Not so fast." She smiled, her eyes twinkling; a confident Siren bent on killing him with lust had replaced the tentative woman. She ran her tongue along his lips until he opened them for her, then scorched him with another kiss.

He rolled his pelvis to bury the head of his cock inside her.

She gasped as he pushed. She dropped her head into his neck and sucked on his tender skin.

Lyon groaned. "By the goddess, you're killing me." He thrust harder, because his body gave him no choice. She rolled her hips to meet his thrust and his entire head entered her wet heat.

He arched his back. His muscles shook as they strained against his restraints.

Persephone panted. "Holy mother."

He fought to relax. "Am I hurting you?"

She shook her head, then looked at him. One corner of her mouth twitched as if she was trying not to smile. "Just. Need. A. Second."

Lyon wanted to puff out his chest and tell her to take all the time she needed to adjust to his girth, but before he could she grabbed the bedding on each side of his head and pushed her body back.

His cock disappeared inside her, impaling her all the way to the hilt. His body bowed again, the pressure of her passage nearly undoing him. His ego declared there was no way he would climax first, but then she withdrew.

He sucked in air, then exhaled an explosive *whoosh* when she impaled herself again.

Persephone rocked back and forth slowly, rhythmically, until Lyon thought he'd pass out from the pleasure of it. He bit his bottom lip until it bled.

She closed her eyes and pushed her upper body off of his chest. Her head dropped back until her long, silver hair brushed his thighs.

"Faster?" she asked between breaths.

"Yeah," he answered with a grunt.

Persephone, the sweet, compassionate woman he'd met only days ago, morphed into the bed partner from his fantasies. She rode him hard and slow, teasing his approaching explosion, pushing it away, then pulling it close again. And just when he thought she couldn't get him any closer to the edge without falling, she found his hidden corners, the parts of him that even he had forgotten existed, and demanded that they open to her. Together, his two souls answered. He quivered for the release that she controlled.

"Please," he begged.

"Don't close your eyes."

He nodded.

She leaned over him and untied his right wrist, then the left.

"Wait. No, don't."

She nailed him with her eyes. The quirk in the corner of her mouth silenced him. He clapped one hand on her waist, and slid the other over her belly until his thumb found the shy, tight nub hiding in her folds.

Persephone shuddered and moaned. "Oh…" she said, her face flushed, her eyes half-closed. "Do it."

Permission granted, he drilled her over and over, their bodies sliding, grinding, slapping. Heat and tension filled him. Closer and closer he came, there, there, there. He shuddered, his lungs stopped filling with air.

Persephone placed her hands on his chest.

He stared into her eyes and found the steel that protected her, the grit that gave her the strength to love despite a terrible childhood, the strength that made her his…his inamorata.

She took his nipples between her thumbs and forefingers and rolled them. "Now."

He growled. "Now."

She pinched the tender buds.

He pressed his thumb against her swollen nub.

Their twin growls changed to roars, and together they fell into blessed oblivion.

30

LEONA SAT IN A CHAIR in the darkest corner of her brother's room, the tip of her blade cutting fine lines in her sensitive fingertips. The heavy smell of sex gagged her, but the locket hadn't stopped vibrating since she'd entered the room, the heavy pulses of energy jacking up her heart rate.

Finding Lyon with the Pondera was a gift. But catching her brother with Persephone in his bed? That was the ribbon on the gift, the jam on a biscuit, better than a table full of fairy heads with layer upon layer of sugared gossamer instead of hair, in shades of red or purple or gold.

The muscles in her body twitched, eager for action, but she forced herself to sit still and wait. The last living embers popping and shifting, the soft scuff of leather slippers in the hallway… She concentrated on every sensory detail so she could recall—with exacting clarity—the moment when she finally had the upper hand with Lyon.

She imagined severing their throats with the slightest flick of her wrist; the squirt of their red blood soaking her clothes, their wide-eyed terror when they figured out they only had minutes to live. But that was too easy for Lyon.

She had held the blade so close to Persephone's face that her breath steamed the metal, her desire to carve his whore's pale flesh so deeply and thoroughly that the only thing holding her face together would be a web of scars, had been near impossible to stave off. It was past time for Leona to pass the 'Untouchable" mantle to someone else, but she stayed her hand so she could savor his horror at being found so vulnerable. 'Vulnerable made you dead' had been drummed into both of them. Time to show Lyon how very true that saying was—and how far he had fallen.

Lyon rolled over and pulled Persephone into the curve of his belly. His sex throbbed, hungry and searching. He opened his eyes and immediately saw Leona sitting in a corner, using her favorite blade to trim her fingernails, a vicious, triumphant smile on her face.

"Holy shit." Lyon jumped out of the bed and crouched, his body between the two women. He grit his teeth and fought the desire to attack Leona for her not-so-subtle threat to Persephone. "How the hell did you find me?"

Leona studied her fingernails. "I came here seeking sanctuary. Imagine my surprise," she said as she gestured at him with one hand.

"Sanctuary, my ass. What are you doing here?"

"A girl can't make new friends?"

"Answer the question." The few hot embers in the fireplace didn't offer much illumination, but Lyon could still see the sickly pallor of Leona's skin, the deep shadows under her eyes. Her face sagged, distorting the four scars, and her full lips were cracked and dry. Her long blonde hair was tawny like his, but this morning, instead of being groomed, it was a rat's nest on her head. There wasn't much that frightened him but the changes in his sister scared the shit out of him. Add to that her proximity to Persephone, and he was near paralyzed.

Rein it in man. She can't know how much Persephone means to you or she'll use it against you.

Leona smirked as if she knew what he was thinking, but said nothing. Her bottom lip started to bleed.

Lyon watched a large drop of blood hang on the edge of her lip, waiting for Leona to wipe it away, but she didn't move. A slave to gravity, the drop fell to her chin and hovered there, clinging to her skin, then lost the battle and landed on her robe, just over her heart.

He picked up his robe and dressed, then pointed to the door. "Get out."

"I missed you too, big brother. Are you going to introduce me to your whore?"

"Watch your mouth."

Persephone sat up, her hair also a rat's nest, but the rest of her was perfect. The sheet slid down, exposing her breasts. "Lyon?"

"This is Leona. My sister."

Persephone gasped and clutched the sheets to her chest. She started scooting to the edge of the bed opposite Leona.

"No, stay. Leona is leaving."

"Ah, what, no family reunion?" Leona asked, her pout belied by the gleam in her bloodshot eyes.

"Why aren't you by Llewellyn's side?"

"I've come to realize that he's the wrong horse to bet on. I need to find my own path. What providence that I should find you here, dear brother."

Leona stood and started to walk to the bed, but Lyon blocked her before she could reach Persephone. A fog of rotten eggs, blood, and infection enveloped him.

Leona peered around Lyon's bulk and leered at Persephone. "You are lovely, but definitely not my brother's type."

Lyon walked into Leona and physically pushed her back to the door. "What have you done to yourself?"

"I'm a new beast. Carved and molded by the deftest of hands."

Lyon leaned close. "Goddess, no. You didn't."

Leona threw her hands in the air. "Tada," she said. "I'm the first female Zodiac."

She grinned at him, her eyes wide and way too crazy for Lyon's comfort. He thought of his first days as a Zodiac: the euphoric high followed by an epic low when he realized he'd killed his mother and maimed Leona. He'd suspected she was involved with the demon in some way, but being turned into a Zodiac... *Aw, hell.*

"I'll go now, but I will be back." She looked at Persephone pointedly, then grinned at Lyon before leaving.

Lyon stared at the closed door, waiting for his heart to stop pounding. Sweat rolled down his spine. "Get dressed," he ordered without looking at Persephone.

"Are you okay?"

"No...yes. Just do it, and quickly."

Lyon escorted Persephone to her room. He went inside first and checked it thoroughly before allowing her to enter. "Stay here, and don't trust Leona for a second."

"Why? I'll admit that was a creepy way to meet her, but she is your sister."

He cupped her face. "She may be my blood kin, but she's not family to me."

"But—"

"No buts. I'm afraid she'll hurt you if given the chance, and I couldn't live with that." He pulled her into his chest and held her. *I love you, I need you, I would die for you.* The words danced on his tongue, eager to be released into the world, but the thick layers of fear and pain and regret clamped his mouth shut. Nothing like the slap of reality to cut through a post-coital glow.

Persephone frowned. "If she's a Zodiac like you, why does she look like she's sick? Did that happen to you?"

Lyon pulled back and released her. His moment of weakness had passed. He ran a hand through his hair and walked to the door. "No. It took me a few days to get used to having demon soul inside me." He looked past Persephone. "Leona... She's done something different." He opened the door. "Lock it behind me."

"Where are you going?"

"To get the whole story out of Leona. Maybe she knows what this madness is about." Lyon left the room.

Once. Just once he'd let his guard down, just once he'd ignored his hard-and-fast rules, and not only did Leona know that Persephone was here, his sister could call down the Zodiacs on his ass.

Love had made him weak, and it sure as shit had made him vulnerable. The question that sent him reeling was, could he overcome his weakness before it killed Persephone, and him?

Persephone paced her room, itching to follow Lyon. The animosity between Lyon and Leona was painful to watch. Physically they were similar—tall, same amber eyes, same thick, tawny hair. There was no doubt that they were related. But the manic, psychotic glee in Leona's eyes belied the dark torment Persephone could see, and it chilled her to the marrow.

A knock on the door stopped her. Before Persephone could answer, the lock opened and the queen swept in, followed by a retinue of young women. Behind them was an old woman, bent at the waist. Her long bones were curved and twisted, her fingers swollen and crooked. She shuffled into the room and closed the door.

The first group of maids bore armfuls of clothes: gorgeous gowns and leather pants and vests that looked more like armor than clothes. The next group carried velvet slippers with intricate embroidery, boots decorated with gold thread and buckles, while others had heavy soles for traveling and thick shafts to protect the wearer's legs. Another group brought in lacy underthings, the kind that Abella wore daily, but that made Persephone itch and rode up her crack. The last group carried a huge copper tub, buckets of hot water, and bottles of shampoos, soaps, and perfumes.

The queen picked out a teal, raw-silk gown with an empire waist and silver and gold threads, and held it up. She took a step forward, but Persephone backed away, her heart racing. The queen smiled and handed the gown to a serving maid. "We're having a feast tonight in honor of our new sisters. This will be perfect." The queen waved over the old woman. "Betta will be tending to any grooming issues." She laid a hand on Betta's shoulder. "She has been with me for years, you can trust her."

The queen clapped her hands. The maids hurried out of the room. As fast as the women had invaded Persephone's room, they disappeared, leaving Persephone alone with Betta.

She turned to the old woman, unsure of what to say.

Betta placed a hand on Persephone's shoulder. "Come, lady. Let's see what we have to work with."

31

LYON STOOD AT THE ENTRANCE of the Pondera cavern, searching for Leona. He'd used his senses to track her, but she'd remained one step ahead of him the entire day. When had little sister become so talented at evasion?

Dozens of women and a smattering of males raced around the space with platters of food and tankards of ale. After spending a few days in the Overworld, the scene reminded Lyon of a medieval castle. Gowns, robes, tankards… He could be in another century.

His nose twitched, and his stomach growled as a platter of meat was carried past him.

A stir at the entrance opposite him heralded the entrance of the queen. The warriors stood at attention, and the room reverberated with the sound of benches and stools scraping across stone.

The queen glided across the floor to the dais, her gown of gold shimmering with each step. Her hair flowed down her back, lengths of gold and silver beads woven in the grey strands. She smiled at her warriors as she passed them, her love for her subjects evident. Had this woman ruled the InBetween, his life and the lives of so many others might have been different.

The queen took her seat.

Lyon turned away. No sense in staying here drooling over the food, he had a sister to find. But before he took a step, he heard the boots of more warriors.

Two women were escorted through the same entrance as the queen.

Leona held her head high, her blond hair piled on top. Her scars were hidden, but nothing could disguise the changes to her face. She'd always despised him for scarring her, for making her the "Untouchable." So what must she think of herself now that her actions were destroying the rest of her beauty?

A chill coursed through him. *What if she didn't care?*

The flowing gown of copper-colored material she wore accentuated her protruding bones, making her look haggard, even cadaverous. He didn't need a healer to tell him what was happening to Leona. She was dying. Instead of bones, she had desperation; instead of muscles and entrails, she had malice; instead of a heart, she had hostility. A walking, talking corpse propelled by her odium for everyone and everything around her.

Lyon pulled his attention away from his sister and glanced at the other woman. Her slim body was encased in a blue-green dress that emphasized her tiny waist and pushed up her firm breasts. A green and blue gemstone-laden net hid her hair, but it emphasized her pale eyes, porcelain skin, and delicate bone structure. She paused at the entrance, as wide-eyed as a doe, then brushed her long, slender neck with one hand as if moving her hair, a nervous gesture he'd seen before.

Persephone. His heart jumped and the rest of him came to attention, stretching his muscles and skin as tight as one of Sag's bows.

She lifted her skirt and climbed the dais steps behind Leona, then took a seat next to the queen.

Lyon pushed past several Pondera guards to get to the dais, but before he reached it a dozen women surrounded him, their swords pointed at various soft spots on his body.

The queen slowly rose. "This is a feast to celebrate the two women who have asked for sanctuary. You, Zodiac, are not invited."

Lyon bared his teeth and hissed.

Persephone rose out of her seat, her face flushed, her chin set. "If Lyon is not welcome, then I must excuse myself."

"Persephone, no," Lyon said.

The queen remained silent.

Persephone stepped away from her chair.

The queen's guard pulled a dagger and crouched. "Shall I slit her throat, my queen?"

Lyon mirrored the warrior's aggressive stance and, with a flip of his hands, his claws extended. He growled low and long.

The queen glanced at Lyon and then turned back to Persephone, her smile incredulous, with a hint of amusement. "Stand down, Ailith."

The warrior straightened and backed away, but did not sheath her blade.

Persephone laid her crushed cloth napkin on the table and raised her chin higher without breaking eye contact with the queen.

The queen nodded. "I can see you're serious. Bring a chair for him."

Lyon pushed past the guards.

Before he could reach Persephone's side, the queen pointed to Leona. "And place it next to his sister. I'm sure you both have plenty of catching up to do." She smiled at Lyon, but it didn't quite reach her eyes.

He stopped cold. She wasn't going to make it easy for him, or pleasant. But at least he'd be able to keep an eye on Persephone. He changed direction and sat in the chair next to Leona. He remained silent while the servants laid a plate and utensils for him.

Persephone took her seat. "Thank you."

The queen patted her hand. "Of course, dear. It's refreshing to be schooled in manners after so many years."

The red flush covering Persephone's face flowed south, blooming across her neck and chest. At least she understood the queen's rebuke and how close she'd come to trouble.

"Your whore isn't going to last long if she can't observe the niceties better than that," Leona hissed in his ear. "But what does she need with longevity, right?"

Lyon looked at her. "What the fuck do you mean by that?"

Leona smirked.

He gripped her elbow and squeezed. "And spare me the cryptic crap. I've had it spewed at me at every turn."

Two males stopped behind Lyon and Leona, their hands full of food and drink. Lyon wanted to order the servers away and get answers, but this wasn't the time to make a scene. He released Leona's arm and sat back, waiting for the males to finish. He glanced down the table and saw Persephone scowling at him. *Goddess help me, I'm surrounded by unhappy females.*

The servers backed away and Lyon dearly wanted to go with them.

Leona giggled. "My, you are smitten with her." She tsked and turned her attention to her plate.

Lyon reached for her arm again, but she glanced at his lap. He followed her gaze to find her five claws extended and hovering over his crotch.

"Hands off, brother."

"Answer my questions and I will." He returned Leona's stare until she turned her attention to the food.

"I have nothing to tell you," she said as she ripped a whole chicken in half.

"I know that's not true."

She slurped the meat off the breastbone. "Huh, you got me. More like, I'll never tell you."

"Hell, Leona, do you hate me so much?"

She dropped the bone and looked down at her plate. A shiny line of fat ran down her chin. "More than you could possibly imagine."

Lyon grit his teeth and pushed away his full plate, his appetite gone. "All right, I deserve that. But why become a Zodiac?"

She turned her head slowly and looked Lyon in the eye. All of her sarcasm and pretense were gone, leaving only the essence of the woman. In the seconds between one breath and another he had his answer. His gut dropped to the floor. "You did this for Llewellyn."

She blinked and the cold, hard steel returned to her warm amber eyes before she dropped them back to the chicken. "Originally, yes. No longer."

"Then for goddess' sake, stop."

She bared her teeth. "Not until I have crushed him under my boot. Not until he sees what his neglect and contempt have wrought. He carved me into a new animal," she hissed, "and I am ravenous."

Lyon swallowed hard to push down his fear. "At least tell me why Llewellyn wants Persephone and her friends."

Leona turned away and started speaking with the queen. Her non-answer was her answer; she wouldn't be helping him in any way.

Lyon pulled his plate closer and worked his way through the food. It tasted like ash, but he forced it down—his body needed the fuel, but to keep his mind clear, he drank sparingly of the wines offered.

Lyon pushed his empty plate away and sipped his wine. A wave of exhaustion rolled over him, his eyes itchy and dry. He pushed his chair back, but when he tried to stand, his legs wobbled. The cavern undulated before him. He blinked to stop it, but when he looked again, the space was surrounded by a growing blackness, like he was moving backward in a dark tunnel.

"Lyon?" Persephone asked.

He opened his mouth to answer, but nothing came out. Several hands grabbed his arms and kept him from hitting the floor. The queen's order to take him to his room was the last thing he heard before the world slipped away.

Persephone raced after Lyon's escort, manners be damned. Before she could catch them, a hand clamped down on her shoulder. Persephone slid to an awkward stop, jerked out of the hold, and turned.

Leona raised her hands. "Sorry, didn't mean to surprise you."

Persephone took a deep breath.

"You care very much for my brother, don't you?"

"Yes. Why don't you?"

"For reasons that aren't important right now, we are estranged. But I'm afraid Lyon's life is now forfeit. The other Zodiacs believe he murdered their fathers. Without proof to the contrary, Llewellyn has no choice but to let them have the justice they demand."

"But he didn't kill those men," Persephone said. "He was with me."

"Then you're his alibi." Leona took Persephone's hands. "You care about Lyon, maybe even love him. Come with me to the InBetween and tell Llewellyn what you know. It's Lyon's only chance."

"I must speak with Lyon, convince him to go with me."

"You know how stubborn he is, how proud. He'll never accept your help."

Persephone studied the floor. Her body flushed hot then cold as she imagined how angry he would be. But how could she not risk his ire if it meant saving his life? Besides, going to the InBetween meant rejoining Abella and Taryn, which was a definite bonus. "You're right, he would be angry at me for trying. But it's his life—I have to convince him to come with us."

Leona's eyes flashed and Persephone thought she saw triumph in the amber. She blinked and looked again, but Leona's expression was flat—there was no glint or glimmer, just concern.

"Okay," Leona said. "Use this to find me, with or without Lyon." Leona handed Persephone a folded piece of paper. "On one side are instructions on how to get out of this labyrinth. The other side has a map to a meeting place. I'll wait for you until midnight. If you show, I'll get you safely to the InBetween, where we can straighten out this mess with Llewellyn and the Zodiacs so Lyon can return home. If you don't show…" Leona shrugged her shoulders, and walked away.

32

PERSEPHONE HELD LYON'S HAND while the Pondera healer gave him a bright purple draught. "Will this wake him?"

The woman wiped his lips and nodded. "He will wake soon."

"Did someone drug him?"

The flames in the fireplace wavered. "I'd like the answer to that question, as well," the queen said as she walked into the room. She stopped at the end of Lyon's bed.

The healer bowed her head. "Yes, I believe his wine was drugged."

Persephone gripped Lyon's hand tighter, fury and frustration and fear battering her. "I thought we were safe here." She released his hand and stood, her body trembling. "As soon as he wakes, we're leaving."

A hand took hold of her wrist and squeezed. "Persephone?"

She sat and took his hand between hers. "Hey, there you are. You gave me a fright."

He struggled to sit up. "What happened?"

The queen walked to the side of the bed and stood behind Persephone. "You were drugged, and I take that as a personal affront." She looked at the healer. "Take good care of him." She patted Persephone's shoulder, then left the room.

"Could all of you leave us?" Persephone asked.

After the women walked out, Persephone helped Lyon sit up. She sat on the bed, but what she really wanted to do was dance around the room. "I have great news."

He rubbed his face with both hands and yawned. "Oh?"

"Leona is willing to help us get into the InBetween."

Lyon's expression remained neutral, but he dropped his hands and fisted the blanket.

Persephone's stomach sank. This wasn't going well. "But…wait, that's not all. She said if we come back to the InBetween with her, I…we can speak with your father. We can prove you didn't kill those men."

Lyon's face crumpled into a deep frown. "Persephone, no. I told you not to trust her. You don't know my father. He's brutal and cruel and Leona's learned her best tricks from him." He shook his head and took one of her hands. "No, you're not going. You're staying with me, here, where it's safe."

Persephone's heart skipped a beat. Sweat rolled down her spine. She stood. "And what about Abella and Taryn? I'm supposed to leave them there?"

He held out a hand for her. "We'll find a way to get them out."

Persephone crossed her arms and backed out of his reach. "When? In a week, two weeks, a month? What will happen to them while we figure out what to do? Will he hurt them?"

Lyon sagged back. "He is capable of that, yes."

Frustration and pain filled her. She paced the room to burn off her mounting anger before it exploded inside her and she said something she'd regret. "You said you don't know why your father wants us. The queen says something is about to happen, something bad, and it involves the paranormal children. Do you agree with what she said about sacrifices having to be made? Do you think those children's lives mean nothing? That they don't matter? You can't show me this world of yours, so filled with pain, and expect me to turn my back on it. Because if you do, you're not the man I thought you were."

He opened his mouth to speak.

Persephone held up a hand. "I'm not done yet."

He crossed his arms and shut his mouth.

She wrung her hands, her throat tightened with unshed tears. "Whatever is about to happen, Abella, Taryn, and I are at the core of it. And you have to help me stop it."

"I can't go back." Lyon threw back the bed covers and rose. "My mission is over. I failed. Llewellyn will never remove the demon soul now. He'll throw me in the lowest dungeons for the rest of my life, which will be decidedly shortened when the demon takes permanent control of me. If I have you, I still have a chance to earn my freedom." He reached for her.

Persephone covered her mouth and staggered back, her eyes burning with her welling tears. "So nothing has changed—I'm still just a means to an end? Your prize?"

Lyon raked his fingers through his hair and started pacing. "Yes. No. Hell, I don't know anymore. You make me forget who I am, what I am."

"If, after everything we've been through, you really believe I would choose safety over my family…" She shook her head. "Making you forget who you are? Right now, I think that's a good thing."

He stopped in front of her, his face bright red, his eyes glowing gold. "No. It's the very worst thing."

She stepped into him, her fists clenched. "Why?"

He turned away and resumed prowling the room. "You make me weak."

Persephone followed him. "Why?" she demanded.

"You just do," he shot back.

"Answer the question!"

"Because!" He stopped moving, and she ran into his back. He turned around and grabbed her arms. "Why won't you drop this?"

Persephone's mouth fell open. Her heart flip-flopped in her chest. "Because I love you."

Lyon released her and stepped back, his face a dark red. He bared his teeth and hissed like a wounded animal. "No! You take that back before it...before *I* destroy you."

Too late. Tears filled her eyes. She bit the inside of her cheek and willed them away. She had bared her soul, and he acted like it was the end of the world. *I'm such a fool.* "How can you believe love is such a bad thing?"

Lyon's shoulders sagged, and he rubbed his forehead. He dropped into a large chair by the fireplace. "I became the first Zodiac when I was sixteen. I was young and foolish and I royally fucked up my first mission. When I returned to the InBetween, Llewellyn and I argued."

Persephone stepped closer to him, but said nothing.

He stared off in space as if the memory was playing in his head. "I was so angry and defensive, and the demon was clamoring for control. My mother and Leona tried to stop us, but Llewellyn just kept pushing, berating me about my failure."

He blinked and looked down at his hands. "My mother came up behind me. She touched my shoulder—" He cleared his throat and scowled, then looked at Persephone, his eyes flat and distant but unable to hide his agony.

"I killed her, Persephone—all but gutted her. Leona tried to stop me and I shredded her face. They were the two people I loved most in the world, and I destroyed them."

Persephone sat next to him, her heart aching for the boy who had made a mistake and the man who suffered still. She covered one of his hands, but remained silent.

He pulled away from her. "Now you know why you and I... It could never work. Loving me is a death sentence."

"Would your mother want you to give up on love because of an accident?"

He sat silent for a moment before shaking his head. "No, but that doesn't mean she'd be right."

Persephone shook her head. "I don't believe that, and I don't think you really believe it, either."

"Why?"

"Everything you've done since the moment you saved me from Scorpio. You saved my friends and me, despite the odds against us. Back in the caves, you fed all of us, including the dogs, before you fed yourself. You carried Candace, even after she ralphed down your back."

"The mission demanded it."

"Perhaps some of it did, but not all."

He took her hands. "Stay here, and let the Pondera keep you safe. I'll find a way to get Abella and Taryn for you."

Persephone pulled away in utter defeat, her body suddenly hollow and folding in on itself. "It's late, and you need to rest."

"Persephone?"

"We'll talk in the morning." She slipped out of his room and ran to escape the pain but it dogged her, choking her until she made it to her room and vomited.

Lyon climbed into his bed, exhausted. He closed his eyes, but the look on Persephone's face chased away sleep. So much pain, and he'd put it there. But he'd had to do it: he had to wall off his feelings to keep her safe.

"What a fool you are," the demon whispered.

"Shut up."

"You love her."

"Stop talking."

"You love her."

"Yes! I love her! Are you happy?"

The door opened and two guards stepped inside.

Lyon shook his head. "I'm fine."

They exchanged a glance and backed out.

"Go to her. Tell her."

"No. My mother died because I lost control. Losing Persephone would be the end of me."

"Haven't you lost her already?"

Persephone paced in her room, checking the time with each turn. Her heart broke for Lyon. A boy barely out of his childhood had been made a killer, and expected to control the active, evil entity attached to his innocent soul. Then, after he'd killed his mother and maimed his sister, he was thrown into a dungeon and left to rot, mired in mental agony and subjected to extensive torture, if the web of scars that covered his body told the tale.

She had fallen in love with a demon-tainted assassin from a paranormal world who had committed unintentional matricide. Small wonder he was afraid that he would lose control and kill her. *So why aren't I afraid of him?*

She sat on the bed and ran her fingers over the leather clothes still laid out for her. She was no closer to real answers now than she had been the night Lyon saved her. As much as she hated leaving Lyon behind, he didn't love her. Abella and Taryn were her family and they needed her. It was time to go.

Maybe, while she was there, she could convince Llewellyn that Lyon was innocent so the Zodiacs would be called off and Lyon could come to her. It wasn't much to hang her hope on, but she had to try—for both of them.

She unzipped the gown, and the lovely silk fell to the floor. She held up the leather pants. "So not me." She wriggled into them, then donned the vest and laced up the heavy-soled boots. She walked to the full-length mirror and stared at her updo and red eyes. She pulled off the jeweled net and removed the pins holding her hair in place. The silver locks flowed down her back.

"You can do this," she said to her reflection. She wanted to smile, to stand up straight and true like the warrior Ailith, but she didn't have the energy to pull it off. *Guess clothes don't make the girl after all.* She sighed and looked around the room. Persephone opened the note containing the directions Leona had given her.

"I'm coming, my sisters."

It took her two hours to work her way through the Pondera caves, avoiding guards as she went. When she finally reached the outside, she breathed deep the crisp air and admired the bright stars and moon before starting the hike. After what seemed like hours, covered in sweat and dirt from the three face-plants that had turned her black leathers brown, Persephone finally reached the meeting place and looked around for Leona. She checked the map again. "This is the place. Am I too late?"

A *click-click-click* drew Persephone's attention to the ground. A scorpion scurried over a rock, only a couple of inches from her boot. Before she could think, she stomped on it.

"That's no way to treat your escort's pet." Leona appeared from the darkest shadows. "I'm glad you've decided to come."

Persephone took a step, then stopped. A huge dark figure loomed behind Leona. It stepped forward until Persephone could see his face.

"You!" She lunged at the Zodiac, her fingers curved to inflict the most damage. She swiped at his face and neck, stripping several pieces of skin from him.

Scor blocked her other attempts to scratch him, but didn't hurt her.

"Persephone, no. We need his protection."

"Screw that, I'm going to flay him alive."

"And who will speak for Lyon if you are hurt or killed? If you want to save him, then accept Scorpio's help."

Persephone backed away, but kept her claws at the ready. She pointed at Scor. "You. Stay away from me."

"Gladly."

The three worked their way down the steep hill.

Persephone slipped on vegetation for the third time. "Why does Llewellyn want my friends and me? And what about the stolen children? How do they figure into this? Do you know what the Quietus is?"

Leona remained silent.

Persephone repeated the questions.

Leona growled. "Goddess, grant me peace." She turned on Persephone and punched her in the face. Persephone fell to the ground. Leona stood over her for a moment before kicking her in the ribs and gut. Persephone curled into a ball and wrapped her arms around her head, trapped between the desire to faint so the pain would stop and the fear that she would never wake if she did.

Suddenly, the kicking ended. Persephone opened her eyes. Scorpio had his back to her, his arms extended to block Leona. "I love a good beating more than anyone, but not when they can't fight back."

Persephone watched as Leona circled around him, Scorpio blocking her step for step. "Out of my way, Zodiac."

"No."

Leona crouched, raised her fists, then punched Scorpio in the gut. He flew backward over Persephone and landed several feet away. He doubled over and writhed.

Persephone wanted to cry, but it hurt too much to breathe. Squeezing out a few tears would be agony.

She rolled her head back in time to see Leona grab a handful of Scorpio's black hair and lift his head. "The old ways are over. When I'm done, there will be new Zodiacs to replace all of you inept relics." She patted his cheek. "But don't fret, you'll be kept alive. We'll be needing breeders, after all."

Leona pulled Scor to his feet and pointed to Persephone. "Pick her up, big boy. There is much work to do."

33

TARYN AND ABELLA HUDDLED close in the back seat of the Hummer whispering, while Libra and Taurus scowled at their truck stop, microwaved burritos.

"So we go to the bathroom together, then sneak out the back door," Taryn said quietly.

"And find a trucker willing to give us a ride," Abella finished.

"Then what?"

"What do you mean?"

"Where do we go? How do we find Persephone?"

"I don't think we can."

Taryn frowned and dropped her head lower. "We've been together since we were in diapers. Why don't we have that thing?"

"Okay, you've lost me."

"Come on, you know—that thing. That we're-so-close-you-have–to-scrape-us-apart-with-a-spatula thing. Where we can feel each other from thousands of miles away." She clenched her hands and leaned closer. "Back in the caves you said you were sure Persephone was alive, that you'd feel it if she wasn't. Where did that go?"

Abella stared at Taryn. "I don't know. We're too far away now? You seriously expect me to have an answer?" She ran a hand through her spiky hair. "Pump the brakes on the tangent and bring it back to getting out of here."

Libra cleared his throat. "What are you two doing?"

Taryn hit Abella's thigh.

"We need to go to the bathroom." Abella looked in the rearview mirror to catch his eye. "Who's taking us?"

"Together? I think not," Libra answered.

"Why? What could we possibly do?" Taryn asked.

Libra and Taurus turned around and looked at the women, their eyebrows arched high.

Libra snorted. "Does the word destruction ring a bell?"

"Oh, right." Abella sat back. "How about one of you joins us in the bathroom. We can't get up to anything then."

Taryn jerked her head to Abella. "Have you lost your mind?"

"They wouldn't be in the stall with us."

Taurus raised a hand. "I volunteer."

Abella watched Libra's smile fade. "Both of us are going."

Ignoring Taryn's death stare, she shrugged her shoulders. "Let's go."

The men unlocked the Hummer doors from the outside and each took a woman by the arm. The large truck stop was an oasis of fluorescent light and food and fumes in the dark of the cold and rainy North Texas night. The foursome crossed the shiny tarmac, weaving through semis and the occasional car until they reached the store.

Taurus stopped short of the double doors. "You give us trouble and we will separate you two for the rest of the trip."

Abella sneered at the huge man but held her tongue, mostly because she had no clue what she could do to get free of them. She ran through scenarios as they stopped and started through the many customers shopping the rows of junk food, porn mags, and soda fountains.

Before she could devise a brilliant plan, they were at the restroom. "And for the first time in history, there's no line," she muttered under her breath.

Abella scanned the large space. Six individual stalls on the right, same amount of sinks on the left. On the back wall were four showers tiled in a wild, hippy-dippy-color pattern, great for the woman truckers to get rid of the hours-old crotch stink that is the bane of all folks who sit for a living, fodder for the snap-happy tourists who see their entire vacation through a viewfinder, and salvation for the mothers who spend half of their time in the car with baby puke on their shirts and diaper ooze on their pants.

Libra and Taurus released them and locked the door, then leaned against the wall and crossed their arms.

"Go to it ladies," Taurus said.

Taryn stamped her foot. "Ugh, at least put your fingers in your ears."

The Zodiacs glanced at each other, then laughed.

Taryn whirled and stomped off to the last stall, then slammed the door.

Libra elbowed Taurus.

Abella cocked her head and looked at the men standing so close their arms were almost touching. She took a step back, a smile cracking her lips, before she retreated to the stall next to Taryn's. *Plan officially formulated.*

"What are you doing, Abella?"

"Togetherness is a good thing."

"Not while I'm on the loo."

"I'm telling you, togetherness is good. We've been in the fire so often, working together was the only way we got through."

Taryn's hand appeared under the stall wall, her thumb up.

She got it.

"Come on you two, enough chatter, time to hit the road," Libra said.

Abella finished her business, then washed her hands avoiding Taryn's eyes. No sense giving the Zodiacs a clue.

Taurus waved them forward.

They walked to the men.

Abella held up both hands, then slammed her palms on their chests. "Now!"

Taryn slapped her hands on top of Abella's. Unlike in the cave, the glowing yellow energy surged through them and into the Zodiacs in an instant.

Libra and Taurus flew back and crashed into the door. They slid down the wall, clutching their chests before collapsing on the floor.

Abella and Taryn checked their pulses. "They're alive. Let's go," Abella said.

They shoved Libra aside and opened the door. Abella glanced in the hall then pointed to the back door. "There." She ran to it and shoved the push bar hard. The emergency alarm shrieked, chasing the women as they staggered through the doorway and into the night.

"Hustle up, Taryn, we need a ride."

They ran to the closest row of trucks and waved. One, two, three truckers looked away, ignoring their cries for help. Finally, the fourth trucker honked. A woman opened the cab door and waved them over. "Come on."

Abella and Taryn ran to her.

Abella looked back at the store. "Please. We need a ride."

"Those two boys with you didn't look too friendly."

Taryn swiped at her face as if she was crying. "If we don't get away from them, they're gonna hurt us bad."

The trucker frowned. "I hate a man who hits. Get in, Thelma and Louise. Let's put some miles between you and them."

Abella and Taryn ran around the truck and clambered in.

The trucker released her emergency brake and pulled forward, easing her way through the other semis. Finally, they reached the interstate ramp and the truck picked up speed.

Abella sat back and closed her eyes. They made it. "Where you headed?"

"Down 35, then west on 10."

"You going past Sonora?"

"Yep."

"Perfect."

Taryn yawned.

"Climb on back. There's room to stretch out."

Taryn worked her way over Abella without touching and disappeared. A muffled 'thank you' came from the back. In seconds came the first soft snore.

"Y'all must be tired."

"It's been a long few days."

"Strap in and get a little shut eye. I'll wake you when we're there."

Abella closed her eyes and drifted. Minutes may have gone, maybe hours, but before she could fall into a restful sleep the trucker cursed. Abella opened her eyes and her heart leapt to her throat.

In the dark and wet, on the blessedly empty interstate, a Hummer was parked across the dividing line between the two lanes, leaving no room for the semi to pass without going onto the grass and dirt. At the speed they were traveling, that was a death sentence.

Taurus stood several feet in front of the vehicle, his legs and arms spread, and his knees soft as if he planned to tackle the truck.

"Holy shit." The trucker slammed on her brake and fought the wheel, but there was no way to stop in time. "Brace yourself!"

Abella grabbed a strap with her right hand and an edge of the console with her left. "Taryn, get down and hold on!"

The truck bucked and tried to jackknife, but the woman was experienced. She growled. "Get the fuck outta the way!"

Taurus lowered his upper body.

Abella blinked.

Horns erupted from his head. His body thickened until he looked like a bull. He stood rooted in place until the truck was only a few feet away from crushing him, then he charged the cab.

"What the hell?" the trucker yelled.

Taurus rammed the grill.

Momentum threw the women forward and the cab and trailer up in the air. The world went topsy-turvy. The refrigerated rig landed upside down in the road. Pallets loaded with boxes of steaks flew in every direction.

Abella hung from her seatbelt, too dazed to move when her door was ripped off the hinges and Taurus appeared, his eyes wild and his nostrils flared.

He pulled a blade and cut her seatbelt but didn't try to catch her. She landed on the back of her neck, then slowly toppled out of the cab.

Taurus said nothing. He just grabbed her, threw her over his shoulder, and marched to the Hummer.

She was too dazed to fight him or complain when he threw her inside and slammed the door. She watched, numb, as Libra retrieved Taryn and returned.

The men climbed in the front seat. Libra looked out the front windshield. "Do that again and I'll kill the human helping you. Understand?"

Abella nodded and closed her eyes, but said nothing. *What is there to say?*

34

AFTER HOURS OF ALTERNATING between pacing in his room and flopping under the sheets, Lyon slipped into the passageway and made his way to Persephone's room. He hid in a dark alcove near her door and listened for several minutes, but the hall was deserted. No one had followed him.

He slipped inside the room. The fire was nearly out, but the chill in the air wasn't from the lack of fire. The room felt…empty. She was gone. He could feel it to his core.

He walked to the bed and lifted the covers. A vice grip of fear squeezed his heart, his gut. He stepped back until he tripped on the dress she'd worn for the feast—the one she'd been wearing when she said she loved him.

He stormed out of her room, his heart pounding as fast as his shifting emotions. The demon surged forward, doubling down on his dread and loss. He wanted to run, but the numbing weight of guilt slowed his feet and legs. Slogging through thick mud would have been easier.

He shoved his way past the Pondera guards and entered the queen's quarters, interrupting a meeting. The warriors surrounded him, their weapons drawn.

"Stop, let him go." The queen stood and waved the women away. "Why are you here?"

"Where is Persephone? What have you done with her?"

"What do you mean?"

"She's not in her room."

The queen snapped her fingers and four of the guards stepped forward. "Find her."

The guards left the room. The queen waved to a chair. "Sit."

He did as she asked, but he couldn't stop his legs from bouncing. He needed to move, to run down the halls, anything to burn off his nervous energy.

The queen sat down and steepled her hands. "You're obviously agitated. Why do you care, Zodiac? It's not like your demon soul can be removed."

He stopped twitching and stared at her.

"Answer the question, Lyon."

The four guards rushed back into the room. One of the women shook her head.

Lyon jumped up. "What the hell did you do?"

The warriors hissed, but the queen waved them away. "I did nothing to her. She is important to me as well, Zodiac." She picked up a hairbrush. A maid took it from her and started brushing the queen's hair. "Take him to his sister. See if she knows where Persephone is."

Ailith and her warriors walked Lyon out of the queen's chambers. She ordered them to hold him in the hall, returned to the queen, and took a knee.

"My queen, he is Llewellyn's son, he must know something that will help us learn the truth. Please allow me to question him and find out what he knows."

The queen shook her head. "He doesn't know anything that will help us. Even if he had answers, it's too late to stop it. Quietus signs are everywhere. We need to ready ourselves here to minimize the destruction." The queen touched the warrior's bowed head. "Now go. Take the Zodiac to his sister's room. And send out word to our warriors to watch for Leona, Persephone, and Persephone's friends, if it's not too late. They are not to let them any of them pass into the InBetween."

"If they do capture them?"

"Bring them here and keep them under guard at all times. Maybe they will be enough to stop what's coming."

The women escorted Lyon to Leona's room and watched as he tore the room apart. Nothing. Leona was gone.

Two maids tried to leave, but he cornered them. "Did you remove anything?"

They squeaked and cowered away from him, too frightened to speak.

Ailith shoved him aside. "Back off."

He snarled.

She aped him and stepped into his space until he relented, then turned to the maids. "The bedding has been changed and the waste removed?" she asked the frightened girls. They nodded.

"Where are they?" Lyon demanded.

They pointed to two sacks in the hall.

Lyon upended the contents onto the floor. He dug through the bedding, shaking each piece. Nothing. He ripped open the bag of trash and dumped it on the bedding. He crawled on his hands and knees checking every scrap of paper until he found a wadded piece of parchment.

He opened it. *Thank you, brother, for handing me the key to the kingdom. Too bad your lover has to die for your ineptitude.*

Panic set in. Lyon's belly rolled; vomiting was next. "Take me back to your queen. Now!"

Moments later, Lyon strode to the queen and slapped the note on her vanity. "What does she mean by 'die'?" He slammed his fist down and cracked the wood surface. "Damn it, you were supposed to protect her. Leona did this—and under your nose, no less."

The queen held up a hand.

Lyon glanced around and saw more warriors had entered the room and were surrounding him, ready to tear him apart. But his rage was too far gone, he didn't care. "You have to help me get Persephone back."

The queen shook her head. "I want to find her as well, but I can only spare two of my warriors to help you." She snapped her fingers. Ailith and another warrior stepped up. "The rest are needed to stop your father."

"You said she was important. You said—" He paused as the meaning of her words registered. "Damn it, you won't get within a hundred miles of the InBetween. He has too many on his side, and the rest are too cowed to go against him. Even if you managed to get to the entrance of the InBetween, no one from the inside will help you breech it."

"There is one person who can get inside." She stared at Lyon.

He rotated the metal wristband. Fessa, the old woman at the outpost, had warned him not to lose his band—it was his only way back in. "Even if I can get back inside, I don't have the strength to fight my way through to the main entrance."

"You could, though," she said, her stare unblinking. "Everything you need is already inside you."

He backed away from the woman until a chair hit the backs of his knees and he sagged into it.

The queen clapped her hands. The maids left her room, leaving only the two of them. She lifted a decanter. "You must ask yourself, what are you willing to do to change your fate? To change hers?" She filled the glass with a dark amber liquid—fairy liquor, no doubt. "Take your time. I'll be back." She walked out of the chamber and closed the door.

Assimilation. Melding his soul with the demon soul—permanently. That's what the woman hinted at. After Lyon had lost control of the demon soul, Scorpio had been created—and soon after, went off the rails. Two Zodiacs, two failures. Llewellyn and the demon king realized Lyon and Scorpio had failed because the two souls inside them were not assimilated. So, the remaining

Zodiacs had a second ritual to help them fuse their souls. Even knowing that assimilating would end his suffering, Lyon continued to fight it. He was too afraid that accepting the demon soul would result in the loss of his free will and he would cease to be.

But Persephone's life was at stake.

What he'd once considered a sacrifice was now the only clear path to saving her. Instead of fighting the part of him that came from the demon, Lyon needed to work with it. He needed to let go of his past and integrate the dark and light inside him.

Fear raised its ugly head, demanding answers to the questions that filled his mind. What kind of man did he want to be from this moment on? Should he run and hide and live with what had defined him to date? Or dare to become a new man with a future unwritten?

If this was his moment, if this was his time to make a stand, then he had to be the best version of himself he could possibly be. He had to let go of his fear of change, be unafraid to shed his old identity, and forge a new one.

He had to give up the only thing he'd ever wanted for the thing he now desperately needed: the strength to save the woman he loved. It was time to stop fighting the demon soul, and accept it as a part of who he was meant to be.

Lyon sat up, his choice clear. "Yes." He rushed to the door and opened it.

The queen stood in the hall with her guards, her arms crossed.

He shouldn't have been surprised that she knew exactly what he was doing. "Seems we're on the same page. You know someone who can help me?"

"Come with me."

She led him down several passages, then down an iron spiral staircase so wide he could drive a car down it. A guard stopped at a wood door and opened it, then gestured for Lyon to enter.

A blast of hot air hit him when he stepped inside the huge chamber. Rickety wood shelves sagged under the weight of jars and bowls filled with goddess only knew what. Three fires roared, the flames dancing up the sides of huge iron cauldrons. Their boiling contents released a hovering, misty cloud of tear-inducing sulfur and excrement and rot.

Scattered around the room were several old crones garbed in robes of various muted shades of brown, green, and ochre. They stopped their stirring and grinding and turned to Lyon and their queen. Another hag, dressed in a crimson robe, shoved the others aside and stopped a few feet shy of the queen. She leaned one way then the other, her joints complaining as she sagged. The rest of the women followed her down into a painful, slow-motion curtsy.

Lyon winced at the cacophony of *snap-crackle-pops*.

"My queen," the crimson-clad elder crone said, "what can we do for you?"

"Stand, ladies, do not tax your joints so."

The crones rose as one, their struggle painful to watch.

The queen turned to Lyon. "If you're sure."

"I'm sure."

The queen waved the elder crone over. "Come, he needs your help."

The crone nodded and hobbled to Lyon. She looked him up and down, then pinched his cheek. She 'humphed' and held out her hand to him.

He took it and followed her deeper into the room. The women surrounded him. He looked back, but the queen was gone. "You can tell me how to assimilate?"

The crone nodded.

"I need to stay awake for this so I can leave right after it's done. Can you do that?"

"It will be painful, but if you are properly motivated, you can survive the ritual awake. But be warned, just because it can be done doesn't mean it should be done."

"What do you mean?"

"Ripping open a soul is nasty business. It will weaken you for a time."

A memory of Persephone smiling swept through him. It filled him with hope, then morphed into an image of her face pale in death. "I have no choice."

The elder crone shrugged. "If you are to stay awake for this, then find a memory, a good, strong one, and hang on to it. It will be your touchstone, your way back."

"My way back?"

"To the light," she said as she looked around the chamber. "Whatever you do, don't let your fear control you, or you will be lost forever."

"I'll die."

She nodded. "Yes. Your fear will kill you."

Lyon rolled his shoulders. The crone pointed to an old chair and he sat with his palms flat on his thighs in hopes his pants would sop up the sweat. He watched the women scurry around selecting various herbs and blobs of goo that he didn't want to recognize. He closed his eyes and shoved his fear aside, leaving a vacuum that was filled with Persephone. "Let's get this done."

The crimson crone secured his ankles and wrists to the chair. "This first part...well, you're not going to like it."

"I never heard that the assimilated Zodiacs had any particular difficulty or pain."

She patted his head and shook hers. "That's because their souls were open, exposed, not yet sealed shut from the wound the demon inflicted, allowing the foreign soul to mesh with theirs. Your soul, however, has been sealed shut against the demon soul for many years."

"So that's what will hurt? Opening my soul again?"

She nodded once, then turned her attention to the others when they began bickering. "No, no, not the salamander heart! For goddess' sake, do you want him to grow a second head?" The woman threw up her hands and marched away muttering.

Lyon closed his eyes and tried to tune out the women arguing over the ingredients that might give him two heads or shrivel his cock to the size of a bean. He thought of Persephone and what being her mate might be like: the years passing, love and grey hair, babies and grandbabies, laughter and hope. A family, his family—by choice, and by blood.

A hand swatted his head. He opened his eyes, and the crimson crone pinched his nose.

"Open your mouth and drink this." She poured a smoking stench into his mouth, then clapped a hand over it, forcing Lyon to swallow, before releasing his bindings and stepped out of arm's reach.

Lyon gripped the arms of his chair and shook his head. "Damn it, you could have warned me."

"Gird your loins, boy, it's about to get harder," she said with a cackle. "Come." She waved for him to follow.

Lyon pushed out of the chair and followed the crimson crone. She weaved through the benches and shelves to the darkest corner of the room, where a small bed was tucked against the wall, the mattress sagging in the middle under the weight of piles of brightly colored blankets.

The crone snapped her fingers and pointed to the bed. "On your belly."

Lyon hesitated. His stomach rumbled. His body grew heavy and he labored to breathe. He sagged onto the bed, one hand gripping the modest painted headboard as the room around him wavered. "What did you give me?"

"A potion to relax you." The crone opened an ancient chest and removed four red braided strings just like the enchanted collars his fenrir-wolf escort had worn when he was taken to the pit death match. "And to relax your grip on your soul."

The crone pushed on his chest with one finger.

He fell back. The numbness that had started in his hands and feet was rapidly stealing over the rest of him. Any moment now, his whole body would be useless. "You will not take any of my soul for yourself?"

She smiled, but said nothing.

He rolled onto his belly while he could. What choice did he have? This was the only way. He spread his arms and legs and turned his head to watch the crone bind him.

She turned away and barked orders at the other women.

He pulled on one binding. The frail braided thread not only held, but a sharp zap of electricity shocked his wrist, then traveled up his arm and straight to his heart. His back bowed. He growled through the pain.

The crone rushed back to him, her hands filled with two flasks and a long glass tube with a cone on the open end. "Stop fighting the thread before you stop your heart."

He snarled at her as he relaxed. "When I get back to the InBetween, the first thing I'm doing is freeing the fenrir-wolves of this torture."

She patted the top of his head as if he were a canid, then slit open the back of his shirt. She rubbed something warm on his exposed skin between his shoulder blades, right over the scar Asmodeus had created. "They're just beasts," she said.

"Even beasts deserve compassion—far more than their masters do."

"And you would know about that, would you?"

Lyon grit his teeth. Shifting images of being beaten, of fighting in the dark for every scrap of food—stabbed his brain, setting up a throbbing migraine of anguish and isolation. "Yes. I would."

She tsked. "You are not your father's son."

Lyon jerked against the restraints, but the four shocks subdued him. "You know Llewellyn?"

"I thought I did, once." She turned away from him and clapped her hands. The women ran to her side, some with their hands filled with knives of various sizes and other tools that looked appropriate for torture, others with bowls balanced in their hands to prevent spillage.

They spread the items out on a small table next to the bed and then surrounded Lyon, leaving no space between them.

"What the hell are you doing?"

"Put on your pendants," she ordered.

The women surrounding him slipped a chain over their heads. At the end, a large, iron pendant with an intricate symbol was etched into the metal.

"What is that?" Lyon asked.

The crimson crone nodded and the women laid their hands on Lyon, holding him down.

"Precautions." She lifted her pendant and showed it to him. "It is a devil's trap."

"What could I possibly do now?"

She leaned close. "Not you—the demon soul. It's not going to understand that we're assimilating you. It could resist. It could even try to possess us. I'll not have my healers harmed."

Lyon nodded.

The crone picked up a small metal tool no longer than Lyon's hand, with a curved blade on one end. She held it up to the light and turned it, her soft smile morphed into a calculating grin that transformed to something maniacal.

Lyon's gut churned. He closed his eyes and took a deep breath.

A hand settled on his left shoulder, a thin line of cold metal pressed just to the left of his spine. The cold glided a few inches down his back, then stopped. Rivulets of warm liquid flowed down his spine and pooled in the small of his back. He waited for the pain to start, but instead the cold spread until he sank into a frigid lassitude.

"Time to conjure your memory, Lyon. And for goddess' sake, don't let go. It's your only tether to this plane."

"Just get it done." He reached for his memories of Persephone. The moonlight shining on her silver hair, her earnest expression when she spoke of her love for Abella and Taryn, her face smattered with engine grease as she explained the difference between an air filter and an oil filter. Her soft skin and shy smile when she looked at him—

A wet crunch followed by breath-stealing agony broke the memory. His body thrashed against his bindings, the stabs of electricity jacking his adrenaline higher and higher.

The women cried out and tried to hold him down.

"Lyon, the memory!" the crone yelled. "Grab it. Now!"

He fought through the flashes of black and white behind his eyes and found Persephone standing in front of him, calling out that she loved him. He reached for her arms but his hands pushed through her image, distorting it as it flowed over his skin. The memory shifted to the small cave, and Persephone pulling him from the water. His lungs burned when he gasped for air, and his heart pounded in his scorched chest. He crawled in the dark until he found her and pulled her tight to his body.

Just as he had relaxed into the past, a bright white light washed away the dark and the cold and even Persephone. It filled his vision, obliterating everything around him and burning his eyes. He tried to turn away but the light coated his body, climbing up his legs and arms until it consumed him. He opened his mouth to scream, and the creeping luminescence flowed over his lips and flooded his mouth.

He clawed at his face, fighting for purchase before he drowned, when a tiny dot of black appeared in the white. It grew larger, bobbing and weaving as if eluding something inside the light. He stared at it, willing it to save him.

"Lyon?"

Persephone's voice called to him. He shook his head. *No, she's not here.*

"Lyon, help me."

He looked around for her. *She can't be here.* "Persephone?"

The darkness advanced until it was only a few feet away. A hand jutted out of it and reached for him. "Please."

He tried to raise a hand, but the white held him fast. He tried again. The white squeezed his body tight, like a snake suffocating prey. His pure soul had made its wishes known: no demon blight would be allowed. He had to make the decision, here and now and at the most basic level. Choose Persephone and forever be tainted with the black demon soul. Reject the black to reclaim his true essence, and lose Persephone, her friends, and probably his own life, as well as countless paranorms if Llewellyn was successful in whatever he hoped to do.

Persephone's face emerged from the dark, her expression pinched and frightened. He fought the white to free a hand. The black around Persephone pulled and gathered behind her head. Larger and larger it grew, until a distorted face formed. Long, broad, and hideous, the face of a man undulated behind Persephone. A wide slit of a mouth opened revealing sparse, jagged teeth and a tongue that had been split into three pieces and braided.

Its hands reached for Persephone.

"No!" Lyon took a deep breath and roared his fear and frustration, his hate and anguish. Not again—no one would be hurt again because of him. He freed one hand, then his arm. He doubled his effort, straining against the white until one leg broke through.

Persephone screamed. The monster had a grip on her shoulders and was pulling her back into the dark.

Lyon heaved his body forward and touched her outstretched fingertips. "Fight! For us! For me!"

She jerked away from the monster and surged forward.

Lyon grabbed her hand and pulled until he could wrap his arm around her waist. The monster's face morphed into Asmodeus.

Lyon growled. "Let her go."

The demon image grinned, then released Persephone. She sagged. He held her tight, exhausted but exhilarated that he had won.

The image of Asmodeus wavered then vanished. The only sound was the demon's fading laughter. All around Lyon, tendrils of black wormed their way into the white.

Lyon's skin crawled, as if something as ephemeral as his soul had enough mass to affect him physically. But it didn't matter; Persephone was safe. He looked down at his inamorata. Her lovely face faded away. Just like a puff of smoke in the wind, she dissipated.

The black encircled him, until that was all he saw. He shielded his face with his hands. The black hadn't touched him yet, but the pressure of the grappling of black and white squeezed him until he couldn't breathe.

A sole tendril touched the back of his right hand and pain exploded inside him. The black wiggled like a worm, then broke through his skin and dove deep. The agony consumed him, and he dropped to his knees. More tendrils attacked his back and legs and face, drilling inside him and setting up a chain of excruciating waves far worse than any torture he'd experienced in the dungeons. His heart pounded, sweat ran down his face and back and belly, and his lungs screamed for air. He fell onto his side and curled into a fetal ball.

He was dying.

The black folded in on him and he screamed.

35

LYON PACED IN HIS ROOM, much more jazzed with energy than he thought he'd be after the assimilation. The last thing he remembered was the pain of dying. Then he'd woken to see the crimson crone's face hovering over his.

He clenched his fists to test them. They were still stiff, as was the rest of him, but they were working. In fact, everything was working just fine, except the ubiquitous scratching and roiling of the demon soul seeking purchase inside him. That was gone.

He tried the door again, but it was still locked. He punched it, then went back to pacing. Shit. He'd made the decision of his life so he could help Persephone and her friends, only to end up locked in a cage…again.

The lock in the door turned. Lyon flattened his back against the wall next to the door. It opened and warriors entered.

He grabbed one of the women by the neck and squeezed. She flailed, but he gripped her throat tighter until her feet were off the floor.

"Release her," the queen ordered.

"And I should obey after you locked me in here?"

The warriors behind him lowered their spears and pressed the tips against his body.

"You're not going to kill me."

The queen tipped her head and pursed her mouth. "I don't want to, that's true. But I will not allow you to threaten any of the Novi."

Lyon released the woman.

"Please, take a seat." The queen gestured to the chairs by the fireplace.

He didn't have time for this, but this was not the moment to make a break for it. He was outnumbered. He sat down facing the queen.

She studied him for a moment. "You look well."

"Release me."

"No."

"What the hell are you playing at?"

She frowned at him and leaned forward. "A Zodiac? Under my control? That is a rare and precious gift. With you, the odds of success tip in our favor."

"I never agreed to that."

Her face reddened and she sat back. "For once, you arrogant son of the House of Leo, stop thinking this is all about you, or your precious Persephone. I'm fighting to stop what's coming, and you *will* help me."

She snapped her fingers and pointed to the bed. "Bind him."

The warriors pushed their weapons against him. The tips sank into his clothes and pierced his flesh. They herded him to the bed and bound him with the same enchanted thread the crimson crone had used. He wanted to fight against the bindings, but his memory of the pain of resistance was too fresh.

The queen walked to the door and looked back. "You get us into the InBetween, and you can see your Persephone. Fight me on this, and you'll never see her again."

Lyon opened his eyes and stared at the ceiling. Sleep eluded him—his rage and churning gut wouldn't permit it. The room was empty of guards, but he could hear the heavy sound of booted footfalls outside his door.

Why the hell hadn't he seen this coming? He'd been in the dungeons too long. Lyon was ruminating over the few options still open to him when he heard two muffled cries and a crash outside his door.

The door opened, and a very tall, very broad-shouldered woman dressed in an Amazon-style leather vest and skirt with a robe draped over her shoulders entered his room with two trays of food. The hood of her black robe covered her head and hid her face in shadow. Her demure body language was belied by her girth and her mincing gait.

She placed the two trays on the closest chair.

Lyon raised his head and watched her drag the unconscious guards out of the hall and inside the room. She looked down the hall before shutting the door and securing the guards with the same leather thongs used to bind the women's long braids. She threw back her hood and returned to the food.

Lyon shook his head. "Sag, what the hell? What did you do to yourself?"

"Man, I'm hungry." Sag stuffed his mouth before he pushed his robe back and showed Lyon the rest of his outfit. A leather vest strained to cover his massive chest and arms, but left his belly exposed. The skirt barely covered his legs. He was one bend at the waist away from flashing his man bits and ass. Small wonder he'd added a robe. *Thank the goddess.*

Sag walked to the only mirror and straightened the long, black wig. "I had a witch mix up a spell to rid me of leg and chest hair, but unfortunately the spell ghosted every hair from head to toe." Sag lifted his skirt and flashed his totally bald-as-a-baby package.

Lyon turned his head. "Shit. Now I'll never get that image out of my head."

Sag twirled, amused by Lyon's discomfort, then stopped short and leaned closer to Lyon. "Son of a bitch. You assimilated!"

"Why are you here? To kill me?"

"Oh no, back it up. You assimilated. Why?"

"The why isn't your business."

"And I was so sure you wouldn't be a dick after."

"Sag!"

Sag popped a grape in his mouth. "I'm not here to kill you. I'm your damned rescuer." He pulled a blade and cut Lyon's bindings.

Lyon got a good look at Sag in the firelight, then ran a finger down the Zodiac's face. "Makeup too?"

"How the hell else was I supposed to move through the Pondera?"

Lyon crossed his arms. "And just how did you know I was here in the first place?"

Sag grinned. "My Hermes hawk. Who do you think found you at the cabin in the desert?"

"That message was from you?"

"Yep."

Lyon advanced on the Zodiac. "If you know so much, then tell me. Where is she?"

"Who?"

Lyon grabbed Sag's neck and backed him to the wall. "Persephone." He swiped Leona's note from the desk and jammed it in Sag's face. "Leona said Persephone's going to die. Why?"

Lyon felt a sting in his belly. He looked down.

"Release me," Sag said quietly, a sharp blade poised to eviscerate Lyon. His sharper stare left no doubt that Sag was willing to do it.

Lyon let go, and took a step back. He looked at his hands. His claws hadn't emerged. There was no blood in his mouth from his leonine canine teeth tearing his gums. The roiling pain and rage he'd carried for years had been replaced by a disquieting calm. "We need to get out of here."

Sag opened the wardrobe and found a voluminous hooded robe. "Put that on. And for goddess' sake, channel your feminine side or we'll never pull this off."

Sag straightened the padding in his bra, then looked in the mirror. "Look what you did to my makeup."

Lyon's mouth twitched. The featherweight of hope freed him, and he grinned. Laughter exploded from him, startling both men. Lyon shook his body as if the mirth had coated him like water on a dog.

Sag paused, his mouth open wide. "Man, that shit is fucked up. Please, don't do that again."

Lyon growled and threw the robe over his head.

"Yup. There's that growl we all know and love," Sag said. He opened the door. "Shall we go before we're discovered?"

Lyon followed the Zodiac down a maze of halls until they reached a large vent. They hauled their huge bodies into the steeply sloped shaft.

"Now I know how a baby feels during birth," Lyon complained.

They reached a turn and Sag stopped. He laid flat, arms over his head. "Correction. This is the womb portion," he said, using his toes and fingertips to inch forward.

"Why are you here?" Lyon asked to keep his mind occupied so he wouldn't dwell on his rising claustrophobia. "You aren't doing this for me."

"Got that right," Sag grunted. "I'm doing it for her."

"Persephone? You don't even know her."

Sag snorted. "Even assimilated, you are such an ass."

Lyon growled.

"Not the lineage kind. The my-head's-up-my-ass kind." Sag paused at a junction before crawling left. "Didn't count on you being such a champion dumbass to boot." He curled his body around the corner. "I'm talking about Leona."

The shaft widened slightly, allowing the men to move more rapidly.

Lyon clawed Sag's leg. "What about her?"

Sag stubbed one of Lyon's fingers with a single toe. He craned his head around until Lyon could see his face.

"If you'd bothered to pay attention to her, you'd know something is very wrong."

"From my cell? What, I'm a Portend now, able to see Leona through yards and yards of rock?" Lyon shook his head. "Sounds like you've been paying enough attention for the both of us."

Sag didn't respond to Lyon's barb. "Don't tell me you haven't noticed."

Lyon hesitated, not sure if he wanted to tell Sag the truth. But, for the first time, he had an idea of what Sag was feeling. Hell, he was sick at the thought of Persephone being harmed. "I saw something when she took me to Llewellyn."

"What?"

"She was angry at me and I taunted her. Then she grabbed my throat and choked me."

"That's all?"

"She was ten feet away."

"Shit."

"And her eyes turned—"

Sag stopped. "—black?"

"Does that mean something to you?"

"Yeah. Yeah, it does." Sag shook his head.

"The demon?"

"Asmodeus has done something to her. I don't know what. But she reeks of demon, and I think they are lovers."

Lyon remained silent. What could he say? Sag loved her, and he had lost her to a demon king. That had to hurt, but Sag deserved to know everything. "She does reek of demon—and far worse."

"And you know this how?" Sag asked, his voice low with an edge.

"I saw her here. Asmodeus did far worse than bed her—he made her a Zodiac."

The two men reached another junction, each shaft tall enough for them to stand. Sag had climbed to his feet, his shoulders slumped as he started down the passage, when Lyon clapped a hand on his shoulder.

"I'm sorry, man."

Sag shrugged him off and continued walking.

Lyon followed Sag down the shaft. "So, I ask again, why come for me? You hate me."

"Hate you? Yes, I did. But not now."

"What could possibly have ended your animus toward me?"

Sag turned to him. "Because I've learned a truth, brother. And soon, you will too."

36

LYON CRAWLED ON HIS BELLY to the top of the tallest hill overlooking the main entrance to the InBetween. He waved Sag up. "We're screwed." He pointed to the valley, where a sea of ginger-headed woman stood, their backs to the entrance, facing the Pondera warriors. "There's a huge line of Bathory Berserkers holding the Pondera Novi back."

"How the hell do we get through that?" Sag asked.

"We need a diversion, a big one."

Sag just stared. "What's your big idea?"

"We need help, is all I've got."

Someone behind them cleared his throat. "Like us?"

Lyon and Sag rolled over and slid down the embankment. They stopped just shy of Libra, Taurus, Abella, and Taryn.

"You son of a bitch," Libra growled. He leapt for Lyon's throat, but Taurus stopped him with one arm.

"This bastard is mine." Taurus grabbed Lyon's throat and squeezed.

Lyon clawed at his hand, choking.

Sag jumped up and shoved Taurus back, breaking the link.

Lyon gasped and sucked in air.

"He didn't kill your father, Taur." Sag hit Taur in the chest with both hands, pushing the huge Zodiac back again.

"What do you mean? Their blood on the pieces of his claws—"

"Lyon was framed. I have the proof." Sag motioned with his head in the direction of the entrance. "In there."

Abella pushed Sag and Taurus out of her way, and marched to Lyon. "Where is Persephone? Why isn't she with you?"

"She must be in the InBetween," Lyon said.

"How could you do that? Why didn't you protect her?" Taryn demanded.

Lyon's skin flushed. Shame for not protecting Persephone, and fear for her life flared hot on his skin. "She thought you were here. I tried to convince her not to come but she wouldn't—" He stopped talking. Defending himself wouldn't get him into the InBetween any faster, or mitigate his guilt. He was a man of action, not words, and right now, he needed to break something. Channeling that anger into saving Persephone was better than using it to pummel her friends. "Speaking of being here, why didn't you beat us here? And why do you all look like hell?"

Taurus and Libra exchanged a look of disgust, then nodded toward the women. Libra rolled his shoulders back. "Cooperation was in short supply."

Sag stepped in between Lyon and the women. "The 'whys' will just chew up time that we have precious little of." He turned to Lyon and cocked his head. "I have an idea."

"What?" Lyon asked.

"You don't want us to march you up to the entrance looking so pretty, do you? The Bathorys might think the great beast, Lyon, didn't put up a fight."

Lyon nodded and grinned, but before he could steel himself against the coming blow, Sag punched him in the mouth. Lyon hit the ground, his vision swimming. He opened his mouth and moved his lower jaw around to make sure he still could. He climbed to his feet and rolled his neck. "Again with no warning, you—"

His breath whooshed out of his lungs and he went down again, his arms around his gut. He looked up at Taurus and growled. "C'mon Taur, you can do better than that."

He struggled to gain his feet, then swayed before the Zodiacs, blood dripping off his chin. He glanced at Libra. "What are you going to do? Beat me about the head with a scarf?"

Libra's lips twitched. "I wouldn't risk pulling a thread in my cashmere." He looked past Lyon. "Besides, I don't think any Zodiac could do worse than they could."

Lyon turned around, and the two women kicked him in the groin, in unison. He fell to his knees, and then his side, before the blessed relief of unconsciousness took the pain away.

Lyon's shoulders twitched as the Zodiacs marched him—his hands bound behind his back— through the crowd of hostile Berserkers. "Libra," he hissed. "This has to be the worst idea in a long history of bad ideas."

"I agree," Abella said.

"And did you have to tie my bindings so tight?" Taryn asked.

"Shh," Libra responded.

A huge Berserker covered in blood-red tribal tattoos stopped the Zodiacs and their captives at the main entrance.

"Her tattoos." Abella said under her breath as she glanced at Lyon. "I've never seen that color red in a tattoo."

"That's because they mix the red color with their victim's blood."

"There are so many. The other women don't have that many," Taryn whispered.

"Yeah, she's covered in them. I've never seen a Berserker with that much ink," Lyon said.

"Does that have a particular meaning?" Abella asked.

Lyon nodded. "It means that she's had the most kills."

Sag snorted. "More like she's the boss bitch."

Taurus and Libra nodded.

The woman stalked to the group. She circled them once, then stopped in front of Libra. "What have you here?"

"Llewellyn is expecting these prisoners. Let us pass."

"Why should I believe you?"

Libra shrugged his shoulders. "Send for him. If you dare."

The Berserker studied him in silence. She grunted, and her warriors parted down the middle all the way to the two carved wood doors.

Libra led the group past the women and slipped inside before they were stopped again. The doors closed with a deep *thunk* and vanished, replaced by a solid wall of rock to keep humans oblivious to their presence.

Sag stepped out from the group and looked around. "Libra, Taurus, you need to round up the other Zodiacs so they don't gank Lyon without asking questions. You all want proof of his innocence. I can give you that and tell you who *did* kill our fathers."

Sag turned to Taryn and Abella. "I'm afraid we need you to go with Libra and be his captives."

Abella stepped up to him. "Persephone is here?"

"Yes," Sag answered as he cut Lyon's bindings.

"Then let's go," Abella said.

Lyon held up a hand to stop the women. "I'll do everything in my power to save her."

Taryn looked in his eyes, then nodded. "I believe you will." She shoved Libra with her shoulder. "Let's go, girlie man."

Libra hissed and leaned away. "You little termagant."

Lyon shook his head as they walked away.

"We can't stay here, someone will see you," Sag said as he pulled on Lyon's arm.

"I need to go to the fenrir-wolf pens first."

"Are you nuts?"

"Definitely. But I have a feeling they have a role to play."

"What are you? Part Portend?"

"No, but I did have one throw up on me once."

★ ★ ★

Sag let Lyon into his room, a scowl darkening his face. "Fenrir-wolves, you say. Important, you think." He threw off his filthy clothes and disappeared into the bathroom. "Fucking trolls? Really?"

Lyon heard the shower start.

"I understand releasing the stag fairies and the moon swans, even the banshees, gremlins, and harpies. But the innocent demonica?" Sag poked his head out of the bathroom and shuddered. "Why the hell release them? And what the fuck were those bony cats with the glowing red eyes?"

"Necrofelidae."

"I have no idea what that means, but anything with a name that complicated pegs out my creepy meter." Sag disappeared.

Lyon heard Sag whoop. "What?"

The Zodiac opened the bathroom door and appeared, sans clothes. "Hey man, my hair is back."

Lyon rolled his eyes away. "Really? Your hairless shit wasn't enough to turn my stomach?"

Sag grinned and disappeared again.

The Zodiac had a good point. Lyon had no idea why he felt the need to release all of Llewellyn's captives. Lyon reeked from wrestling the ungrateful fenrir-wolves to the ground to remove their red enchanted collars, and the multiple aches covering his body promised a roadmap of bruises by tomorrow. What had started out as a simple release of the fenrir-wolf pack turned into a freedom day for all of the imprisoned just to quiet them. It was a bitch of a job, but they'd managed to free all of the creatures Llewellyn had collected. The 'why' was trickier to wrestle—even he didn't understand it. The tickle that had started when he reentered the InBetween became an all-out burning impetus that he couldn't ignore. Only after releasing all of Llewellyn's experiments did the itch stop.

Sag rushed through the shower and redressed. "Stay here. I have to get something. And keep your head down—if the other Zodiacs realize you're back, they'll kill you without stopping for a Q&A." His nose wrinkled as he dressed. "And for goddess' sake, take a shower before the Zodiacs sniff you out by your stench alone."

Lyon showered and dressed. He had paced the room for several minutes when Sag returned with an old hag.

Lyon recognized her crouching stance, her slow, lame shuffle. It was his healer, the old woman who'd tended his wounds for years. He shoved Sag away from the woman. "What are you doing? Is this a game to you?" Lyon gently turned the healer around.

"She wants to be here."

"Is this true?" Lyon asked.

She nodded.

Lyon led her to a chair and helped her sit. He walked away, rubbing his forehead. *I don't have time for this.*

He stopped in front of the woman and crossed his arms. "What is it?" Lyon asked.

She dropped her head and lifted her hood, revealing a cloud of white hair so sparse he could see the pale pink and cream skin of her scalp. Then she raised her face to him. Tears rolled down her cheeks freely, until they were diverted to the jawline just under her ear by the network of scars that marred her face.

Someone had worked her over. He grimaced when he thought of the pain she must have experienced.

"Do you have the sunglasses I gave you?"

Lyon pulled them out of his pocket, and held them out to her. "Don't know what you were thinking, these did nothing but muddify things. Couldn't tell what I was seeing."

She snorted. "Put them on."

Lyon glanced at Sag first. The Zodiac nodded. Lyon slipped the glasses on, looked at the healer, and gasped. Her face shifted and shimmered like the heat waves coming off the lava in the pit. Finally, her face settled into beautiful features that were so similar to his mother's face, Lyon's heart skipped.

"Lady Martina?" Lyon whispered. "We thought you'd died." He dropped in front of the woman and bowed his head until it rested in her lap. She leaned forward and laid her cheek on his head and cried, wetting his blond hair even as he soaked the lap of her old, brown robe.

"Welcome home, nephew."

Martina gripped his shoulders and gently pulled him until his head rested against her chest. She wrapped her arms around him and rocked. "Ah, child, it's me, and I'm very much alive."

Lyon pulled away, his mind and heart reeling. The pain of looking at her made it hard for him to breathe. "But how—why did you disguise yourself this way?"

"When your mother died, I was so filled with rage. All I could think of was revenge."

"Against me," Lyon whispered.

"I'm ashamed to admit it but yes, against you."

"You've had years to end me, why didn't you? And the disguise?"

"A spell, just like the spell Sag used to infiltrate the Pondera. I showed up as your healer and no one thought to question the old scarred hag with a bag of smelly unguents. I was poised to end your life, but then I saw how young and frightened and devastated you were by what happened."

"I lost control and killed my mother. Scarred Leona so badly that she hates me. I would have welcomed death."

"I know, boy, and that's what stayed my hand. What happened wasn't your fault, and your mother knew that. I came to understand it, as well."

Lyon stood, and walked to the opposite side of the room. "I wish I could believe you, but how could you possibly know what my mother knew?"

Martina laid a hand on his shoulder. "You can believe me because I knew my sister better than anyone. It's one of the perks and the pains of being a sister. I felt her heart stop. I heard her say, 'I love you,' as if I was standing next to her instead of being miles away."

She swiped at her tears. "Every night, I stood over you and watched you thrash and cry in your sleep, calling for my sister, screaming, 'I'm sorry,' over and over. And every time I stopped myself from taking your life, until finally I knew I could never hurt the son my sister loved beyond reason. If I was to honor her, I had to protect you as much as I could."

Lyon placed his hand over hers and nodded his bent head, his tears falling to the floor.

Sag cleared his throat. "I'll be back in a few." His door closed quietly.

Lyon turned to Martina. "And what about Scorpio? Does he know you're alive?"

She looked away, her body tightened. "My son was lost to me long before my sister died. His father made sure of that." She drew a shaky breath. "There is no going back, I'm afraid. My sins against him are too grievous."

Lyon touched her shoulder. "I have recently been made aware that it's never too late."

Martina nodded. "Your mother told me that many times." She lifted her tear-stained face to his. "I wish I had listened."

They slipped into each other's arms and silently mourned the woman they'd both loved and lost.

37

SAG LIFTED HIS FIST TO KNOCK on Leona's door, but stopped when he heard her talking with Asmodeus. Rage bloomed, heating his skin and sending the churning in his gut into overdrive. He pivoted and stood with his back to the wall, then cocked his head and closed his eyes to listen to Leona. The soft, lyrical voice that had once sent shivers down his spine had changed to a deep, dark gravelly pit of anger and corruption. But he couldn't help it, he still loved her—had loved her since they were children.

"…but I don't trust them. They will try to double cross us when the gate is opened," Leona said.

"I have a plan."

"What is it?"

"Mmm, you smell delicious."

Sag heard a soft slap. He clenched his fists. His stomach roiled.

"Not now, Asmodeus."

"Always now."

"No. The plan."

"You just stay by my side. When the gate opens, the chaos will either be our best cover, or their best opportunity to gank us. You stay close and I'll give you the ride of your life on the coattails of my army."

Asmodeus and Leona stopped talking.

Sag heard footsteps closing in on the door. He had no time to escape, he'd have to to brazen it out. He turned to face the door, and knocked.

The door opened.

Sag expected to see either Leona or Asmodeus, but they were across the room. He took a step inside the room and checked behind the door. Nothing.

"What do you want, Sagittarius?" Leona asked.

He opened his mouth to speak when her eyes shifted from amber to glowing gold.

"Spit it out, boy," the demon said.

Sag looked at the demon and took another step, his need to end the bastard for what he'd done to Leona overriding his normally healthy fear of all things demonic.

"Sag," Leona said.

He pulled back from his posturing to look at her.

"Leave. Now."

He backed out of the room.

"Smart move." She lifted her hand and waved it just as he cleared the doorway.

The heavy wood slammed in Sag's face. He heard Asmodeus clap and congratulate Leona. He leaned against the door, listening to their whispering. His gorge rose high in his throat. He needed to walk away from her, let her live the life she had chosen. Hell, he needed to run away from her before she killed him.

Leona was lost to him, for now, but he wouldn't mourn her. No. He would fight until the last beat of his heart, and hope that it was enough to save Leona from the demon—from herself.

He pushed off the door and walked away.

Sag returned to his room. He sat on the edge of his bed, slumped and silent.

Lyon stared at him for a moment before speaking. "Sag, I'm glad you're back. Martina was about to tell me what's been happening."

From there, Martina explained to Lyon about the evidence she had found, and how it had proven he didn't murder the Twelve. Then, she unwrapped the stiff, blood-encrusted glove and handed it to Lyon.

Lyon sniffed it, then nodded. He could smell the blood of the Twelve.

"Smell the inside," Sag said.

Lyon rolled down the wrist of the glove, then held it to his nose. "A woman wore this."

Martina nodded. "Yes, and I know who she is."

"Circe," Lyon and Sag said at the same time.

"How do you know that?" Martina waved a hand of dismissal. "It doesn't matter. The important thing is that this is enough to implicate Llewellyn in the butchery, and prove that Circe did the deed."

"We have a glove and a note. That's pretty flimsy—hardly enough to exonerate me."

Sag slapped Lyon on the shoulder. "It was enough for me, and it will be enough for the other Zodiacs."

Lyon rubbed his forehead. "Why raise the woman who killed you? What's the point? And why does Llewellyn want Persephone and her friends?"

Martina patted Lyon's shoulder. "I don't have those answers. But I do know two things. One, it's a ritual that demands a blood sacrifice, and two, it's happening soon."

"Leona's note said Persephone would die. Maybe her death is for the blood sacrifice," Lyon added.

Martina cocked her head. "Then why bring Persephone's two friends here? I've never heard of a blood spell that required more than one death. And even those only required the sacrifice of an animal, not a human. Who or what are they that a witch goddess needs their blood for a ritual?"

"Well, they did cleave a house in two just by touching each other," Lyon said.

Martina crossed her arms. "Interesting. I need to do some research." She placed a hand on Lyon's arm. "There's one other thing you should know. When Leona returned with Persephone, Scorpio was with her. He must be taking orders from Llewellyn now."

Lyon nodded, thinking. "Sag, find out what you can and get back to me. We need to know what their plan is so we can stop it. No one, especially Persephone and her friends, are dying for some ritual."

Sag raised his head. Lyon blinked when he saw the despair on the Zodiac's face. "What is it, Sag?"

"I overheard Leona and Asmodeus talking about gates and chaos and his army."

Lyon's breath caught in his throat. "Gates? Army?"

Sag nodded.

Lyon handed the glove to Sag. "Scrap what I said earlier—you need to find the other Zodiacs and make sure they know I didn't kill their sires. We're going to need all the help we can get." He gripped Sag's hunched shoulder. "Now, Sag. Go."

Lyon waited for the Zodiac to leave. "Martina, can you take me to Persephone? I need to see her."

38

PERSEPHONE HELD HER FACE in her hands, crying. Leona had made promises, and Persephone had yet to see one fulfilled. This had always been a possibility, but... She jumped up and moved around the room, willing someone to come to the door. At this point, anyone would do. The irritating creak of her leather clothes was only outdone by the painful chafing she'd sustained. But there were no clothes to change into, and Persephone sure as hell wasn't going to prance around naked. She squirmed in the leather, pulling it and her fancy undies out of her butt when, as if the heavens had heard her wish, the doorknob turned.

Persephone ran to the closest marble statue, raised it over her head, and hid behind the door.

A robed figure appeared.

Persephone yelled and attacked.

The woman dropped to her knees, then kicked Persephone's legs out from under her. She clutched Persephone's robe, and raised a fist to punch her when a second figure stopped her.

"Abella, look."

Abella flipped her hood back. "Persephone!"

Martina led Lyon through the halls until they made it to the entrance of a maze of hidden walls built throughout the InBetween. She pressed a small stone. A soft clunk preceded a small door yawning open. "There are only a handful of these hidden doors in all of the InBetween. But all the rooms I've come across have peepholes."

He marveled at their existence. Tiny, narrow stairs here and there took them to new levels, miniscule alcoves that backed up to private quarters with peepholes that exposed the dark secrets of the occupant's true nature.

Martina remained silent as she led him up stairs and around corners until he was truly lost. Finally, she stopped. They squeezed into an alcove and she reached behind Lyon's head. A heavy, black velvet curtain dropped. Martina raised a hand, palm facing the material, stroking it as if it was alive. She whispered *"Dissimulo"* and with a soft snap, the folds smoothed out and became rigid, forming a thin wall. She said *"Tegere"* and the material transfigured into solid stone, as if the alcove had never existed.

"Now we can talk without anyone hearing us."

"Fuck me. Where'd you learn that?"

"Language," she fussed. "Your mother and I had training."

"Training?"

"That story is for another time. I've discovered it's amazing what you can learn when you're a servant, especially when you're an old hag. I'm invisible, inconsequential, and, apparently, they think I'm deaf because they will say anything with me in the room. But this," she said as she pointed to the peephole, "makes me privy to what no one wants known."

"Bloody brilliant," Lyon said, "but what's this got to do with Persephone?"

Martina touched his face and smiled. "Look," she said as she pushed a peephole cover aside.

He leaned in and saw Persephone sitting at a small desk, her back rounded, her hands covering her eyes.

"She's crying," he said. He placed both hands against the wall as if he could push it open. A growl started deep in his chest. He turned to the solid curtain and pushed, but it didn't budge.

He hit it with a fist. "Let me out. I want to go to her. Now."

"Watching and listening are all you can do for now. We can't risk you being discovered." Martina laid her hands on his fists. "Now, quiet. Listen."

Lyon looked through the peephole again. Persephone had risen from the chair and stood facing the door, wiping her tears away with a sleeve. The bolts opened. Persephone grabbed a statue, hid behind the door, her arms raised.

Lyon hit the wall with the heel of his hand.

Two cloaked figures stepped past the threshold. Persephone screamed and attacked, but the taller woman knocked Persephone to the ground. Before Persephone got punched, the other woman stopped the fight.

"Abella, look." Taryn flipped her hood back.

Abella did the same. "Persephone!"

The three women smiled, then cried as they crowded together as close as they dared without touching.

Persephone's door opened again. The women backed away as a cloaked figure entered the room. The visitor flipped back her hood, revealing red hair, pale skin, and green eyes.

Martina hissed. "Circe."

"Persephone needs me." Lyon pushed back from the peephole, his protective instinct in high gear, but Martina stopped him with a hand on his arm.

"Circe isn't going to harm her, not before the ritual, and we need information."

Lyon twitched with pent-up frustration. He was itching for a fight, but she was right: Circe wouldn't harm Persephone…for the moment. And they desperately needed information if they stood a chance of stopping the ritual.

Lyon returned to the peephole in time to see Abella advance on Circe. The two women stood toe to toe. Circe was relaxed, her eyes half-closed, while Abella's hands were clenched into fists, bouncing on her toes as if ready to throw down. Abella towered over the more diminutive Circe, but the menace radiating from both women was equal.

"So you're the bitch in charge?" Abella asked. "We'd like to lodge a complaint about the accommodations."

Circe giggled. "All that bluster. Add a little garlic and Bathory tripe and you'd be a carnivore's delectable delight." She ran a finger down Abella's chest, delving deep between her breasts. Circe slipped the finger into her mouth and closed her eyes, moaning.

Abella flushed bright red.

"Abella, please," Persephone said.

Abella held her tongue.

"Obedient little bitch, aren't you?" Circe clapped her hands and three servants trotted into view, each carrying a tray loaded with covered plates and goblets filled with wine. "Please partake. I suggest the wine first to prepare your palates."

The servants offered the wine to each woman.

"You go first," Abella said, her voice soft but tight with rage.

Circe turned her back on Abella, and smiled at Taryn and Persephone. "Gladly." She held out a hand and a tiny girl ran to her, a goblet in one hand and a flask in the other. Circe filled her cup to overflowing, ignoring the stains to her gown and the rug beneath her feet.

"To…new beginnings." She downed the wine, then held out her goblet for more. "Come, join me. It's delicious."

Lyon's hair stood up on the back of his neck, not from fear but from the electrical charge that buzzed around him. It was as if Circe was raising the static in the air. The glee and anticipation in her voice raised his alarm bells. He wanted to shout a warning, but he didn't know if it would help or makes things worse, if they even heard him.

Martina put her hand on his shoulder and shook her head. He frowned, but her unspoken plea kept him silent as he watched Persephone and the others drink their wine. He held his breath as he waited for them to fall to the floor, writhing in pain from poison, but nothing happened.

Circe waved to the guards. They uncovered the food, then took their positions in the room. "Please eat. Enjoy the repast I chose for you. Oh, and I suggest you rest. Tomorrow will be a very long day," she said as she walked out of the room. "And one you will never forget."

The door closed and bolts were pushed home, locking the women in.

Taryn picked up a fork and dug into the food. She chewed carefully, then nodded. "It's good." She tried the mystery vegetables. "Very good."

Abella and Persephone attacked their plates and their eyes rolled back in ecstasy.

Persephone covered her full mouth. "Oh. My. God."

Abella swallowed, then frowned at the pile of food. "Good enough for a last supper, isn't it?"

Persephone and Taryn stopped chewing.

"Well, if it is, then I'm going to gird my loins by filling my gut," Taryn said. She raised her goblet to Abella and Persephone. "And worry about tomorrow…tomorrow."

"To girding," Persephone said.

"Screw girding. To loins," Abella said.

Martina led Lyon back to Sag's room. Lyon slipped into the dark room ahead of her and saw Sag bound in a chair.

Sag shook his head, then looked at the fireplace.

Lyon put a hand out to stop Martina, but before he could back the woman into the hall, the door shut.

Scorpio leaned against the wall, his arms crossed.

Leona stood by the fire with an arm draped on the mantle. "Hello, brother dear, it's good to see you again. And so soon."

Scor shoved Martina and Lyon to the middle of the room and pointed to a chair. "Sit."

Lyon and Scor sneered and circled each other, the need to kill sharp and pungent.

Leona grabbed Martina's throat. "Stand down or the old woman gets it."

"I claim the right to take his life for the life of my sire," Scor said.

"I think Sag has made a convincing argument that Lyon didn't kill any of the Twelve," Leona said.

"I don't care," Scor snapped back. "I have other reasons to end him."

"Well, there are plans for Lyon and they require he be alive...for now. Bind him."

Reluctantly, Scor tied Lyon to the other chair.

"Stay with them to make sure no one frees them before tomorrow," Leona said when Scor finished. "By then, it'll all be over." She shoved Martina out of the room. "If you try to help Lyon in any way, I will kill you. Understand?"

Martina nodded and scuttled away.

"Leona, please, you're not yourself. Come back to me—I can help you," Sag said.

Leona sat on his lap and kissed him. She leaned back and looked at both men.

"Look at her eyes," Sag whispered.

"They're glowing gold," Lyon said.

Leona grinned. "Yeah, ain't it great?"

Lyon's heart stopped. "Why did you let that demon rape your soul and make you one of us?"

She nipped and nibbled on Sag's mouth. "Mmm, just as warm and soft as I remember when you introduced me to kissing." She traced his bottom lip with her thumb. "I have one more task to perform before my transformation is complete. My first kill," she said as she stroked his face. "Dear Sag, you've figuratively given me your heart. Tomorrow, I will take it literally, and you'll watch me eat it as you die." She dismounted and walked to the door. "In case I forget to say it tomorrow, thank you for your sacrifice."

"Well, if you're planning to eat me tomorrow," Sag said, "I suggest you feed me now. Wouldn't want all this lovely flesh to be made sour by an empty belly."

"Get them fed," Leona ordered Scor before leaving the room.

Scor pulled a cord hanging next to the door twice, then settled into a chair by the fireplace and stoked the meager embers until a flame erupted. He stacked several logs and watched the fire grow, the light illuminating the strain on his face.

"You know she's mad," Sag said.

Scor remained silent.

"What has the demon done to her?" Lyon asked.

"Don't blame the demon for giving her what she wanted. The House of Leo is rife with madness, and so filled with its own imperiousness that it chokes anyone in its sphere."

"So why are you answering to Llewellyn and Leona? Are you such a masochist that you enjoy our asphyxiating presence?" Lyon asked.

The corner of Scor's left eyelid twitched, giving Lyon a microsecond warning. He braced for the blows. Scor didn't disappoint. The first punch was to his face. The second to his flank, and the final blow, to Lyon's solar plexus.

Lyon tried to bend at the waist to relieve the agony, but his bindings stopped him. He struggled to breathe, but his diaphragm wasn't having it. He remained conscious, but he really wished he hadn't.

"My reasons are my own."

"Your mother disappeared right after Lyon killed his. Basically, he stole her from you," Sag said.

Scor turned on Sag. "What makes you think you know anything about me?"

Sag leaned into his bonds. "I know his ineptitude ruined Leona, then and now. I know that with one blow, he killed off the sweet, loving girl she once was, and created the Untouchable, a woman with no legacy and no future. I know he drove her into the arms of those who would use her for their own gain, and she has been made mad by her desperate desire to be the son Llewellyn always wanted, not the scarred daughter of no use." Sag took a deep breath before continuing. "That's what I know about it. So you can take your brooding anger and shove it up your ass."

Scor stared for a moment, then nodded his head. "Maybe you do understand."

Sag scooted his chair closer to Scor. "Then release me, brother, and let's have a go at the bastard."

Scor leaned into Sag until their noses nearly touched. He reached around Sag and put a hand on the rope.

Sag smiled. "That's right. Let's take Lyon out together. Get him out of our blood by spilling his."

Just when Lyon thought Sag had managed to sweet talk the irascible Scor into releasing him, Scor stood and backhanded Sag so hard the chair fell back. Sag slammed against the floor.

Scor righted the chair, and held out a hand. One of the tattoos rose from his skin. He lifted it by the tail and dropped it into Sag's lap, its stinger already dripping with venom and poised to strike.

"Oh, not my man bits, guy. C'mon."

"Keep your mouth shut, keep your dick. Up to you." Scor returned to his chair and stared into the fire.

Lyon leaned in. "You were so close. You really don't know when to shut your mouth, do you?"

Sag spat out blood, and went back to contemplating the bug on his nuts.

Lyon bit the inside of his lip to keep from laughing at Sag struggling to remain silent. Sad commentary when a man had to think about the choice between talking or body parts.

If only the choices that faced Lyon were so clear, so simple. Freedom was the big, fat carrot Llewellyn had dangled to motivate Lyon and he'd lunged for it, even though a part of him had suspected his father had no intention of freeing him. But he desperately clung to the dream because he'd needed hope.

He needed to believe there was a place of quiet and peace waiting for him, a place devoid of pain and hatred. Even captive, with the weight of utter desolation bearing down on his chest until he couldn't breathe, he had hoped. Even with the looming prospect of living the rest of his life in the darkness of his cell, he had hoped.

He had assimilated his souls so he could save Persephone. He would sacrifice his hope, and his life, if it meant he could see her survive this.

But, like a grotesque, mythological Cerberus—Llewellyn, Asmodeus, and the witch goddess, Circe—couldn't be destroyed when acting together. It would be suicide if he took them on alone. Just shy of impossible even with backup.

The only way Lyon could defeat them was to turn them on each other; fell them from within. But which head needed to be lopped off first? Who was the weakest? Who could be bought? But the most pressing question was, how the hell was he going to get out of this room?

39

LYON STARED AT THE DANCING FLAMES. His whole world had changed in a matter of days, and this was the first moment he'd had to take it in. He'd heard love was glorious and fulfilling, but all he'd felt since admitting he loved Persephone was rage and fear. When were the softer feelings his mother sang of in lullabies supposed to set in? Take over?

A quiet rap roused him. The door opened and closed. Scor jumped up from his chair and bowed his head.

Lyon heard a whisper of fabric, felt the suddenly frigid air stir around him, carrying with it the putrid stink of musk and death. He looked over his shoulder then jerked back when something slashed at him. The sticky heat of fresh blood ran down his cheek. He bared his teeth and hissed like a wounded cat.

Several Creepers surrounded him.

"Circe."

"This is Circe?" Sag asked.

"Hello, my pets," Circe said as she circled the bound men, a book clutched in her hands. She laid it on a small table and approached Lyon. "I expected you'd come back." Circe trailed a hand over the contours of his chest and arms and back. "I was disappointed when you failed to bring my pretties, and a bit jealous that you dipped your wick into that vapid waif."

"Why are you doing this? What's the endgame?"

She leaned over and placed her mouth by his ear. "You, my dear, will be in the front row to watch me shred your little pretty and her friends."

Lyon struggled to move, but his bindings kept him immobile. "You hurt her, I will hunt you down and skin you alive."

Circe danced around him, giggling like a mad woman. "Promises, promises. Too bad you won't survive the arrival."

He kept his eyes on her until she turned away from him, then took a quick glance at the spine of her book. He blinked to focus and concentrated on the faded words: *Descensus ad Inferos. The Descent into Hell.*

She snatched the small, thick book from the table and held it in front of his face. "Is this what you're interested in?"

"At least tell me one thing. Persephone and her friends—who the hell are they?"

Circe bent at the waist and looked in his eyes. "Blood of my blood, fruit of my womb, their creation one of the most powerful and pure forms of dark magic. Your father has his faults, but he could have been a great sorcerer had the fates not made him a human."

"So they're just another one of his experiments?"

She giggled. "Oh, no. They're far more than that." She ran a hand down Lyon's face and cupped his chin. "They're my daughters."

He should have figured it out when Persephone and her friends destroyed their house. You get three witches in the same room who don't know how to control their power? The havoc would make an extinction-event meteor strike look like nothing more powerful than a stone skipping across a pond.

But mix together three descendants of a witch goddess, a black magic grimoire, add a dash of demon, a pinch of a mad mother, and one resurrected, megalomaniacal prince, and what do you get?

The end of everything.

"You can't use your magic, not these days," Lyon said. "The human population has exploded since your time. They outnumber us, and when they're afraid, they're vicious. If the humans learn about you, they'll overrun the InBetween and kill every paranorm."

Circe heaved a sigh. "I don't know why I bother."

"You can't do it. Millions of paranorms will die."

"Not just paranorms. When we're done, millions of the weakest, most useless paranormals *and* humans will either be killed or be possessed. Those strong enough to survive the first wave will serve me as I devour my way through the rest."

"Why?"

She sat in the chair on the other side of the fireplace and raised a forefinger. "Answer number one—because I can—seems too cliché." She added her middle finger, "Answer two—I have mommy issues—is close to the truth, but pathetic." Last, she added her ring finger. "But, answer number three—I always finish what I start—is dead-on true."

"So this is just a 'fuck you' to mommy for putting you in a centuries-long time out?"

"Crude, but accurate." She caressed the cover of the grimoire. "I have to say, I couldn't have done it without Leona's pathological need for Daddy's approval and your lack of control. A beautiful one-two punch you Leos dish out."

She tucked the book in the waist of her skirt and straightened. "Did you know Llewellyn drones on and on in his sleep? 'Out of the darkness, into the light.' It's his most fervent desire, and he'll do anything to get it—even sacrifice his family."

Lyon's breathing increased. Sweat formed at his hairline. "I don't believe you."

Circe laid a hand over her heart. "I have no need to lie about this. Asmodeus warned him about what could happen, that you were too young to be made a Zodiac, but Llewellyn didn't care. All he's ever wanted is to reclaim his birthright."

"No. No, that's not true."

"Oh, yes, it is." She leaned forward. "Despite the absence of the Master of the Dark—and my 'time out' as you call it—the sorcerers continued to thrive and grow and spread his word. Llewellyn knew your mummy was one of the most powerful of the Master's followers. He also knew that he could use her blood to find me. So he married her, filled her belly twice, then, when she reached the height of her skills, he put mummy in your path and waited for the inevitable. And, wow, you didn't disappoint."

Lyon's body jerked and flailed like a man being electrocuted. His mind raced, his heart pounded, as he tried to comprehend this reality shift. Everything he knew about himself and his culpability was tossed on its ear. It still didn't mitigate the fact that he had delivered the killing blow. His gorge rose in his throat. Lyon wanted to strangle the bitch for the gut shot she'd so gleefully delivered.

"I have much to do. That front-row seat to the big show is calling your name, so don't go anywhere." Circe twirled and swept out of the room.

Lyon couldn't organize his thoughts. He closed his eyes and pulled up an image of Persephone's smiling face. He held it tight while he pushed everything else to the back of his mind. There wasn't enough time to sort through the revelations and betrayals. He needed to get free and get Persephone out of the InBetween.

"That was seriously messed up," Sag said.

Lyon dropped his head back. What was there to say? Sag had nailed it.

Several minutes after Circe had swept out the door, three maidens bearing trays entered the room, their eyes wide, the dishes clattering in time with their shaking limbs.

"Put the tray down here," Scor said, pointing to the dining table. They hurried to do his bidding.

"You'll need to feed them," Scor said.

The three whimpered and hugged each other. The smallest of the three burst into tears.

"For goddess' sake, they won't hurt you, they're tied up," Scor yelled.

The girls screamed and ran.

Scor growled as he slammed the door.

"Your charm is working overtime there, old boy," Sag said with a snort.

Scor snapped his fingers. The scorpion hovering over Sag's crotch lowered its stinger to only a millimeter above the fabric.

"Oh, ho, ho. Easy now, bug boy. Just messin' with you."

Scor lifted the plate covers. Steam rose from the three huge plates of food. Tankards of beer overflowed with a beautiful head of foam.

Sag sniffed and moaned. "I'm starving."

Lyon's stomach growled.

Scor looked from the food to the Zodiacs.

"You have two choices: feed us by hand, or untie us and let us feed ourselves," Sag said. "Two against one isn't even a fight for you, Scor. I've seen you up against much worse odds."

Scor untied Sag, but he remained sitting.

"Go. Sit. Eat."

"Uh," Sag said pointing to the bug still sitting on his balls.

Scor removed his scorpion and set it on his hand. "Go."

"Gotta hit the head first."

Scor hissed, but nodded.

Lyon squirmed in his chair. "Untie me, I won't try anything."

"You can eat when Sag is done."

Sag returned and joined Scor at the table. He dove into his food with gusto, groaning with each bite of food and swallow of beer.

Scor shook his head. He'd just picked up his utensils when a log popped and fizzed, then broke into two pieces. One piece stayed in the hearth, while the other rolled onto the rug. Embers ate at the wool fibers.

"Shit," Scor muttered. He rose from his chair and kicked the ember back into the hearth.

Lyon and Sag glanced at each other. Sag nodded briefly and smiled.

Scor stamped out the remaining sparks on the rug until it stopped smoking, then returned to his chair. He looked at his food, then grabbed Sag's wrist before a large piece of steak disappeared into Sag's mouth.

"You dared to touch my food?" Scor asked.

Sag paused.

Lyon's heart raced. *Don't blow it, Sag.*

Sag shrugged his broad shoulders. "Your steak looked better than mine."

Scor pulled the steak off the fork and jammed it in Sag's mouth. "Let's see if you're lying. Chew."

Sag chewed the steak for several seconds, then swallowed. His eyes rolled back in his head.

Lyon inhaled, and held the breath.

Sag opened his eyes and smiled. "Just as I thought, your steak is better than mine."

Lyon sagged in his chair and exhaled.

Scor loomed over Sag, his face dark. "Don't do that again."

Sag raised his tankard. "To no more food theft."

Scor shook his head.

"C'mon, Scor, can't deny a dying man's last toast."

Scor scowled, but raised his beer. The two Zodiacs hit the metal tankards together, then drank deeply.

Sag belched, and smiled before finishing his food. He rose from the table and walked back to his chair. "It's time, brother," he said to Lyon.

Scor pushed back from the table and rose. He swayed, then placed his hands on the table to steady himself. He looked at Sag, and blinked. "I'll kill you, you bast—" Like a felled tree, Scor hit the floor, unconscious.

Sag crossed his legs and smiled. "How much do you love me now, big guy?"

"Untie me," Lyon demanded, his voice a low growl.

Sag shook his head. "Impossible."

As soon as he was freed, Lyon went to the table and shoved handful after handful of food in his mouth.

Sag stared. "I've seen trolls eat with more manners."

Lyon glanced at Sag and grunted. He raised beer to his lips. "I assume you didn't drug this, too."

"I don't drug friends. Even I have standards."

Lyon paused, the term 'friend' so foreign to him he had to delve deep in his memories to remember what the word meant. His heart stopped for a second. He couldn't speak, so he growled and continued to stuff his mouth.

Sag raised his tankard. "To…new friends, and many, many sunsets." He held his beer and waited for Lyon.

Lyon stared at Sag, then the tankard. He lifted his beer to acknowledge Sag's toast. "And less fucking secrets."

Sag smiled. "So, what's first?"

"I need to get a message to Persephone."

"You can't do that."

"Why?"

Sag leaned forward. "Right now, we're a nuisance, not a problem. If they find out that Persephone's been warned, that you're loose in the InBetween, they may move up the time of the ritual. We need all the time we can get."

"For what? Last-minute hopes that we can stop this?" Lyon stood and wiped his mouth with his sleeve. "I'm here for one thing only, and she's in a room a stone's throw from here."

"You would save her and leave the rest of us to die, or worse? Ruled by the man who ordered our father's murders, and the bitch who did the killing?"

"What would you have me do? What is your big hero plan?"

"I say we help the Pondera infiltrate so they can help us fight. I say find the paranorms Llewellyn has imprisoned and release them so they can stand by our side. I say be the big brother who, for once, puts Leona's needs ahead of his own!"

Lyon's hands curled into fists. "Well, maybe I should do that!"

"Maybe you should!"

Lyon stood there, panting, his body trembling with the need to thrash Sag, but he held back. As hard as it was to admit, the guy was right.

"So what do we do first?" Sag asked.

"Did you see Circe's book?"

"I was more worried about freezing to death. Bitch packs a frigid punch."

"It said, Descensus ad Inferos."

"The descent into hell?"

"It was the definitive spellbook for all things demonic until it disappeared centuries ago."

Sag said nothing.

"The darkest rituals known?"

Sag rolled his eyes. "Just spill it."

"The last ritual in the book is for opening the gates of hell."

"By the goddess." Sag rubbed his temples. "That's what—"

"Indeed."

"Holy shit. What do we do first?"

"We need help. This is too big for two."

"The other Zodiacs."

"No, absolutely not. I don't trust them. Besides, this is too huge to stop outright. I need to get to the women and get them out, quietly."

"You think the Zodiacs don't know how to slip in and out without detection? We're a damn sight more experienced at it than you. I can't think of a better group to help us get this done."

"I said no!"

"Man, you and your sister are just alike. Must be a Leo thing." Sag slammed the empty tankard on the table. "I'm only saying this once, so hear me clear. You walked away from us when we needed you. You rained down destruction on the people who loved you most and never had the decency to apologize."

"My apology was allowing Llewellyn to lock me away. I could have run—hell, I could have killed dozens before leaving. But I stayed away. What more was I supposed to do?"

Sag rubbed his temples so hard his skin turned red. "You should have stayed with us, not hidden yourself in a cell. You should have stayed and cleaned up the mess you made. Learned from your mistakes so you didn't repeat them. Instead, you locked yourself away. You took your rage and guilt into the death pit and killed your opponents without mercy until all that was left of you was a beast."

Lyon gritted his teeth and clenched his fists. Acid bubbled up and burned his throat.

Sag held his ground. "If you had stayed, maybe Llewellyn and Asmodeus would have been content with just you as the sole Zodiac Assassin, and the rest of us could have had normal lives. If you had stayed, we wouldn't have been forced to share our soul with that of a demon king. We wouldn't have been forced to kill time after time. But you didn't stay and we've had to carry the burden of your hubris and wrath ever since."

Sag lowered his voice until it was a mere whisper. "But the most egregious sin? You abandoned Leona when she needed you the most. Her big brother, the man she adored, turned on her, ripped her face—and her life—wide open, then walked away."

"Damn it, I walked away for her."

"No, you walked away for you. You chose what was easy for you over what was right for her and everyone else."

Lyon paced the room, waves of hot and cold racing through his body as he thought about Sag's words. He finally stopped in front of the Zodiac. "We don't have time for this. We need to go."

Sag nodded. "You're right, this isn't the time. But be warned, you will deal with this—if not for your sake, then for Leona's." He snatched up the wrapped glove, walked to the door, and stopped with one hand on the knob. "I will see her made well and whole, no matter the cost." Sag walked out, and the door closed with a soft click.

Lyon stood rooted to the floor. He couldn't stop his racing thoughts, his plans of escape wriggling around in his brain like a man floundering to puzzle his way through a maze. Every idea went *splat* as it hit a dead end. He needed more help than just what the Zodiacs could provide—a lot more. And the timing had to be just right. He slid his hands in the pockets of his pants. Something poked his right forefinger. "Shit." He pulled his hand out and found a tiny drop of blood oozing out of the sensitive tip. He slid his hand in his pocket again and pulled out a tiny black feather.

"Collas."

He nodded as a new idea formed. Of course, it hinged on his ability to find the entry to the wall passages. He tucked the feather back in his pocket and cracked open the door. He looked both ways, then slid out of Sag's room.

40

LEONA ENTERED PERSEPHONE'S room followed by several maids carrying food and fresh clothes. Despite their protests, Persephone, Abella, and Taryn were stripped, bathed, covered with henna symbols, and dressed in black robes covered in more symbols embroidered with gold thread.

"What's happening?" Abella asked.

"We're going to a party," Leona said with a smirk.

Persephone backed away from the much-taller Leona and wrapped her arms around her abdomen. Her bruised belly and back still burned from the beating Leona had given her. "We don't want to party, we want to leave."

"Aw, aren't you cute?" Leona stabbed Persephone's breastbone with one finger. "This party is for you. It would be rude for you not to attend." She snapped her fingers and two Creepers lined up in the hallway. "Make sure they don't leave."

Leona looked back. "Rest. Relax. I'll collect you later." She smiled. "This is such a thrilling time. You three are going to help us change the worlds." She closed the door behind her. The guards in the room shifted, but remained standing.

Abella waved Persephone and Taryn closer to the fireplace. "What's going on, Persephone? Libra told us nothing."

"Despite her wiles," Taryn said. "I was impressed with his restraint."

Persephone stared into the fire, mesmerized by the dance of the flames. "What do you think she meant by 'change the worlds'? I don't think it's a good thing, and not just for us." She looked at her two best friends. "Don't get me wrong, I'm terrified, but if we're needed to kick-start whatever is coming, then we can also stop it."

Abella glanced at the guards and lowered her voice. "If we're needed, wouldn't leaving be the best way to stop it?"

"You have a way out?" Persephone asked. "Because I don't."

Abella drummed her long fingers on the mantle. "We do have one weapon that would guarantee a way out."

"Yes," Persephone said, "but I think we need to stay and save that *gift* for later. As you said, it's a one-off."

Taryn leaned closer. "But if we're the key, why not go now?"

Persephone rubbed her temples. "How do you know we're the only keys? Do you want to escape, then find out someone else took our place? I won't take that chance."

Taryn grinned. "Color me shocked."

"Our little dove has traded places with a raptor," Abella said. "I like it. I'm staying, too."

"Well, it won't be a party without me. Besides, you're gonna need my gypsy magic," Taryn chimed in.

"So we're in agreement?" Persephone asked.

"We're all in," Abella said.

Scorpio opened his eyes and looked around the room. He sat up and cracked his twingy neck before pushing off the floor. His head was fuzzy from the drug Sag dosed him with, but he could move his limbs. More importantly, Lyon and Sag were gone. Scor staggered to the door. *To hell with this, it's time for Lyon to be taken out.*

He made his way to Llewellyn's quarters and pounded on the door. A servant opened it and Scor shoved the little man aside. Llewellyn glanced up, then returned to his meal.

Scor stopped at the dining table and slammed a fist on the thick wood. "It's time for me to get my due. When I find Lyon, I'm taking him down," Scor said.

"Go to your room and wait for instructions," Llewellyn ordered.

"No. I've waited long enough."

Llewellyn slowly placed his knife and fork down. He gathered his linen napkin and blotted the corners of his mouth before laying it aside and rising. He stepped toward Scor. "You'll wait…until I tell you otherwise. Do you understand me?"

Scor hissed. His scorpions writhed under his skin, but he backed away. He might be able to take Llewellyn one on one, but sometimes it paid to bide your time. He left Llewellyn's quarters for his own to wait…for the last time.

"Enter," Llewellyn called out, his ire peaked. First, that little bitch Scorpio, now another interruption. A man can't even eat his meal in peace. He placed the sugar-frosted fairy head on his plate and wiped his hands clean.

He shoved his chair back and stood as Asmodeus, Circe, and Leona filed into his quarters followed by a cowering, quivering servant.

Llewellyn threw his linen napkin onto the table. "You, servant. What do you want?"

The man bowed his head and genuflected once, twice—his knees cracking and popping with each effort. "My lord. I have news from the laboratory." He dropped to his knees and remained there, his body shaking. "Bad news."

Llewellyn stalked to the man, his temper rising with each step. "Speak."

The servant crouched low to the ground as if anticipating a blow. "The creatures have been released," he muttered.

Llewellyn crossed his arms over his chest. "What did you say?"

The man turned his head to look at Llewellyn. "The creatures in the lab... They have been released."

Llewellyn clenched his hands into fists, his face burned hot. Rage filled him and he wanted to beat the messenger to death. He drew a ragged breath. "Get out."

The servant scuttled back a few steps.

"Get OUT!" Llewellyn yelled as he advanced on the man.

The servant scrambled to his feet and ran out of the room.

Circe cleared her throat. "Before you allow yourself to be distracted by the inconsequential, has the word been spread about the ritual being performed in the morning?"

"Yes," Llewellyn said.

Leona looked at Circe, then Llewellyn. "Why does that matter?"

Asmodeus touched Leona's arm. "We don't want anyone interrupting us."

"But I thought the ritual needed to be done at dawn."

Circe held out a hand, as if admiring her long black fingernails. "It's a misdirect. The ritual requires no specific hour, just the right blood—which we have now."

"And the Berserkers?" Asmodeus asked.

Llewellyn nodded. "They're engaging the Pondera Novi."

Circe moved around the room. "What about the parents of all those yummy children?"

"They've been collected."

"What are you doing with them?" Leona asked.

Asmodeus and Llewellyn looked at each other. Llewellyn tilted his head as if giving permission.

Asmodeus rubbed his hands together and grinned. "As soon as the gate is opened, the parents will be sacrificed to help my army rise."

"And your daughters?" Llewellyn asked.

"They've been prepped," Circe answered.

Llewellyn downed a shot of whisky. "Lyon is loose."

Circe tapped her pursed lips with her forefinger. "Let him be a distraction for the Zodiacs. They want revenge, so their focus be on him and not on us during the ritual. Don't want them growing a conscience at the last minute."

Leona stepped up to Llewellyn and opened her mouth to speak, but Circe tapped her on the shoulder. "Come, child." Circe walked Leona out of the room. Her grip tightened when Leona tried to break free.

"Release me." Leona said, her teeth bared, canines dropped.

"I, too, have felt that rage for a parent who ignores you, little one. He doesn't see you, doesn't understand the power you have—so much anger, so much potential. Your body is so tight that your skin aches and itches and if you don't move to relieve it, you jerk and flail like a cod on a river bank."

Leona stiffened. "How could you possibly know?"

"I recognize twitchy when I see it." Circe crooked her arm and offered it to Leona. "Come, tell me what you would do as leader of the InBetween."

Leona sneered at the witch, rejecting her arm. "I won't be staying here once the ritual is done."

Circe drew close and cocked her head. "Your energy, it has changed. Grown." She held her hand up close to Leona's heart, her palm nearly touching the girl's shirt.

The locket hummed and lifted off of Leona's skin. She gasped and stepped back, her hands on the locket, pressing it against her chest.

"What do you have there?" Circe demanded as she followed Leona. "Show me. Now." Circe reached for her again but Leona crouched, threw out a fist, and struck the witch goddess in the solar plexus sending her flying into the wall.

Circe slumped on the floor.

Leona ran.

Scor paced his rooms, wearing a path in the rug. Rage fueled his agitation, the need to rip Lyon's head off his body clouding his thinking. He'd asked for one thing, only one—to have a go at Lyon, but Llewellyn kept refusing. And ordering him around like a drudge.

"Screw waiting," Scor muttered. He headed for the door to leave when he heard a muffled voice behind him. He turned, but he was alone in the room. He cocked his head and listened. A soft growl came from his bookcase. He walked to it and leaned in.

A soft scrape and curse sent his adrenaline through the roof. He grabbed the bookcase and pulled it down. The shelves and books landed with a loud bang. He froze when he saw a small peephole. He ran his fingers over it, then pressed his face against the wall to see through it, but all he saw was black. "Son of a bitch."

He reared back and punched through the wall until he'd opened a hole large enough to stick his head inside. Dark ruled. A faint scrape sounded to his right. He stepped back and grabbed the wall with both hands. He ripped it down until he could step inside the passage. He waited for his eyes to adjust, then went right.

There was a rat in this secret maze, and Scor was in the mood for some extermination.

41

SAG GRABBED LIBRA'S ARM and pulled him around. "I'm just asking…" He stopped and faced the wall while two maids laden with dirty laundry scurried past them. He slapped the grey glove against Libra's chest. "I'm just asking you to smell this glove."

"I can smell the blood on it already, including my father's. What's this about?"

"I told you I had proof, and this glove is it."

Libra shoved Sag against the opposite wall. "Here's the truth. Lyon slaughtered our fathers. He tore into them and ripped them apart until all that was left were piles of blood and bits of bone." He dropped the glove on the floor. "If I find him first, there won't be even that much left of him." He walked away.

Sag pulled a dart from his pocket and aimed. It flew past Libra's right earlobe, then bounced off the wall and landed at the Zodiac's feet.

Libra turned slowly. "Seriously?"

"Dead serious. Now smell the inside of glove or by the goddess—"

"All right, I'll smell the damn glove." Libra snatched it from Sag. "But there will come a time…"

"I know—I owe you one."

Libra rolled the leather down to expose the interior, then brought it to his nose and sniffed. He frowned and took a longer sniff. He closed his eyes. "A woman wore this."

Sag nodded. "Exactly. And that means?"

"Lyon was set up."

Sag pointed a finger at Libra and nodded.

"Who?"

"The woman did the deed, but it was Llewellyn who sicced her on our fathers."

Libra adjusted his suit jacket, and looked down the hall. "Give me her name."

"Circe."

"The witch goddess?"

Sag nodded. "The same."

"Do the other Zodiacs know?"

"Not all them. We still need to show this to Pisces and Aquarius."

Libra rubbed his chin. "We need to get the rest of the Zodiacs together—with Lyon—and figure out what the hell is going on."

"You get the Zodiacs living along this corridor, and I'll get the rest. We meet in my room."

Libra walked to the nearest door and pounded on it. "Taurus! Pull your dick out of the wench, and answer the door."

"I'm not in there, you ass," Taurus said.

Libra and Sag turned. The rest of the Zodiacs, save for Lyon and Scorpio, were grouped together and led by several Creepers.

"We're keeping mum about this, right?" Libra whispered.

Sag tucked the glove in his back pocket. "For the moment."

"We've been summoned," Pisces said. "Llewellyn wants to see us."

* * *

Leona stormed into her room, her hand on the door, itching to slam it off its hinges. She stopped when she saw a pair of long legs crossed and hanging over the side of a chair. The legs unfolded and a tall warrior stood.

"Ailith."

The Pondera Exemplar strode to Leona and leaned in, crowding her. She wrapped a hand around Leona's back, pulled Leona tight against her body, and leaned in until her lips hovered near Leona's. "The walls have ears," she whispered. "Is it time?"

Leona slipped a metal cuff into Ailith's cleavage. "This will gain your warriors access to the lift. Have them in place within the hour." She looked at the cloth bag on her bed. "The rest are in there, as well a map."

Ailith released her, walked to the bed, and looked inside the bag before removing a parchment.

"That'll take you to a small, remote outpost manned by an old couple named Hiram and Fessa. It's the best place to infiltrate: quiet, and poorly guarded. Hell, you just look at them wrong and they'll disintegrate into a pile of ash and bone."

Ailith turned her head until her lips hovered over Leona's. "Anything else?"

Leona stood her ground. "Make sure your bitches understand, Circe and Llewellyn are fair game. If they have a shot, take it."

"What about the demon?"

"Do what you want. Kill him, trap him if you can, whatever. I don't care anymore."

"I would have sworn otherwise." Ailith crossed her arms. "Must have been a hell of a find in the reliquary for you to go from being the demon's little bitch to not caring about his fate."

Leona leaned her head to one side, then the other, until her neck cracked. She smiled and leaned close to the impudent warrior. "You're going to have to get a lot smarter if you expect to survive knowing me." She walked into the taller woman and pushed her hard into the wall. Her canines dropped, splitting her gums. Blood filled her mouth with a salty, metallic taste but she ignored the blood—even when it ran down her chin. "You do want to survive, yes?"

"And thrive." Ailith licked her lips and looked away.

The show of submission cooled Leona's anger. "You do as I ask, and the InBetween is yours. No more hiding in the shadows for your people." Leona pushed off of the warrior. "One hour. And Ailith? Make no mistake. You challenge me again, I will kill you."

Lyon cursed under his breath when he slammed his forehead into another low beam. Squeezing sideways through the narrow passage was bad enough, but a few more head slams and a concussion would take him out of this fight. Finally, he came to a small door. He looked out the peephole and saw a long, empty hall ending in a door he hoped to never see again.

The dungeon.

He heard a scrape behind him. He dropped down and stared into the darkness. A squeak above startled him. He looked up and saw a rat scurrying along a wood beam.

Lyon rose. *Damn.*

He tried to shake off the heebie-jeebies, but the tight passage and ratty noises were brutal reminders of his time in the lower dungeons. He took a breath and rechecked the hall. Still empty.

Time to revisit your old digs, boy.

"Shut up, demon," Lyon said, as he opened the door to the hidden passage. He took a last glance up and down the hall, then stepped out and pulled the door shut behind him.

He ran for the entrance to the dungeon, pulled it open, and slipped inside before closing the heavy wood and iron door behind him. He leaned against it for a second before reaching up and removing a large ring of keys from a hook. The thick, rough iron ring was heavy in his hand, but it weighed heavier on his psyche.

"Pull it together, man. This is for her."

He swallowed hard and started the descent into his personal hell.

Scor watched Lyon sprint to the dungeon door, then enter it. He waited for a few seconds before he stepped out of the passage. He loped to the dungeon door and pressed his palm against it, waiting to give Lyon time to get far enough away so he wouldn't know Scor was on his tail. Then, he opened the door a crack, pulled back a sleeve, and touched four of the scorpion tattoos. They writhed under his flesh, rose out of it and dropped to the floor.

"Be my eyes and track Lyon," he whispered. They scurried away, dropping down the stone steps and disappearing into the dark. Scor glanced back before entering the dungeon and closing the door. *Time to claim my pound of flesh.*

42

"WELL, WELL, LOOKS LIKE my little birds are ready for the party," Circe crooned as she walked to Persephone, Abella, and Taryn. She ran a hand down each woman's face.

"We don't know what you want with us, but you ain't getting it," Abella said.

"Oh, but I am." Circe snapped her fingers and the Creepers grabbed the three women. "Come. Let's take you to another room that's closer to the great cavern."

The Creepers forced them out of their room and down a hall.

Circe stopped at a door and looked at Persephone. "This will be especially interesting for you, poppet." She pushed the door open.

The hinges creaked in protest; cobwebs tore and floated down to face height.

Persephone crouched under the webs and looked around the sparse space. A huge king-size four-poster bed dominated the room, leaves and vines and swirls carved into the gold-painted posters. A chair sat on one side of a cold fireplace, a small dining table with only one chair opposite. The walls were barren of decoration. A dust-covered dresser had one lonely frame. This cold, desolate room had been abandoned long ago.

She turned to Circe. "Whose room is this?"

Circe ran a finger across the top of the picture frame, stirring up dust. She wiped her finger on her robe, then picked up the frame. She turned it around for Persephone to see. "Your lover's room. Exactly like it was the day he killed his mother and maimed his sister. The day he went down in the dungeons and never came back."

The self-satisfied smirk slid right over Persephone.

Circe cocked her head and laughed. "I see my revelation is old news."

"No matter what you do to us, Lyon is out there, free, and hungry to kill you."

Circe grabbed Persephone's bottom jaw. "He's not 'out there,' he's here. I promised him a front-row seat to watch the three of you die."

Persephone closed her eyes. *Oh, Lyon, no.*

Abella shoved her body against Circe's arm, breaking the contact between the two women, freeing Persephone. "Why us? If we're to die, at least tell us the reason."

"You three are the blood of my blood, and that means you have the power to open the gates for me."

"Blood of my blood? You mean…?" Taryn whispered.

Circe backed away from Abella and threw her arms open. "You can call me mummy."

Lyon descended all the way through to the lower dungeon with no paranorm parents in sight. He reached the last cell and punched the door. A screech and scuffle sounded, and small thick hands grabbed the cell window. A head slowly appeared. A wild tangled mess of dark hair preceded a filthy squat face and needle-sharp teeth. Gremlin.

The little beast chattered its teeth and hissed. Its throat undulated.

"Don't you dare spit on me, you little shit." Lyon stepped to the side and back to stay out of range.

The gremlin smiled. "Why for here, Zodiac?"

"Where are the paranorms?"

The gremlin frowned. "All paranorm."

"I know we're all paranorms. I'm talking about the newest group of paranorms in the dungeons."

"New group, new group." He raised one forefinger and pointed it at Lyon's hand.

Lyon raised the keys. "Is this what you want?"

The gremlin chattered again.

"Tell me where the group is and I'll set you free."

The gremlin shook his head. "Free now, then show."

"Tell."

"Show."

"So you don't know how to tell me where they are, but you will show me?"

The gremlin nodded.

Turning one gremlin loose wasn't a deal breaker, but it was close. Just one could wreak havoc. But Lyon needed a hand. "Okay, but know this: if you fail to find them, I'm locking you back up. Got it?"

The gremlin nodded again. His hands released the bars and he disappeared.

"This is a bad idea," Lyon muttered. He worked his way through the keys until he found the right one. He opened the door and the gremlin flew out of the cell and down the hall. "You little shit." Lyon took off after him, following the freshest stench until he saw the creature take a right. He skidded around the turn and saw the gremlin hopping up and down at a set of double doors.

It was the spectator entrance to the pit.

Lyon slowed to a walk. He reached the door and laid a hand on it. He hesitated, girding himself for a fight. He picked out the sole gold key and inserted it. "You can go, gremlin."

The little creature smiled and nodded, but remained.

"Okay, stay here then." Lyon unlocked the door and eased it open. The heat swept over him, the orange-red glow illuminating the empty cave.

He stepped inside and let the door close. The gremlin bumped into him. He threw out an arm. "Get outta here."

The gremlin ran to the pit ledge and bounced on his toes.

Lyon followed him. He looked down and saw dozens of paranorms on the floating rock at least forty feet down—probably more, because of their weight. They clung tight to each other, chained and standing because there was no room to sit. Sweat poured off their faces. Their clothes were drenched.

Lyon backed away. How the hell was he supposed to free them? If there was room, he might be able to jump down and remove their chains, but there was no room for him to land. If he tried, someone would have to die to make space for him. Even if that happened, how could he get them off the ledge and out of the pit?

It was a no-win scenario. He needed to get out of the dungeons and figure out how he could stop the ritual without backup. He turned to the door—and saw Scorpio standing there.

Scor sneered. "I've waited for years to feel the crunch of your bones under my fists. To paint my body with your blood."

Lyon dropped the keys and opened his arms. "Give it your best, then."

The Zodiacs crouched and circled each other.

The double doors opened wide and several Creepers entered the cave. They paused, then made for Lyon.

Scor held up his hands. Scorpions poured off his skin and out of his clothes. The insects chased back the Creepers. "He's mine."

Lyon snorted. "Aw, you brought backup. How adorable."

The Creepers backed away from the scorpions. They surrounded the hole in the floor and waited.

"Not backup, they're here to take the paranorm parents to the great cavern."

"What? Is an audience needed?"

Scor crouched. "Not an audience—more like a snack for all the ravenous mouths coming to the party."

Lyon backed up to watch the Creepers and stay out of Scor's reach. Ten more Creepers entered the cave with a long ladder. They lowered it until the ladder spanned the diameter of the pit. A line of Creepers walked on the ladder, then dropped down on the rungs and held out their freakishly long arms to the paranorms. One of the men grabbed an arm and the Creeper pulled him up.

One by one, the Creepers lifted the next man or woman on the chain. As soon as the levitating rock was within reach, the Creepers on the ladder dropped to the rock, the others lowered one end of the ladder, and the rest of the paranorms climbed out of the pit.

Lyon waited for one of the skeletal creatures to attack him, but the Creepers herded the paranorms out and closed the doors behind them without a second glance.

"They're starting the ritual now, aren't they?" Lyon asked, but he knew the answer. If he were a megalomaniacal asshat like his father, he'd do the same thing. "C'mon Scor, I need to go."

"Not a chance."

Lyon and Scor stalked each other, moving in a smaller and smaller circle until they were within striking distance. Scor lunged and slammed a fist into Lyon's face. Blood exploded from Lyon's nose. He staggered back a couple steps, then charged the Zodiac.

He hit Scor's belly and slammed him against the wall. Scor's air came out in a great *oomph*.

Scor sagged against Lyon's back.

Lyon loosened his grip and Scor slammed his fists into Lyon's kidneys.

The flank wound broke open, and Lyon faltered.

Scor kneed Lyon in the gut and shoved him away.

Lyon staggered back, bent at the waist. He placed his hands on his thighs and turned sideways to Scor, the pain so great his lungs refused to work. Before he could get a deep breath, Scor charged.

Lyon waited for Scor to get within arm's length, then dropped into a roll.

Scor lost his balance.

Lyon kicked both feet into Scor's hips and let gravity and momentum carry Scor over him.

Scor landed on his back. Lyon slammed one leg down on the Zodiac's neck before rolling away.

Scor grabbed his throat with both hands and gagged.

Lyon got to his hands and knees and crawled to a wall. He sat against it, resting until the fire gripping his body cooled enough to allow him to rise.

Scor rolled to his hands and knees and dry heaved.

Lyon staggered to Scor and grabbed his hair. He lifted the Zodiac's head and punched him in the face.

Scor sank to his knees.

Lyon kicked him in the jaw.

Scor fell back and landed in a heap.

Lyon stood over him, his jelly legs spread wide to stay on his feet. He spat out a mouthful of blood. "Are we done here?"

Scor raised a hand.

Lyon took it and helped Scor to stand.

Scor nodded, his eyes down.

Lyon released him and started to turn when Scor grabbed Lyon's head and kneed him in the face.

Lyon fell.

Scor took a handful of Lyon's blond hair and smashed his fist into Lyon's mouth. "You never look away," Scor said. He punched Lyon in one eye, splitting the skin.

Lyon clawed at Scor's arm, but couldn't gain purchase.

"Until your enemy," Scor punched Lyon again, then released him, "is dead."

Lyon collapsed to the floor. Scor straddled him and sat on his chest. He raised his fists to deliver a fatal blow, but stopped when the doors to the pit flew open and banged against the wall.

"Stop! Llewellyn wants him alive." Sag and Libra ran into the pit cave and tackled Scor.

His scorpions skittered to Lyon and crawled on him, their stingers poised.

Sag pulled a blade. "Call them off, bug boy."

Scor turned his head and spat, then slapped one palm against the ground. The remaining scorpions skittered to him and flowed up his arm and over his body before sinking back into his skin.

Scor shook his head. "He's mine. Leave now and I won't kill him...yet."

Sag and Libra backed to the doors. "Llewellyn wants Lyon front and center," Sag said.

"Go. Now," Scor answered as he wrapped Lyon's long hair around one hand.

The two Zodiacs scowled but left the pit.

Scor jerked Lyon's hair, pulling the man to his feet. "I've waited for this day for years."

Llewellyn sat on the gold dais watching the priests finish carving the huge sigils in the great cavern floor. More intricate than a circular maze, the highest point was in the center, perfect for letting gravity do all the work. His voluminous gold robe hid a leather shirt and pants with protection symbols carved into the dried skin. He patted his thighs, the HellHawk throwing knives strapped to them reassuring. Just a few more minutes and he would be free of this hellhole.

The priests stopped; the sigils were done. They looked at him, and he waved them away. A Creeper appeared in a doorway at the opposite end of the cavern. It looked around, then continued in.

Behind him, guarded by several more Creepers, were the shackled paranorms—the parents of the children who'd been plucked from their arms. Corvus Wards, Portends, Indigos, Kellas Cats, Harpies, the list of species was long, the menu perfect for feeding a starving demonic army. They shuffled into the great cavern, herded by the Creepers.

Llewellyn shifted in his chair to look at the demon. "How close are we?"

"The Berserkers are engaging the Pondera Novi."

"Are they holding?"

Asmodeus straightened his tuxedo bowtie. "Oh, yes. Definitely no-holds-barred blood, boobs, and bare-ass naked. It's enough to make a man quiver."

Llewellyn remained silent. He watched the Creepers herd the paranorms around the sigil until the living ring closed. Once done, the Creepers took up positions between the sigil and the paranorms. Outside the layer of paranorms, the final ring of trolls and fairies, Amazons and reapers stepped into place to guarantee no parents could escape and no interlopers could pass.

He drummed his fingers on the table. He'd just opened his mouth to ask where the rest of the party was when Leona strode in dressed like a warrior. She looked at him and frowned. She climbed the dais steps and stood on his left.

Llewellyn shook his head. "You look like hell. What have you done to yourself?"

She placed a hand on his shoulder and squeezed.

He tried to pull away. "Damn you, let go."

"Am I hurting you?" she crooned.

He looked in her face and jerked back. Her eyes were a swirling, glowing gold, her skin covered in thick makeup that didn't disguise her pallor or the black circles around her eyes. She smiled, exposing her elongated canines. "Get off me," he demanded.

Asmodeus touched Leona's shoulder and she released her sire.

Llewellyn rubbed his hand. "You're rotting even as we sit here. What makes you think you'll live long enough to help me in any way?"

"What? Starting the fun without me?" Circe said from the foot of the elevated table.

PERSEPHONE WATCHED THE TENSION between the players. Circe seemed calm, confident, as did the demon. Llewellyn may have wanted to seem the same, but she could feel the fear coming off him in waves. But it was Leona who scared her.

In the short time since Persephone had seen Lyon's sister, the woman had changed—and not for the better. She looked sick, inside and out: her complexion—though pale to begin with—was cadaverous, drained of blood, her flesh white and blue at the same time, the skin peeling as if she was decomposing before their eyes. Even her thick blonde hair was now limp and patchy.

Abella leaned over. "Who's who?"

"Leona is Lyon's sister, the blond man is Lyon's father, and were I to guess I'd say the man standing is the demon king, Asmodeus."

Taryn leaned over. She opened her mouth, but before she could speak she tripped and fell against Persephone and Abella. The women grabbed her arms to stop her from hitting the floor. It wasn't until Taryn was righted that Persephone gasped.

"Taryn? Abella? Look."

The women were holding each other, and nothing was happening. No wind, no thunder, no catastrophic weather anomalies.

Circe chuckled from behind them. "I prepped you, remember?"

The three flinched away from her.

"The food?" Persephone asked.

"And the drink, all laced to render you normal." Circe clapped her hands. "I need your blood, not your chaos."

Three Creepers dragged the women to the middle of the elevated innermost sigil ring. They placed Persephone at twelve o'clock and Abella and Taryn at nine o'clock and three o'clock, then pushed them down until they lay on their backs. The creatures bound them and backed away.

Persephone choked on her fear. Her breathing increased until she was hyperventilating and her vision swam. She shook her head hard to gain control, but her body rebelled against her will. A shout echoed through the huge cave. She turned her head and gasped.

Just like in her vision, Lyon was struggling against Scorpio, his face swollen and so bloody he was close to unrecognizable. Scor cuffed the back of Lyon's head, then dragged him to the edge of the outer ring and forced him down on his knees between a troll and a reaper, directly behind Circe.

The other Zodiacs took up places around the circle, a space open for Scorpio.

"Lyon!" Persephone strained against her bindings to get Lyon's attention, but he stared at the dais. "Lyon?"

His shoulders jerked when she cried for him, but he didn't look at her. She struggled until her skin was chafed. Her frustration and pain restraining her as surely as the bindings.

Circe walked to six o'clock and knelt. She removed a small dagger, and nodded to the three Creepers guarding to her daughters. They pulled identical blades.

Circe drew the sharp metal down her wrist, opening her vein. She tilted her wrist and let the blood drip into a small well. She raised her hand, laid a poultice over the cut, and within seconds the wound had healed.

She stood, then nodded to the Creepers. "Do it."

Persephone's Creeper cut her wrist, but didn't stop at a few millimeters. It opened her vein and her blood pumped into the wells with every beat of her heart. The blood pooled then spilled over, traveling to the middle of the sigil before running down the maze of carved symbols.

Circe opened two books, then raised her arms and chanted.

"Conjuro potentiae Lucifer
Patefacio a porta ad inferos
Et tua deamones transire
Sic urantar mundi."

The ground rumbled and bucked once, then fell quiet again.

"Conjuro potentiae Lucifer
Patefacio a porta ad inferos
Et tua deamones transire
Sic urantar mundi."

The stone heaved, stretching, straining like something was pushing it from within.

"Conjuro potentiae Lucifer
Patefacio a porta ad inferos
Et tua deamones transire
Sic urantar mundi."

The Creepers fell back. The paranorms screamed and fought their chains. Persephone struggled against her restraints, but she had grown too weak. "Lyon!"

44

LYON STAYED ON HIS KNEES, tortured by the need to run to Persephone and free her, to soothe away her hurt and fear, but the only way he could get her through this was to ignore her. *Wait for it. Wait for it.*

The other Zodiacs stumbled back from the buckling ground. His skin itched, his gut roiled, but, for the first time, it wasn't the demon soul searching for control. It remained a steady presence just under his skin, undemanding—patient, even—as if waiting for his signal. Shit, what a change these last few days and an assimilation had wrought.

The energy of the ground beneath his feet vibrated through him, growing in frequency and depth. He looked left, then right. The Zodiacs fought to get back in formation. They each returned his glance.

They were ready.

The middle of the sigil cracked, and steam exploded out. The screams of the paranorms were as loud and distracting as the eerie whistle-whine of the steam. Mother Earth had split at the seams and she was shrieking her rage and insult. The floor heaved again. The crack widened.

The terrified paranorms pushed and shoved at the line of trolls and fairies, Amazons and reapers, but the powerful captors didn't budge.

How the hell were Lyon and the other Zodiacs supposed to break through the three rings to get to Persephone and her friends? He looked for anything, a distraction, a moment that screamed 'now.'

A deeper rumble started slow, but picked up momentum. Asmodeus' army was coming.

Lyon grit his teeth and dropped his head. *Goddess, I need your help...now.*

A howl broke through the screams of the paranorms.

Lyon opened his eyes and glanced to his right. There in the deep shadows stood a huge male fenrir-wolf, its eyes reflecting the light, making them look silver. Another pair of eyes appeared, then dozens more. Behind them, gremlins, the stag fairies, and more waited. The beasts looked directly at him, giving him chills—and hope. He nodded once, then struggled to gain his feet.

The fenrir-wolves raced into the cavern and leapt at the outer circle of guards. Screams and roars pulled attention away from the inner circle and the three women dying there.

The ground heaved again. Scor released him to fend off the long, razor-sharp claws of a necrofelidae. Lyon staggered away from the Zodiac, his arms pinwheeling to stay upright. A pair of hands gripped his shoulders and kept him from falling. Lyon glanced back.

Sag jammed two daggers into Lyon's hands and pointed to the women. "Free them." He pointed to the chained paranorms. "We'll take care of the parents."

They nodded.

Lyon turned and saw Fessa and Hiram—the old couple from the outpost—stagger into the space, holding each other up, their clothes bloodstained.

Hiram collapsed to the ground bringing Fessa down with him. "Help," Fessa yelled. She rolled off of Hiram and sat up. "Lyon, we're under—"

A triple-bladed throwing knife flew across the sigil, and buried itself in Fessa's chest. She fell to one side, her hands gripping the hilt.

Lyon tracked the knife trajectory back to Leona. She dropped her hand and rose from her half-crouch stance, her expression flat.

Lyon raised his daggers, the need to run Leona through hot in his gut. Instead, he focused that rage on the Creeper closest to Persephone.

Screams filled the cavern as the other Zodiacs attacked the guards not already being pulled down by the beasts.

Lyon dodged the slash of filthy nails, whirled, then lunged, driving his blade deep into the Creeper's chest. Another clawed Lyon's back, shredding his shirt and the skin underneath it. He grabbed the Creeper's wrist and elbow and slammed it against his knee. The bones cracked; the creature screamed. Lyon jammed his blade under the Creeper's chin. It froze, then slowly slumped to the floor.

Lyon ran to Persephone and dropped to his knees to cut her loose. Her lips were blue, her eyes barely open. "Come on, love, stay with me."

He gathered her in his arms and looked around for a safe place. Taurus, Aries, and Aquarius were hacking away the chains binding the paranorms. The freed men and women ran at the Creepers and trolls with nothing but their bare hands and snapping teeth. The melee became a din of yells and shrieks that competed with the surging, buckling floor.

Lyon turned and saw Martina waving both arms at him from a dark, narrow servant corridor. He pushed his way through the crowd and carried Persephone to her. The old healer laid a wad of goddess-only-knew-what green moss on Persephone's wrist, then wrapped it tight. She chanted some words over the bandage then released Persephone's arm.

"Do you have a weapon?" Lyon asked the healer.

She raised the hem of her robe and pulled out a sword. "I won't let anything happen to her."

Lyon nodded. A battle cry rose behind him. Before he could turn, Martina lunged at him. He tried to move before the woman could run him through, but instead of feeling the cold fire of steel in his belly, the sword ran under his arm and a pained grunt sounded behind him. He turned and watched the body of the now-dead Berserker slump to the floor.

"Son of a bitch." He glanced at Martina. "I'm glad you're on my side."

"Lyon." Martina pointed at Circe. "You need to kill her. If you can't kill her, get her books—they'll be on her person. She's strong in her own right, but with her grimoire and the other book…she's unstoppable."

Lyon nodded. "I understand."

Martina flashed a smile. "Go kick it in the ass, boy. For all of us."

Lyon ran into the cavern and assessed the situation. At least a dozen Berserkers were fighting the Zodiacs. The paranorms were being slaughtered, but they just kept charging forward, a wall of enraged flesh set free to avenge the theft—and possible murder—of their children.

He looked at the center of the sigil. Abella and Taryn lay immobile over their wells, their skin blue and their faces blank.

Lyon ran over the body of a dead troll, and past several parents huddled together in confusion. One of the men grabbed Lyon before he passed. Lyon whirled on him, his daggers poised to kill, when he saw the man's face.

"You're the Corvus Ward," Lyon said.

"What can I do?"

"You know how to fight?"

The Corvus Ward male nodded.

Lyon gave the man one of his daggers. "They took your children, your blood. It's time to take theirs."

The Corvus male wrapped his fingers around the grip and nodded.

Virgo was under siege by two Berserkers. Lyon joined him, and they hacked and slashed at the tattooed women.

One Berserker dropped to the floor and kicked Lyon's legs out from under him. She jumped up and straddled him, then reared back with both hands on her sword. Lyon raised his dagger and ran the blade up under her ribs, piercing her heart. She screamed and fell to the floor.

Virgo was still fighting the other Berserker. Lyon ran his sleeve over his forehead to get rid of the sweat and started for Taryn. He fought his way to her and freed her wrists and ankles.

Lyon turned to look at Abella, loathe to leave her on the altar when time was so critical, when something slammed into his back and rolled off. He whirled, and ran his dagger through a reaper. He had squatted by Abella's head when he saw Scorpio emerge from the deep shadows, oblivious to the fighting, the blood, and the death around him. Scor entered the sigil, pushing his way through the Berserkers as if they weren't there, as if the slashing blades were no threat.

Lyon rose to his feet and raised his blade, waiting for Scor to attack, but the Zodiac ignored him.

Instead, he knelt and touched Abella's face, a caress both gentle and possessive. He freed her wrists and ankles, then scooped her up and carried her to Martina without a word.

Lyon grabbed Taryn and followed Scor's path through the fighting.

He saw Scor lay Abella down and watch as Martina applied the herb wrap. Scor spoke to Martina but she ignored him. The Zodiac drew a dagger and pressed the tip against Martina's neck.

Lyon picked up the pace. The spell that disguised Martina from the world was about to get her ganked by her own son. He'd be damned before he'd let Scor carry that burden.

Martina turned her head to the Zodiac and nodded once.

Scor disappeared into the melee.

Son of a bitch. What was that? Lyon skid to a stop next to his aunt and lowered Taryn to the ground. "Are you okay?"

"Yes."

"What did Scor say?"

She pursed her lips and shook her head. "It's not important, get back to it."

The women were safe for now, and, if Martina was half the healer he believed her to be, the three would survive. He glanced around to see where he needed to go next. Circe's forces were running from the attack by the paranorm parents. The men and women may have been armed only with their pain and rage and grief, but they were greater in number and driven by a clawing, kicking, biting murderous frenzy. Their opponents didn't stand a chance.

Then he saw Llewellyn sitting on the dais, drinking wine and eating, like death and dying were part of his daily entertainment. Asmodeus and Leona had retreated to one corner of the cavern, Sagittarius hot on their trail.

Another lurch of the floor shook the cavern. The table on the dais leaned to one side, then collapsed to the floor. Llewellyn stood and blotted his mouth before he descended to the floor and joined Circe at the outer ring.

Lyon growled. His mission was a go, two of his targets in sight.

Circe smiled.

Lyon lowered his head and fought his way through flying fists and bloody blades. A Creeper stepped in his way and he barely glanced at it when he slit its throat. The twitching body fell at his feet, but Lyon stepped over it, his focus on Circe.

"It's over, bitch," Lyon growled.

She walked backward around the circle until she stood behind Llewellyn. "You have your inamorata and her friends, I'll give you that. But this is not over."

She raised a hand, then curved her fingers like a claw.

Llewellyn pulled his blades but before he could defend himself, Circe closed her fingers in the air.

Llewellyn coughed and gagged. His knives clattered to the floor. He clasped his throat, fighting against her invisible grip.

"Isn't that sweet, Llewellyn? Your boy is here to give you a schooling," she said. She dropped her arm.

Llewellyn collapsed to his knees.

Lyon's body raged with heat and turmoil. His hands itched with the desire to carve into his sire until the man disappeared, but he couldn't do it. "No."

"Come *on!*" Circe frowned. "What a disappointment."

She released Llewellyn.

He climbed to his feet. "Just like your mother. Weak, sentimental, a waste of space on two legs," he said before he punched Lyon.

The blow sent Lyon back a step. He returned the punch. Over and over, father and son pounded each other until Llewellyn staggered and fell to his knees.

Lyon grabbed his throat.

Llewellyn grinned through the blood. "Do it. Kill me like you killed your mother. If you can."

Lyon squeezed until his sire choked. All his hate and frustration and grief poured through him, into his hands, clenching Llewellyn's throat tighter and tighter.

Lyon jerked when a hand settled on his shoulder. Persephone stood behind him, still pale, but standing.

She shook her head. "No, Lyon. You don't have to do this. You're more than a killer."

"Am I?" he asked. Blood and saliva dripped from his mouth and ran down his chin. "Right now, I'm happy to wear that mantle."

"You going to heel like a bitch?" Llewellyn asked, his head cocked to the side, his grin bloody and his bruised eyelids nearly swollen shut.

Lyon sneered. "She's right." He released his sire's throat and leaned back. "You don't deserve to get off that easily. You have a lot to answer for—enough for many lifetimes. But I do owe you this." Lyon clenched a fist and punched Llewellyn one more time. The man fell back and laid still.

Persephone helped Lyon rise.

"He'll live," he said. He smiled at Circe. "Your turn."

"Give it your best shot."

He grabbed his dagger from the floor and went after Circe. When he was close enough, he gathered a bunch of her robe and pulled her to him. He raised the blade.

Before he could strike the killing blow, Leona tackled him. They rolled and she ended up on his chest. She punched his face over and over, the heavy blows punctuated by her shrill screams.

Lyon rolled and shoved her off him. He jumped to his feet. Leona rose slowly. Her skin was dusky and peeling, her breathing labored. The deep dark shadows around her eyes looked like she had one foot in the grave already.

"It's over, Leona. Please, let me help you."

She grinned at him, her teeth yellow and pointed. Her eyes shifted between her normal amber color to glowing gold and back again, as if she couldn't decide what she was or what she wanted. Her grin transformed into a broad smile that cracked the flesh over her prominent cheekbones and her plump lips. Blood slowly rolled down both sides of her face and down her chin. Without looking, she held out a hand. The pile of debris of the wrecked dais blew apart and a large pouch flew across the cavern and to her. She caught it with both arms and lifted the single strap over her head and settled it across her chest, then walked backward to Asmodeus.

In the span of a moment, the fighting and screams stopped, and the screech and whine from the large crack in the floor softened. Circe's remaining allies were huddled in a corner, trapped by the surviving parents.

"Give it up, bitch, you're done," Lyon said.

Circe laughed. She helped Llewellyn up and cupped his face. She gave him a soft kiss, and dragged him with her as she backed into the inner ring. She slid her hands down and wrapped them around Llewellyn's throat. Her long, sharp thumbnails ran up and down as if taunting Lyon, daring him to watch. Then, in one slice, she sliced open Llewellyn's throat.

Llewellyn collapsed to the floor, his blood flowing into a shallow groove in the stone. It mingled with the women's blood until it finished the depiction-in gory red detail—of the sigil of the gates of hell.

Circe crouched by Llewellyn's side. "You didn't really think you'd get to rule in the Overworld? You were always my fall back plan, little prince, in case this happened. All of my mother's delicious goddess blood inside you will raise the demons I need to rule all the worlds."

The ground rumbled. New cracks formed inside the sigil. The tapestries on the walls fell to the floor. The great cavern's columns of stalagmites and stalactites crumbled, sending the crowd into a panic, scrambling to get away.

The center of the blood-filled maze cracked into two pieces, then four, then eight, until all that remained was rubble. Circe leapt out of the center and danced over the wreckage until she reached Asmodeus and Leona.

With a final rumble, the stone debris fell away and disappeared into a massive hole, then blew back out with deadly ejectas of steam and sulfur that punctured the ceiling of the great cavern.

The earthquake stopped. Silence gripped them.

Within seconds, a thunderous scream ripped out of the hole and ricocheted around the cavern.

"Back! Everyone get back," Lyon yelled.

Circe slapped a hand on Asmodeus' shoulder. She leaned close and whispered in his ear, then backed away, grinning. The demon jerked hard to the left, then right. He reached for Circe, his eyes wide, and his mouth slack as he fell to his knees.

"No!" Leona screamed. She lunged for Circe, but Sag grabbed her waist. She punched and scratched his arms and legs, but he held her tight as he headed for the closest passageway, ignoring the damage she inflicted and her screams.

Lyon ran to them. "Sag? What are you doing?"

"She needs my help, and by the goddess she's going to get it."

Leona calmed and sank into Sag's arms, her back against his chest. Her shoulders shook, her head dropped, and she covered her eyes.

"Are you crying?" Sag asked.

She sobbed even as she shook her head.

"Aw, hell." Sag stopped and lowered Leona so she could stand.

Lyon held back to give Sag time to say goodbye. Sag gently turned Leona's face toward him. Lyon cringed when he saw her, her eyes red from tears brought on by the acrid stench of the gases filling the cavern, the snot coming out of her nose, her disintegrating face.

But Sag acted like he'd never seen her so beautiful. Lyon's heart broke for both of them.

Sag touched Leona's face. "Please. Don't cry."

Leona looked into his eyes. She gave him a soft smile, then wrapped her arms around his neck.

"Sag. Watch yourself," Lyon said. He reached out for the Zodiac, but Sag shook his head and pulled Leona close.

She kissed his neck and cheek and then his lips, a soft kiss that tore Lyon apart. Goddess only knew how hard it was for Sag. Hope surged and Lyon took a step, but Leona shifted in Sag's arms, threw her head back—and sank her teeth into the side of his neck.

Sag grunted, but didn't pull away.

"Leona!" Lyon pulled on her until she released Sag, then shoved her away.

Leona staggered back, her grin a slit in her blood-coated mouth. She lurched around the huge hole until she reached Asmodeus.

Sag started to follow, but Lyon held him back. "It's too late, she's chosen her side. If you go to her now, she'll kill you."

"I'll take my chances." Sag struggled to free himself from Lyon's grip, his despair and need heartbreaking.

Lyon tightened his hold. "I know this is hard, but Leona will need you to help her through the long, dark fall that's coming." Lyon waited until he felt the Zodiac's body relax, before releasing him.

Together, they watched Leona help the demon stand.

"I promise you, we'll get her back," Lyon said.

Before Sag could respond, Circe threw her hands in the air. "Out of the darkness and into the light, my pretties!"

Thick, writhing black smoke exploded out of the hole. It circled the cavern as if it was sentient, exploring sections of rock until it reached the roof. The smoke hovered below the ceiling, the undulating mass growing in size until no more smoke exited the hole. The earthquake ended; the rocks stopped screaming. The mass consolidated, then it pushed at the network of punctures that dotted the ceiling leading to the Overworld. The waves of smoke quivered as if excited, then bunched up and blew out of the cavern, leaving destruction and silence in its wake.

45

LYON LOOKED FOR CIRCE and Asmodeus, but they were gone. Only Leona remained, a step away from the huge rift in the floor.

Sag surged forward.

Leona grinned, bent her knees, and jumped backward into the massive hole. She fell out of view for a moment, then slowly reappeared, hovering in midair. This level of magic was beyond anything Lyon had ever seen or thought possible.

A flash of movement caught his eye. Sag was racing to the hole. "No!" Lyon raised a hand. "Someone stop him!"

Before Sag could launch himself at Leona, still floating inside the abyss, Taurus t-boned him. The pair of Zodiacs hit the floor and slid several feet, Sag kicking and punching the larger male.

Lyon caught up to the pair and gripped one of Sag's arms, stopping the fight. "If you really love her, you have to stay alive." Lyon shook Sag until he acknowledged him. "Do you hear me?"

Sag stared for a moment, then nodded as Leona sank out of sight. "What makes you think she will survive this?"

"With all I've seen lately, I have to believe." Lyon released Sag's arm. "We're good, Taur."

Taurus shook his head as he pushed off the floor. "I'm never fucking falling in love."

Lyon held out a hand to Sag. "You and me together. We'll find her."

Sag took Lyon's hand and rose to his feet. "I'm holding you to that," Sag said as they walked back to the gathering group.

"What just happened?" Persephone asked, her head craned back.

"A demon army has been loosed on the humans," Lyon said.

Libra joined Lyon. "It's hell on earth, figuratively and literally."

Lyon looked around at the destruction of his world. He dropped his dagger and walked from the Zodiacs, checking the bodies of the fallen for a pulse. So many lost. He continued until he found the Corvus Ward male laying in a heap. He squatted down and laid his palm over the man's heart.

The male grabbed Lyon's wrist. He opened his mouth and blood gurgled out. He choked and sputtered for a moment before finding his voice. "Did we stop it?"

Lyon shook his head. "No, but we will."

The male turned his head. Lyon followed his sight line and saw the man's sister lying dead a few feet away. A Memoria soul-keeper worked her way through the fallen until she reached the dead Corvus woman. She lowered her body, careful to keep the crown of iridescent blue and black butterflies on her head from tipping, and held out a hand. A golden glow enveloped the Corvus woman for several seconds then winked out, revealing a butterfly on her chest. It unfurled its wings, then flapped them several times before rising in the air and joining the other butterflies. The Memoria rose to her feet and looked at the Corvus male next to Lyon.

"I never thought dying could be made so beautiful," the Corvus whispered.

"Your sister had the heart of a warrior."

"And the soul of a mother—pure and beautiful."

Lyon dropped his head. Shame swamped him. He should have done more. "I'm sorry."

"Don't be sorry," the male whispered. "Find Collas. Find him, and make sure he's okay."

The Memoria kneeled next to the male and looked at Lyon. This was not the place for him. He started to rise, but the Corvus grabbed his hand. "Stay?"

Lyon nodded and gripped the man's hand tight. "I vow to find him and tell him how much he was loved."

The male took a deep breath, then exhaled a final time, his eyes now blank and fixed.

Lyon waited for the man's soul to flutter up and join the souls of his family. He rose and watched to see if the Memoria would walk away or begin the Lines End Release Ritual.

Persephone leaned against him and slipped her hand in his. "Why are you watching her?"

The Memoria smiled at him and made her way out of the cavern. He released his breath: the boy Collas must still be alive. Had the child been dead, it would have meant that his Corvus family line had come to an end, and the Memoria would have performed the release ritual so all of the collected souls could travel together—as a family—to the other side. It was a beautiful ritual, but sad in its finality.

"I'll explain later." He kissed the top of her head, then looked at the bodies all around him, and the many Memorias busy collecting souls. Butterflies of different colors and sizes fluttered and rose in the air, softening the horror of the bloody carnage. He shook his head. "This shouldn't have happened."

"So, what are you going to do about it?"

"Me?"

"Yes. You, and the rest of us," she said as she waved a hand at the other Zodiacs in the cavern. "All of us. With eleven Zodiac Assassins, and the three daughters of the most powerful witch goddess ever known, we should be able to put the genie back in the bottle."

"Aw," Taurus said from behind Lyon and Persephone. "She's adorable."

Lyon agreed, but he was smart enough to keep his mouth zipped.

The Zodiacs gathered with Lyon and, together, they moved the injured out of the unstable cavern to a smaller cavern, while the women helped set up a makeshift ward where Martina and several other healers could help the wounded.

They worked for hours to free every dead body and lay them out with respect.

Persephone, Taryn, and Abella called the Zodiacs together and fed the exhausted men.

Lyon held out a hand for Persephone. She took it and sat next to him. He looked in her eyes and saw the love she had professed in the Pondera realm. His heart swelled with joy and pride and love. For the first time, the need for connection that had been buried so deep under layers of anger that he'd never even known he desired it, swamped him. He wrapped an arm around her waist and pulled her tight against his side. "Are you okay?"

"I'm alive. My sisters are alive." She looked at him. "My love is alive." She touched his swollen face and winced. "You are Lyon, right?"

"Yes," he said with a snort, "and you are my inamorata. My love."

She beamed at him, her face flushed.

He touched her cheek and leaned close, gently pressing his lips against hers. Her soft, warm breath tickled him.

Catcalls echoed.

Lyon pulled away from Persephone and looked at the Zodiacs. "All right, all right. If you have enough energy to heckle us, you have enough to talk strategy. The demons need to be found and shoved back into hell. But I can't do this alone." He stood and placed his right fist over his heart. "Who will join me?"

One by one, the men got to their feet and placed their fists over their hearts, until the eleven stood in a united circle. Abella, Taryn, and Persephone stood with the men, their fists over their hearts.

"Brothers?" Lyon asked.

The Zodiacs said *"brothers"* in unison.

"Don't forget sisters," Taryn added.

Lyon smiled. "Naturally."

"*Sisters*," the men said, their voices echoing around the cavern.

Lyon looked at each Zodiac, truly seeing each man standing with him for the first time. "We have work to do. Let's go kick it in the ass."

46

SCORPIO WATCHED THE GROUP of Zodiacs and women hug it out. It made him want to puke. They broke apart, but the women remained standing in one place. Abella ran a hand through her short hair and swayed.

He jerked forward, his every instinct screaming to go to her, claim her before one of the other Zodiacs did. One day he would have her, he swore to himself. And if anyone had a thought to stand in his way, Scor would end him.

But first he had work to do, and it only called for one.

He backed down the unlit passage, and melded with the darkness.

EPILOGUE

P ERSEPHONE PUSHED THE WHEELBARROW to the last troll in a ring of the pungent beasts guarding the steaming hole in the great cavern, the pack of fenrir-wolves trailing her as they had done since the demon army had been released. She stopped and heaved out a huge watermelon, then staggered to the creature and placed the fruit at its feet. The troll's mouth fell open and drool threatened to drench her…again. She stepped back several feet and crossed her arms, watching the trolls' faces light up as they bit into the sweet treat.

She ventured between two of the beasts and stopped at the rim of the bottomless breach in the earth's crust.

Abella worked her way through the ring of animals surrounding Persephone and stopped next to her. They stared into the darkness together. "What are you doing?"

"Looking in the dark."

"No, I mean with the trolls."

Persephone blinked and looked at their contented munching. "I thought I'd try increasing their fiber to help with…" She waved a hand under her nose.

Abella's eyes widened, then she smiled. "Ah, yes. Good thought."

"Hey, a little help here," Taryn said.

Persephone and Abella turned and rushed to Taryn. They caught several journals at the bottom of the stack in Taryn's arms before they hit the floor.

"Here, just put them down," Taryn said with a jut of her chin.

They set the journals on the ground and Taryn straightened the stack.

"What are these?" Persephone asked.

Taryn stood and wiped the sweat off her forehead before arching her back. "These are Llewellyn's journals. He kept pristine records of every experiment and breeding, his successes and his failures. He was a monster, but he also was a hell of a scientist."

"That's a lot of notes," Abella said.

Taryn squatted. She held up the top three journals, her face beaming. "These are about us."

"What?" Persephone asked.

Taryn handed her a journal, then passed one to Abella. "Our names are on the first page, as if someone was tracking us and knew what names we picked for ourselves."

"That's disturbing," Abella mumbled.

They opened the journals together.

"There must be a hundred pages in here," Abella said. She thumbed her way through the book and frowned.

"It's written in code," Persephone said.

Taryn smiled. "There *is* a living primer, if we can find her."

Abella and Persephone nodded and handed the journals back to Taryn.

"That's a lot to go through," Persephone said with a nod to the stack.

Taryn looked at the pile. "Oh no, this is just what I could carry. There's a room filled with hundreds of journals."

Taryn looked at Persephone and Abella. "Don't you see? If we can find Llewellyn's 'primer,' then we can find out who our fathers are—find proof about what species we are."

Persephone flashed a smile and looked away. "That's a great find, Taryn. But if those three journals are about us—"

Abella snapped her fingers. "How many of these other journals are about people like us, half witch goddess and half something else?"

"And how many have waking powers they have no clue how to control?" Taryn asked.

Persephone turned back to the massive hole. Taryn and Abella joined her.

"There's something else we haven't considered," Abella said. "There are four worlds: the Overworld of the humans, the InBetween, Hades, and Hell."

"Seriously with the redundant?" Taryn groused.

"So what else might have risen with the demon army?" Persephone asked quietly as she rubbed her chest.

Abella pointed to her and nodded.

Persephone backed away from her sisters and the rim of the depths. There was too much to think about, too many questions coming at her in waves, each wave higher and more terrifying and spawning a host of more questions with no answers.

She had reached her limit on worry yesterday—she had no more to give.

She picked up the wheelbarrow and headed for the secondary cavern they'd been using as a medical area, her heart pounding when she just wanted it to stop.

The last time she'd seen Lyon was right after the gate opened. He'd made this lovely speech about brotherhood and working together, then disappeared. Not to-the-bathroom disappeared, not an I-need-a-shower-because-I-have-blood-and-guts-all-over-me disappeared...

He hadn't been seen for three days—no calls, no messages, no sightings, nothing.

She'd been so busy helping the wounded and trying to feed the rest she hadn't had time to think about him. But, she was officially out of busy work, and the pain she'd kept at bay came crashing in, filling every part of her until she thought she'd choke on it.

"Honey, you've barely slept or eaten since he left," Abella said behind her.

"You really think that matters right now?"

Abella passed her and raised her hands to stop Persephone. "You're gonna make yourself sick."

Persephone's shoulders heaved. A dry sob erupted from inside her. "I need him, Abella."

Abella opened her mouth to speak, but stopped.

A flood of paranorms streamed out of multiple passages and filled the great cavern without saying a word. Only a slight hiss of their slippered feet sounded.

Persephone looked to the right and sighed. "What now? If I have to listen to one more telling of the great battle, I think I'll be sick. Puke all over the shoes, or hairy feet, or the whatever of the endless number of paranormal creatures I've met."

"Uh, Persephone?"

Persephone threw up her hands. "I know. I shouldn't complain. But," she placed a hand over her heart, then fisted her shirt, "I hurt so much."

"Persephone!" Abella hissed under her breath. "Look."

Persephone turned around and saw the large group of paranorms clustering around one of the passages leading into the cavern. The chatter grew louder; her head pounded. Just when she thought it would explode, a mane of tawny gold appeared. At least a head taller than the crowd, Lyon worked his way through the mass until he broke free.

Persephone's heart stopped for a beat. Anger, joy, and more anger flashed through her.

Lyon finally looked up and saw her. He grinned, then looked behind him at the tiny silver-haired girl clutching his huge mitt of a hand. Behind her, two Dobermans—one black, the other red—clung like velcro to their little charge.

"Candace," was all Persephone could manage before her tears rendered her speechless. She squatted down and held out her hands.

Candace squealed and raced across the open space to Persephone. She launched her tiny body into Persephone's arms, the dogs right behind her. The foursome sagged to the floor.

Persephone looked at Lyon. "M&M," she mouthed quietly.

He frowned and shook his head.

She gripped Candace tighter and rocked, her face buried in the child's silver hair to hide her tears.

Lyon stood over her, frowning, his arms crossed over his chest. "All right, that's enough, you three scamps. You've already stolen my first kiss. Time to go slobber on someone else."

He wrapped an arm around Candace's waist and lifted her off of Persephone. He gently set the child on her feet, pointed her at Abella, and watched the baby Portend totter off to Abella's open arms.

Persephone scrambled to her feet and shoved his chest with both hands. "Where have you been?" She wiped the tears from her face and shoved him again. "I was sick with worry."

"I can attest to that," Abella said between Candace's squeals and the Doberman doggie kisses.

"Give me a minute, and you'll have your answer. But first," he pulled Persephone into his body and kissed her thoroughly, his claim loud and clear.

Persephone swayed when he released her. "Hey, I'm really mad at you. If you think a kiss is going to make me forget that you left me here for three days—"

He cupped her face and smiled. "Hopefully, this will help make it right." He looked over his shoulder and nodded.

Persephone peeked around him, and saw that the ragged group of paranorm parents—still missing their children—had gathered together. So many had been lost in the fight, while so many others had succumbed to their injuries. The distraught men and women clung together, their eyes red from grieving, their clothes draped on their protruding bones like hangers. The others, having lost their children before the battle and a mate during it, remained still, their faces slack, the shock pulling them down, paralyzing them. They clutched at each other as if believing that what little remained of their world would unravel if even one of them strayed.

Lyon kissed the top of Persephone's head. "I'll be right back." He strode to the beginning of the passage and looked down it. He lifted a hand and waved someone forward.

The hairs on Persephone's neck and arms rose, and goose bumps raced over her skin.

Lyon gave her a huge smile and a wink, then walked backward a few steps. She heard the soft patter of feet. Then, like a flood, children ran into the cavern and huddled around him, their eyes wide and their bodies trembling. The group stayed next to Lyon until all of them were together, nervously looking from him to the adults.

A cry echoed in the huge space, and one woman broke free of the group of parents. Her long black hair had only one feather left, but it was enough to identify her as a Corvus Ward. She ran to the children and dropped to her knees in front of one child, a little girl. Mother and daughter clung to each other, sobbing and touching each other's faces. The woman picked up her baby and stepped aside.

Lyon looked at the children and nodded. "Go. Find your family."

The children ran to the group of adults. Parents and children mingled, cries of joy reverberating for several minutes before they slowed as families stepped aside, reunited.

Lyon grabbed Persephone's hand and they waited with Abella, Taryn, and the other Zodiacs.

"That was a good move, man," Libra said. "But what about the orphans?"

"I have that covered." Lyon walked to the remaining children and gathered them close. He pulled a piece of vellum out of his back pocket and held it up to them. "This piece of paper is for you, if you want it. It is your choice to stay or to go. Whatever you choose, I promise you'll always have family here. Do you understand?"

The children nodded.

Lyon backed away from the group until he stood several feet from them, alone. "Persephone? Would you read this out loud?"

She took the vellum, opened it, then looked at Lyon. "What is this?"

"Please. Read."

She nodded. "Arrona."

A tall slim, Kellas Cat girl stepped forward. "I claim the name Arrona," she said.

Persephone glanced at Lyon, confused.

He bowed deeply to the girl. "It is my honor to meet you, Arrona." He rose and held out a hand. The girl accepted it, took her place by his side, and turned to face the other children.

"But didn't you say a Kellas Cat can't be named until they have their familiar?" Persephone asked.

Lyon smiled at Arrona and she flushed red. "We will find Arrona a familiar." He looked back at Persephone. "Go on, love, or we'll be here all night," Lyon teased.

"Candace."

The little girl squealed and ran to Lyon, her arms raised high for a hug.

He knelt and squeezed her tight before standing again.

Persephone nodded and cleared her throat before reading the next name on the list. "Collas."

Lyon raised a hand. "I know who Collas is." He held out a hand to a young black-haired boy.

A tiny Corvus Ward with one thumb in his mouth toddled out of the group and stopped in front of Lyon.

"You are Collas."

"Cowwas."

"Close enough." Lyon scooped the baby boy into his arms and stood, resting him on one hip. He pushed the riotous curls out of Collas' eyes. "Your mother and father and uncle were the bravest people I've ever met. They loved you very much." Lyon kissed the boy's forehead.

Tears welled in Persephone's eyes. One by one, each orphan stepped forward to claim a name, then joined the growing group standing with Lyon.

When Persephone finished, she folded the vellum and looked around.

The Zodiacs, the parents and their reunited children, and many other paranorms surrounded Lyon, Persephone, and the orphans. "I don't understand. You said only parents are allowed to name their children."

Lyon set Collas down. "If they agree, I claim these children as my own. My family—not of my blood, but of my choice."

The orphans squeezed in, and wrapped their arms around Lyon and each other.

"That's lovely," Persephone said quietly. She leaned over the sea of children to hand the paper to him.

He shook his head. "You missed a name."

She unfolded the paper, and glanced at the list. "I didn't miss any."

He smiled. "Oops, I forgot." He reached into his other pocket and pulled out another piece of vellum. "Read this."

She opened the worn, oft-folded page and gasped when she saw her face—the outline drawn in pencil, the lines smeared, while her features had been newly drawn in ink. Below it was one name. *Persephone*.

Lyon took a knee and held out both hands. "You haunted my dreams before I found you. You've *made* my dreams come true ever since. My family would not be complete without you. Will you have me? Will you have us?"

The children looked between Lyon and Persephone, then dropped to their knees and held out their hands.

She covered her mouth. Her tears flowed freely. She touched each child's hand as she worked her way to Lyon. Too choked to speak, she nodded.

He swept her up and held her body close as he kissed her.

She whispered, "You are mine."

"And you are mine, my inamorata. Together, we'll never be alone in the darkness again."

The End

ABOUT THE AUTHOR

It all started with the title, "The Zodiac Assassins".

While studying writing craft, I struggled to decide what I wanted to say and what genre in which to frame it. Most of my childhood was spent moving from one military base to another with friends coming and going out of my life so I turned to books like the "Wizard of Oz" series for entertainment. Getting lost in each new world fed my wild imagination. That, paired with my adult philosophy that "Anything is possible", primed me to be drawn to the worlds of fantasy and the paranormal.

That's when the Zodiac Assassins came to me. I wrote the first book with the Zodiacs as vampires. Then scrapped it. Why try to fight for a place among the great vampire stories already out in the world?

So I started over. Creating the InBetween and the many creatures needed to inhabit it was great fun, but I asked myself, what could I do with it? How could I make these unique creatures interesting and relevant to the human experience?

I've always been fascinated by the stars, the universe. The notions of infinity and infinite possibility appeal to my soul. But here on earth, humans are also a source of fascination. Who are we? Why do we do what we do? Then, the Hubble telescope started sending us images of astounding beauty that fired up my imagination. At the same time, I was reading books about astrology and the enneagram personality system. BAM! I had my males and a way to make them speak to all of us.

Twelve paranormal males ruled by the shadow side of their zodiac signs who need to overcome the needs, beliefs and fears that have formed who they are, to become, maybe not whole men, but at least less damaged. Fear of emotional attachment, fear of losing control, needing independence are just of a few of the issues that will be explored along with the themes of free will versus fate, good versus evil, and my favorite for this series, the brilliant quote from the television series Leverage, "Sometimes the bad guys are the only good guys you get."

The Zodiac Assassins and the creatures of the InBetween will face a battle within and without against human, paranormal, and supernatural adversaries. I hope that at least one of the journeys the males must make will resonate with you. You can learn more at www.artemiscrow.com.

A percentage of the author's proceeds will be donated to a national animal rescue group and an animal shelter.

ACKNOWLEDGMENTS

The process of writing a book then getting it ready for publication involves many people, too many to name here, so I'll limit the list. Thank you to my editor, Jen Blood, at Adian Editing for taking on a new writer and teaching me so much, all while remaining patient and kind. Thank you to Derek Murphy of Creativindie for his stellar formatting, beautiful cover design and answering my endless questions. Thank you to Laura Baker, author and instructor of the amazing Discovering Story Magic online classes, without whom I wouldn't have the bones of this story. Last, thank you to authors Emilie Rose and Sarah Winn, for not falling out of their chairs laughing when I announced that "The Zodiac Assassins" was the perfect name for a series.

Made in the USA
Middletown, DE
24 September 2015